The Highland Thistle

by KJ Fay

This is a work of fiction. Names, characters, places and incidents are either the product of the author's imagination or are used fictitiously. Any resemblance to actual persons, living or dead, events, or locales is entirely coincidental.

Copyright © 2021 by KJ Fay

ISBN 978-1-7368737-1-7

Contents

Prologue

Kinneil House, West Lothian, Scotland, 1584

"What news from the Highlands?" Captain Stewart, the Earl of Arran asked the man standing before him. The earl sat in a sumptuous velvet chair before a roaring fire, the only light in the room on this night, absentmindedly swirling a glass of brandy in his right hand. A tall, lean man stood a few feet away, his cold eyes glinting in the firelight, his jaw clenched.

"Dangerous rumblings, milord," the man answered. "The natives, as they say, are getting restless."

"They are always restless, James," the earl said. "And frequently dangerous."

"Aye, sir, but of late more so than usual. There is very real talk of another move against yourself, and perhaps even the king again."

"And no doubt the loudest talkers are our old friends Mar and

Angus?" the earl asked.

"They are, but those *good earls* be joined by many others. The treachery of the Highland lords runs deep. Perhaps it is time we deal with this problem permanently."

"I agree," the earl stated. "But our position in the Highlands is weak. We need to further divide them, to secure more allies and lands, deny our foes the safety of the whole of the region. What of our young friend in Nairnshire? Is he still willing to be of use to us?"

"Willing, milord? He is that and more," James said. "He is like a hound who has caught the scent of a hare and awaits only his master's permission to run it down."

"Then I shall put him to task at once. And I know the perfect place for him to start," the earl said with a wicked smile.

1

Errogie, The Scottish Highlands

Arabella Fraser ignored her brother's cry to slow down – as usual. Instead, she leaned low in the saddle and slapped the heels of her leather riding boots even harder against her filly's slate-colored flanks. The wild moorland pony sped up, pulling farther ahead of her brother Douglas and his mount. Another horse and rider raced past on his left, Molly MacBain giving him a quick wink as she went. The heather and gorse of the hillside flew past the two women in a pink and yellow blur. An ancient fence of stacked fieldstone stood before them, losing a slow struggle against time but still presenting a formidable challenge. At the last second, Douglas Fraser pulled back on the reins, stopping his mount. Arabella and Molly continued, driving straight at the wall. With whooping yells, first Arabella and then Molly soared over the barrier. Arabella landed cleanly but Molly's horse came down hard, nearly launching her from the saddle. She stayed mounted – barely - and brought her horse under control next to Arabella's. Both women turned back to Douglas with a triumphant grin.

Douglas Fraser led his horse along the old stone wall to a section where it had long ago crumbled into a low pile of moss-covered rocks. Though three years older at two-and-twenty and as experienced a rider as any in these Highlands, he had never been able to match his sister's skill - or daring - in the saddle. He was taller than her at six feet, though only by a few inches, and sported the same fiery red hair. Their familial resemblance was unmistakable, the green eyes, fair skin, lean but wiry build, both broad of shoulder and iron strong. Even their clothes nearly matched today, both wearing rough woolen trousers and riding boots, with Arabella sporting the same saffron-colored man's linen shirt as her brother, her collar scandalously open. Douglas' beard drew an instant distinction, of course, a tangled thatch of a red bursting from his face.

"Very well, ladies, I yield! You win! Again," he added, shaking his shaggy head.

The girls led their horses back to him at a jaunty trot. Arabella's usually fair cheeks were flushed from the exhilaration and danger of the race. The sun's rays sent streamers of light through her dark red tresses, untied and uncovered, causing the tangled mane to glow as if afire.

"Your hat, Molly," Douglas said, handing the young woman a dusty flat cap retrieved from the bushes. Arabella's best friend since childhood, Molly sported the same red locks and fair skin, though she stood several inches shorter and carried many stones more weight. The boys loved her curves though, including Douglas, which she often displayed by wearing daringly low-cut bodices. Today her skirts and been pulled high for riding, showing her white linen bloomers, and her chemise pulled low, exposing a good deal of cleavage. She caught Douglas staring as she took back her bonnet.

"Gramercy, kind sir," she said, batting her eyes with a devilish smile.

He looked away quickly, his cheeks going red. "And quit gloating the both of you," he said. I let you win."

"Oh bother," Arabella answered. "You have never beaten me over that wall and you never will."

"What I meant was, I let you ride the faster horse today, that is all." He said this as the three of them headed at a more leisurely pace back toward *Ban Tigh*, the ancestral Fraser home.

"Of course, dear brother, and I thank you for allowing me the honor of riding *my own* horse this fine day. And by God, a lovely day it is," Arabella said, gazing toward the Great Glen spreading before them as far as the eye could see, its greens dotted abundantly with little patches of yellow and purple and pink. To the south towered the Monadhliath Mountains, the blues and grays and browns of their peaks raking the sky and disappearing into the mists. Just ahead lay the village of Errogie, nestled snuggly on the shores of Loch Mhor. The small rough-stone houses with their thatched roofs looked for the most part as they had for centuries, though recently some owners had taken to whitewashing the rocks and painting their doors in bright hues, as was the current fashion in Edinburgh.

"I really wish you would not ride so recklessly, Ara," Douglas told her. "I dread to think what father would do to me if I brought you home in pieces."

"He is right, Ara," Molly chimed in. "For a change. Have you forgotten, we have a rocking to attend later, and we must look our best for the lads."

"I did not forget, though I had hoped you might," Arabella said, rolling her eyes. "What is the point, Mol? 'Twill just be the same local boys as the last rocking, and the one before that, and the one before that."

"Oh bollocks. I rather fancy some of the local lads," Molly said, glancing slyly at Douglas. "Besides, who else would be there but us locals?"

"There are plenty of clans in these Highlands, Molly MacBain, and you know it. 'Twould be nice to see a few new faces."

"Or mayhaps an old one?" Molly asked.

"Whatever do you mean?" Arabella replied innocently.

"Methinks you are still pining on that handsome Campbell lad you encountered last year while away in France."

"Do not be silly, Mol. He had his chance and showed no interest. Why, I have all but forgotten him."

"Liar!" Molly teased, smiling. "I have known you too long for you to fool me. You still carry a torch for him, fool that he may be."

"And an arse," Douglas interjected. "And one of ill temper and ill-repute at that."

"The Campbells are not of ill-repute!" Arabella said. "A finer family is not to be found in the Highlands."

"'Tis not his family, I speak of, Ara, but Duncan only," Douglas said. "He has sent more than one man to the grave while in a rage, though his father's wealth and good name has so far kept him from the gallows."

"I do not doubt," Arabella said, "that he has dueled a time or two, either in anger or in honor; what Highlander has not?"

"You are the one to talk, Douglas Fraser," Molly said. "I have heard a tale or two of your own taphouse duels!"

"Youthful indiscretions they were and well behind me now," Douglas answered stiffly.

"As with Duncan, I am certes," Arabella said.

"If you say so," he muttered.

"If you are quite finished, I should like to hear no more of you and your pub mates gossip about young Master Campbell," Arabella said with finality.

"The Campbells are indeed a fine family," Molly said. "And Duncan Campbell would be a fine catch for any lass. Do you know he is next in line for the Thanedom of Cawdor? After his brother Colin, that is."

"Do not be so quick to bury their father, Lord John," Douglas said. "He is not much older than our own dear gaffer."

"You know she meant no disrespect to Lord Campbell," Arabella said. "She only meant that Duncan is-"

"Second in line for the Thanage of Cawdor, with greater prospects yet," Molly answered, giving her friend a wink.

"Oh stop, Molly," Arabella said. "A title and a bit of land mean nothing to me and you know it."

"A bit?" Douglas said. "Cawdor is a magnificent estate, Ara. Not a drafty auld *bothy* on a wee piss of land like our home."

"*Ban Tigh* is not a *bothy*!" Arabella cried. "It is a lovely and stately auld manor, perhaps more – venerable - than some but no less grand and as charming as any. And father's estate is no wee plot. Besides, as I said, such things mean nothing to me. For true love, I would marry a poor tinker with no prospects at all."

"Oh, so a *dafty* like me," Douglas said, a wry smile on his handsome face.

Arabella hated to hear him speak so of their family fortunes, yet she could not deny their father had suffered greatly these last few years. The same could be said for most Highlanders.

"Dearest Douglas," Arabella said. "Please do not begrudge Duncan or anyone else their fortunes. The Earl of Arran's vile policies have hurt all the Highland lords, including the Campbells. You know they have opposed him just as vigorously as our father, perhaps even more so if the rumors are to be believed."

"Worry not, sis," Douglas said as they entered the paddock behind their manor house. "The fault is mine for being so thin-skinned about it."

"Ara is right," Molly told him. "True love cares not for fancy titles or grand estates." She and Douglas looked into each other's eyes. After a moment, Molly looked away in a rare bit of self-consciousness. "Fie, what is all this talk about love and marriage? Sure'n we are putting the cart before the horse. First things first, Ara, we have to away to get dressed, do our hair, and sure'n we will have a damn fun time tonight whomever shows up. We are both nineteen already; nearly auld maids! Perhaps this year, some lads will pluck up the courage and ask for our hand." Now she looked straight at Douglas as his cheeks burned crimson once more.

"*Ban Tigh*," he squeaked before clearing his throat. "Home."

"Not mine," Molly said. "I will expect to see you shortly at the rocking. Both of you," she added, continuing on the lane to the nearby shire of Ault-na-goire where she lived.

Douglas and Arabella reached the rear courtyard and walked their horses into the old stone barn. They stabled their own mounts, as they had been doing since their father had let his last groomsman go nearly a year ago. Douglas remained behind to tend to a neglected gate repair while Arabella continued to the house. She gazed up at the squat timber and stone structure with great affection, ignoring the large flakes of fallen whitewash and mortar dotting the ground like so much snow. Despite it's dilapidated state, she had missed the old place terribly while away in France, having only recently returned. Her home had always been full of love, even in the difficult times after her mother Elizabeth had left her father, Sir William, effectively abandoning her and Douglas as well.

Arabella was only three years old when this happened and, though saddened and confused, she was at least spared knowledge of the scandal this caused, or the greater scandal that followed when her mother gave birth only six months later to a daughter, Alexandria. Elizabeth made it clear the child was not Sir William's, confirming her infidelity and, in the process, greatly humiliating the old knight. But the greater surprise was when James Stewart, Earl of Arran and the most powerful noble in Scotland save the king, admitted the child was his. The earl was of course already married, but his wife refused to grant him a divorce, not willing to give up her title and lands to this new usurper. Elizabeth remained his consort and, eventually Lord Stewart convinced the king to grant her a baronetcy, making her Lady Elizabeth. She almost completely ignored Arabella and Douglas after the birth of Alexandria, but Sir William did his best to make up for it.

"Ah, there she is!" William announced as Arabella entered the house. The old knight was well into his fifties, his beard and hair – what little remained of it – snowy white. He matched Douglas' height but not his lean cut, Sir William's paunch growing larger with each passing year. He sat in the great room at the head of the long dining table, a plate of neeps and tatties before him, the bones of a small char on a side dish. He stood and embraced his daughter with a warm hug and an even warmer smile. "Riding again?" he asked, looking concerned. Arabella said nothing. "Auch, daughter, now how would you look attending today's festivities black and blue and broken from a fall?"

"Pish posh, father, I have not been dismounted in years. 'Twas but a short ride, not too fast and with only a wee jump here and there. Besides, I am not even certain-"

"Do not say it, daughter. Do not tell me you mean to not attend the rocking," her father admonished. "Ara, ye are getting on in years, 'tis nigh you give up your tomboy ways and find a husband. You do not want to be an-"

"Auld maid?" Arabella said. "I heard that already today. And since when does a little riding make one a tomboy?"

Her father gazed at her current garb, more lad than lass, before answering. "'Tis not just that, Ara, though you indeed ride better - and more daringly - than most men. There is also your fondness for swords and pistols and the like. Or have you so quickly forgotten Paris?"

"How can I, father, when you will not let me? So I have taken the time to learn to protect my kith and kin, and my honor, should the need arise. 'Tis only prudent, in times such as these."

"Swords and pistols and riding are all fine things to know – for a son, which I have," William said. "But how be your skills at cooking and cleaning, at knitting and sewing and darning, at gardening or caring for a household? These are the things a good man wants from a wife, Ara, and I want you to find a good man "

"I know," she sighed, seeing the sincere love in his eyes, which failed to hide just a hint of disappointment. "Of course I will go to the party."

As Arabella retreated to her room to get ready, her thoughts returned to Duncan Campbell. They had first met as children many years ago and, though Cawdor Castle and the Campbell lands lay but two days ride away, she had not seen him again until a chance meeting in France, almost one year ago.

2

The *Maison des Petits Palets* was rumored to be the oldest house in Dol de Bretagne, France. For this reason, the son of Monsieur Concino, the Marquis of Ancre, insisted on hosting a Hogmanay celebration here for his many Scottish friends, so far from hearth and home on a dreary New Year's Eve. Arabella had been in France for some months now and was indeed homesick. The Earl of Arran had traveled there on business for King James. Lady Elizabeth had accompanied him and insisted Arabella come and attend her. Elizabeth told Arabella she wanted her to learn there was a whole world beyond the 'dreary and culturally-backward' Highlands, to learn the ways of courtly life and perhaps find herself a husband. For many months,

Arabella served as a lady-in-waiting to her mother, learning etiquette, improving her reading and writing skills, and mastering the many other arts necessary and appropriate to fulfil her duties. She had a great thirst for knowledge and proved a quick study at almost everything she tried. She mastered French very quickly and even picked up a little Latin, adding these to the Scots Gaelic and English she already spoke.

As a condition of giving his blessings for Arabella to make this trip, Sir William had insisted that Lady Elizabeth keep him regularly informed of his daughter's learnings and activities, both academic and otherwise. To his surprise, Elizabeth did exactly that, for she reveled in every opportunity to remind William of the wealth and status the earl was able to provide for her and Arabella, and how much more cultured and civilized was Paris than Errogie, Scotland.

One particular morning, Elizabeth informed Arabella there would be no courtly duties for her for several days, as the gentlemen of the court were away in the country hunting foxes or quail or some such. "Use the days as you wish, daughter," Elizabeth instructed. "Take in the city, immerse yourself in its culture, its art and music, food and wine, its great poets and authors. Gaze upon Notre Dame and try to imagine anything so grand in Errogie, or even all of Scotland."

"As you wish, mother," Arabella answered, ignoring the smirk on the lady's face.

Arabella wandered about the city for some time with no particular destination, simply letting her feet and instincts guide her. She saw many a board above the doors of quaint little shops proclaiming fine art, fine food, fine wine, and she thought it all fine and dandy - and utterly boring. Then she noticed a large and highly-detailed sign with an *epee* prominently displayed above the words, *'Academie des Maitres en Faits d'Armes.'* Now this looked intriguing!

She entered and found herself in a large, open room, well-lit by very tall windows and torches in wall sconces. Weapon racks lined the walls. A handful of instructors and spectators watched several pairs of men fencing against each other. One of the fencers turned his head to look at her and his opponent lunged at him, scoring a point. The other fellow quickly turned back to his foe and with rapid ferocity knocked the man's sword to the ground and scored what would have been a killing blow but for the protective pads. They bowed to each other and then to their instructor, before the winner removed his helm and approached Arabella. He was, she noted, the very definition of tall, dark and handsome, and likely not too many years older than she. In fact, he looked familiar, and she realized she had seen him at court.

"Madam," he said with a sweeping bow. "Welcome to the *Academie*. You are a stranger here, though I have seen you before, I believe."

"At court, monsieur, though please forgive me if I do not recall your name."

"Jean Louis de Sayssel, at your service. And you are?"

"Arabella Fraser." She hesitated while he grinned at her as if this should mean something to him. "I attend the Lady Elizabeth, who attends James, the Earl of Arran," she added.

"Ah, the Earl! Yes, now I remember. So what brings you here? Do you enjoy watching?"

"Yes, but I enjoy *doing* more. I want to learn."

"Learn what?"

"To fight, of course," Arabella answered.

"But you are a girl!" Jean Louis replied.

"I am glad you noticed. Will you teach me anyway? And not just the epee, but firearms as well, like the petronel and pistolet."

Jean Louis stared at her for a long moment, a quizzical smile on his handsome face. Finally, he laughed.

"You Scots are crazy! But it would be so very rude of me to refuse your request. It will be my pleasure to train you."

Lady Elizabeth soon noted that her daughter had finally begun to take a serious interest in men. In fact, she was spending a great deal of time in the company of several young lords and esquires, all from the finest families, of course. Blissfully and, thankfully, unaware of Arabella's true interests, Elizabeth dutifully updated Sir William on the latest news, even hinting he might soon expect to receive a letter from some nobleman to announce their daughter's engagement.

Sir William was again sitting at the long table in the great hall, though this time his food sat untouched as he struggled to pay far too many bills with far too little coin. His valet, an aged fellow named Thomas, stepped into the room.

"Sir William, a messenger has arrived for you from France."

"What say you? France, was it? Is it from Lady Elizabeth?" the knight asked.

"No sir," Thomas replied. "He said his lord sent him, a marquis I believe."

William jumped to his feet and nearly knocked his aged valet over running past him to the door. A young messenger in very fine livery met him there.

"I am Sir William. To what do I owe this honor?"

"Sir William, my master, the Marquis d'Aix-La Chambre, has directed me to deliver to you the following message. Um, if you will pardon me, sir, but these are his words, not mine," the lad said, unrolling a scroll of parchment.

'To whomever claims responsibility for the sauvage of a woman-child known as Arabella Fraser: you Sir, should be ashamed of yourself for allowing a female to partake in training in the manly and dangerous use of arms at the most prestigious Academie des Maitres en Faits d'Armes! I had heard of the reputation of the Scottish Highlanders for their barbaric frenzy in battle, though I was unaware this attribute belonged not to the Highland men but to their women. Please Sir, if you are of good conscience, you will remove your daughter from the Academie at once. I implore you this not simply because she soundly and publicly defeated my son in a fencing match, but because of my sincere concern for not only the egos of the young men at the school, but for their safety!'

Some weeks after this, Lady Elizabeth received a letter from Sir William. He told her he was outraged to learn from others that she had allowed Arabella to partake in such dangerous pursuits and for having somehow *forgotten* to inform him she had enrolled in the *Academie* at all. It was only after Arabella returned home many months later that she learned the shallowness of her father's anger, noting the pride in his voice whenever he told friends and acquaintances how his daughter had bested the best lads in her fencing school, a story he found excuse to relate surprisingly often. Arabella was, of course, forced to withdraw from the *Academie* after this. Still, she continued to pursue her tomboy ways during her remaining time in France. She simply learned to do it more discreetly as she grew into womanhood, learning as she did just how fragile the male ego could be. And Arabella did indeed grow to womanhood, realizing rather suddenly she was no longer the tall, awkward girl of her youth. Mirrors showed she had grown curves, while the boys let her know - often when they thought she could not hear them - that those curves were 'in all the right places.'

Their enthusiastic attention was far from one-sided though, for Arabella also began finally to notice the men in her life, and as more than just instructors, riding opponents or dueling partners. As if a veil had been pulled from her eyes, she wondered how she had missed for so many months the fact that France abounded with an amazing assortment of very handsome and dashing men. These included her riding instructor, her fencing partners, the young - and not so young -

lords at Court, the knights who were constantly going off to fight the king's wars, and an alarming number of strangers she passed on the street. Her social life picked up considerably and Lady Elizabeth finally had some encouraging news to send home to William. Though amazingly well-informed by her spies and gossips, Elizabeth never did learn about 'the one that got away,' as Arabella called him, the young many she met at that New Year's Eve Hogmany party.

The *Maison* was indeed ancient but also quite small and, as such, the guests kept bumping into each other - a good or bad thing depending upon whom one bumped into. In Arabella's case, she happened to stumble over a young gentleman's exquisite calfskin riding boots and nearly fell. Luckily, the fellow had superb reflexes and caught her, saving her from a very embarrassing tumble into a large silver bowl of Scottish ginger wine. When she looked up to thank her savior, his ice blue eyes struck her speechless - a very rare thing with her. About her same age, he was tall, several inches over six feet, and powerfully built. He was impeccably dressed in the latest French fashion, from the beret atop his blonde hair sporting a beautiful, silver *enseigne*, to his dark velvet doublet, his codpiece and hose, down to those fabulous riding boots. He wore no beard or moustache, which suited him, for his chin was square and strong. After a time that she felt was all too brief, the young man unwrapped his powerful arms from around her and set her back on her feet.

"Apologies and gramercy, sir," Arabella said, blushing.

"A bit too much wine, perhaps?" he smirked. "Please do watch your feet, girl. Or, if you cannot watch yours, at least watch mine. These boots were terribly expensive."

"You are a Highlander!" Arabella exclaimed, detecting the brogue at once. "And you look familiar. Have we not met before?"

"Perchance," he said, taking a harder look at her. "Duncan Campbell, Esquire."

"A Campbell, I thought as much! I am Arabella Fraser, my father is Sir William. You and I met in our youth."

"Fraser, eh?" Duncan said dispassionately. His eyes left hers and wandered about the room almost of their own accord. "Well neighbor, how find you this *fete*?"

"'Tis a bit reserved for my tastes," Arabella answered. "Though I appreciate the Marquis holding it for us."

"Reserved is not a bad thing if the guests are at least somewhat impressive," Duncan said. "Sadly, this party is a complete bore, with no one of interest beyond the Marquis himself."

"Excuse me?" Arabella said.

"So few people from good families, of wealth and nobility, I mean," Duncan said. "Well, I pray your leave, Annabelle, I must thank our host before departing." With that, Duncan turned on his heel and left.

"Arrogant git," Arabella cursed under her breath. "Though a damn handsome one."

Arabella managed to run into Duncan several more times over the next few months, often with great effort on her part. And though he slowly warmed to her and became more friendly, she doubted he was as smitten with her as she with him. Shortly thereafter, the earl's business in France concluded and he, the Lady Elizabeth and Arabella returned to Scotland.

Arabella arrived home shortly after her nineteenth birthday, with neither an engagement nor a host of suitors following. Even worse as far as her father was concerned, she seemed more high-spirited and independent than ever. And though she had learned many customs and courtesies that would serve a lady at court, she had not learned a thing about the important domestic duties of a wife and mother, in William's opinion. His frustration overflowed one eve when Arabella burnt his supper once again.

"Damn that mother of yours!" he blurted. "I must write to her yet again to express my disappointment at her for allowing you to waste your time in France learning not how to be a goodly wife and daughter, but an undisciplined, rowdy son! Which I already have!"

"Father, no!" Arabella cried. "She knew nothing of my martial activities in Paris, nor most of what I did when I was not attending her at court. The blame, if you will, lies completely with me, and so too should your anger."

"Nay, I will not hear it, daughter. She was responsible for you, at her side or not. Because of her, you may have squandered your best and perhaps last opportunity to find a worthy husband!" He said no more, but he did not have to; the disappointment in his eyes said it all.

"Have you your rock and reel? And your wool?" William asked his daughter for the third time as she walked beside him and Douglas into the village. She was dressed most splendidly. No longer looking the lad, she wore a beautiful dress of green and black plaid, a white linen chemise underneath, high of collar and with long billowy sleeves, with a black woolen bodice around her waist and bosom. Her hair was tucked not so neatly into a snood that matched her dress, with several locks refusing to be contained and framing her handsome face. She was barefoot, as was common in the Highlands.

"I would look a fool trying to make yarn without them, father," she answered, rolling her eyes. "And Douglas, are you not the fine looking one!"

Her brother wore his finest *breacan-an-feileadh*, or great belted plaid, over his best – or at least cleanest – saffron tunic, the tartan wrapped up and over his shoulder then belted at the waist. The plaid was of his clan colors, the red matching his hair and the green his eyes. He was bare of leg though not of foot, choosing leather rullions for his feet, which he thought made him look terribly sophisticated. A flat cap completed the outfit, slouched rakishly on his head. He had bathed in the crik, and Arabella was certain she smelled rosewater perfuming him.

"Ah, this auld getup," he answered. "'Twas but lying about."

Arabella smiled and shook her head, though said nothing.

Soon they arrived at Auld Man McNarty's barn, largest in Errogie, tall and grand in great timbers and stone. The animals and other sundry had been cleared out to make room for the unattached lasses, who gathered now with their distaffs and spindles to spend the day spinning yarn. Several young men had shown up already, mostly the younger and more anxious ones, to visit and make merry. No staid event, those young men who knew an instrument played hearty rigs, with the lasses often joining them in song. Boards had been set with milk and cheese, fish and mussels, wild berries and smoked venison. Soon, the older lads arrived, bringing with them strong ale and whiskey sweetened with heather honey. At first distributed only amongst themselves to buck up their courage, as day turned to evening and the torch lights were lit, the drink eventually found its way to the lasses as well.

Molly was on her third mug of short beer and Arabella had just finished her second when Molly gasped, looking toward the barn door.

"Now there is a stranger, and a most handsome one," she said. "But who is he?"

Arabella followed her gaze and gasped as well. "I do not believe it! 'Tis Duncan Campbell!"

Duncan was again dressed very smartly, though this time dressed as a proper Highlander, his attire similar to Douglas' though noticeably finer. Arabella could not help but notice the blue in his plaid accentuated his eyes. Molly noticed this too.

"Well bundle me now," Molly said, her hand going to her bosom. "You were not exaggerating, Ara. He is a braw man indeed!"

"Hey," Douglas said, putting his arm around Molly's shoulders and pulling her close. "Am I not your man? Are you not my lass?"

"Am I? Be you announcing it publicly, Mister Fraser?"

"Well I...I..." he looked from her to the dashing young Mister Campbell and back to her again. "By the good Lord I am, Miss McBain!" Douglas had had a whiskey or three himself and his courage now ran hot within him. "I have feelings for you, lass, strong ones. I have no *fede* ring but prithee wear my brooch," he said, removing his cloak pin. "If'n you will have me, that is. And if so, I will go first thing in the morn to your father and ask proper for your hand!"

"'Tis so?" Molly cried, embracing him tightly. "Drunk, in jest or dead serious, you have said the words and I will hold you to them, Mister Fraser!"

"Molly, I am so happy for you!" Arabella exclaimed, hugging the couple. "Both of you."

"Congratulations," Duncan Campbell said as he reached the small group. "Two joyous occasions this night: a betrothal, and me reuniting with the most fair Arabella Fraser."

"What imposter is this?" Arabella asked with a broad smile. "Last we met you could not run from me fast enough."

"A fool I was, Miss Fraser," Duncan said, stepping close and taking one of her hands in his. "A smitten fool, to be certes. Your beauty and charm struck me as hard as iron. I was stunned, at a complete loss for words. A fool I was, so I ran, as you say."

"Mister Campbell," she said, blushing. "This is most unexpected. Pray tell me you are not playing me the fool, for I would never forgive you."

"As the Lord is my witness, 'tis no tomfoolery. Ah," he said, noticing the wooden mug in her hand. "You are empty. Please let me refresh your drink."

When he returned, Arabella noticed the cup did not contain beer, but whiskey, as did his silver *quaich*.

"To the happy couple!" he toasted to Douglas and Molly, and they all drank. "And to you, Arabella," he said, his clear blue eyes staring intently into hers as they drank again.

When he next went to refresh their cups, William Fraser sidled up to the group, grinning a drunken fool, though he was only half-drunk.

"Congratulations my son, and to you Molly!" he said, clasping Douglas about the shoulder. "A lovelier lass could not be found in these Highlands, lest it was our own Arabella. And speaking of Arabella, well - Duncan Campbell," he said, giving his daughter a wink. "Now he would make a fine husband, indeed."

"Father! Surely you speak in haste. I barely know the man."

"Bah! What is to know? We are practically kith and kin with the Campbells. Auch, you have known them since before you could walk. And the Thane and I go back even farther than that. A fine family, a great family!"

"Father, you are making a spectacle of yourself," Arabella told him. She could not deny, though, the joy in his eyes and how his happiness made her happy.

"All right daughter, all right," he said, backing away as Duncan approached. "Though if he come speerin' me for your hand, I will not be beukin' him."

The night wore on, with most of the lads and lasses pairing off, the young men carrying their lady's spinning tools home when the time came. Some time and many trips to the cask later, Duncan called loudly to Sir William that he had something important to say.

"Good Sir Knight," he said, swaying slightly. "I am in love with your daughter! Nay, I have always loved her, since first we met as children. Our reuniting in France was surely nothing short of Providence. And though I could not bring myself to tell Arabella my true feelings then, when she left Paris and returned to Scotland, I felt as if my heart had been ripped from my breast and traveled with her. I realized I could not bear to lose her again." He reached into a leather pouch and produced a beautiful and intricately-carved silver *fede* ring. Molly gasped loudly again. Arabella's cheeks burned crimson and she had to sit on a nearby stool for fear of falling. "Sir, I ask for your daughter's hand in marriage."

Sir William stood mouth agape in stunned silence for a long moment. He looked from Duncan to Arabella and back again. His mouth moved a few times though no words came out until he finally found his voice. "A…a…aye. You have my permission and my blessing, laddie. But what say you, daughter?" he said, turning back to Arabella.

Arabella was speechless. Her head swam and her heart pounded, though from emotion or alcohol or both she could not say. She looked at Duncan uncertainly. She turned to Molly and Douglas. Molly was beaming a smile as wide as the Firth of Forth and nodding her head *yes*. Douglas was a harder read, a bemused smile on his lips but a crease in his brow. Finally, she looked to her father. He smiled broadly, his face glowing, a small tear in the corner of one eye.

"Yes," she said softly, then louder. "Yes!"

"Huzzah!" Molly shouted, and everyone joined in.

In the ensuing days and weeks, Sir William could not hide his joy.

Duncan's father, Lord John Campbell, Thane of Cawdor and brother to

the Earl of Argyll, had long been a close friend and ally. It mattered not

to him that Duncan, as the second son, was not likely to inherit his

father's title or lands. The Campbell name and prestige were more than

he could have hoped for for his daughter, and her financial future was

no longer uncertain. A weight had been lifted from William's

shoulders. Arabella could not remember ever seeing him so happy.

Duncan wasted no time in making their wedding arrangements, even

choosing a date that was none too far off.

"So soon, Master Duncan?" Arabella asked.

"Why wait?" he answered matter-of-factly. "Besides, Paris is

lovely in the spring, as you know."

"Wait. Paris?" Arabella said, surprised. "No one said anything

about Paris. What is wrong with the Kirk in Errogie?"

"What is wrong with the kirk in Errogie?" Duncan repeated. "How

can you possibly compare a run-down shanty in some backwater

village to…to…well, anything in France?"

"Run down…backwater…?" Arabella stuttered. "How can you say

that? Errogie is a lovely village, and the kirk, while obviously no Notre

Dame, is beautiful and quaint. I always just expected I would get

married there."

"Ah, but you never expected to marry a Campbell, did you?" Duncan asked. "No, Errogie simply will not do. It is Paris, child, where we were reunited, and it will be Paris where we wed."

"But what of all my friends here?" Arabella asked. "I cannot bear to think they will not be in attendance."

"Then we shall bring them!" Duncan announced. "On my father's ship."

"Lord Campbell has a ship?" Arabella asked, her eyes wide.

"My father," Duncan explained, "recently purchased a magnificent sailing vessel, per my recommendation, mind you. Not only shall it serve to conduct trade and carry cargo between Scotland and ports both here and on the continent, it is just the thing for a trip to France. It is a splendid vessel, I assure you, large enough to accommodate the entire wedding party."

"Oh, Duncan, this is a most wondrous surprise!" Arabella said, unable to contain her smile. "You could not know this, but I love the sea and sailing! Something about it sets my heart astir. I know we shall have the grandest time!"

"Of that, my dear, you can be certain," Duncan told her, now grinning himself.

The days rushed by in a whirlwind of wedding planning and travel preparations, and soon it was time for the Frasers to leave *Ban Tigh* for the journey to Cawdor Castle. A paltry four servants accompanied them, the only ones who could be spared from the already too few tending the manor and its grounds these days. In addition to Auld Thomas, Sir William's valet, came Robin and Christopher, who served in the fields and would perform the duties of porters and grooms of the chamber at the wedding, and dear old Bess, originally Arabella's nursemaid and now simply her maid. The procession from *Ban Tigh* set out just as the first rays of sunlight shone over the rugged peaks of Carn Ghriogair. Their packhorses carried nearly every stitch of clothing the Frasers owned and a score of other little items deemed necessary or appropriate for their journey and the wedding. Molly MacBain would of course be one of Arabella's bridesmaids, and she joined their group in the shire of Ault-na-goire. Though they had last seen each other but two days ago, the girls hugged and kissed and danced a silly jig around an imaginary Maypole. Douglas had to remind his fiancé and his sister three times they had a schedule to keep before the girls finally mounted their horses. Molly gave Douglas a quick kiss but quickly fell back to ride side by side with Arabella, taking up their same conversation from two days ago in mid-sentence as if there had been no break at all.

"So, is your sister still agreeing to be your other bridesmaid, or has she changed her mind again?" Molly asked.

"Half-sister," Arabella corrected. "And yes, Alexandria is still in the wedding party. In fact, she is to meet us in Nairn, where Lord Campbell's ship is at port.

"And is she still a disagreeable, spoilt brat?"

"Molly! She and I are kin, and that means the world to me, regardless of how our parents feel about each other. Oh, I try so hard to be friendly to her, but she meets all my efforts with something between icy indifference and outright rudeness."

"So yes," Molly said. "She is still a spoilt brat."

"Well at least she agreed to take part in the wedding, even if only at the very last."

"Aye, and I am certain 'twas done purely out of familial love," Molly said, "And not the opportunity to visit Paris again with its multitude of handsome men and fabulous parties."

"Oh, you are terrible, Mol, just awful!" Arabella said, as both girls laughed and turned their conversation to other topics.

The weather proved cooperative during the two-day trip to Cawdor, and everyone remained in high spirits. Upon their arrival at the castle, Lord John himself welcomed them and did so as if they were royalty. He threw a grand feast that night for all and would have done so every night if they could have stayed longer. There was no time though, and bright and early the next morn the wedding party set out once more, this time joined by the Campbells and their retinue. And a grand host it was. In addition to the thane, his eldest son Colin and of course Duncan, they were joined by a troupe of four minstrels, several gentlemen ushers including the distinguished Sir Robert Rose of Kilvarock, Sir Henry MacQueen of Tomatin, and Master Rob Roy, hailing from Invernesshire, as well as valets, pages, cooks, potboys and servers, a seamstress and a laundress. The Reverend Minister Edward Keith, who would be officiating at the ceremony, accompanied them as well. The group now consisted of more than a half-dozen wagons and travel became much slower. Still, Nairn was not far from Cawdor and the group expected to arrive before dusk.

The air grew cooler and less settled as they approached the coast, and now the sky doused them with an occasional drizzle. And though the showers dampened their heads, it did little to dampen their spirits. Sir William and Lord John, both bachelors, genuinely liked each other and got along very well. The two gentlemen rode side-by-side at the head of the group.

"Tell me, Sir William," Lord Campbell said during a break in the rain. "Do you know if Arabella's mother and the earl shall be attending the ceremony?" He asked the question quite innocently yet quickly regretted it, seeing Sir William's jaw clench and his brow furrow. This passed almost immediately and William again became the picture of genial composure, putting on a friendly smile as he answered.

"Aye, the lady intends to be there."

"And the Earl of Arran?" Lord Campbell pressed.

"I think not," William said. "Something about 'royal business' preventing him, apologies and best wishes and all that rubbish."

"I shall consider myself the more fortunate for it. The man is a damned snake and I care not to see him."

"We are of the same mind, brother," William told him. Most of the Highland lords knew Sir William to be an outspoken critic of the earl, though few who did not know him well could say whether his real hatred was for the man or for his policies. His close friends knew it was both.

"My disdain for the man," Lord John said, "is perhaps less personal, to be sure, and rather more political, if you will."

"Aye, and I second you in that regard as well," William said.

"He is just so…" the thane paused, searching for the right word.

"So un-Scottish, if you catch my meaning. There is too much of France and England in him, I say, and too little of Scotland."

"Verily, and well met, dear friend," the old knight answered. "If only our brave cousins at Ruthven had been more successful."

"Softly, Sir William, softly," the thane said quietly, drawing his horse closer to William's and looking about nervously. "We must not be accused of treason, mind you."

Despite being in the Highlands and among friends, Lord John felt uneasy speaking of the incident just two years ago when a group of Highland nobles led by Lord Ruthven, Earl of Gowrie, seized the teenage Scottish King James hostage after a day of hunting. The nobles had not been upset with the king so much as with his policies and the men who formed them, including the Earl of Arran. The king escaped after a time and returned to power, though he judiciously refused to punish most of the conspirators, dismissing the matter as little more than 'a disagreement amongst gentlemen.' King James well knew the political power plays that were a standard of his young reign, and in fact the reigns of most of his predecessors. One faction or another always conspired for control, with the sovereign often a prisoner – either figuratively or literally - of some combination of the powerful nobility. The faction who controlled the king administered the laws according to their own caprices or resentments, with the expected banishments, forfeitures and even executions ensuing. When the king was freed from the domination of one faction, it was often only to fall into the snare of their rivals, who retaliated without mercy. Caught in the middle, the king had to play his hand very carefully, typically with benevolence and moderation. James, the Earl of Arran, however, had neither benevolence nor moderation. He grasped at any means to destroy everyone involved in what had come to be known as the Raid at Ruthven, as well as those who did no more than sympathize with them. And as Lord High Chancellor of Scotland, he wielded the power and authority to do so.

After looking over both shoulders, Lord John reached into his pocket and withdrew a silver flask. "Here is to Ruthven," he said, drinking deeply before handing it to Sir William, who did the same.

They had not but finished their toast when they heard the unmistakable sounds of horse and rider galloping fast toward them from behind. The image of the Lord Chancellor with his legions of spies and king's guards flashed through the thane's mind. Then, he recognized the rider as a man from his own household. He paused, bidding William and the others to continue while he allowed his man to catch up. William removed himself to a discreet distance but went no further. He watched as the rider breathlessly whispered a message into Lord Campbell's ear. The thane's expression changed from concern to joy and then quickly back to grim concern. Lord John shook his head and William heard him tell the page he had thought correctly in coming to give him this news at once. His message delivered, the servant turned his horse and began his journey back to Cawdor. Lord Campbell rejoined Sir William. The two men rode in silence for some time before the thane finally shared his news with the old knight, who by then was on the verge of bursting with curiosity but knew it was improper to pry.

"Queer that we were but a moment hence speaking of the Ruthven lords," the thane told him quietly. "I have just learned they have once again put themselves deep into a het pint."

"How now, milord?" William asked. "Do not tell me that cur James has finally discovered some cause to have them arrested?"

"Discovered? Hardly, for the Earls Mar and Angus have *given* him cause. By God, man, they have seized Stirling Castle!"

3

"God's death!" Sir William exclaimed. "They seized Stirling? And what of the king? Was he taken as well?"

"Nay not, for he escaped just in time. Apparently, Earls Mar and Angus got wind that the Earl of Arran was preparing to move against one or more of them with some evidence he had acquired - or fabricated - and so they struck before he had a chance. Earl Gowrie is also suspected of having a hand in the plot, though word is he was not present at Stirling for the actual siege."

"God love 'em!" William said, taking out his own flask and tipping another toast. "But what hope do they have?"

"Without the king as hostage, little, I fear. From the sound of it, their move was hasty and ill-planned. The king's forces, led by Arran of course, are already on the move. They will no doubt surround and lay siege to the castle in a very short time. The earls and their supporters cannot possibly hope to hold out for long."

"Then that is it; they will surely face the headsman's axe this time." William took another long draw from his flask before passing it to Lord Campbell.

"Not necessarily. There is a chance they will come to their senses and abandon the castle before the king's army reaches them and cuts off any retreat. If so, they may yet escape."

"Still, the earl will have their titles and their lands at the least."

"Aye," Lord Campbell muttered. "May God and King James have mercy on them all!"

The wedding party reached Nairn and the coast just as the sun began its slow descent toward the western hills. There, they found Alexandria and Lord Campbell's ship, *The Thistle*, awaiting them. Arabella warmly embraced her sister, who put on an almost convincing act that she was pleased to see her as well. This task done, Alexandria ordered the nearest deckhand to carry her luggage aboard and show her to 'her suite.' For her part, Arabella wanted to be nowhere else right now than where she stood, taking in the sight of this lovely ship. She thought *The Thistle* a most handsome vessel, one of the finest three-masters she had ever seen. Two pennants fluttered in the stiff breeze atop her towering flagstaff, the higher bearing the blue and white St. Andrew's Cross while the lower proudly bore Lord Campbell's family crest, a rather angry-looking duck wearing a gold crown.

"I only just purchased her," the thane told her proudly, noting her stare and the admiration reflected there. "I put Duncan in charge of preparing her for this voyage and you will notice she has received fresh paint from stem to stern and her hull is freshly scraped and as smooth as a baby's erse. She sports new masts and spars and the finest Norwich canvas money can buy. But fear not, for I did not expend all my coin on her exterior. You will find her interior as comfortable and well-appointed as one could hope for, and Duncan assures me her holds have been filled with the finest food and drink my money would buy. My nephew Fergus is one of the hands aboard her; I am sure you will meet him. Ah, there is her captain. Allow me to introduce you."

A stocky man of perhaps fifty years approached, a bushy white beard erupting from his sun-kissed cheeks. He had been scowling a moment before but smiled broadly when he saw the thane and Arabella.

"Captain Darby McMullins at yer service, ma'am," he said with a

nod, his accent clearly Irish. He then shook Lord Campbell's hand.
"Milord."

"You look troubled, Darby," the thane said. "Is all well?"

"Oh, just the usual ruddy confusion and calamity that always seems to strike just before setting sail. Nothing to concern yerself with, sir, by the by. Here, me men will help with yer baggage and show ye to yer quarters."

The thane of course had the largest and most sumptuous cabin, the one normally reserved for the captain. Two huge, painted-glass windows ran along the back wall, giving Lord Campbell a stunning view of the sea. A small porthole sat low between these to accommodate a long-barreled bronze cannon of exceptional quality, a three-pound chaser bearing the Campbell duck. Lord John called it "Big Quacker." The thane's suite consisted not only of his sleeping quarters but another small cabin used as his dayroom and chartroom. Both rooms opened onto a large area containing the lord's dining table in the rear part and the helm in the fore. Three more cabins stood within the ship's sterncastle, one each for Sir William and Captain McMullins, while Lord Campbell's page George and his valet Ian shared the last. The remaining gentlemen, gentlewomen and guests had accommodations on the lower deck, where several small cabins lay neatly in the corners or under the ship's knees. These typically housed the ship's officers, masters and mates, who had been temporarily displaced by the wedding party.

Because the men had been put in the stern section and amidships, the bow had, for the most part, been left to the women. The four cabins in this section were separated from the rest of the ship by a long bulkhead running athwart *The Thistle* and set with double doors. The plan had been for Arabella to share one of the cabins with her nursemaid Bess, while her two bridesmaids bunked together in the cabin next door. Alexandria, however, refused to share a room with anyone and thus Molly was forced into Arabella and Bess' already cramped quarters. Typically, Miss MacBain was not one to hold her tongue when confronted with such outright rudeness, but Arabella knew well her friend's temperament and quickly silenced her with a kick to the shin and a look that said, 'No fighting during my wedding, please!'

Isla and Dorothy, Lord Campbell's seamstress and laundress respectively, shared the third bow cabin. Arabella could have moved into the last cabin except it had already been assigned. Placing this cabin's occupant, however, had presented something of a dilemma as there were no more women aboard but there were certainly those who still needed a room. Eventually, Thane Campbell and Captain McMullins had decided the cabin should go to William's valet, Thomas. At seventy years of age, they felt Thomas would be beyond the impropriety the situation would have caused had a younger man bunked there. Nonetheless, they allowed the Reverend Keith to have the final word in the matter of whether such quartering arrangements might offend the Good Lord. To his credit, the normally severe minister quipped that if a seventy-year-old man could cause 'impropriety' with one or more women both young and mature, then it would certainly be a miracle. And since all miracles were God's prerogative, then certainly the Almighty could not be offended by such. Thomas, for his part, approached the matter with his typical dignity, reserving only icy stares and stony silence for the jocular comments made at his expense. Secretly, however, he rather enjoyed the entire affair and, thinking of the fetching Miss MacBain, silently prayed for just such a 'miracle.'

The remaining porters, groomsmen, yeomen waiters and potboys shared the open area of the lower deck with the crew, either sleeping in hammocks or on straw palliasses on the floor. Although these men enjoyed little if any privacy, they had plenty of room, as the ship was lightly manned for this voyage and could easily have accommodated at least another two or three score guests and crew.

The ship weighed anchor and set sail with the evening tide. Most of the passengers stayed below or in their quarters if they had them, not being used to the sea and most taking ill. Duncan had so often made the Channel crossing, however, that he rarely became seasick anymore, and Arabella, by fortune, had never suffered from that affliction. She stood on the deck with Duncan, watching the waves dance. After a while, Lord John and her father strolled past. She gave them a broad smile which they returned. The men had not spent quite as much time at sea as their children but knew enough to resort to the old sailor's standby of a stiff drink to 'confuse the humours upset by the tides.' As the ship sailed into the North Sea, a gentle wind kissing her canvass, the sun sank until the orb lay completely below the mountains and only its glow remained.

"Is it not the most beautiful thing?" Arabella asked, gazing at a horizon ablaze with oranges and yellows and purples flowing from one shade to the next.

"Pardon, Arabella?" Duncan said distractedly. "'Tis just a sunset, child, like a thousand before it and the next thousand to come."

"Fah," she said with a frown. "'Tis not just the sun I was speaking of but everything: the water, the open skies, this grand ship and her towering sails. It is all so like a dream."

"Pity you were not born a man; you could have been a sailor," Duncan teased.

"She always was more lad than lass," Sir William called from nearby. Arabella gave him a stern look but the hint of a smile played on her lips, for his comment was true and had been said with love.

Lord Campbell approached them, his attention focused not on the horizon but on the ship itself and its trappings. He addressed his son. "Duncan, dear, was the ship outfitted entirely as to my wishes?"

"Sure'n it was, father; I saw to it myself. Whyfore do you ask?"

"I seem to recall paying for several cannon but note they are not on the gun deck. Topside, I see only the small swivel guns in the bow and stern and, of course, Big Quacker in my cabin."

"Cannons?" Arabella asked. "Oh, I should very much like to see them!"

"So would I, milady," the thane said much less enthusiastically.

"But Your Lordship, why should we be needing such on this fair voyage?" William asked.

"Pirates, of course, and other such vermin as prowl these waters," John answered.

"Pirates?" Arabella gasped, her eyes going immediately to the seas around them. "Sure'n we are in friendly waters, are we not?"

"Yes, we are," Duncan said, putting a protective arm around his fiancée's shoulders. "Really, father, you are scaring Arabella and quite unnecessarily I am sure. One does not greet honored guests bristling at arms like a king's warship. I am sure your guns are simply stowed below, ready to be brought out at the first sign of danger. Not that there shall be any of that, as Arabella is quite correct; we are in friendly waters and shall, I am confident, encounter no trouble at all."

"Indeed, I am certain you are correct on both counts, my son," Lord Campbell said, smiling reassuringly at Arabella. "My apologies to the lady."

He and Sir William removed themselves to the stern section of the ship, presumably to examine their position on the charts in the helm but to really give their children a bit more privacy, or at least what privacy one can find on the deck of a ship at sail. Arabella and Duncan stood in silence for a few moments watching the last minutes of an absolutely beautiful sunset. The few crewmen on deck, busy about their numerous tasks, tried to give them their space, muttering sincerest apologies when their duties carried them near. The sun set completely, plunging the world into darkness. Soon after, Arabella and Duncan joined their fathers and most of the wedding party in the great room, where they found them enjoying a late snack of bannocks and some of Lord

Campbell's scotch while the minstrels played a hearty rig.

The ship sailed south for several days, hugging the coast for safety and as a guide. Near dusk on the third day, the ship sailed into Aberdeen Harbor and dropped anchor. Truly, there was no need for the ship to port here, as they had provisions enough to reach France without stopping. Still, Lord Campbell correctly discerned that most of his guests could use a respite on *terra firma*. Indeed, several of them had not left their cabins since the ship had left Nairn. The two families and their guests walked the short distance into town to the bright and welcoming *Mathair* Cameron's Inn. Here, Lord John gave another magnificent feast. Spirits were high, the food was hot and the ale was cold as the minstrels played with all their heart. The music continued long into the night and Arabella spent most of it dancing wildly and joyfully, exhausting everyone with her energy.

The next morning they set sail again. Before long, most of the passengers acquired their sea legs and began to actually enjoy the journey, spending more time above deck in the fresh air. The weather remained fair for the most part with only the occasional squall. Alexandria still remained unsociably cloistered in her cabin, which Molly and Arabella agreed only made the voyage more pleasant. Unfortunately, Duncan also spent most of his time below decks as well, which Arabella did not so much like. He explained he only wanted to take advantage of the opportunity to relax a bit before they reached France and things became chaotic. It was no secret though that he had a great love for gaming. He spent hours playing at cards or dice with Colin or Douglas or anyone else willing to indulge him. Arabella joined him occasionally and tried her best to relax as well but found this easier said than done. Idleness made up no part of her and she usually found herself topside before long, doing as she had on her previous voyages: immersing herself in the sailors' duties and the workings of a great ship of the wind. This meant she generally made a complete nuisance of herself, but luckily she was a nuisance the sailors found easy to look at and talk to and so they did not complain

Lord Campbell's talk of pirates had greatly intrigued her, and she asked many questions about what they would do if they encountered any, what sort of ship's maneuvers and weapons and tactics should be used. The sailors patiently responded to each of her endless questions and observations, even when their duties really did not allow them time for such. The truth of the matter was the ship had sailed short-handed owing to some sort of mix-up in Nairn, and each of the crewmen and officers seemed always busy. Still, they had just enough hands to manage the ship and did so with the practiced expertise of the veteran sailors they were. Arabella happily pitched in whenever the crew let her and her father and Duncan were not about, for the two men did not approve of such behavior. To the surprise of many among the crew, she proved not the hindrance they had expected. Quick study that she was, she rapidly mastered half the tasks aboard *The Thistle*, though the sight of her working in her long skirt and petticoat, boned bodice and billowy chemise always gave the crew a good laugh. She begrudged them not for this though, and became friends with most, taking the time to learn their names and a bit about them. The first mate, an Edinburgh man named Duff Selkirk, commented that if marriage did not suit her, he would happily give her a position aboard the ship.

Arabella was not the only passenger who found it hard to do nothing. Lord Campbell also made something of a nuisance of himself with his frequent prowling about the ship. He inspected her from stem to stern and from her orlop hold to her top deck, and would have climbed into her tops if Duncan and Sir William had not stopped him. He inspected each of her holds and all her cargo and stores and talked in turn to every member of the crew to ensure they knew well their duty. He also spent a good deal of his time with Captain McMullins and the ship's Portuguese sailing master, a man named Benito De Rivero.

After several more days, *The Thistle* sailed into English waters. Here she veered east to sail around Emmanuel Head on Holy Island, with its newly-constructed English fort. Not that they had anything to fear, for the two nations were presently at peace, but it was natural for the Scottish to not trust the English and vice verse. Lord Campbell stood on deck and watched as they passed the fort, the sun sinking low on his right. Assured all was well, he nodded to Captain McMullins and went back to the stern castle common room. There he found his two sons along with Sir William, Molly and Arabella already seated for supper. They stood as he entered and he bade them sit with a wave of his hand. His countenance was dark and he wore a scowl on his lips.

"What ills you, good sir?" Arabella asked when she saw that Duncan would not.

"Oh, 'tis but a little thing, my child," he answered, smiling with some effort. "Ship's business, 'tis all."

"Do tell, father," Colin pressed.

"Oh, it is just that I have noted some disturbing discrepancies in my inspections of the ship and her stores. Duncan, my boy, you will note that I was correct about the cannons; they either were not purchased or were not put aboard."

"To hell you say!" Duncan spat, crimson coloring his cheeks. "I saw to their purchase myself father, just as you directed. I tell you, I never did trust completely that harbormaster."

"And that is not the whole of it," his father continued. "As we have all no doubt noticed, the ship's crew is short by a full third. Some sort of mix up at the docks."

"Most regrettable," William said. "What is to be done?"

"Nothing at the moment, William. There is naught we can do while at sea, nor even after we reach France most likely. I fear this will all have to be settled upon our return to Scotland."

"And meanwhile, that bastard of a harbormaster will have likely disappeared with our gold!" Duncan cursed.

"Language, son," his father admonished. "The lasses."

"Your pardon, Arabella, Molly," Duncan said. "I just hate the thought of a thief."

"Auch, I have heard far worse language from these two," Arabella said, jerking her thumb toward her brother and father.

The two men looked sheepish and suddenly decided they needed to find another decanter of scotch. They had just removed the stopper when the sound of thunder rent the air. They could hear the crew shouting and running about the deck. A moment later, First Mate Selkirk charged into the room.

"Begging your sirs' pardon, and the ladies," he said, whipping off his hat. "We are beset by two ships; the captain fears they may be pirates!"

4

Lord Campbell jumped to his feet and rushed from the room, followed closely by everyone else. Arabella tried to follow but Duncan barred her path. "Stay, my dear! I beseech thee. If it is as he says, it will not be safe for you on deck!"

"If it is as he says, it will not be safe for me anywhere. I want to be with you and my family!"

"A ship a'fight is no place for a girl! If I cannot trust you to stay safely indoors, than I must ensure it." He pushed her into the cabin and yanked the door closed. "Forgive me, Arabella," he said, making fast the door with a belaying pin wedged between the handle and the jamb. He left her pounding on the door and ran to join his father and the others on deck.

There, activity was fierce. Crewmembers scrambled to and fro frantically trying to adjust the sails to urge her to greater speed. Those few hands not in the tops raced to load and prime the small foredeck guns, all the while cursing their lack of greater firepower. The captain grimly watched the two ships draw ever closer. Both looked to be at least equal in size to his own. In fact, one of them could have been *The Thistle's* double except for her different paint - though both of the other ships carried far more guns and hands. One vessel came at them from behind and the other from ahead, their decks lined with dangerous-looking men. Captain McMullins counted at least eight cannon and four swivel guns pointed his way between the two of them

"Who are they? Can you tell?" Lord Campbell asked.

"I thought at first they might be English king's ships, for they both sailed from behind Guile Point shortly after we passed. And see there," he said, pointing toward their flagstaffs. "They both fly the St. George to make us think so. But I recognize that ship closing on our stern, the large caravel; she is the *Gunsway*, a pirate vessel last rumored to be sailing in the Irish Sea. I cannot make out t'other."

"Do you know anything of this *Gunsway*?"

"Not much, milord, though last I heard she was under a Captain

Boggs."

"And what is his measure? Is he a mad devil or can he be reasoned with?"

"He is no butcher, if that is what ye mean. Still, I should like to know who he is in consort with."

"They must have been lurking out of sight in the bay until we came near," First Mate Selkirk said, having joined the men on the quarterdeck. "They were upon us a'fore we knew it."

"Can we not outrun them?" his lordship asked.

"We cannot, sir. They are at least as fast as us and they have the weather gage."

"The weather gage?" Douglas asked, strapping on his sword belt.

"The advantage of the wind and their position in it to ours, young sir," the captain explained without looking at him. The thunder erupted again as the pirates lobbed another shot across their bow, encouraging them to douse sails and surrender. "Answer 'em back with the swivel guns!" McMullins barked to his deck crew. "Let 'em know we are not a'feared to fight! Maybe they will break off and go in search of easier prey."

A moment later, the two peterero on deck burped their deadly contents toward the *Gunsway*. The nerves of the gunners showed though, with one shot hitting the sea fifty yards from the vessel while the other hit her side, sending large splinters flying but otherwise causing no damage at all. In answer, sharpshooters with muskets in the crow's nest of the *Gunsway* opened fire on the two sailors manning the forward gun. Their shots killed one and chased off the other. The pirate ship adjusted her helm slightly to present her entire larboard gun battery to *The Thistle*, the gunners' hot-matches smoking and ready to fire.

"Well, they are not of a mind to give up. 'Tis folly to try to run or fight, sir," the captain told Thane Campbell. "We shall do so if you give the order, of course, but we shall not prevail. If we surrender now, they may simply take our possessions and leave us be."

A fighter at heart, Lord Campbell hated the thought of giving such an order. Still, he saw clearly the futility of his ship's position against the two vessels with more guns and more men. Unable to say the words, he simply nodded to the captain. Moments later, *The Thistle* dropped her sails and hove to. The *Gunsway* and her consort dropped their English flags and their pretense, taking positions on either side of them. They grappled her tightly and put some sixty sea dogs aboard. The pirates knew their prey offered no resistance and so did not savage them, proceeding in a surprisingly orderly fashion. The captains of the two pirate vessels marched side-by-side up to the quarterdeck, where *The Thistle's* officers and the noblemen awaited them. The first pirate stood tall and very heavy, his fat belly hanging over a thick belt, his hair and beard a tangled mass of black flying in the breeze. The second captain was fairer of hair, wore no beard and stood even taller than the first, though lean and ramrod straight. His eyes were cold and hard. The thane stepped forward and inclined his head slightly in salute to both men.

"I am Lord John Campbell of Cawdor, and this ship and crew are at your mercy; we offer no resistance."

"Wisely so," the fat captain said. "Samuel Boggs at yer service," he added, his eyes sweeping over the assembled nobles on the deck, lingering on Duncan for a moment before returning to the thane. "Tell yer boys to lay their weapons on the planks. If everyone cooperates, we will be done with our business and away before ye know it." The men on the quarterdeck did not need to see Lord Campbell's nod to know what was expected. Claymores and rapiers and daggers clattered to the boards.

The crew and wedding guests similarly cooperated for the most part and the pirates quickly disarmed everyone else, stripped them of their valuables and then assembled them on the main deck. They divided the prisoners by class or, more precisely, their potential worth. The rovers quickly found Arabella and Alexandria and dragged both kicking and screaming from their cabins. Arabella saw that the pirate holding Molly had blood cascading from his nose, which had clearly been broken. In addition, four crimson scratches on his face and three more on his forearm told Arabella her friend had not been captured without a fight. Despite her fear, Arabella smiled at Molly, who gave her a wink in return. Arabella also noted how efficiently the pirates went about their work of looting the passengers and ship. They rushed to and fro like ants, racing from the main deck to the lower decks and back again, carrying armloads of swag and depositing everything at the base of the mainmast. Regrettably, she saw that a good deal of their loot consisted of wedding gifts meant for her and Duncan. Captain Boggs saw this as well and seemed quite pleased with the haul. His attitude improved markedly, in contrast to the other pirate captain who said nothing and still wore a dangerous scowl. As the last pirate deposited his goods amidships, Boggs called out to a scrawny little man who stood at the mast with scroll and parchment in hand.

"Squid Lips! Have ye yer inventory?"

"Aye, aye, cap'n!" the purser responded, smiling.

"Bobbing John, ye mark that," Boggs called to his quartermaster, a hulking brute of a fellow.

Bobbing John looked over the list, compared it against the pile of looted goods and only then put his mark on the parchment. "All right, ye dogs," he called out. "Get this swag back to our ships! Ye will get yer shares later. After."

"Ain't we gonna divvy it 'ere and now?" one of the pirates asked.

He had barely finished the question when the quartermaster jerked a heavy cat-o-nine from his belt and struck the man hard in the face. The fellow dropped instantly to the deck, covering his face with both hands and cowering. His mates laughed at him.

"That man and the ones to either side of him!" Boggs shouted. "Five lashes each before they get their liquor tonight!"

"Aye aye, cap'n!" the quartermaster replied. "Now get yer scurvy arses to work and get this loot aboard ship. Now!" This time, the men jumped to the task without any questions.

Boggs turned back to the nobles standing near him, a greasy smile again on his face. He removed his hat and bent his leg in a sweeping bow. "Yer generosity be most appreciated, good gentles. We be nearly finished with ye."

"*Nearly* finished?" Lord Campbell said. "Damn your avarice man! You have stripped my ship and the people upon her near to the bone;

what more is there to take?"

The smile on Bogg's face actually grew before he answered. "We 'ave most of yer valuables, yer lordship, but not all. We be taking yer ship as well, though we will allow yer the first opportunity to buy her back from us."

"Damn you, you cur!" Lord Campbell cursed.

"And lest I forget, we are taking the crew and passengers hostage for ransom. Ye look surprised. Ye did not think I were going to leave so many valuable prisoners behind did ye when there is coin yet to be made from selling them? But again, because I am a fair man, I will give ye first chance to ransom them back before I sell them on the Barbary Coast."

"You would not dare!" Lord Campbell protested.

"Damn your black heart, scoundrel!" Sir William cursed.

The two pirate captains ignored them, letting a handful of their men guard the nobles while the captains quickly divvied up the prisoners. They sent roughly half to the other pirate vessel, the one so similar to *The Thistle*, then directed their men to secure the remaining prisoners below decks on this ship.

"Almost finished," Boggs said. "Now, I will be granting your release, Lord Campbell, and yours, Sir William, on yer gentlemen's honor to pay yer own ransoms and so ye can raise the money for the other hostages, assuming ye are so willing. But lest ye should forget yer promise once me sails are 'yond the horizon, we will be taking yer young'uns with us."

"No, I beg you!" Sir William cried.

Boggs again addressed the other pirate captain. "So which do ye favor, Woode?"

"I will take the Campbell lads," the other pirate captain answered after a moment's pause. "You can keep the Frasers." He nodded his head and several pirates moved forward to secure his prisoners.

"Woode?" Lord Campbell said suddenly, looking hard at the pirate captain. "By Mary, I thought I recognized you. You are James, Lord John Spotiswoode's brother!"

The pirate captain's eyes flashed from dangerous to deadly. Without a word, he stepped close to Lord Campbell and appeared to give him a rough hug. The nobleman gasped and the pirate stepped back to reveal a long dirk plunged deep into the Thane's stomach. Spotiswoode twisted the blade savagely and the nobleman dropped to his knees, trying to speak but only spitting blood onto his killer's sleeve.

"Father!" Colin screamed. He tore his arms from the grasp of the men holding him, hurling one clean over the railing and into the sea. He jerked the cutlass from the other sea dog's sheath and lunged for Spotiswoode. The villain threw himself backward, tumbling to the deck and narrowly avoiding his death while four other rogues jumped forward to battle Colin.

"Filthy pirates!" Douglas swore, throwing off his own captors and sliding a hidden dagger from his boot. He spun and slashed one of the pirate's throats. Before he could do more, Captain Boggs shoved two feet of cold steel through his back.

Arabella, bound and still on the main deck, watched as Douglas fell to his knees. Their eyes met and held for a long moment before Douglas' flickered, rolled back in his head and he pitched forward, dead. Arabella opened her mouth to scream but nothing came out.

"Goddamned blackguard!" Sir William cried, lunging for Boggs. The pirate captain hit him hard in the face with the metal handguard of his sword, knocking the old knight to the planks.

"Damn you pirate scum!" Duncan screamed, finally shaking off his shock and trying to wrest free from his captors. The men beat him savagely to the ground, silencing his cries before dragging him away.

"No!" Arabella cried, finding her voice at last. She fell to her knees and stared in horror at the sight before her. Atop the quarterdeck, only

Colin Campbell still fought. He smashed one pirate to the planks with his brawny fists and ended another's life with his cutlass. A third rover finally managed to bring the pommel of his sword down on the back of the young man's head. Colin staggered and the fellow hit him again and again. The Scotsman crumpled forward into the arms of two more pirates. Captain Spotiswoode calmly rammed his sword into the young man's heart, killing him instantly. A sudden silence loomed over the quarterdeck before Spotiswoode ordered his men to toss the corpses into the sea.

"Get her below with the others!" Boggs barked, turning back to the pirates holding Arabella.

They half-carried, half-dragged her from the main deck. Before she disappeared into the dark, she turned toward the pirate ships in the water, marking them in her memory. The breeze had blown the second ship, Captain Spotiswoode's, around just enough to allow her to read the name on its stern: *Sea Rover*. She would not forget it.

Sir William awoke and struggled to rise. Boggs kicked him hard in the chest and pushed him flat onto his back.

"Don't be a fool, Sir William," he hissed. "Even a pitiful old knight like ye must know when the battle has been lost. Right now, ye should be concentrating on staying alive long enough to raise yer fair daughter's ransom if'n ye ever want to see her again. And I will be expecting ye to give the same message to Lord Campbell's kin so they can fetch poor Duncan from the hell that awaits him otherwise. Do I make meself clear?" Sir William nodded, tears stinging his eyes and choking off his words. Two pirates came forward and shoved him into one of *The Thistle's* oar boats. "The shore is that way," Boggs called down to him, pointing west with a cruel smile.

A moment later, the three tall ships unfurled their sails and turned toward the open sea.

The pirates hauled Arabella below, not to her cabin but to a hatch in the floor of the lower deck, roughly amidships and secured with an iron bar. They opened the portal and carried her down into the bowels of *The Thistle*. The air here was dank and lifeless, with no light save for the sputtering lanterns the men carried. She hesitated to go into this dark hole. One of the pirates shoved her forward, causing her to fall. Not waiting for her to stand, they grabbed her arms and dragged her like a sack of grain until they reached the ship's forward storerooms. In the gloom, she could just make out two hatches before her, perhaps three feet to a side, also secured with iron bars. The pirates unlocked one and shoved her in. Soft hands reached out and caught her, pulling her in and cradling her. The comforting voices of Molly, Bess, Isla and Dorothy welcomed her. Alexandria also shared their dark cell, though she sat away from the rest, sniveling dejectedly in a far corner. The cramped hold in which the six women found themselves measured only four feet wide and seven feet long, while the low ceiling hung just over their heads even while seated. The rovers slammed the cell door shut, plunging them into total darkness.

The women huddled together, most of them sobbing. Bess, the eldest, remained calm, doing her best to soothe the others. Arabella could not keep silent and told them of the horrific and cold-blooded murders she had witnessed on the quarterdeck. More tears came from everyone now and continued for some time. Eventually their grief gave way to a heavy, despairing silence. Beyond the wooden walls of their prison they heard only the sound of the sea rushing past, telling them they yet sailed, though to where they could only guess. After some time, Arabella inquired as to the other prisoners aboard their ship, the men among the wedding party and crew. Molly told her they had all been brought down together, with the men placed in the hold next to theirs, though she could not be certain who by name shared their prison.

"Well then, let us see if we can remedy that," Arabella said.

She called out to the nearby hold and instantly received a reply. The captives could just hear each other through the bulkheads if they shouted. The pirates had kept more than two dozen men aboard *The Thistle*, cramming them into three separate holds in the nose of the ship. The girls learned that Captain McMullins had been placed aboard the *Sea Rover,* but First Mate Selkirk remained on this vessel. Among the other remaining officers and crew were Mister De Rivero, master gunner John Browne, their Danish carpenter Mister Ejnar Jonassen and six sailors including Lord Campbell's nephew Fergus. Of the gentlemen from the wedding party, the two knights had been taken aboard the *Rover* but Duncan's remaining gentlemen ushers, Rob Roy MacIntosh and Angus Brodie, were here along with the Reverend Keith, Ian and Michael, two of the Campbell family's valets, Lord Campbell's page George, all four of the minstrels and a handful of potboys and porters. The two groups conversed with each other at length, talking and exchanging information until their voices went hoarse from yelling. Arabella learned that, thankfully, the pirates had murdered no one else, though they had been most cruel to many of the men and boys. They had not molested any of the women, however, which was another cause for thanks.

After this, the women again fell silent, though Alexandria

continued to sob, hovering on the verge of panic. Arabella moved to her and tried to comfort her, holding her and rocking her gently back and forth while stroking her hair, though to little avail. Arabella did not hold this against her sister, for she found her reaction completely understandable considering the circumstances. It was her own reaction she found odd, recognizing the sharp contrast between her and Alexandria and wondering at her own lack of hysteria during all of this. Surely she, of all persons, had the most reason to lose control, to succumb to panic and fear. And yet panic did not consume her despite a sadness almost too powerful for words and her very real concern over what her captors might yet do to her and the others.

Hours later, Arabella still lay awake even as the steady breathing of the others told her that blessed, exhausted sleep had finally come to them. The sadness and pain she felt crushed in upon her, as complete as the blackness of the dank hold. Now, as the others slumbered, she allowed herself to weep, and did so until her tears ran dry some hours later.

There, she thought to herself. *That is enough. I am a Highlander and a Fraser and I will cry no more.*

5

Although *The Thistle* had remained within sight of the coast, the pirates had dropped Sir William into a rowboat nearly a mile from shore. Daylight was quickly fading. He was no stranger to working the oars however, for he owned a small boat of nearly this size and used it often to fish on Loch Mhor. Still, his struggle to reach the shore this night proved anything but a leisurely stretch on the thwarts. His head throbbed painfully from Bogg's blow and blood still oozed from the wound, while powerful swells and an offshore current fought him every inch of the way. It was late at night when he finally dragged himself onto the rocky shore and collapsed. Emotionally and physically spent, he fell asleep right there on the beach.

He awoke the next morn, cold, stiff, wet and completely shrouded in a thick fog. His head still smarted terribly and now his stomach ached for its breakfast, though for this he knew he would find no relief anytime soon. Not knowing what else to do, he pushed himself to his feet and began walking inland. The fog began to thin and he soon came across a well-traveled road roughly following the shore. He turned north, toward Scotland. He hoped by following this track he must come upon a town or village at some point.

Two hours later he walked into the English village of Elwick, nestled snuggly within the gentle slopes of the Kyloe Hills. He stopped at the first inn he found, famished and parched. He called for food and drink and ate like a man starved near to death, consuming two large platters of meat and vegetables and a prodigious amount of ale. Only upon finishing his meal did he learn the inn would not take credit but expected him to pay at once in gold or silver coin. Of course he had none, having been thoroughly dispossessed by the pirates, and tried to explain this to the proprietor. He told the fellow he was a knight of Scotland and as such his word was as good as gold, and that he would send back payment in full the moment he reached Edinburgh. The man laughed in his face and called him a liar, eyeing with disdain his wet, torn and bloodied clothes and bedraggled hair and beard.

Sir William grew incensed. He cursed the man a fool and swore he would take his life on the field of battle for questioning his honor and good name. The innkeeper's wife ran out and fetched the shire reeve. The old knight soon found himself occupying the town's one small gaol cell. He would remain there, the reeve told him, until his debt had either been paid off or worked off.

6

The pirates gave their prisoners neither food nor water their first day of captivity, nor did anyone come down to check on them. The women could tell night from day only by the most miniscule amount of light that reached them through uncaulked seams in the boards of the deck above them. By evening, their bellies grumbled and their throats felt like sandpaper. It was the smell, however, that proved the worst. Foul dampness permeated their wooden prison and mingled with sweat, mud, mold and human waste. The pirates had not provided them with a bucket and so the women had to crawl to a corner and relieve themselves there. No air moved within the small cell and the stench increased with each passing hour, stinging their noses and choking their lungs. And still the ship sailed on. Though she did not express her fears, Arabella grew increasingly worried when they did not quickly port somewhere. *How far away from Scotland - and their ransoms - were they going?* she wondered.

Late on the second night, Arabella felt the ship slow and heard the rush of water against their hull diminish. *Surely we must be entering a harbor, soon to be released if not from bondage at least from this hellish hold,* she thought. The ship continued, however, without turning or slowing more. In less than an hour, *The Thistle* once again increased its speed, dashing Arabella's hopes. Duff Selkirk announced from the other hold that the captain of one ship had likely wanted to go aboard the other ship to discuss something with his counterpart, and thus the two vessels had slowed to facilitate the crossing. By mid-morning of the next day, the prisoners found themselves in a terrible state. They had gone beyond discomfort and faced the prospect of suffering real harm from neglect. Poor Alexandria, accustomed to a very pampered life, suffered the worst. She spent most of her time weeping inconsolably and the rest moaning that she was surely to die at any moment. Molly wondered aloud if this was not what the pirates wanted for all of them, to simply let them die.

"What then," Arabella countered, "was the point of kidnapping us?

The pirates could just as easily have slit our throats on the first night and tossed the lot of us into the sea."

She had no more finished this sentence when the door to their hold swung open. Several pirates stood without and Arabella could not help but think her words had leapt into reality and they had come to slaughter them all. She prepared to fight.

"Pray tell us you have brought food and water," Molly croaked.

"Aye, we got yer vittles," one of the men grunted. "How is the young'un faring? She do not look so well," he added, implying Alexandria.

"She suffers, as do we all," Arabella told him.

"Is it true she is the kin o' Earl Arran?" he asked.

"What does that matter?" Molly asked.

"Cap'n says 'e did not know it when 'e took 'er. Says she is too valuable a hostage to risk dying in these stinkin' holds."

At that, two of the men reached in and grabbed Alexandria, dragging her from the cell. The other women did not know whether to grab her and hold on or let her go, worried for her safety but knowing another day in this cramped prison might be the death of her anyway. They chose to let the pirates take her.

"Do not touch a hair on her head!" Arabella told them.

"Captain's orders, she is not to be mistreated in any way; on pain o' death," he added, though the women were not certain whether he spoke to them or to his mates.

"And what of the rest of us?" Molly demanded. "Are we to be left here?"

"Aye. Guess yer should have had wealthier dads!" The pirate laughed and placed three buckets into the cell before slamming the door shut again. "One is food, one is water and the third be empty," he called from the other side. "I am sure ye can figure out what to do with that'un."

The prisoners found themselves in darkness once more. Nearby, they heard the male prisoners also receive food and water. The girls reached for the buckets, the first containing two small loaves of hard, stale bread, a boiled hunk of what might have been pork and various vegetable scraps, most likely the leavings from other meals. They ignored this for the moment and passed around the water bucket, quenching their thirst and ignoring the brackish taste and odd smell, its contents as welcome to them as cloutie dumplings on Christmas morning.

The next day, the little door to the hold creaked open again. The

same pirates as before stood without, looking worried. Behind them,
Arabella saw the Reverend Keith, looking just as grim.

"Which one of you was the blond girl's kin?" a pirate asked.

"What do you mean, 'was,'?" Arabella replied, fear gripping her
stomach.

"Miss Fraser, please accompany us," the reverend said.

Arabella looked at him but did not move. The priest's eyes
beseeched her to come, if for nothing more than to complete an
unpleasant but necessary task. Finally, she crawled from the hold and
tried to stand. Her legs would not support her though, either from being
cramped in the hold for so many days or from a physical unwillingness
to go where these men wanted to take her. One of the pirates stepped
forward and supported her, then helped her up the ladder and to the
decks above. Finally, she was able to again stand. Once topside, she
filled her lungs with the fresh sea air, gulping it in like a drowning
swimmer freshly risen above the water's surface. She closed her eyes
and let the wind caress her, billowing her tattered and stained skirts and
untangling her matted hair. A hand touched her arm and she opened her
eyes, immediately returning to stark reality. The Reverend Keith guided
her to the port railing on the main deck. There, a small number of
crewmen and ship's officers stood solemnly around what appeared to

be nothing more than a bundle of rags on a long board. Only when she stepped closer could Arabella see that a body lay beneath those rags, small and frail. The corpse had been shrouded head to toe in sailcloth in the tradition of a burial at sea. A bulge near the feet would be a cannonball, she knew, placed there to ensure the body sank. Arabella's head swam as if she were ill or in a dream. The hold did not seem such a terrible place at this moment, so long as it was anywhere but here.

"Reverend," she said to the minister, who stood with his bible in hand. "Can this be true?"

"I am sorry, my child. I gave her Last Rites some hours ago. If it is any comfort, I believe she passed quietly in her sleep."

"Dear God!" Arabella gasped, leaning on the ship's rail for support. Though she and Alexandria had never been close, she felt the pain of the girl's death intensely.

"And ye will swear to that," one of the pirates growled. He seemed to be a man of some authority, perhaps the first mate, for his dress set him apart and the other men seemed to treat him with deference if not outright fear. "We did nothing to her. Her death was due to natural causes, aye Reverend?"

The priest nodded his head curtly. Arabella felt the color return to her cheeks.

"Natural causes? Hardly!" she blurted. "Being confined in that hellhole is what killed her! She had not the constitution for such excitement and fear and barbaric treatment as you subjected her to - all of us to! How dare you call her death 'natural.' You murdered her as surely as if you had slit her throat!"

"Shut yer hole, girl!" the first mate barked. "We got her out o' there as soon as we known who she was! Gave her her own quarters and treated her to good fare and drink. It is no fault of ours her weak constitution, as ye yerself admit. The reverend ha' prepared a document attesting to that fact and ye will sign it as a witness to our innocence if ye value yer own life! Now let us be done with it."

After a moment's pause, the minister began a brief, though heartfelt service. Arabella remained silent during this out of respect for both he and Alexandria, though for sure she had more to say. The pirate who had spoken seemed to know this and stayed clear of her, refusing even to look at her. After the eulogy and several prayers, two crewmen lifted the plank and the body slid quietly into the sea. Only a small splash echoed up to the deck, followed by silence.

"Gramercy, father," the pirate said before turning to his sailors. "Now get 'em back below - after they has marked that document."

Both prisoners soon found themselves shut into the darkness once more, leaving Arabella to again wonder if it had all simply been a terrible nightmare.

***

It was near evening on the day after the funeral when the prisoners once again felt *The Thistle* slow. This time, however, they also felt the ship turn in a long, sweeping arc. Within an hour, movement ceased entirely and they heard through the thick wooden walls of their prison the unmistakable sounds of a busy seaside dock. Ships' bells rang, gulls cried, stevedores cursed and cargo clattered as it was loaded and unloaded. Arabella and her fellow prisoners believed they would finally be freed from this accursed gaol, taken from the ship and allowed to breathe fresh air once more while awaiting their eventual release. The hours passed though and no one came for them. No one came for them the next day either, during which the ship took on additional supplies and cargo. With the evening tide, *The Thistle* weighed anchor and headed out to sea once more.

The following day, the hatch barring the hold swung open yet again. Several pirates stood outside the portal, their light blinding everyone within. This time, they dragged Arabella from the hold. Arabella screamed and struck one of the men hard in the face. She followed this with a swift kick to his groin and he crumpled to the floor. His mates laughed even as they grabbed her and quickly wrapped leather cords around her wrists and ankles. They slammed the hatch shut and carried her up the ladder to the lower deck. This time they did not continue to the upper deck, carrying her instead down a passage to the forward section of the ship, the same area in which she had berthed at the beginning of the voyage. The rovers took her to a small cabin just opposite the one she had shared with Bess and Molly and dropped her onto a thin straw mattress. One of the dogs knelt beside her and rolled her onto her stomach, all the while leering at her with his one good eye. He took a dagger from his belt and Arabella winced as she felt the cold steel touch her ankles. The blade severed the rope pinioning her legs and she feared the worst. One of the brute's hands moved up to her backside and rested there a moment before he slit the bonds securing her wrists.

He stood, and a second later the door to the cabin slammed shut. She heard the bolt thrown, locking her in. For the first time in many days, she was alone. All of the furniture had been removed from the cabin, leaving only the palliasse upon which she now lay. A chamber pot, a bowl of gruel and a pitcher of water had also been placed within. She stood and tested the door just to be certain, finding it indeed locked and very stout. Despite the sparseness of her new surroundings, she could not complain. This cabin was a palace compared to the pit she had so recently occupied, tall enough in which to stand or lay comfortably and with a small porthole in the wall providing light and a view of the ocean but a few feet away.

She gazed out the window for several minutes before remembering the food and how hungry she was. She wolfed down the gruel and nearly wept with joy when she saw that a hunk of bread had been thrown in. She devoured every crumb, despite its foul taste and the weevils living in it. After eating, she returned to the porthole. A dozen thoughts at once went through her mind. She worried about her father first and foremost, praying he had not been hurt too badly and that he had safely made it home. Still, he would be alone now, without his son or daughter at his side just when he needed them most. This thought led to her next, the dread question she could not stifle no matter how hard she tried: what ransom could the pirates honestly expect from her father? God knows he loved her and would do anything necessary to free her, but they had so little these days. What if he did not have enough money to satisfy these greedy devils? She continued to stare through the porthole at the limitless sea as another thought came into her mind: did the pirates really mean to ransom her at all, or any of their prisoners for that matter? She could not shake her apprehension that they had traveled too far to easily accommodate a ransom, and certainly not a visit from anyone who wished to confirm their health and well-being before paying such. What devilry were these rogues up to? Where were they taking her and her fellow prisoners, and to what fate? These thoughts and a score of others occupied her for the remainder of the day and well into the night. Finally, at some point very late, exhaustion took her and she slept.

A noise awoke Arabella and she sat up with a start. Captain Boggs stood in the open doorway leering at her. By the light peeking into the room, the heat of the day and the hungry ache in her belly, she knew she had slept for a very long time. She sat up, pushing her skirts down to cover her bare ankles.

"Miss Fraser," Boggs said, removing his hat and bowing as if he were a country gentleman come a'calling. "We were not formerly introduced before: I am Captain Samuel Boggs. I have assumed command of this ship and now captain her as my own." As he spoke, his eyes roamed over her body from head to toe, leaving her feeling violated. It was his failure to look her in the eyes that prevented him from seeing the fire there a second before she launched herself at him.

"Murderer!" she screamed, one hand clawing at his face while the other grabbed for the dagger in his belt.

The big man yelped and stumbled backward. He shoved a hand into her face to push her away and she bit down on his thumb. The nails of her right hand carved four crimson furrows into his cheek as her other hand closed about his dagger. He smashed his fist into her stomach, blasting the wind from her and causing her to lose her grip on both him and the weapon. She fell to the floor, gasping for breath and Boggs kicked her hard in the ribs. She felt such pain she nearly blacked out but refused to give him the satisfaction. Unable to speak from the ache and lack of air, she simply glared up at him from the floor as he held a silk kerchief against his bleeding face. His own glare burned as hateful and dangerous as hers.

"Damn, but ye're a hellcat! I am trying to be civil to yer but one more outburst like that and I'll slap ye in irons and throw ye back in the hold!"

"Then do so!" she croaked, able to speak once more. "You should expect no civility from me! Why was I brought to this cabin? What are your intentions?"

"To talk, for sure, not to fight!"

"Go to the devil!" she spat, rising to her knees. The captain took another step backward. "You murdered my brother and by God I am going to see you dead if I have to do it myself!"

"Softly, lass, softly! I had no wish to harm yer brother or anyone else; he made me do it when he attacked me and me men. Believe me, I am as sorry for his death as you." Arabella chortled derisively and the captain smiled. "Oh, do not get me wrong; 'twas not the loss of his life I regret but the loss of his ransom."

"Pig!" Arabella spat.

"But let us speak no more of the dead, for yer tears and anger can do them no good. 'Tis the living ye should be concerned with and that is what I have come to talk to ye about. Ye do care about yer friends and mates in me hold, do ye not?" Arabella said nothing, continuing to glare at him, so Boggs continued. "As ye know, ye are all held prisoner until such time as a ransom can be delivered. As me prisoners, ye have me word ye shall not be molested or cruelly abused."

"Your word? So I am now to be taking the word of a pirate and a murderer?"

"Take what ye like, lass, but thank yer stars that ye are more valuable to me pure and untouched than t'other way." His clenched jaw and roving eyes told her he would much rather have had things 't'other way,' though just what was stopping him from doing so she could not fathom. Did he really believe her father would refuse to pay her ransom if she were 'ravaged and spoilt?' She prayed the presence or absence of her maidenhead would make not a whit of difference to her father - dowry and future husband be damned. Or was it that the threat of a future rape of his daughter meant to compel Sir William to meet the pirates' demands in a timely fashion? She could not dwell on it, though, before the villain spoke again. "Until such time as ye are properly paid for, ye should consider yerself not me prisoner, but me guest. Assuming ye behave, that is."

"Fah! No host treats a guest so poorly as you have treated me and my fellow captives, who I must assume yet linger down in those stinking, black holds."

"This is no sultan's luxury ship, missy, and accommodations are first reserved for me officers and crew."

"What of proper food and water? Is there not enough of that aboard for all of us?"

"Which brings me to me point. There are enough victuals on this ship, but little can I spare any of me men to prepare them and dish them out to yer, at least not on a daily basis. And so I mean to offer that task to ye."

"To me? So that is why you brought me to this room so far removed from the holds, to make me more amenable to your 'offer.'"

Arabella shifted a bit and smiled to see that the captain took another half step back. "You were only too willing to take us captive, but now cannot be bothered with feeding and caring for us?"

"As I said, this is a working ship and we have no butlers or yeomen of the pantry aboard. If ye want yer friends to eat, than ye must do it yerself."

"'Tis not a lack of food that will be the death of them, 'tis being locked in those Godforsaken holds, stinking and damp. One has died already and yet you leave them down there."

"I cannot have a gaggle of prisoners running amuck on me ship, girl. Am I to give them all individual cabins and have me men sleep on the open deck, exposed to the elements?"

"Then give us the forward section of this deck, the four cabins here in the bow. Sure'n it would be cramped, but 'tis a far sight better than those bloody holds."

"Do not make demands of me on my ship, missy!" Boggs growled. "Ye can care for yer mates under my conditions or not at all. If one or two more of them pass in the holds, what is it to me?"

"And what of your precious profits from their ransom?"

"Ransoms have been paid for dead folk before, Miss Fraser, so long as those doing the payin' do not yet know they be dead. And know this: each time I send me men down to feed and water them there be a risk. This is a ship full of lusty men, and I cannot watch all of them at every moment. Some of me hands were particularly eyeing the old gray-haired lass."

"You are scum!"

"Aye, and then some. So let us have yer answer, miss: what say ye?"

"Care for my comrades or let them suffer? 'Tis no choice at all and you know it. I will do it, but on two conditions."

"And I told yer ye are in no place to make demands!" Arabella just stared at him with a look of firm resolve in her eyes. After a moment of intense silence, he waved his hand as if to brush off a pesky gnat. "Let me hear them already and I will decide."

"First, everyone, the women and the men, come out of those holds. And second, you swear the women will not be ravaged."

"And if I do not agree to yer terms?" the captain asked with a smug grin. "Ye see, in matters such as this, ye have to have something of value to be offerin' back."

"And so I do. If my terms are not met, I will take neither food nor water for myself, though I may starve. Not only will I save my father a hefty ransom he can ill afford to pay, but I will rob you of whatever value I may have."

The smile slid from Boggs' face. "Ye would not."

"Try me," she said, her green eyes blazing. There was no baseless bravado in that stare and the captain, to his credit, realized it.

"Fine, then," he sputtered after a moment's pause. "Yer terms are fair and of no consequence to me. But know this, missy, and know it well: ye had better be on yer best behavior, all of yer, or it is right back into the holds! Now quit yer lollygaging and get up to the cook's cabin; yer mates will be gettin' hungry." Arabella knew the way. She rose and moved toward the door and Boggs gave her wide leeway to pass, his hand on the hilt of his sword. As she reached the ladder he called after her. "And when they be slopped and ye 'ave scrubbed the galley pots and pans clean, ye can head back down into the holds with a brush and bucket. Thirty prisoners can make a right foul mess with nowhere else to relieve themselves!" Captain Boggs burst into roaring laughter, his hoots following her all the way to the main deck.

Once there, she again stopped and stood, taking in the smell of the salt air and the feeling of the wind on her face. She listened to the sound of the waves rushing past the ship and of the sails and rigging snapping in the breeze. Looking up, she was not surprised to see that Lord Campbell's pennant had been taken from the flagstaff, though it did sadden her somewhat. The St. Andrew still flew there, though its position had moved to below an English St. George. The pirates must have raised this after taking the ship, to fly no doubt while they sailed through English waters and just as surely to be replaced with a different one as soon as they entered another nation's seas. She turned and scanned the horizon, searching for the *Sea Rover*. She knew there was little hope of actually seeing Duncan, but just to see the ship that carried him would be enough for her right now. She saw first the land, falling away to the west. Turning, she spotted another ship at a great distance that looked to be paralleling them, though at this range she could not discern whether it was the *Rover* or the *Gunsway* or some other vessel. She saw no third ship. Still, she gazed at the vessel for some time, wondering if Duncan were aboard. She wanted to think so, to believe he was there, that he was well and perhaps even thinking of her at this very moment.

The crack of a whip near her elbow shattered her peace, making her jump. She spun about and saw the cruel eyes of the pirate quartermaster called Bobbing John glaring at her, the cat dangling in his calloused hand.

"The galley is that way, wench."

Despite her loathing for Captain Boggs, Arabella lived up to her end of the bargain, as she would not sacrifice the welfare of her fellow prisoners simply to satisfy her thirst for vengeance. She became the cook, server and maid to the thirty-plus prisoners. Surprisingly, the captain kept true to his word as well, bringing them up from the hold and placing them in the forward bow of the lower deck. The pirates allowed only Arabella to roam about the ship, while the rest remained confined to the lower deck twenty-four hours a day. The women had the largest of the cabins on the starboard side, while the men had the remaining three cabins as well as the floor space in between. The bow was cramped and overcrowded to say the least and the situation would have been appalling under different circumstances. No one complained though, for each of them knew it was far better than being in the holds.

And though she felt some guilt and regretted terribly that none of her fellow prisoners could join her, Arabella enjoyed her newfound freedom, her access to the ship's outside decks, the feel of the wind or sun or even the rain upon her skin. This freedom, however, was her one pleasure. For unlike her long days of worry and boredom in the fetid hold, she now lived days filled with unending toil. Even the outside air she so loved had its drawbacks, for although they sailed during the springtime and there were few violent storms, she often found the cold winds and waters of the Atlantic anything but pleasant. She most disliked the nights and early mornings, for they were often bitterly cold, especially on days when the fog hung thick. She often cursed the thin dress she wore. Not only was it ponderous, with its billowy sleeves and long skirts, but it became entirely too revealing when wet, which happened often. It also saddened her that the once fine garment had become torn and stained in more places than she could ever hope to clean or repair.

On most days, she was the first to enter the galley in the morning and the last to leave at night. Captain Boggs insisted she prepare the prisoners' breakfast before the ship's crew ate, but she was to fix their supper after the crew had been served their final meal of the day. This had been done, she guessed, at the insistence of Boggs' cook, a gross, lazy slug of a man everyone called 'Biscuits.' The galley was bitterly cold in the morning until she lit the cook fire. Once the fire began roaring though, the tiny cabin quickly overheated. Late in the day, after Biscuits and his mates had fed the crew, Arabella prepared supper for the prisoners, but not before she first had to clean up after the pirate cooks, who always left their mess for her. To serve the prisoners required making dozens of trips from the hot galley across the wind-swept deck and down into the stuffy lower deck, followed a short time later with a plunge into the frigid wash water to tend to the used plates and bowls and tankards and kettles. Between the morning and evening meals, Arabella kept busy with innumerable other chores, doing all for the prisoners they could not or were not allowed to do for themselves. They had no access to wash water for instance and thus Arabella laundered all their clothes. She also did the mending and darning since the captives were not allowed needles or knives. And of course, there were always the chamber pots to carry topside and dump and rinse out before returning them to the prisoners. She rarely finished the last of her chores before midnight.

The prisoners were extremely grateful for everything she did for them, helping as much as they could and never failing to express their gratitude. The pirate crew, however, delighted in making her life miserable. They lost no opportunity to make sport with her and often abused her verbally if not physically. Her trips across the ship's deck never went unnoticed or uncommented upon, and the pirates constantly harangued her with disgusting catcalls and rude comments. They ogled her in a most indecent way, rarely letting their eyes rise above her neckline, and made comments such as she had never heard despite growing up surrounded by men. She was actually thankful she had no idea what some of the comments meant, though she knew they were disgusting and unfit for civilized men. And despite the captain's orders that she not be molested, the crew had no qualms about swatting her on the arse as she passed by or 'accidentally' brushing against her breasts any time their duties carried them near her.

Complaining would have been pointless, she knew, and likely would have only made matters worse. For the most part, she made light of their jibes, often returning their insults with salty words and phrases of her own, things she had learned from the men in her life and on her previous sea voyages. Once they saw their rude comments would no longer get a rise from her, most of the pirate crew gave up trying. At the same time, she made an extra effort to get to know the sailors personally, to engage them and show an interest in them as people. In this way she not only subtly encouraged them to do the same with her, but also won valuable allies among them. Soon, instead of harassing her, many of these men began to urge their mates to 'show the lady some bloody respect' as she went about her duties. There were, of course, those sailors who refused to treat her or any woman as anything but a sexual object and a victim, things Arabella refused to be. She ignored these brutes as best she could but made clear she would not tolerate any physical violation of her person. The message did not truly sink in until the day a sailor went too far with her and Arabella cut off a large piece of his ear with a galley knife she had hidden upon her person, promising him he would lose other, more significant parts of his anatomy if he ever touched her again. This earned her the respect of most of the crew, though Bobbing John was furious at her for daring to raise a hand against one of his men. He begged the captain to let him punish her but Boggs refused. Not only was he protecting a valuable asset, but in Boggs' view, the sailor had only received what he had coming to him for disobeying his orders.

The Thistle continued ever south, each day moving farther away from Scotland. Soon, Arabella recognized the narrows between Calais and Dover, for she had seen this passage before on her own voyages. Scores of ships from most of the nations of Europe plied these waters, and she thought that if this ship was ever to be stopped by an English or French 'king's ship' it would be here. This did not happen, however, and the pirates sailed through the Channel without incident. Arabella's hope for deliverance by a royal ship diminished with each mile they traveled, only to be replaced by fantasies of Duncan coming to her rescue.

In her mind's eye, she saw him standing proudly on the bow of the *Sea Rover*, having led his fellow prisoners in revolt, overpowering his captors and seizing control of the vessel. He of course would immediately come for *The Thistle* and Arabella, and neither Man nor Nature would stop him from liberating her. This fantasy made her smile and gave her at least some hope, though she knew deep down it was little more than that – a fantasy. The pirates might be uneducated savages, but she could not deny they knew their business. While they might let her move freely about their ship, they would never do so with Duncan. What was she to them, she thought, but a young girl and a rather slight one at that, while Duncan was a grown man, tall and powerful and dangerous to his foes.

No, she thought, *I cannot rely on childish fantasies. No one will save me but myself.*

A few days later, Arabella left the galley and was walking across the deck when a sailor climbing up into the rigging suddenly stopped. He hung motionless for a moment as all the color drained from his face before pitching backward and crashing to the planks right at Arabella's feet. And though the morning was a cold one, she noted he was drenched in sweat.

"Do not touch him!" another sailor called out, rushing over. "He is with fever; he must be quarantined. Somebody notify the captain!"

As the first mate ran off to do this, Arabella looked around and noticed several other sailors appeared to be ill as well, their skin pale, sweat beading on their brows, one even on his knees vomiting. The illness quickly spread, affecting crew and prisoner alike. It began with a fever that came on fast and hit hard, bringing weakness, violent nausea and terrible pain in the joints. The captain reacted swiftly, quarantining anyone complaining of the symptoms in the aft section of the lower deck, and placing everyone else in the stern. He even moved the healthy prisoners out of the bow, despite the protests of his crew. Their words fell on deaf ears, for the health of the prisoners meant more to Boggs than the health of his crew. The way he looked at it, every dead prisoner was a loss of income to him, whereas every dead sailor represented one more share of ransom among the survivors.

Arabella remained unaffected by the illness despite her movement about the ship. As such, she not only continued her cooking and cleaning duties, but added caring for the sick to her long list of tasks. She spent every second she could below decks, bringing the afflicted water and cooling their foreheads with cold compresses, changing their clothes and sheets when they soiled them, emptying their vomit buckets, or just sharing a few words with them to comfort them. She did not limit her ministrations to the prisoners, either, but gave care to all, even those pirates who had so abused her. This was not because she had forgiven her tormentors or forgotten their cruel acts - for she had

not. It was simply not in her nature to deny assistance to those who

needed it, even the likes of these pirates.

The illness raged for several days, spreading to nearly three-fourths

of the crew and an equal number of the prisoners. Here it seemed to

peak, reaching its climax on a bitterly cold night as a violent storm

wracked the seas. Most of those who died from the epidemic died on

this night, including the Reverend Minister Keith. For his burial and the

burials of the few ship's officers who passed, Boggs allowed relatively

proper, Christian services. For the others, prisoner and common sailor

alike, he simply ordered them tossed over the ship's railing.

After that hellish night, the rest of the sick began to slowly recover.

In another few days, most of them were up and back at their tasks. Dear

old Thomas however, Sir William's valet of so many years, continued

to suffer. He had turned seventy only a few short weeks before and

Arabella smiled to remember his birthday gala. It was celebrated in

grand style at *Ban Tigh*, lasting several days and involving a great deal

of ale, ginger wine and whisky punch. As Arabella remembered this,

she realized she had never known a day at *Ban Tigh* without Thomas.

Now she feared for the worst but refused to give up, neither sleeping

nor eating but spending every moment she could spare, borrow or steal to be with him.

Four days after the storm, Captain Boggs brought up to the main deck three of the male prisoners. This was the first any of them had been allowed outside in the fresh air in more than two weeks. The captain stood scowling at them, his stern-looking first mate and hulking quartermaster at his side. The quartermaster held a crumpled piece of parchment in his hands and struggled to read it. Finally, he stepped to the fore and barked out a name.

"Benito De Rivero!"

The small man from Portugal hesitated a moment and then took a step forward. "Si. Here."

"It says here you were the pilot of *The Thistle* under her previous captain."

"Si, signore, I was the pilot," the man replied in his Castilian-accented English.

"Right. Our pilot is dead. We need a new one. Are you familiar with the waters beyond England, say points south and east?"

"I am."

"And are ye willing to serve the captain loyally, doing as ye are told with no tricks, on pain of death, until we can find another man to replace ye?"

"On pain of death, you said?" Mister Rivero asked.

"That is what he said," the captain growled. "Ye can serve me honestly and live, ye can serve me sneaky-like and die, or ye can refuse to serve me at all and go over the side right now. Them's yer choices."

Oddly, the man thought about it for a long moment before he answered. "Si, I will be your pilot."

"Good. Next!" the captain barked.

"Which one o' yer be John Browne?" the quartermaster called.

"I am," a big Lancashireman responded, stepping forward.

"Master gunner," the first mate stated. "We did not see much gunplay from this brig when we took her. Then again, we did not see many guns. Know ye yer trade?"

"I know my trade. 'Twas not my fault we had no guns aboard ship under McMullins," Mister Browne answered.

"Same offer to ye," Boggs told him.

When the pirates had seized *The Thistle*, they had placed four large minions, or four-pounders, aboard her, two on her larboard and two on her starboard side, as well as a good deal of shot and powder. This had not gone unnoticed by Mister Browne.

"Since I do not swim," he replied. "I am your man."

"Fine, step back," the quartermaster told him. "That leaves only ye, longshanks," he said to a tall Dane standing with De Rivero and Browne. "Yer must be Jonassen."

"Ejnar Jonassen, master carpenter," the man said proudly. "I know my choices and have already decided. My adz is yours. Get it? My *adz*!" He laughed hard at his own joke, though nobody else did.

With his masters replaced, Captain Boggs had other prisoners brought up and gave them a similar choice, although without the threat of being tossed overboard. The tasks the masters filled were critical to the running of his ship and he could not afford to sail without them, whereas he had plenty of sailors but always sought more to lessen the work and strengthen his numbers. Most of the prisoners agreed to serve Boggs, some gladly and others with heavy heart, feeling they were betraying Lord Campbell and their former captain. Still, none wanted to return to the misery of remaining locked below deck twenty-four hours a day with nothing to break up the tedious monotony. Working for Boggs, they would at least have a bit of freedom to move about the ship and a chance to breathe fresh air while doing so. One who did was Fergus Campbell. He had heard how they murdered his uncle and stated he would die before aiding them in anything except a swift and bloody exit from this world. As such, he remained one of the few prisoners. Upon hearing of his loyalty to Lord John, Arabella felt proud he had nearly been kin to her and hopefully still would, and told him so at the first opportunity.

On the same night the Reverend Keith had passed, Biscuits the cook had died as well. His mates Keith and Ken – though everyone called them Spit and Polish – had been filling in but were young and utterly inept. Preparing meals aboard a ship took some skill, for little of it was fresh and one had to know how to properly make ready salted meats and hard tack before it was palatable. The food the mates dished out was barely edible. In addition, the crew had needed to put out three gallery fires in as many days. Captain Boggs had sailed long enough to know that a well-fed crew was generally a happy crew, all other things being equal, whereas poorly-fed men were always unhappy, and unhappy men had a nasty habit of mutinying. He thought that a wench might be more capable in the kitchen, assuming she had been raised 'properly.'

With this in mind, he headed down to the sick deck for the first time since the epidemic had struck. He cast a disgusted eye toward where Arabella sat at Thomas' side, mopping his brow with a cool, damp cloth, then looked about for the other women. He did not ask Bess or Isla or Dorothy, though, for he did not think they would be up to the physical demands of the task at their age. This left Molly. It warmed Arabella's heart when she told him to go to hell. After a litany of curses and threats that Molly returned in kind, Boggs reluctantly asked Arabella if she would take on the duty of ship's cook in addition to her many other tasks. She refused him, albeit somewhat more politely than Molly, as she was in fact far too busy to take on any more work just now.

"Ye are only too busy because ye waste time on hopeless causes," the captain barked. "Why not spend it taking care of those who will benefit from it?"

"That is exactly what I am doing, Mister Boggs."

"Ye are not. Ye are but wasting time on infernal pampering o' the dead."

"The dead you say, sir?" she asked, color rising in her cheeks. "May I remind you that most of those I tended to recovered, and Thomas here yet has that chance. And every life saved benefits you as well as the survivor, I might add."

"Some lived, some died; 'twas naught but luck or fate," he said dismissively, refusing to even acknowledge that such outbreaks aboard ship typically took a full half or more of the afflicted, while he had lost less than a quarter this time. "Now this old gaffer here, the little profit in him is not worth all the effort on yer part. Yer time could be better spent elsewhere."

"I say it is well-spent right here, sir, and here is where I shall remain until dear auld Thomas is hale again."

"Or until he passes?" Boggs asked.

"If it comes to that."

"Right." Boggs drew his cutlass. Arabella saw the murder in his eyes and stood, placing herself between him and her patient. "Step aside, lass! 'Tis but a mercy killing for one who is already gone."

"I will not step aside and I will not let you murder this man, not while I still have breath in my body!"

"Get away, girl, and let me do me work!" he said, shoving her forcibly aside.

He took a step toward the bedridden man and Arabella jerked her own blade, the one with which she had cut off the ear of the pirate who had tried to molest her. She again stepped between Boggs' blade and Thomas.

"Raise that sword and you will be dead before he is."

The captain hesitated. "Stand aside, Goddamned you!"

"Never! You will have to kill me first - if you can."

"Damn yer Scots' stubbornness!" Boggs growled, advancing menacingly. Arabella stood her ground. He glared at her with hatred in his eyes, his greed clearly battling his rage. Finally, his shoulders slumped and his sword lowered. "Fine. Waste yer damn time on a dead man if ye will. What does it matter to me except that there will be more coin in me pocket come the end o' the voyage?"

He stuffed his sword back in its sheath, turned on his heel and stomped back to his cabin. Arabella breathed a sigh of relief and turned to see Molly flashing her a broad smile.

7

Sir William remained in the Elwick town gaol until such time as he received funds sufficient to pay for his meal at the inn, three weeks 'room and board' in the care of the shire reeve, and a small fine for disturbing the peace. This money came in answer to a letter he had been allowed to send north to a friend in Invernesshire, and included additional monies meant to aid him with his journey home. With little money to spare after paying his fines, Sir William resisted the temptation to acquire a young trotter and instead purchased an old swaybacked nag. As William left Elwick, the reeve was kind enough to advise him that the coast road leading from the village would take him all the way to Edinburgh. However, he should take care to stay to the road despite its twists and turns and cutbacks along the rugged shoreline and not give in to the temptation to cut straight across country and so shorten his journey. The rough wilds of the border area between England and Scotland were notoriously dangerous, owing to the reivers. Sir William knew well of the Border Reivers and even had some sympathy for their situation, for their lands had been subject to wars and invasions for centuries, with towns and villages on either side of the English-Scottish border constantly in the path of one army or another, and suffering the fate of all such places. Most of the villagers who remained in the marches along the border could no longer work the land, their farms and crops so frequently burned, their livestock ever stolen or slaughtered. So they turned to thieving, with great bands of men roving the border area and preying on any and all who crossed their path.

William rode north into the warm spring afternoon and made good time on the old road, passing without stopping through the shires of Fenwick and Cheswick before finally reaching the great walled town of Berwick-upon-Tweed. Berwick lay on the south side of the River Tweed, the occasional border between his country and England. The town had changed hands many times, with each nation improving its defenses in the hopes of holding off the next attempt to take it. At the present, the English possessed Berwick and it was a veritable fortress. William entered through the massive Southern Gate and quickly found a cozy little inn, spending some of his remaining coin on a bottle of whisky in the hopes it might help him forget his woes, if only temporarily.

Memories of the pirate attack burned fresh in his mind and his thoughts troubled him greatly. His son and a good friend had been murdered and his daughter seized, along with several servants, some of whom had been with him for decades. He had no idea how he was going to raise Arabella's ransom, let alone enough for Thomas or Bess or his young porters. Mostly, however, he worried about how Arabella would be treated by the murderous sea dogs. That night by the fire, he drank to Lord John and Douglas and Colin and prayed for Arabella and Duncan, drinking to them as well. When his first bottle ran low he bought another. He drank into the wee hours of the morning, sitting before the slowly dwindling embers in the old inn's rock hearth. The innkeeper found him there in the morning. He let him sleep for a bit but woke him as midmorning approached, telling him he would need to either pay for another day's stay or take his leave. Not wanting a repeat of the events in Elwick, Sir William departed, his heart heavy, his head throbbing and his steps slow.

He crossed into Scotland before noon, passing through the village of Burnmouth a short time later. He chose not to stop there despite his hunger, for his shillings were few. He thought he might try his hand at catching some small game in the nearby woods, a rabbit or pheasant perhaps. He had always been a proficient hunter, though his lands held little game, but he knew well how to set a snare. Besides, he could use a quiet nap while he waited for some unsuspecting prey to fall into his trap. In no time, he lay beneath the broad arms of a gray-trunked and wonderfully shady oak, his hat pulled forward over his eyes and a line of rope wrapped around one foot, trailing away to the nearby snare. In the warmth of the afternoon, he dozed. The jerking of the line awoke Sir William and told him his trap had done its trick. Or more precisely, it had *nearly* done its trick, for when he sat up he saw his supper bounding off into the forest. A long line of cord trailed after the great, fat hare. In an instant, the old knight scrambled to his feet and raced after the coney, convinced he could grab the line trailing from the little bugger and still eat for free tonight.

The hare was fast and led him a merry chase deep into the woods, the rope always tantalizingly close. As exhaustion threatened to take him, Sir William dove for the line. He heard the unmistakable 'twang' of a bowstring and saw a shaft pierce the hare, sticking it fast to the ground. William pulled himself to his knees, clutching the line and staring dumbly at the arrow, not comprehending what had just happened but grateful the chase had finally ended. He looked up, shocked to see he had charged headlong into the outskirts of a large encampment. Hundreds or more men stood or lounged around scores of tents, with paddocks for horses and cattle and sheep and all manner of animals, draft and otherwise. One of these men had launched the fatal bolt that had downed the coney. Others carried bows as well, many of them pointed directly at him.

"Bloody reivers," Sir William muttered, standing and raising his hands in surrender.

"Stand fast!" one of the archers growled. The old knight did as he was told, though he slowly folded his arms across his chest and tried not to look frightened. "Touch not your blade," the fellow added.

"Go on, then," Sir William called back. "Here is my coin pouch, though it is frightfully light. Sure'n, by the looks of things, you are eating better than I of late. But go, take it. And you can choke on it as well!"

"Who are you?" the bowman asked, approaching with several of his mates. Most had lowered their weapons, for Sir William had but a small dagger and no sword and appeared to present little risk to this group.

"Who wants to know?" he replied boldly.

"He is a Highlander, all right," one of the men said with a laugh. And sure, this bloke clearly had a Scottish brogue as well. Now that he looked, Sir William noted many of the men in the encampment wore the kilts of the Highlands as opposed to the trousers or leggings of the English or the Lowland Scots. Odd, he thought, that so many of these reivers should be from the Highlands.

"Come now, old gaffer," the first man said. "What clan do you hail from and what brings you to these woods?"

"All right then: Clan Fraser," Sir William answered, puffing out his chest. "I am traveling north to reach my home in the Great Glen."

"A Fraser, eh?" the man repeated, giving his mates a knowing glance. "Know you Sir William Fraser, perhaps?"

"Sir William? I might and I might not. What is it to you, boy?"

"Our master knows of him, has heard his name mentioned in certain circles. He is rumored to support rebellious ideas, and thus there are some who question his loyalty to the king."

"Sir William is loyal to the king, and any who know him knows this!" the old knight barked. "It is those damned scoundrels who surround young James that concern him. Now who is this master you serve?"

"What if we told ye we serve the Earl of Arran?"

"Arran!" William spat. He jerked his dagger and his knuckles went white around the hilt. "If you serve Arran, than you serve the devil! And to the devil with you all! No wonder you are a bunch of sodden thieves; your hearts are black and your bellies are as yellow as the sun!"

"Easy, good fellow, easy," the man spoke, a broad smile splitting his face. "If you can restrain yourself from stabbing anyone for a few moments, we would like you to join us for supper. Especially since you supplied the rabbit."

"Fah! I would rather starve than sup with the likes of supporters of the Earl of Arran!"

"As would I, Sir William," a deep voice called from nearby.

William spun and saw a richly-dressed nobleman seated atop a chestnut mare some twenty paces away, surrounded by several similarly-dressed men. This, however, was not the Earl of Arran, but another man William recognized as having recently been in the service of King James. "Earl Mar!" he sputtered.

"Pardon the ruse by my men," the earl said. "One can never be certain of another's loyalty in these times. We had heard you were no friend of the king's momentary favorite, of course, but wanted to be certain."

"You heard rightly, milord," Sir William said, finding his voice at last. "Though I almost wish your men had been his, for I was looking forward to teaching them to dance a Highland jig to the tune of a little chin music!"

The earl laughed out loud, joined by several of his fellows. "By Mary, you are a thistle, Sir William! Now come. I trust you were not chasing that rabbit for sport but because you are hungry. Let us adjourn to my trestle and see if we can rouse up a meal."

A short time later, Sir William found himself seated at a lengthy table under a gaily-colored canopy at the center of the encampment. He was joined by not only Earl Mar, but his fellow rebels Archibald Douglas, the Earl of Angus, and Lord Russell, as well as many other knights and men-at-arms. What Sir William had taken to be a large gang of bandits now looked to him much more like an army, an army of several thousand men. He had resisted asking more questions of his host out of courtesy but was dying to hear the story of how the earls had escaped Stirling. Luckily, his host told it, though not before making certain his guest had all the food and drink he could desire.

"You are curious, no doubt, how I find myself in these parts," Earl

Mar said. "Just as I am curious as to how you ended up here, so far from Loch Mhor and your home. But as you are my guest and I your host, I will start, though I must beg your forgiveness in that I am a poor storyteller and my tale a brief one. I trust you heard that I, Lord Douglas and these other good gentles at table recently gathered some hearty lads and took Stirling by force, our goal being to talk some sense into young King James without Arran whispering incessantly in his ear?"

"I did," Sir William responded, taking a bite of pheasant and following it with a biscuit he stuffed whole in his mouth. "Though by your presence here," he said when he could talk again, "I must assume all did not go as hoped."

"In faith. Our force was smaller and the king's larger than we had guessed, and they arrived sooner than we had thought possible, the Earl of Arran leading them, of course. Our position was untenable and so we departed."

"Hastily," Earl Angus added, taking a long draught of ale and wiping his mouth on his sleeve.

"A prudent move considering the fate of Earl Gowrie," Lord Russell said.

"Gowrie?" William asked. "What happened to the good earl?"

"He was arrested," Lord Russell told him, "in Dundee by Colonel Stewart, and immediately taken to Edinburgh Castle. Eleven days ago, they convicted him of treason and beheaded him."

"God's wounds!" William exclaimed, horrified.

"Not God, Sir William, but the devil to be sure, as you so rightly put it," Earl Mar said. "For that fiend stalks Scotland in the person of the Earl of Arran, just as surely as he and not King James rules this land. Thusly, after retiring from Stirling, Earl Angus and I led our forces south, ostensibly into England's safe arms. But we held no true desire to leave our beloved country, just as we held no trust for England's promises of protection. As such, we encamped here to regroup and consider our next move."

"Though the hope of encountering and joining with Lord Maxwell and his forces did, of course, aid our decision to come to these parts," Earl Angus added.

"Lord Maxwell?" William repeated, wracking his brain to recall why he should know that name. Then he remembered: Lord Maxwell had been Warden of the Western Marches and one of the king's favorites until he and the Earl of Arran had quarreled over some land that Maxwell possessed and the earl wanted. When Maxwell refused to accede the estates, the earl cobbled up charges against him and issued a warrant for his arrest. The man wisely fled instead of surrendering himself to the earl's 'mercy,' becoming a rebel from the king's justice. He was rumored to be somewhere in these parts and to have gathered about him a sizable force of men-at-arms, a force made more dangerous by Maxwell's widely acknowledged brilliance as a military tactician. "Oh, Lord Maxwell, of course," William said. "Aye, he would be a valuable ally; I hope you find him," he added, raising a toast.

"Here, here," Earl Mar answered. "And gramercy, good sir knight, for your kind words. But as I mentioned, my tale would be brief and so you have heard it. I will not insult you with admonitions that what you have seen and heard here this day must remain concealed, for you have proven the fealty that others have long vouched for. But enough on that matter, dear sir. Pray tell us what brings you to these parts? Surely you are not looking for me, are you? You must know you are welcome to join my little band if you should wish."

"No offense, milord, but I was most certainly not looking for you or anyone else this day, just as I was not looking to find myself riding an old nag from England to Scotland when I should be at my daughter's wedding in France."

"Please to tell, good sir," Earl Mar encouraged.

And so, William told the story of his journey to Cawdor and then to sea, and the unspeakable events that followed. The table grew quiet, with all eyes on him. When he finished, a great hue and cry arose from the assembled lords. They loudly expressed first their heartfelt sorrow over his losses and the murders of Lord Campbell and the others, then their anger and disgust at the pirates who had committed these foul deeds. Few of them had heard of Captain Boggs, but most of them knew of James Spotiswoode, and that his brother was in the service of the Earl of Arran.

"Damn Spotiswoode to Hades!" Earl Angus, swore, standing and banging his fist on the board.

"His brother John is one of Arran's wolves," Lord Russell commented. "He enforces the earl's judgments to steal the lands from those who cannot pay their taxes."

"Clearly, the entire family are thieves and cowards," Earl Mar added. "Though James does it out in the open! To murder the thane in cold blood, though, and then take hostage a young lad and lass en route to their wedding, why, it is just loathsome!" The earl jerked his leather coin purse from his belt and tossed it onto the table in front of Sir William. It hit with a heavy thunk. "To help pay the ransom, sir knight, and buy a stone for your son."

Within moments, other purses of gold and silver and rings and necklaces had been collected and deposited before him, despite his protests. These from fellows who almost to a man had lost their homes and lands and in some cases their fortunes for opposing the Earl of Arran. As the gathering of lords and knights promised more assistance to Sir William, financial or otherwise, the old knight could not hide the tears welling in his eyes.

8

Arabella cared for the ailing Thomas ceaselessly for another two days, eating little and sleeping less. Finally, with luck, her care and his stubbornness, the man's fever broke and he slowly began to recover. Thomas had been the last of the afflicted and, with everyone else well, Arabella sought to return to her other duties. She found she was too exhausted to do so though, both physically and emotionally. The captain ordered her to her cabin and to bed, refusing to take no for an answer despite still needing her to take over the duties of ship's cook as soon as possible. Arabella spent the remainder of that day and all of the next sleeping, interspersed with an occasional hearty meal and tankard of fortified wine.

She emerged the following day refreshed anew, much to everyone's relief. As she strode across the deck toward the captain's cabin to tell him she was ready to return to her duties, her eyes sought out their companion ship. She thought she saw it not too far off but realized its shape was different, that it was neither the *Sea Rover* nor the *Gunsway*. After several moments of searching, she realized the ship carrying Duncan was no longer within sight. Her heart caught in her throat and she looked about the deck, finally spotting a sailor she recognized from when Lord Campbell was still master of the ship.

"It is Mister Urquhart, is it not?" she asked.

"Aye, miss," he answered, pleased she remembered.

"What happened to the other ship that has been traveling with us these many weeks?"

"Oh, I heard one of the mates say we separated from her in the storm. I should not be too concerned though, for such things happen often at sea. The captain expects we shall meet up with them again later, as we are both bound for the same destination."

"Thank you," she said. Her eyes returned to the sea and caught sight of a mountain of rock towering before them and, miles away to the south, a great landmass. England was far behind, she knew, which ruled out her suspicion they had sailed around the Lizard and back up to Wales or even Ireland. "Pray pardon," she asked again. "But do you know where we are bound?"

"I am truly sorry, miss, but I do not, other than that we have traveled almost due south since leaving the Channel. The officers tell us nothing except what to do and when to do it, and they do not like us asking too many questions."

"Well, thank you again," she said.

Arabella continued on towards the captain's quarters. She found him there, engaged in the activity in which he spent the bulk of his time: drinking. The truth was, a ship well-manned and with a crew that knows their business needs little direction from its captain except during emergencies or when engaged in battle. As such, Boggs had little to do and even less inclination to do it. He presented no fair sight as Arabella entered his dayroom, his shirt soiled and torn, his trousers undone at both the waist and knee, no stockings and his hair and beard a tangled, matted mess. Worse than the vision, however, was the smell; it reminded Arabella of an animal, though she had never quite identified exactly which kind, despite living on a farm. Boggs was raising the bottle to his lips as she marched into his room. He hesitated then tipped the decanter to her in salute before continuing. After a long draught, he smacked it down on his table and pushed himself to his feet. He bowed, almost tipped over, caught himself and then decided against standing entirely, plopping heavily back down into his chair.

"Ah, recovered, I see," he slurred, drinking her beauty in along with his whiskey.

"Still a drunken sack of dung, I see," she shot back.

"Recovered yer cheery disposition as well, ye 'ave," the captain grumbled, rolling his eyes.

"Where the hell are you taking us?"

"'Tis no concern o' yers, missy."

"We are far from my home and my ransom, sir. And the shores off our bow are neither Britain nor France, I am certain. And though I have never seen the Pillars of Hercules, I have read their description and would bet my last shilling that the rocks I just now saw were they. I can fathom no reason that would warrant a trip to these waters if you were sincere in your intent to ransom us back to our families. So I ask again: where are you taking us?"

"The Pillars already, do yer say?" Boggs sounded genuinely surprised. "God and Mary, I best finish this bottle quickly so I can sober up all the faster. The Med is no place to be without one's wits."

"The Mediterranean!" Arabella cried. Dread filled her heart as she realized there was but one reason a blackguard such as Boggs would carry prisoners to these waters: to sell them into slavery on the Barbary Coast.

"Oopsie, did I let that slip?" the captain said, laughing and taking another slug.

"So we are to be sold into slavery despite your promise of ransom?" Arabella asked. The captain said nothing, continuing to stare at her with that damned grin on his fat face. "You planned this all along, didn't you? You never did intend to allow our ransoms to be paid, despite your promise to my father!"

"Not true," Captain Boggs protested, rising from his chair again. "We 'ave every intention o' letting yer ransoms be paid. We just never intended to give any of ye back afterward!" The man broke into uproarious laughter, falling back into his chair and clutching his large belly.

"Bastard!" Arabella spat, ire turning her alabaster cheeks scarlet. "You filthy, despicable pig!" Rage filled her heart and she jerked her dagger from its sheath. Boggs put both feet against his desk and shoved it forward. It smashed into Arabella's thighs and knocked her legs from under her. She fell to the floor but was up a moment later, her dagger held before her. Boggs now stood – unsteadily - facing her, his cutlass in one hand and his pistol in the other.

"You will not kill me," Arabella snarled, her voice sounding more confident than she actually felt.

The captain was drunk and had lost his grin, his beady black eyes once more reflecting the dangerous animal he was at heart. He raised an eyebrow and then smiled, lowering his pistol's aim from her chest to her thigh. "Nay, I will no' kill ye. But as God and Poseidon are me witnesses, I will take an arm or leg if need be. Yer true value do not lie in them parts."

Arabella wanted nothing more than to kill him but knew he would follow through on his threat if she even flinched. *Another time*, she told herself. *There will be another time.* She slowly lowered the dagger and backed away. "And what of the other ship, the one my Duncan is on?" she asked. "Are they all to be sold into slavery as well?"

"That be the plan. But look on the bright side: assuming ye behave for the rest of the voyage and I don't 'ave to throw ye overboard, ye and yer fiancé could soon be reunited!" The captain burst into laughter again and Arabella stormed from the cabin.

She started to march away but stopped and just stood there on the deck. She wanted to cry, to scream, to leap overboard even and take her chances with the angry sea. Instead, she just stood there feeling helpless, ignoring the stares of the crew. The sun was warm on her shoulders but a fit of cold shivering suddenly took her. Taken to a foreign land and sold into slavery! How would she survive? Would she even want to? She had heard stories of the horrors suffered by those sold to the Saracens, of the torments, the abuses, the brutal, unending labor. Worse were the reported depravities suffered upon female slaves. Standing there amidst the sway of the deck on the rough seas, she now realized why the captain had insisted that she and the other women not be ravaged; they would indeed be more valuable this way to potential buyers. She wondered then just how a buyer could determine a prisoner's purity, for surely they would not accept the word of a pirate, nor even the word of the prisoner themselves. No doubt it would involve some sort of degrading physical examination, and likely in a place public enough to appease the doubts of all those at the auction. At the thought of this humiliating violation in some filthy desert bazaar, a wave of nausea rushed up from within her. A moment later and for the first time since they had set sail from Nairn, Arabella fell to her knees and fouled the deck with the contents of her stomach.

The Straits of Gibraltar were still some hours off and a number of the hands lounged about, having few duties to attend. The nearby crew, swabbing those same decks, pointed her out to their mates and many laughed cruelly at her discomfort. The quartermaster had issued double shares of drink to steel the men's courage before they entered the dangerous Mediterranean. Arabella could feel the eyes of many of them upon her. A shadow came over her and she looked up. Bobbing John stood there, his face hard and angry.

"Clean yer filth from me decks, ye scurvy flaxwench!" He pushed one of the swabbie's water buckets over to her with his foot. "And when ye're through with that, get yer skinny arse to the kitchen and prepare the crew's supper."

Arabella glared at him, knowing he was a man who did not take kindly to disobedience but not caring a whit just now. "To hell with you, Bobbing John," she said. "To hell with you and with the whole stinking crew! You can all starve to death as far as I'm concerned!"

"What? What is this?" he bellowed. "You damned, insolent wench!"

He kicked the mop bucket at her so hard it shattered, pelting her with chunks of wood and drenching her with water. Her cotton dress instantly drew tight against her body and became nearly transparent. Many of the crew laughed aloud once more, the usual oafs hooting and hollering and letting her know how much they enjoyed the view. Their cries in turn egged on the quartermaster, still enraged and fogged with drink. He jerked his ever-present cat-o-nine tails from his belt and raised it high. Arabella flinched but still refused to jump to his commands. He brought it down hard, the leather straps slashing painfully across her arms and shoulders as she tried to block the blow. He drew back and lashed her again. Then again. And again.

Bill Urquhart shouted at the man to stop and rushed forward. Boggs' first and second mates grabbed him and held him fast, enjoying this sport too much to let anyone spoil it. They told him he would feel the sting of the whip next for trying to interfere, and promised the same to any other sailor who butted in. No one else stepped forward. In fact, in their drunken lust, many who ordinarily would have now decided it might be more entertaining to watch the clothes flogged from her back as she writhed in pain.

"Do it, Bobbing John!" one of the pirates shouted. "Whip her bloody!"

"Aye, man, make a show of it!" another called out.

A wicked grin spread over the quartermaster's face and he gripped the cat more tightly, the muscles of his arm flexing. "On yer feet, girl," he growled, raking her across the thighs with the cat. She was loathe to follow his orders but hated even more the idea of remaining on her knees before him. She stood abruptly, her head high and proud, though her blouse was now quite transparent. She remembered her dagger and wondered at her chances of slitting the quartermaster's throat before he or anyone else could stop her.

"Get to it, Bobbing John!" a voice called from the rigging. "Whip that dress right off her!"

Arabella noted the raw, animal lust in the quartermaster's eyes and her hand inched closer to her knife. She was completely surrounded by the crew and had nowhere to run. Still, she refused to submit to such treatment, from this or any man. She closed her eyes, prayed for strength and came to terms with the fact that she was probably about to die. Bobbing John drew his arm back to strike her again and she reached for her dagger.

"Ahoy there!" came a loud voice from somewhere near - but not aboard — *The Thistle*, breaking the dead silence that had fallen over the ship.

Two sailors were so startled by this hail they lost their hold in the rigging and fell atop their mates standing below. The rest of the crew spun to larboard and the direction of the call. A large ship ran parallel with them, not one hundred feet away. Her swivel guns and starboard cannons were manned and pointing directly at them, though Arabella noticed her gun crews wore friendly - if triumphant - smiles as opposed to the bloodthirsty kind. *The Thistle* crewmen did not seem to notice this distinction. Loud cursing and oaths flew from them as they jumped to their own cannons and peterero, frantically trying to get them battle-ready. The ship facing them flew a white pennant with a red saltire from its flagstaff, which Arabella recognized as the St. Patrick's Cross, a common symbol for Ireland and Irish rebels opposed to English domination. She looked for the man who had hailed them and spotted him in an instant. His broad smile gleamed white in the sun and his bright blue eyes were fixed upon her own. He was a hale man of good height, not yet thirty, his skin tanned dark from the sun and the sea, his head uncovered and his long black hair tied tight in a ponytail. Though by no means pretty, he had a rugged handsomeness she found appealing. And she could not deny he cut a dashing figure standing on the ship's gunwale in his knee breeches and shirt, short of sleeve and open to his navel. One hand grasped a bowline for balance while the other rested rakishly on his hip, completing the well-intended pose, the very image, oddly enough, Arabella had envisioned when fantasizing about Duncan coming to her rescue. This man had certainly just saved her from an unpleasant fate, and she had the distinct impression he knew it.

"Avast there, men!" Bobbing John called to his gun crews. "'Tis only *The Raven* and Captain McNamara." Then, in an aside to the hands manning the swivel gun closest to him, he added "But keep yer gun on 'im anyway, lads, just in case."

"You are lucky we recognized you, Bobbing John, and your mates," Liam McNamara called across the water in his strong Irish brogue. "Do you no longer serve Boggs on the *Gunsway*?"

"Nay, we still serve Captain Boggs, just on this new ship now," the quartermaster answered.

"Excellent. Will he receive me, then?" He had clearly addressed John, though he was staring at Arabella, who suddenly remembered her nearly-transparent garments.

"What? Oh, aye, come aboard then if'n ye want," Bobbing John called back. "I will advise the cap'n." He looped the cat back through his belt and lumbered off to the sterncastle, muttering to himself about the "bloody Irish pirate always wantin' to come aboard fer the captain's hospitality and a free meal." As he reached the cabin door, he seemed to remember Arabella. "Back to work, you!" he barked over his shoulder. She glared right back at him for a moment and then grabbed another wash bucket.

A short time later, Captain McNamara climbed nimbly up the rope ladder and stepped onto the deck. Arabella hardly recognized him, so drastic was the change in his appearance. No longer unshaven and unkempt, his square jaw had been scraped smooth and his hair had been rinsed and retied with a blue silk ribbon. He now wore a beautiful black doublet, generously laced with red trim, over a long-sleeved shirt of black silk, the wrists cuffed with frill and tied with silk cords. His slops were also of black and in the Venetian style, with silk stockings below and buckled leather shoes on his feet. He wore a broad leather belt and baldric about him, from which hung a finely-made but obviously well-used cutlass. He had shoved a flintlock pistol into his belt, though whether for function or appearances Arabella could not say. To offset these bellicose trappings, however, he carried in his hands two bottles of fine port. His eyes immediately sought out and found Arabella and he again smiled. Boggs emerged from his cabin, still intoxicated and not at all happy at having to play host for his fellow rogue. His stained and soiled garb, his corpulence and his bleary-eyed besottedness only served to reinforce the differences between the two men. The Irishman tucked one bottle under his arm and grasped the captain's hand in greeting. Boggs gave it only a cursory shake, looking down his nose at the man's fancy dress before relieving him of both bottles.

"Such finery, Liam. I regret to inform ye the queen shall not be dining with us today." He laughed at his own joke and turned to lead the man into the dining cabin.

"Stuff your bloody queen, Boggs. I will get dressed up for her only once and that when they lower her into the cold, wormy earth. Though my eyes did see a woman aboard your ship with whom I would not refuse to sup."

"Oh ho!" the captain cried, clapping his guest about the shoulders and steering him into the cabin. "So the truth outs! I should 'ave known ye did not really want to come aboard just to see me!"

Laughter followed the men into the cabin and the door slammed shut. Arabella pretended to continue her cleaning but moved closer to one of the open portholes so she could hear inside.

"So, is she your woman or just a ransom?" Captain McNamara asked.

"Would it kill yer if I said she was mine?"

"Hardly, she is just a sirrah," the Irishman answered casually.

"Liar. And though I wish I could say otherwise, she is a prize."

"Then she has a price. Excellent."

"Forget it, Irish. She is not for sale to the likes of yer, and even if she were ye could not afford her."

"To hell you say. My money is just as good as anyone else's, not that I am making an offer, mind you. I am merely curious to hear her price."

"And I said forget it. She is going to the Med and will be disposed of there. 'Tis already arranged."

"You have a purchase contract then?" Liam pressed.

"No, not exactly," Boggs answered.

"Then bugger all and sell her to me," the Irishman blurted.

Outside and below the window, Arabella felt an odd ripple run through her at the thought of this rogue's desire to purchase her. She quickly forced this thought from her mind, hating herself for entertaining for a moment the thought of any other man's desires except Duncan's. Inside the cabin, the men continued.

"Sorry, lad, the arrangement has already been made and I mean to honor it," Boggs answered.

"Bah! You have never kept a pact in your scurvy life, Boggs. Since when did you decide being honorable was worth more than being a scoundrel?"

"Since it became worth so much for me to do so!" Boggs laughed. "Besides, I would not be safe anywhere if I reneged on this deal."

"How now?"

"Never ye mind. In fact, I 'ave said too much already. Forget I mentioned it."

"All right, if that is how you want it," Liam told him. "But give a dog a bone, Sam: what is her price? She is worth a good deal, is she not?"

"Aye, that she is, lad, that she is. And there are other hostages too. Truth be told, I expect to make enough from this voyage to retire."

"Retire? Surely not from this one trip alone? Why, you old rascal, you have been doing better than I thought! And sure'n you had me fooled, with your miserly ways and poor fare all these years whenever we have supped together."

"Stuff yerself, Irish," the captain retorted, though with a smile. "I am no rich man, not yet at least. 'Tis this voyage and one more after that will change all that. Now, I know what be going through yer head right now, lad, and let me put it right out. My deal is set on both ends; there be no market for her on the Muslim coast to the man who does not possess the proper authorizations from the Beylerbey to sell her. And even if ye did find a black market buyer or keep 'er for yerself, ye would sooner find a knife between yer ribs than a safe harbor anywhere in the civilized world."

"You wound me, Sam. I would never steal a prize out from under a brother."

"Ha! We both know there is a man in a Spanish dungeon who would say otherwise."

Liam lost his smile and grew serious. "You should not believe everything you have heard about what a scoundrel I am." He looked the captain hard in the eye as he said this, and Boggs saw cold danger there, realizing he had just pricked a too-fresh wound.

"Easy, lad, easy. I meant no offense. I simply meant that we are both pirates and blackhearts, through and through."

"To black-hearted scoundrels, then," Liam said, raising a toast. The two men tapped their mugs and drank deeply before Liam continued. "Let us waste no more time on the girl, then. She was but a pretty thing that caught my eye. So tell me, old dog, what ever came of that little trouble you found yourself in down in Panama? Sure'n we all heard the tales, but I want the truth now!"

The drink continued to flow and the conversation turned from Arabella to other topics. She moved away from the porthole, finally making her way to the kitchen. Once there, she tried not to think about the rakish pirate and why his offer to purchase her affected her so. Then she thought of how he had first seen her, taking a beating from Bobbing John like some errant child. She felt ashamed and wished he had waited but one minute more to make his presence known. Then he would have seen her in a moment of strength, giving the quartermaster a taste of his own medicine. She tried not to dwell on her thoughts and feelings as she prepared the afternoon meal but found it impossible. Her shame soon turned to anger, and not just at Bobbing John for humiliating and victimizing her, but at herself for letting him do so, just as Boggs had done before. She regretted now more than ever not having slit both men's throats, consequences be damned. Well, no more. As the salted beef simmered in the pot, she retrieved from her darning pile an unclaimed pair of trousers and a man's shirt from one of the sailors who had died. She would not leave this room and go back amongst the crew wearing the same dress she had worn today, the dress she had been forced to wear since her capture so many weeks ago. That garment set her apart from the men aboard this ship and thus led them to think of her as something less than they. She cast her dress into the cookfire and watched it burn, standing naked in the firelight without shame.

A short time later, she left the galley garbed in her newly-mended trousers and shirt, bare of foot and with a bandana wrapped around her red tresses. As she stepped onto the main deck, she thought briefly of the Irishman and became suddenly self-conscious. But only for a moment before she carried on, head high. The crew took notice of her right away and let fly with all manner of comments, most questioning whether she was trying to become a boy. Nonetheless, their words were tempered somewhat, as if they might have indeed been speaking to a new crewman. Arabella smiled and knew it would be all right. She saw no more of the handsome Irish rogue though, for he had returned to his ship. She spotted his sails moving briskly toward the horizon, away from *The Thistle* and the perils of the Mediterranean Sea.

That night, *The Thistle* sailed through the Straights of Gibraltar and into the Alboran Sea. The crew's mood and behavior changed abruptly, exhibiting no more of the drunkenness and horseplay that had been their habit throughout the voyage. Most of them had roused from their groggy slumber to watch the massive black rock slip by them to the north. Arabella joined them, abandoning for the moment her pots and pans. Even the captain emerged from his cabin, dressed only in a long nightshirt. He immediately doubled the lookouts in the crow's nest and told the quartermaster to ensure that the men were no longer allowed to take ale or hard liquor aloft with them. He then ordered the crew to lower the English St. George and replace it with two other English flags, the first a red banner emblazoned with three gold lions and the second displaying the green and red Tudor Rose.

Arabella asked one of the hands if he knew why this was, and he explained the St. George was not well-liked by the Muslim nations of the Mediterranean, who had seen far too much of it during the

Crusades. In addition, the Italian city-states of Milan and Genoa bore the same cross on their flags and they were currently at war with the Ottoman Sultan, whose fleets commanded these waters. A knowledgeable sailor as well as a loquacious one, he further told Arabella that in addition to the sultan's fleets, legions of Barbary Corsairs prowled these waters, sailing from scores of ports all along North Africa's Barbary Coast. For the most part, they took their orders from the sultan's regional governors-general, the beylerbeys, and preyed on any ship from a nation not currently at peace with and paying tribute to the Ottoman Empire. And though Spain, France and Italy bordered the Mediterranean on the north, the corsairs were the real power in this sea. Still, the Arab Turks conducted a brisk trade with most of the nations of Europe, even their enemies when it profited them to do so, and European ships were free to ply these waters so long as they had the proper permissions.

"And Boggs has these, I presume?" Arabella asked.

"Well, 'e must," the fellow answered. "Still, I do no' like being in these waters, with or without permission, especially since we 'ave separated from the *Rover*. God knows yer cannot trust pirates, Christian or Muslim!" The sailor chuckled at his humor and moved away to attend to a loose shroud.

As they sailed deeper into the Alboran Sea under the light of a fat, yellow moon, Boggs turned a wary eye to the south and the endless desert sands stretching before him, now in deepest shadow. Arabella swore she heard him mumble a quiet prayer.

9

After another two days as the earls' honored guest, Sir William finally begged his new friends' leave so he could return home and tend to his affairs. The nobles threw another grand feast in his honor and sent him forth with their most heartfelt wishes for a safe and pleasant journey and for the quick return of his daughter. William left them with little fear of his newly-acquired gold falling into reiver hands, for six of Earl Mar's knights accompanied him on the coast road all the way to Edinburgh. There, at the city gate, they bid him farewell, again wishing luck upon him and foul death upon those responsible for the sacking of *The Thistle*.

Four days later, William reached Inverness and his beloved

Highlands. Here, he was warmly greeted again by friends and relations. The old knight had to endure another retelling of the great news of the day, the taking of Stirling Castle and the escape of the rebel lords, as well as the sad fate of Earl Gowrie. William said nothing of his encounter with those very nobles, knowing only too well that the Earl of Arran had spies and informers everywhere these days, even in the Highlands. Once this news ran its course and those telling the tales were finally ready to listen, William had to explain again what had happened on his voyage to France.

The reaction here was just as it had been in the earls' camp. Lord Campbell had been very well liked and much respected among the Highlanders and his death in this manner, while en route to his son's wedding, was an outrage beyond words. Promises were made to immediately send several ships in pursuit of the pirates, while a delegation was readied to travel to Parliament to introduce a bill to make Duncan the new Thane of Cawdor in absentia. Additional monies were promised for the ransom of the hostages, despite the privation of many of the Highland lords who still suffered under Arran's wrath. This outpouring of support toward him and the Campbells did much to bolster Sir William's flagging spirits.

Today, at least, his tomorrows did not look quite so bleak.

10

After several days of uneventful sailing, *The Thistle* left the Alboran Sea and entered the Mediterranean proper. They had sailed a few degrees north to bring them closer to the Spanish coast and Cartagena before turning south again. Arabella had overheard the captain telling the pilot to chart a new course for the waters just to the west of a place called Sidi Ferruch, which apparently would place them within fifteen miles of the great corsair city of Algiers. The winds remained brisk on this leg of the journey and the ship made good time. The pirates reached their destination two days later. They dropped their sails but not their anchor, ready for anything as the ship bobbed gently on the turquoise water. The sky overhead remained storm free, the cobalt blue broken only by the occasional wisp of cloud. The lookouts reported no sails on the horizon, hostile or friendly. This disappointed the captain, who had hoped Spotiswoode and the *SeaRover* might be nearby.

"Are ye sure there be no sign of the *Rover*?" he called up to the crow's nest.

"Nay, cap'n."

"Damn. Well, keep'e a sharp eye there lads, for our mates and for the bloody Mussulmen. Yer know the ships we be looking for?"

"Aye, cap'n," the sailor called down. "Three corsair rigs, fustas and galiots, flying the banner o' Abdullah Reis."

"Which is?" Boggs pressed.

"Two crossed scimitars of gold over a lion's head on a field o' green with a white crescent in the corner," the lookout answered.

"Glad ye could remember it, ye damned dunderheaded ape," the captain muttered loudly enough for the man to hear. The sailor said nothing in reply, knowing the captain's volatile and violent nature. Nothing out loud, that is. Despite the early hour and a fair breeze, the sun beat down cruelly on the deck of the ship. The captain retreated once more into the cool darkness of his cabin, though he poked his head out at regular intervals to demand an update from the lookouts.

Some two hours later, one of them called down with, "Sail ho! Two points off the starboard bow!"

Every eye turned in that direction, nerves tense and hands at the ready to turn the ship about and run for Spain if it was any but their expected rendezvous.

"Is it the *Rover*?" the captain asked, stepping from his cabin.

"Nay; 'tis two ships, both lateen-rigged."

"Just two? Can yer see what flags they be flying?"

"Not yet, cap'n."

"Just two, eh?" the captain repeated, turning to his quartermaster and first mate, standing at his side.

"I thought Abdullah said he was bringing three ships to escort us in?" the first mate commented.

"Aye, that were the plan. That were the plan," Boggs said.

"What do yer think?" the quartermaster asked. "Do we stay and see who they be or run for Spain?"

The captain wrestled with this for a moment before the lookout hollered down to him.

"A sail, cap'n! A sail to the west, heading this way!"

"The *Rover*?" Boggs called.

"Impossible to say at this distance," came the reply. "But it looks like it could be her."

"Can yer make out those damn corsair flags yet?" Boggs yelled

back, knowing even as he asked that it might be an hour or more before

the ships were close enough to read a small pennant flapping in the

tops.

"Nay cap'n, not yet."

"So what be yer decision, Samuel?" the first mate asked, on edge

and sounding irritated.

"It is probably Abdullah," the captain said at last, more to himself

than his second-in-command. "We got separated from a ship in a storm,

maybe they did too. Top! Let me know as soon as ye can read their

flags!"

"Aye, aye, cap'n."

Boggs spun on his heel and returned to his cabin. Those outside his

quarters heard the clanking of liquor bottles and knew he sought

courage and decisiveness in the only place he had ever found it.

Arabella stood on deck and watched the two ships approach, first

visible only as tiny white specks on the horizon, one behind the other.

Soon they grew into two ships, eventually drawing near enough that

she could make out basic details of their shape and structure. They were

unlike any craft she had ever seen, ships of European build typically being tall and stout and having great square sails. In contract, these craft were long and sleek, their decks sitting low to the water. One had but one enormous triangular sail, while the other carried two smaller ones, also triangular. She had seen such sails used on the mizzenmast or bowsprit of some ships before but never as the mainsail.

"Pray pardon," she asked a deck hand who stood nearby. "The man in the tops said the ships we were looking for were galiots and fustas. Are these them, and how do you tell which is which?"

"Hard to say from here, miss; I do not really know me Arab barkies too well. Hey! Limp lance!" he called up to the man in the crow's nest. "Which ship is the fusta?"

"Me staff be stiff enough to shug yer mother!" came the reply

"Only if ye pay her this time, ye cheap bastard!" the first fellow retorted.

Both sailors laughed and then the man in the tops spoke again. "That first ship there is a galiot and the one trailing, the one with the two smaller sails, is a fusta. And yer can tell the captain they both be flying the Sultan's flag up top, though I cannot just yet make out the lower flag to tell us if they be Abdullah's."

The sailor on deck shrugged and headed toward the captain's cabin, leaving Arabella alone. She noted that in addition to their oddly-shaped sails, both craft had huge oars jutting from their waists, though at the moment neither was using them. As the ships grew closer, she saw dozens of colorfully-dressed men in turbans working the sails and rigging, while shirtless rowers sat at the ready along the oar benches. None of the rowers wore turbans and most were noticeably lighter-skinned than their Arab masters. *The oarsmen are slaves!* Arabella though. *Most likely captured European sailors.* A handful of the rowers, however, were so dark she felt certain they must be African tribesmen stolen from their villages to the south of the great Bedouin deserts, the jet of their skin standing in stark contrast to their English and Spanish bench mates. She cringed at the thought of these men toiling under the hot sun in a life of such brutal and dehumanizing slavery.

The ships continued their slow approach, sailing a direct but leisurely course. Arabella had few duties to attend to at the moment, the crew having already had their noon meal. The men were busy about their various tasks and generally ignored her. Boggs placed a hand on her shoulder and she actually jumped. She spun around to find him eyeing her and grinning his usual, stupid leer.

"Since ye 'ave not else to busy yerself with, there be some tidying up in me cabin ye can attend to."

After a moment's hesitation, she followed him in. As usual, the cabin, like its master, was a mess. This was the first time though he had ever troubled her to clean it and she wondered if perhaps he meant to impress the corsair captains if they came aboard. She hardly knew where to start but he did not hesitate to tell her. The hot air outside had long ago seeped into the room, adding its unpleasantness to the stench. She set to her task though, intent on being done with it as quickly as possible. The captain sat in his chair and watched her work, his feet on the desk and a bottle in his hand. The first bottle became a second and then a third, as all the while he ogled her.

"I is going ter miss yer, Miss Ara," he slurred, glancing through the porthole at the closest ship, not far off now. "Ye be a fine sight to watch, whether workin' or just standin' doin' naught. And damned those Muslim devils fer payin' double fer virgins, or I'd a had ye keep me company every night o' this voyage."

"Then let me thank Providence for your damnable greed and this little it has served me," she sneered.

The captain laughed and nodded, then grew confused and wondered if he had just been insulted. He was about to say something when the door to his cabin swung open and his first mate looked in.

"Both ships are flying the flags of Abdullah ibn Rahman Reis," he announced. "But the lookouts have spotted several more corsair sails on the horizon, following the same course as the first two but coming much faster."

The captain shoved himself to his feet and staggered from the cabin, Arabella at his heels. Sure enough, at least four and possibly five more sails could be seen but a few hours behind the first ships. Abdullah's men had also seen them and now piled on all the sail they could carry, adding their oars as well and beating furiously to reach *The Thistle*. Weapons appeared in the Muslims' hands and their gun crews lit the slow matches for their numerous cannons and peterero.

"I do not like the looks o' this, cap'n," the first mate growled.

Boggs just stared stupidly at the ships, the first but a moment away and the second only minutes behind that. "Nay, it do not look right to me either. Issue weapons and man the guns, but tell the hands to hold their fire until I give the word." The first mate and quartermaster raced off to carry out his orders. By the time the first of the Arab vessels came within hailing range, *The Thistle* was battle-ready. "Browne! Fire a shot across their bow!" Boggs called down to the gun deck.

A moment later the gun roared and spit its missile over the approaching Arab ship. The galiot hove to some fifty feet away and the captain came to the railing, a scowl on his face.

"What is the meaning of this, Boggs?" he called in heavily-accented English.

"It is Uluj Ali, is it not?" Boggs asked.

"I am he, and Usain Reis is just there," the Arab captain answered, indicating the second ship.

"Where is your master, Abdullah?"

"Abdullah Reis was called back to Istanbul by the Sultan himself to tend to urgent business. He sends his regrets, but has authorized Usain Reis and me to conduct our agreed-upon transaction under the same terms. Why did you fire on us? And where is your *Sea Rover*?"

"Delayed," Boggs answered. "But near by; right close behind us, in fact. What are them other sails beyond ye? What game are ye at, Ali?"

"There is no game, Boggs," the man answered smoothly. "I know not what those other ships are; most likely a fishing fleet trying to catch tonight's dinner. Come, we are wasting precious time standing in this infernal heat. Do you intend to honor our agreement or not?"

"Do not question my honor, ye Goddamned heathen!" Boggs spat, his fear venting as anger and bluster. "Ye send a man over in a boat, just one man, and let me see these new authorizations from Captain Abdullah."

The Arab captain hesitated and his smile faltered for just a moment before returning, even broader than before. "But of course. They are on Usain Reis' ship, which shall join us in but a moment. In the meantime, will you not have your men stand down? I would hate for an accident to happen that would prove very dear to both of us."

Boggs looked across the water and saw that indeed the other ship was even now drawing nigh. However, instead of pulling up next to the galiot, they looked intent on circling around to the other side of *The Thistle*. Thin wisps of smoke trailed from their gun deck, betraying the fact that the cannons' slow matches were lit. Boggs beetled his brow in concentration, his fear and greed and uncertainty all mingling together and paralyzing him from taking any action. The first ship was drifting slowly closer to *The Thistle*, a feat accomplished by a very subtle manipulation of their sails. Though Boggs seemed not to notice this, Arabella did. She looked hard into the eyes of the smiling Captain Ali and saw something there. A moment later, the man's cheeks flushed slightly and she knew her hunch was right. She had seen that flush a hundred times while dueling, always just before an opponent attacked.

"Damn your ignorance, man!" she yelled to Boggs. "It is a trap! They mean to attack us!"

Captain Boggs' liquor-soaked wits struggled to grasp Arabella's warning. "What? How can you…?" But then he too noticed Ali's ship, now almost within grappling range, and saw that several corsairs had indeed picked up hooks and lines. "It's a trap!" he yelled finally. "We are betrayed!"

One of his crewmen touched off the foredeck swivel gun and sent a blast of grapeshot into the corsairs' midst. Three went down, painting their mates with their blood. The remaining Turks abandoned stealth and whipped the galley slaves into a frenzy, urging them to cover the remaining distance to *The Thistle* as rapidly as possible.

"Get us the hell out of here!" the first mate yelled to the crew. Some grabbed the halyards while others scurried back into the rigging to work the sails. The helmsman made no move, however, turning to his officers for guidance.

"Hard a' larboard and all speed away!" Boggs cried.

The man pushed the whipstaff hard to turn the ship's tiller in the desired direction, while the crew bent every sheet the ship carried to drive her away from the corsairs. The wind had slacked though, and now blew in an unfavorable direction. They had little chance to escape the Turks, who carried both sails and oars. The Arabs aboard the galiot let fly with their grappling hooks, winging their lines across the few yards of sea separating the two ships. Five struck home and three-dozen strong hands began pulling the two craft together. Their mates answered *The Thistle's* one cannon blast with several of their own, sending a hail of grapeshot and sangrenel screaming across her deck. Half-a-dozen Thistles fell to the planks never to rise again. The second corsair vessel, the fusta, continued her wide arc around the combatants, seeking to move into position on their port side. The first mate quickly counted heads on the enemy vessels and compared this against his own fighting crew. Boggs had allowed only his own pirates to be armed, not yet trusting the former crew and prisoners of *The Thistle*. As such, the corsair warriors greatly outnumbered them.

"We are lost!" he cried, turning on Boggs. "Damn ye for letting them fool yer and get so close! We are all sure to be killed or enslaved because of yer blundering ignorance!"

The captain's eyes bulged and his cheeks burned crimson. "I will not suffer such insolence from the likes o' ye, man!" Without warning, he jerked his cutlass from its sheath and rammed the blade deep into his first mate's guts. The man fell to the deck as most of the crew looked on in stunned horror. They too realized the situation was dire, but still looked to Boggs for leadership - and hope. He had none to give them. "It's every man-jack for themselves!" he screamed. "Fight, flee, pray or drink yerself to Old Harry! Ye're on yer own!" Arabella turned to confront him over this cowardly course of action just as his hand closed about her arm. He yanked her into his cabin and slammed the door, his expression crazed. She twisted from his grasp and stepped back as he threw the bolt, locking them in. "No sense saving yer maidenhead now, lass, not if some bloody Arab is just going to rob me of its profit anyway!" He lunged for her and she darted around his hammock, putting it between them as she pulled her dagger. The captain grinned savagely and raised his cutlass, still wet with his first mate's blood. "If that is how ye wants to play it missy, so be it. I will cut ye down and rape yer dyin' corpse if I must!"

He thrust for her, his blade going straight for her midsection – a killing blow. She pivoted sideways and jerked the hammock up, catching the sword in its web. She threw her weight back and the captain, already off balance, stumbled forward. Her hand shot out and plunged her dagger into his throat. Boggs screamed and the cutlass slipped from his fingers. He fell, his hands clutching at his neck in a hopeless attempt to stem the bleeding. Arabella left her blade in him and took up his sword, fire in her eyes. Boggs saw this and grabbed for his pistol. He tugged it from his belt and swiveled the barrel toward her just as she swung. Bone and sinew severed and the pirate's head hit the planks. It rolled into the corner, his eyes still open and staring at her.

"That was for my brother, you son of a bitch!" Arabella growled.

Outside, she heard the roar of cannons and muskets, telling her that at least some of the Thistles had decided to fight. She glanced through the porthole and saw that their strategy was not completely hopeless, as the second corsair ship was still struggling to move into position against a capricious wind. If the Thistles acted quickly and decisively, she thought, they yet stood a chance to defeat the first ship before the second could lend her swords to the battle. What the crew lacked, however, was the leadership they needed to do so. More fighters would help as well - and she knew just where to find them. She peeled Captain Boggs' sword belt from him and threw it over her shoulder, using it as a baldric since its length would have wrapped three times around her waist. She slid her dagger and the captain's pistol into this, then took up his keys. With his cutlass in one hand and the keys in the other, she stepped from the cabin.

The deck of *The Thistle* swirled in mad chaos. Several of the crew had manned the guns and were blasting away at the galiot as quickly as they could load and fire. The corsair, in turn, sprayed their mid-deck with shot from her swivel guns while dozens of Turks swarmed onto her foredeck. A score of Thistles were aloft and alow trying to work the sails and move the ship farther away from the approaching fusta despite being grappled to the galiot. Some of the other pirates had hastily provisioned an oar boat and were now frantically trying to lower it into the water in an effort to flee. Their lines had become entangled with the ship's rigging though, and now these sailors fought with the riggers.

"Men of *The Thistle*!" Arabella yelled at the top of her lungs. "Those needing a weapon, follow me!" She dashed to the ladder leading to the lower deck and threw herself down the hatch just as another blast from the Saracens' guns tore across the deck. A moment later, the iron padlock to the cell holding the few remaining prisoners hit the deck. Arabella told the men to follow her, a moment later using another key to open the weapons locker. "The corsairs have betrayed the pirates, who are presently outnumbered," Arabella told everyone. "If we have any chance of remaining free or even alive, we must come to the aid of Boggs' crew."

"Fight for our captors?" Fergus Campbell asked. "The very ones who murdered my uncle?"

"That score must be settled later," Arabella said. "If we do not act now, we will almost certainly all perish!"

Despite their misgivings, everyone able to take up a weapon did so, even the recently ill Thomas, who told Arabella he would fight the devil himself to repay her kindness to him. Molly did not hesitate to take up arms and the other females tried to follow her lead, including Arabella's aged nursemaid Bess. Though grateful for their courage and support, Arabella realized that only Molly knew how to wield a sword or load and fire a pistol, and as such the others' 'help' might actually be more dangerous than the enemy. She told them to arm themselves with a dagger as a weapon of last resort, but they could best help by filling their arms with as much powder, shot, spare axes and arrows as they could carry. She took another two pistols for herself, ensured their flints and papers were dry, loaded them and shoved them into her belt. Thus armed, Arabella led her group back to the fight.

The scene on deck was, if possible, even more desperate than before. The big guns were silent now on both ships, for the Turk gunners had abandoned their cannons to join their comrades, who swarmed aboard *The Thistle*, wailing like demons and lusting for conquest and plunder. *The Thistle* gunners had similarly joined the fight on the main deck, adding their swords and pikes to the fray. The sailors working the rigging had also been forced to abandon their efforts and now battled the boarders, allowing the cowards in the oar boat to make good their escape. Those men now pulled frantically for the desert shore. The second corsair ship ignored them, knowing they could pluck them from the sands at their leisure once the battle had been won. The fusta was nearly within grappling distance, though their cannons remained silent for fear of hitting their comrades already aboard *The Thistle*. Their help was little needed, though, for the decks ran red with the blood of the outnumbered pirates.

Arabella's group hesitated, aghast at the carnage and the desperation. The only thing in their favor was the fact that the battle had surged past this part of the ship and they had emerged behind the corsairs. Arabella knew her little group had but one chance and one moment in which to seize it. She shrieked a wild, Highlands war cry and led them straight at the enemy's flanks, firing two pistols and killing two men instantly. Her fellow prisoners did the same, firing pistols or arrows if they had them. Before the dead had even fallen, Arabella leapt among them with her cutlass in hand. With bloodcurdling cries of their own, the rest of the prisoners charged in behind her, Molly and Duff Selkirk at her side.

The corsair attack stuttered as confusion and fear at this sudden onslaught rippled through their ranks. They turned to battle this new foe only to be surprised once more to see that the dirty, bedraggled group was led by a screaming, crimson-haired she-devil. Two of the Turks facing Arabella froze upon seeing her, unable to grasp immediately this threat from such an unlikely source. She did not hesitate however, and cut them both down. The Muslim forces recovered quickly and resumed their attack. They now focused their fury toward Arabella and the warriors she led. Though many of the former prisoners had little or no formal training, they fought with all their heart. Several of them, though, were very experienced with a blade, with the likes of Duff, Rob Roy MacIntosh, Angus Brodie and Fergus Campbell, as well as Arabella and Molly, taking a terrible toll on the corsairs. The *Thistle* pirates had little idea of just what had occurred, their vision obscured by the numbers between them and the smoke from the black powder weapons. All they knew was that someone had come to their aid. Their flagging spirits rallied and they threw themselves at the enemy with renewed vigor. The boarders now found themselves between two groups fighting with the desperate ferocity of those who know that surrender is not an option. Scores fell, though not without inflicting great damage on the Thistles. The corsair captain, Uluj Ali, quickly recognized how precarious his position was and called a retreat.

As one, the warriors of Allah fled back to their ship, hacking at the grappling ropes as they passed to free their vessel. Their bosons whipped the galley slaves, and the corsair ship began to slowly move away from *The Thistle*. The pirates cheered their victory and jeered their defeated foe, reveling in their unexpected salvation. Only Arabella saw the reasoning behind Ali's action, remembering the second enemy vessel fast approaching from the west.

"Crew of *The Thistle*! To the port cannons!" she cried, shoving men in that direction. "The fusta approaches!"

The pirates now realized the danger as well and rushed to their guns, hardly taking note that it was Arabella who commanded them. Most of them seemed to neither realize nor care that a third of their number were their own former prisoners, now armed and being re-supplied by women who carried spare powder and shot. The crew ran out the port guns and fired, doing so just as their foes launched their grappling hooks. The minions and swivel guns aboard *The Thistle* burped red-hot steel across the length and breadth of the fusta's deck. The corsairs had seen their brethren flee the vessel but had nonetheless held their fire, hesitant to slaughter the Christians and thus lose the profit they would bring in the slave markets of Algiers. Instead, they had filled their deck with the faithful of Allah, massing to board and overwhelm the ship. *The Thistles'* guns took a horrific toll on them now, cutting down a score or more in an instant. The few grappling hooks that survived their flight through the maelstrom reached the gunwale but had no hands left to pull them.

"Reload and fire again!" Arabella screamed, shouldering a musket handed to her by Bess.

She and Molly fired into a group of corsairs who looked to be officers. Two went down and the third dove unceremoniously for cover. The battle was not entirely one-sided though, for the Turks had weapons of their own and used them. Muskets and arrows flew at the pirates, cutting a swath of death across their decks. The pirates struggled to swab, prime and load their cannons, having been fighting nonstop under the blazing sun for some time now. A few former prisoners rushed below to give them a hand and even some of the women pitched in, braving arrows and cannon fire to bring fresh weapons, shot and powder to the gunners or simply splashing the gun crews with buckets of cold water to cool them. In between, the other women tended the wounded as best they could.

"Molly! To starboard!" Arabella called just then, looking to the east.

There, the first corsair vessel was rapidly beating back toward them. As Arabella spoke, the galiot's guns blazed and hot metal shrieked across the deck, ripping the life from ten more Thistles. Ignoring the danger, Molly led a group to the starboard guns to answer them back. The cannons sent death and destruction into the galiot. One of the gun crews managed a lucky shot that tore a jagged hole in the corsair ship just below the waterline. An instant later, a terrible explosion erupted from within and the entire galiot shuddered violently. Clearly, they had hit a powder barrel stored below decks. The ship listed onto her side and the corsairs began to abandon ship, many ignoring the oar boats and simply leaping into the water and swimming toward the desert shore. With the deck in splinters, the enslaved oarsmen began freeing themselves by yanking their chains from the boards, helping those who needed it. Once free, these men seemed briefly confused as to where to go, looking from the shore to *The Thistle*. Most ran to board the ship.

On the other side of *The Thistle*, the men in the fusta fired another volley before attempting to board again. Unfortunately, this broadside was almost as lucky for the corsairs as the Thistles' had been for them. An entire gun crew completely disintegrated in a crimson spray of bone and gore, while another round smashed directly into the other cannon, hurling its carriage into the gunners with terrible force. Bones shattered and men screamed as another big gun fell silent. A score of grappling hooks flew from the corsair onto *The Thistle*, and this time several dozen men held the lines. Before the pirates could hack them apart, the two vessels were drawn fast together. Arabella's heart caught in her throat as she saw the nearly one hundred Turks prepared to board them, fresh and ready to pay back the price imposed on their brethren in the galiot. Against them stood less than three score Thistles, many wounded and all weary.

"John Browne!" Arabella yelled to the man who had served first as Captain McMullin's master gunner and later as Captain Boggs'. "Loose the starboard cannons from their moorings, shove them to the larboard gunports and load them with grape and sangrenel! Do not worry about lashing them to the futtocks, for we have time for only one shot. Just point them at that corsair's main deck and blaze away!"

"Aye, aye, mistress!" John Browne shouted as he jumped to it. Arabella leapt to the starboard railing and the peterero mounted there.

"Mister Selkirk, Mister Cromartie! Give me a hand with this! Let us get her over to the larboard side for a final shot!"

The two men took boarding axes and helped her hack the small gun free from its mounts on the railing, then carried it over to the ship's other side. Molly was already loading the other swivel gun with sangrenel, having heard Arabella's call.

"Arabella," Duff told her as he loaded their gun. "We cannot hold this and fire it; it needs to be mounted to something."

"There is no time!" she replied. "Butt it against the foremast and clap on for dear life!"

Now the corsairs let loose their high-pitched battle cry and threw themselves over *The Thistle's* gunwales, their curved scimitars gleaming in the sun. Arabella touched the slow-match to the peterero's cook-hole and the gun erupted. A swath of hot shrapnel flew into the Muslim vanguard, shredding a half-dozen of them and drenching their comrades with their remains. Arabella and the two men dropped the hot gun, their ears ringing and their hands numb. Molly pointed her gun directly into the midst of the boarders and fired. Several more men died, with many more wounded. The corsair attackers faltered, their first wave slaughtered the moment they had set foot on the ship.

"Any time now, Mister Browne!" Arabella called down to the gun deck.

A second later, John Browne put his slow-match to the big gun and sent another hail of iron screaming across the deck of the enemy ship, directly into the massed boarders. A dozen or more fell dead or wounded. The cannon, not secured, bucked up and back with tremendous force, flipping on to its side and hurtling across the deck. Mister Browne had expected this, of course, and had made certain the path was clear. Still, this gun would fire no more in this battle. He gave the order to move the last working gun into place for what he knew would be its final shot before his gunners joined their mates topside. The corsairs resumed their charge onto *The Thistle* while those above and behind directed musket and arrow fire into her crew. Arabella dove for cover behind a gunwale and took a second to catch her breath, ragged in her throat from the intense battle. She quickly looked over her crew. She was pleased to see the fire in their eyes, despite their near exhaustion, and knew it was up to her to lead them. She pushed herself to her feet and turned to face the enemy, calling out to the crew to follow her.

No one heard her though, for at that moment the skies exploded with rolling thunder so powerful it shook the seas. Arabella watched as the entire aft portion of the corsair's deck disintegrated into a cloud of splinters and gore. A huge veil of black smoke hung in the air a hundred yards off their port side for just a moment before drifting away, revealing another ship cutting through the green seas, her great square sails billowing in the breeze. The ship had already begun its long, slow turn to come about and bring its other guns to bear. As it turned, she saw Liam McNamara standing on the railing, grasping a shroud and flashing his bright smile.

Those Turks not already aboard *The Thistle* froze in shock and confusion, so focused had they been on their prey that they had failed to notice *The Raven's* approach. Some thirty corsairs had already boarded *The Thistle*; behind them, scores of their brothers lay dead and dying on their ship. The remaining attackers stood motionless, not knowing whether to continue their attack or return to their ship to battle this new foe. The Muslim captain quickly realized *The Raven* had many more guns than he and a fresh crew as well, and thus presented the greater threat. Also, she would be vulnerable only for another moment while coming about for her next attack. He called for his crew to cut their ship free and engage the new ship, trusting that his rovers already aboard *The Thistle* would be enough to win victory over the weary pirates. Despite the arrival of *The Raven*, the Thistles knew the battle was far from over. They resumed their charge at once, their courage buoyed by Arabella's and the knowledge they were no longer alone in this fight. In addition, many of the freed oarsmen joined them, grabbing any weapon they could find and falling upon their former tormentors with savage frenzy. The corsairs had heard the words of their captain and knew they could expect no more help from their shipmates, at least not for some time. It would be up to them, numbering but thirty, to face and defeat almost seventy of the enemy.

The Raven slowly came around, attempting to bring her larboard guns to bear before the corsair could respond. The fusta fired first though, a testament to the speed and proficiency of Usain's crew. A second later, *The Raven* answered back. The two ships savaged each other, though the Turks suffered the worst of it, her rigging and sails shredded and her deck littered with the dead. Captain McNamara gave the command to close on the enemy and board her. His helmsman turned the tiller and the riggers adjusted the sails, turning the ship another two points away from the wind. A powerful gust caught her mainsail just then and an ear-splitting crack rang out. A moment later, *The Raven's* mainmast gave way, a chance shot from the corsairs having split it nearly in two. The towering spar toppled into the water, crushing half-a-dozen men who could not move from its path quickly enough. The mast did not tear away cleanly though but hung athwart their ship with one end in the water. It had taken most of the rigging with it, disabling the other sails. Worse still, where the canvas draped over the cannons, the hot iron and the burning slow matches ignited it. All offensive action stopped as Captain McNamara led his men's efforts to douse the flames and cut away the wreckage. For now, his ship was dead in the water.

The crew of *The Thistle* had no idea of their rescuer's fate, engaged as they were in a vicious fight against a fanatical enemy. Arabella led them fearlessly, taking on any foe who came within reach.

She brought to bear every ounce of skill with a blade she had learned and added to this her natural ferocity. Though many of her opponents on this day rivaled her strength, few could match her speed and accuracy and none matched her sheer desire to win. In a short time, half the boarders lay dead on the planks while some sixty Thistles yet remained, led by the red-haired demon who showed no sign of wavering. The corsairs knew they were beaten and that to continue fighting would only result in their deaths. As one, they surrendered, dropping their weapons. Arabella ordered them bound and taken below.

Only now did she realize that the cannons of *The Raven* had fallen silent. She looked across the water and took in the situation at once. Captain McNamara's ship drifted out of control toward the shore, her crew focused on saving the vessel from burning. The Arabs had fared no better, with many of their crew dead or wounded and almost all of their cannons out of action. The ship listed well to larboard, telling Arabella that one of the Irishman's rounds had holed her and she now took on water. The corsairs had separated from *The Thistle,* but drifted only a short distance away, as they too focused on saving their ship. The battle was at a standstill, victory dangling within the grasp of whomever could first reach out and pluck it.

"Mister de Rivero!" Arabella cried, turning to the bloodied and weary pilot. "Put us alongside that ship!"

Such was the fire and steel in her eyes that he moved to the ship's helm without hesitation. A moment later the sails caught wind and began to close on the fusta.

"You mean to ram her?" Molly asked.

"I mean to board her!" Arabella cried. The crew gaped at her in stunned silence. Most had been thankful just to have survived this battle, which they now thought was over. The idea of carrying the fight to the enemy had not even occurred to them. Arabella jumped atop the foredeck railing and faced them. "Now is the time, Thistles, before they can regroup and come at us again! If we act with speed and courage, that ship and this battle will be ours!"

Molly and Duff thrust their swords in the air and gave a hearty "Huzzah!" Grins broke out among the crew, caught up anew in Arabella's bravado. The two ships slammed together and Arabella was the first to leap over the gunwales.

"Follow me and give 'em hell!" she screamed, cutting down the first corsair who stepped into her path. She put a musket ball into the skull of another and Molly and Duff and the rest of the Thistles followed.

The two crews smashed against each other, metal ringing, men screaming and black powder singeing the air. The decks ran with blood, and though the Thistles and the corsairs stood roughly equal in numbers, the sheer ferocity of Arabella's attack threatened to quickly overwhelm them. Usain Reis surged to the forefront, intent on destroying the crimson-haired *djihn* who led these infidels. The giant of a man raised an enormous scimitar high over his head with both hands, then brought it down toward Arabella with enough force to cleave a bull in two. He sliced little more than air though, as the lithe Highlander nimbly spun sideways and rammed her cutlass into his stomach. The captain dropped to his knees and his men's hearts filled with despair - and fear.

Arabella turned to the corsairs, yanking her blade from the captain's body. One of the Turks threw down his sword and threw up his hands, falling to the deck and pleading for mercy. A half-dozen of his mates followed his lead and in moments, the rest of the crew surrendered. The Thistles gave another hearty cheer, as did the chained galley slaves, most of whom were Christian sailors seized from other ships and who saw their own freedom now at hand. The Thistles quickly secured their captives and freed the oarsmen, then set about stripping the Turks of their jewelry, rings, earrings, necklaces, and any loose coin they carried.

"Take the Arab captain and officers aboard *The Thistle*," Arabella called to Fergus. "Along with the oarsmen. But take care with the captain for he is grievously wounded, yet I should like to question him if possible."

He did as she asked while the rest of the crew set about searching the captured ship, which continued to list as she slowly took on water. It did not take long for them to empty the cabins and holds of their contents, carrying all they found to the main deck and building a great pile there to divide amongst themselves later in accordance with their Ship's Articles.

This task done and their long morning of danger and struggle over, the crew suddenly found themselves at a loss. Some turned to Arabella for direction, while others turned to Bobbing John, the most senior officer to have survived the battle.

"What now?" a sailor asked, looking from Arabella to the quartermaster.

"'Tis clear," Bobbing John growled. "We load the swag aboard *The Thistle* and put this blasted desert behind us."

"Aye, but under whose command?" the man asked.

"There be no question there, ye damned fool!" John retorted. "I am captain now by rank and by rights, and I will teach a hard lesson to any who says otherwise."

"Than you best be prepared to teach me that lesson, Bobbing John," Arabella told him, stepping forward. "For I say otherwise."

11

The quartermaster sneered at her. A muttering in her favor by all of the former prisoners and even some of the pirates gave him pause, though. But only for a moment, for he saw before him not the fierce warrior Arabella had today proven herself to be, but the slim girl who had quailed under his whip only a few days earlier. His face cracked into a broad, cruel smile as he hefted his blade.

"Wench, ye be forgettin' yer proper place."

The quartermaster lunged for her with a powerful and well-aimed thrust, expecting to make short work of her. She met him head on and smashed his sword away with her own. She instantly reversed her swing and slashed the blade across his throat. A crimson line appeared there. He staggered back, his hand going to the wound. He tried to curse her but could not, spewing only blood. A second later, he collapsed.

"Apparently, my place is in command of *The Thistle*," Arabella said, looking at the mixed crew of pirates and former prisoners alike. "Unless anyone else wishes to challenge me!" No one did, though some among the pirates looked none too happy about this sudden change in command. "Then let us get this plunder aboard *The Thistle*. And we will take the fusta's cannons and powder as well. Mister Browne, please rig tackle and pulley and get any gun still capable of firing aboard; God knows we can use them. The rest of you, fill your hands with as much food and water as you can carry and get it over to *The Thistle* as well, for sure'n we will need that too."

"What of the corsair ship and the prisoners, ma'am, er, captain ma'am?" one of the pirates asked. "And them other Turks, the ones whose ship we sank? Most of them swam for the shore."

"I fear we have not the hands to man more than our own vessel right now and so must leave this ship to drown. Nor can we chase after the scattered remnants of her crew, especially with those sails we saw on the horizon bearing down on us. No, we must take what we have and go."

"But there be more than just them Arab crewmen on yonder shore," another sailor said. "What of our hands who abandoned the fight?"

Arabella turned toward that golden shore, its sands shimmering in the bright sun. She clearly saw one of *The Thistle's* oar boats there, its crew of twelve even now being surrounded by some two score corsairs who had also reached shore.

"I will not waste a single grain of powder or drop of our blood on such cowards," Arabella said coldly. "Leave them to the choice they made. Now let us be off this rig before she sinks."

"Avast, there!" a voice called out from behind. Arabella turned to see Captain McNamara clambering over the railing from the gig that had carried him and a half-dozen men from his ship to this one. "Would you forget that my men contributed to this victory or that my ship has suffered for it? We deserve our share of the spoils. Where is your captain? Who is in charge here?"

"I am," Arabella said, stepping forward.

"Hello?" Liam said, turning to her with a surprised and very amused look. He looked her up and down, noting the difference between now and the last time he had seen her. He glanced at the faces of the men behind her to see if they were playing him a fool, but none disputed her words. "You? Your station has improved since last I saw you. What happened to Boggs?"

"I killed him like the pig he was. And his quartermaster for good measure."

"And a good spot more of the heathen dead you see littering the decks around you," Duff Selkirk announced, the pride in his voice unmistakable.

Captain McNamara looked around at her handiwork and his grin widened. "I never did like ol' Boggs. I do not believe we were ever properly introduced. Captain Liam McNamara of *The Raven*, at your service" he said with a bow.

"Captain Arabella Fraser of *The Thistle*." She enjoyed the sound of that.

"Well met, milady. But this does not change the fact that I and my men are owed something for coming to your rescue back there and helping to win the day."

"And how came you to be here, exactly?" she asked, then answered her own question. "You have been following us!"

"Aye, you've nicked me, lass. Tailing you we have been and purely out of concern for your welfare. That is, I mean, the welfare of my fellow rogues in these dangerous waters."

"Just that, then?" Arabella asked, smiling. "Concern for Boggs and his men?"

"Not a thing else to be sure."

"To be sure. But you are right on the score of helping us with these corsairs and you deserve a bit of the profit," she said. "You can have any of the Turks you can pluck from the shore, and the fusta."

"The ship?" he said, losing his smile. "This heap is sinking, milady. In a few moments there will be not be a ship."

"Then you best stop lollygagging here on deck when it is below you should be, making repairs," she told him with a warm smile.

"On the other hand, I see your lads carrying chests of gilt and armloads of swag aboard *The Thistle*, plus you have taken most of the crew and almost all of the guns. It hardly seems fair." He struck what he thought was a menacing pose and let his hand rest on the pommel of his sword, hanging at his hip. His crewmen nodded and muttered their agreement.

Arabella continued to smile, unfazed. "Fair is a matter of perspective, Captain McNamara. From where I stand, my offer to you seems more than fair." She glanced over her shoulder to Molly, on the deck of *The Thistle*, who stood behind one of their peterero, a burning slow-match in her hand. The barrel was pointed directly at Captain

McNamara and his men. "What is it you have in that gun there, Molly MacBain?"

"Sangrenel, cap'n. 'Twould be a pity to touch it off though, for that Irish captain is most pretty."

"Now let us again consider what is fair, Liam McNamara," Arabella said. "You and I both know this fine ship and a gaggle of Muslim prisoners will fetch a pretty penny at any port in the Mediterranean. I think my offer is more than fair, just as I do not think a man with a dismasted ship dead in the water and but six hands backing him under the lee of my guns is in a position to dictate terms to me."

Captain McNamara stared at her and, though he hated to admit it, his admiration increased even more. After a moment's hesitation, he swept his hat off and bowed to her again.

"You strike a hard bargain, lass, but a fair one."

Arabella returned his bow. "And if I may suggest, make a quick patch of her and get her underway as soon as possible. Before the fighting started, we spotted another five sails on the horizon, most likely more Turks, pulling hard for our position. They are likely a fair spot closer by now." Without another word, she turned and climbed the rope ladder back to her ship. Liam watched her go, giving particular attention to her backside as she shimmied up the ropes.

"Fiery colleen, that," he said to his mates with a broad grin. "Now let us do as she said and get below before this rig sinks from under us!"

Back aboard *The Thistle*, Arabella sent a man into the crow's nest to report on the approaching ships. At the same time, she told him to lower the English flags and raise the Scottish St. Andrew once more. The lookout confirmed that the ships had continued straight toward their position at full sail and were now but a little more than an hour away. Arabella went to John Browne, overseeing the work of hoisting the new guns aboard. He eyed them like a midwife watching the birth of a precious babe.

"Mister Browne."

"Miss Arabella," he said, doffing his hat. "Those are some fine guns we captured off that Arab barkie. What be your plans for them?"

"That is what I wanted to talk to you about. In the main though, I want to know if you are interested in continuing to serve as master gunner, and whether you can do so under a female captain?"

"Well, miss, it be right strange for an old hand like me to serve aboard a ship with a lady captain. Still, I have heard and seen plenty of strange things in my days. You saved all our hides back there, including mine, and I owe you that. Aye, I will be your gunner."

"Excellent. Then once these guns are safely aboard do not stow them but move them right away into position for battle, and then please see to the repair of any of our other guns that are salvageable. We may yet need them again before this day is over."

"Aye, aye, *captain*," he replied, returning to his work with new purpose.

Arabella left him and saw Molly and Fergus hovering nearby like protective mother hens. It looked as if the two of them had taken it upon themselves to stand guard near their new captain lest any of the hands try to cut her down and seize the ship by force.

"I can bloody well care for myself," she chided, though with a smile, for she did appreciate their concern.

"Course you can," Molly told her. "And we are here to help you care for yourself."

"'Tis just as well, for I shall be requiring the both of you in a moment. And Mister Selkirk." Duff had resumed without hesitation his former position as first mate out of habit and necessity. He stood even now on the main deck barking orders to the sailors to make repairs to the sails and rigging to ensure the ship could get underway as soon as possible. "Mister Selkirk," she called to him. "A word with you please."

She knew she needed to appoint ship's officers and instill some semblance of order and normalcy aboard *The Thistle* as soon as possible. Not only was the ship still in very dangerous waters with more vessels approaching, but she could not be certain what Captain McNamara would do once he had made repairs to his ships. He was, after all, a pirate and might easily come and demand a greater share of the spoils. These thoughts and several others occupied her, including the idea that she must at some point in the very near future review the Ship's Articles to determine how to properly divide their newly-captured treasure among her crew. She was certain she had seen the document somewhere in Boggs' quarters, and had gathered that the crew deemed the 'agreement' most unfair to everyone except the captain and his hand-picked officers. As Duff joined their little group, Arabella directed them aft onto the quarterdeck where they had a bit more privacy.

"I would like to first say to each of you that your efforts this day and even before have been noted and are most appreciated. But we are not yet out of danger and I will be needing your strength and support still. Can I count on you?" Each assured her enthusiastically she could and so she continued. "What were our casualties from the battle?"

"Boggs' men suffered the worst of it, to be sure," Fergus told her.

"They lost thirty or more hands, including almost all of their officers. But thanks to your leadership and the Good Lord's Providence, our group did right fair, at least as fair as could be expected, considering."

"We took some casualties," Molly said. "We lost Master MacIntosh and our carpenter Mister Jonassen, as well as a couple of the young fellows Lord Campbell brought aboard - God forgive me I cannot remember their names just now. And one of our dear minstrels, Tyrone, who played the lute ever so sweetly. He fought like a demon, though, and killed four men before they got him. And Arabella, I am sorry to say that dear old Dorothy perished."

"Dear God," Arabella muttered, her hand over her mouth and her eyes welling.

"And a few sailors from *The Thistle's* original crew," Duff added. "Bill Urquhart and Jack Cromartie, both good lads."

"Not Bill," Arabella said. "He was always kind to me." She paused a moment before continuing. "Boggs' men still have us in numbers, though they may not realize it. And sure, some of them may actually prefer me being in command, for I heard more than our cheers alone when I cut down Bobbing John. The wild card are the galley slaves we took aboard, for they owe allegiance to neither of us. There numbers would give us the upper hand should things come to a head with the pirates. We must assert our command over this vessel and her crew forthwith, and enforce it courageously if challenged. Mister Selkirk, I would like to officially offer you the position of first mate, and Molly, if you will, I would love to have you as second." Both agreed. "We will let the crew elect a new quartermaster if they feel one is necessary; I understand that is proper?" she asked, looking to Duff.

"Aye and well," he said with a smile, impressed with her knowledge.

"We will need another two mates we can trust, for discipline and security," she continued. "Fergus, will you be one?"

"I will indeed, ma'am."

"And can you recommend another?"

"Aye, there be Angus Brodie. He is training to be a knight and proved himself well-qualified today in battle."

"Excellent. Please ask him on my behalf, assuming he can put his ego aside and serve under a woman."

"If he is truly a gentleman, it should be his pleasure," Fergus answered.

"Our Mister De Rivero is already serving as pilot," Arabella continued. "And since no one else seems capable or willing to take the task, I will officially offer him the position, and also ask if he would be so kind as to act as sailing master until we can find another. And I think auld Thomas will make a fine purser; I know he is good with numbers and accounts. John Browne is doing his duty as master gunner even as we speak and I think young George, Lord Campbell's page, would make a fine gunner's mate for him. I dare say we will need a bosun and I have one in mind. Mister Fionn MacCumhail held the position under Boggs and I noticed just now he did not have the decency to perish in battle. I say this because I have ever found him to be a brutish man of intemperate disposition. Nonetheless, he knows his job and this ship well and I cannot think of anyone better suited to the task. What say you?"

They agreed and in such a way, Arabella quickly filled the positions aboard the ship, primarily with the former prisoners but also including some of Boggs' men. A short time later, Mister Selkirk assembled all hands on deck so he could announce the new ship's officers, masters and mates. He had to fight for their attention though, as the approaching sails, once so far to the east, continued to draw ever closer. Clearly, they could not remain in these waters much longer. But a ship at sea runs on tradition and order as much as anything else and Arabella knew this ceremony was necessary. As Duff rattled off the names and posts, very few of the crew grumbled at the selections, for few positions had changed except to replace the dead, and those appointed were well-qualified. Next, Duff told them to elect a new quartermaster from their ranks as soon as possible. Finally, he stepped aside to allow Arabella to address them. She leapt nimbly atop the capstan to better see them all and allow them to see her. In her hand she held a roll of parchment.

"Crew of *The Thistle*, hear me! I know this is right strange to you, being captained by a woman. I know many of you think it bad luck even. I am certain many Englishmen had the same feeling when first Mary and then her sister Elizabeth ascended the throne. Yet look how strong England finds herself now, stronger even than under their father Henry! So do not listen to the fools who whisper in your ear that all women are weak or unwise and must surely lead men to their doom. In faith, would you say such a thing about your own mothers?" She paused a moment to let this sink in as a good number of the crew chuckled and nodded in agreement. "I have proven myself in battle and in command this day in fair sight of each and every one of you! And I will continue to lead you and captain this ship as best I can, so help me God! I hold here your Ship's Articles, drawn up by Captain Boggs and his officers and signed or marked by each of you, dictating the division of booty and other such spoils as taken in action." The crew's faces grew dark, for each of them knew how unfair those Articles were. Arabella held the hated document before them a moment longer before tearing it to shreds and letting the wind carry the fragments away. After a moment of stunned silence, the sailors erupted into cheers and huzzahs.

"We all fought side-by-side today as equals, and we shall all share in the profits from this day as equals!" Arabella told them. "I ask only for an additional ship's share to replenish the powder and shot we used to achieve our victory. As for the rest, I shall leave up to you any decisions about awarding extra shares to those you feel deserve them." This announcement drew more cheers and broad smiles from the crew. "But right now, we have foreign sails approaching and I do not want to be here to greet them. I know every one of you just fought hard and we are all fatigued, but our work this day is not done. For any man who does not wish to view tonight's stars chained to the oar bench of a Muslim galley, let him find what strength he has left within and continue to do his duty! I promise each of you that, if this night we view the stars together as free men and women aboard this ship, I will have a hogshead of beer brought up to the main deck and equal shares measured out to everyone!" More cheers and huzzahs rang out.

"However," she continued once they had calmed down a bit. "If any amongst you cannot give me and your mates your full support, or if you feel the ship would be better captained under a man, then come forward and challenge me right now and so let us get it over with." An uneasy silence fell over the ship, broken only by the occasional scrape of a foot shuffled across the deck. Then a sailor broke wind, another laughed and the tension broke. A good deal of laughter followed this, with no one stepping forward to confront her. Arabella breathed a sigh of relief. "Then let us unfurl the sails, grab halyards and get that canvas off those gallows! Helmsman, find the wind and bring the ship around until it is in our quarter. I mean to put this infernal desert behind us!"

The crew jumped to their tasks. Arabella crossed the deck to the ship's rail. Below bobbed the wounded fusta with Captain McNamara's crewmen scurrying about.

"Captain McNamara!" she hollered. A moment later the pirate popped up from the hold. He was naked to the waist and in his bare feet, and sweat and seawater glistened from his muscular torso. When he saw Arabella his eyes betrayed the pleasure he felt at seeing her again. "How fare thee?"

"We have plugged the hole, temporarily at least, so she is seaworthy once more. And the sails are repaired and rigged as well. I believe we can have her underway in but a moment. It is *The Raven* that worries me, though. We had a spare mainmast aboard and have got her topside, but my crew is having a devil of a time getting her raised and set. And then, of course, she will still need to be rigged. I fear those approaching ships might not give us the chance to finish."

Arabella glanced over her shoulder, shocked to see how much closer the corsairs were since last she saw them. She swept her gaze across the water to *The Raven*. The ship's cannons were primed and loaded but there would be no one to man them with everyone working to set and rig the mast and sails. "Would you welcome more hands to help?"

"Any you can spare."

"Then you shall have them."

By the time Captain McNamara returned to his vessel, some thirty of Arabella's crew were aboard and helping to rig the giant timber. The work was hard and dangerous, with the men delicately-balanced on the top braces or the spider web of lines running through block and tackle rigged between the fore and mizzen masts. The remaining crew aboard *The Thistle* manned their guns, primed and ready to defend their mates should it come to that. The foreign sails were very close now, as every rigger *The Raven* and *Thistle* carried scurried about her tops.

"Not one shroud more than you have to, lads!" Captain McNamara called up to them. "Just enough to get her underway!"

A short time later, the main sheet dropped, billowed as it filled with air and tugged *The Raven* forward against her anchor lines. Both crews cheered and shook hands, any petty disagreement about the division of booty forgotten. The *Thistle* men scurried over the gunwales to their ship, fast alongside *The Raven*. The captured galley sat close behind, her sails also full and with heavy tow cables running between the two ships.

"What be your heading, milady?" Captain McNamara asked Arabella as she prepared to return to her ship.

"My pilot tells me Cartagena is but a few days journey to the north and west, and that she is heavily defended against corsair attack."

"Cartagena? A fine city. Regrettably, I face a hanging if I ever set foot there. Myself, I am for La Sabina on the Isla de Formentera. Sure'n it is not the fortress Cartagena is, but it does have its charms. Perhaps you could alter your course a bit and join me, safety in numbers and all?"

"My pilot is Castilian and insists upon going to Spain to visit relatives and pay some debts before he too faces a hanging. Since good pilots are worth their weight in gold and we have no other, I am rather at his mercy. Though perhaps we shall visit La Sabina afterward."

"I cannot promise I will still be there," Liam told her.

"I will just have to take that chance," Arabella said with a wink before leaping over the railing and onto her own deck.

The ships ran north at full sail with the corsairs close on their heels, though Arabella's course took her vessel just slightly north-by-northwest. The large square sails of the English ships gave them the advantage while the winds blew fair, though the Arab ships would quickly catch them under their oar power if the winds faltered. Luckily, this did not happen. *The Thistle* drew ever farther away from *The Raven* and her Arab consort, and by dusk they could see no more of each other than specks of white on the horizon. The Arab ships had fallen far behind.

As night fell and the crew's duties slacked, they took the time to elect a new quartermaster from their ranks. Since one of the man's principle duties was to stand up for the crew's rights against abuses - real or perceived - by the ship's other officers, they chose a Dubliner named O'Bannon, a large man with a quarrelsome nature and a stubborn streak a mile wide. The crew next set to deciding how to divide the spoils from today's action, including which sailors deserved an extra share or two, either for uncommon bravery in battle or for receiving a particularly nasty wound. This in turn raised the question of whether the galley slaves they had taken from the corsair ships this morning were to remain free or be sold back into slavery, thus increasing the total take. In the Mediterranean, galley slaves were a commodity, especially experienced ones such as these. The life of an oarsman was brutal, unimaginably harsh and often short. The weak tended to perish within the first month or so, while those who survived were considered veterans and carried that much more value for it. Arabella had taken aboard some thirty galley slaves, almost all of them Christians and most of them sailors taken by the Muslims from captured European ships.

While it was understood that any Muslim crewman captured would be sold in the nearest European port and soon find themselves chained to the oar bench of a galley in the Maltese or Italian fleets, there was disagreement about what to do with the Europeans. One group of pirates felt they should be treated as they themselves would like in a similar situation: set free and given the choice of joining the crew or leaving ship at the first port. Others said the rescued rowers were captured booty same as the Muslims or a bolt of silk, and they should be treated that way. The two sides argued for some time before they realized the captain had never said what she intended to do with them, and that maybe someone should ask her. This task became their new quartermaster's first official duty. Mister O'Bannon set his jaw, squared his shoulders and marched across the deck to the captain's cabin.

"Miss Fraser," he said upon entering. "Me name is Seamus O'Bannon. Not sure if yer remember me but I was one of the top hands, working the rigging under Captain Boggs. The crew has just elected me quartermaster and I 'ave come to announce me position and to discuss another matter, a ship's matter, that just now has arisen."

"I do remember seeing you occasionally and hearing you often," Arabella answered. O'Bannon had a very loud voice and was more prone to using it than many of the other hands, often directing his comments toward her and the other female prisoners. He was one of those who seemed to have a rather low opinion of women. Arabella could not help but wonder if this had played any role in the crew having chosen him as quartermaster. Nonetheless, he had been duly-elected and she would treat him with the same courtesy and respect she would show to any other ship's officer. "Congratulations on your selection, Mister O'Bannon. What issue may I help you with?"

"We was wondering, the crew that is, what be yer intentions with them galley slaves we took off the corsair ships?"

"My intentions? How do you mean?"

"Well, some of the crew think all the men we took off that galley, the Musselmen and the Christians, should be considered booty and sold at market, thus adding a fair bit to the coins in our pocket, see?"

"God's wounds, man!" Arabella said, disgust clear in her voice. "Those rowers we rescued are Christians and our brethren. Are you telling me the crew would see them returned to the hell of the oar bench just to increase their own share?"

"Some o' the crew, ma'am, and ye can add my number to that lot, for sure'n those slaves are not Muslims, but they have some value still, same as anything else taken off a captured ship."

"Well I will be damned if I have a hand in sending those men back into a life of slavery while I am captain. I will address the crew." She strode outside where almost all the sailors stood already assembled, awaiting her answer, though most expected it to come from the quartermaster. "Crew of *The Thistle*, hear me!" she called loudly. "As you know, we rescued some forty or so Christians from the Arab galleys this morning, thirty of whom yet live. Most of those men were sailors just like you before being captured by the Muslims, and as such they are your brothers. As far as I am concerned, they are free men once more, welcome to leave us at the next port and return to their families or to remain aboard and join our ranks if they so wish. I do not have to tell you we could use a few more hands after today's actions. I know many of you feel the same as I.

"And yet I hear that some amongst you feel our brothers should not be set free but should be sold right back into hellish slavery, to have their chains refastened and once again be made to attack their fellow Christians at sea. Who, who amongst you feels we should act hand-in-hand with the Sultan, strengthening his navies while weakening our own, simply for a few ill-gotten shillings? By show of hands, please!"

Not surprisingly, very few of the crew raised their hands, perhaps nine or ten in all, including Mister O'Bannon. The rest kept their arms at their sides and cast dirty looks at those who had lifted theirs. All but O'Bannon and two other men quickly lowered their hands, the rest muttering something about having "misunderstood the question."

"So be it," Arabella announced. "As captain, I will respect your choice as voted here fairly and in sight of all; the rowers are slaves no more!" The crew gave a cheer and welcomed the newly-freed men as brothers, a great many of whom expressed their desire to remain at sea and serve their savior, Captain Arabella. "I believe that settles that, Mister O'Bannon," Arabella said to the quartermaster, who now wore an expression both confused and perturbed. "Now, let us go to the ale locker and fetch that beer I promised the men."

Hours later and well after nightfall, Molly found Arabella in her dayroom, the cabin softly aglow from the dim light of an oil lamp hanging above the table. The lantern swung gently back and forth with the rocking of the ship, illuminating the large map of the Mediterranean Arabella studied.

"Should you not be perusing a map of the Atlantic and the way home?" Molly asked her childhood friend with a smile.

"Nay not," she replied. "For that is not where my course lies."

"Do you mean to say we are not sailing directly to Scotland? Then what was the point of taking back this ship, Ara?"

"To win our freedom and our lives, Mol, and a say in where we go next. Sure'n when I led us into battle, my only thought was to save our skins from the slavers' auction block. Once we had actually taken *The Thistle*, of course I thought first of heading back home. But then I remembered my dear Duncan and the other captive on the *Sea Rover*, still prisoners of that vile Captain Spotiswoode, bound like us for these waters and the same miserable fate."

"Forgive me, Ara, I did not think of them. So what are your intentions?"

"The *Rover* was bound for the *suqs* of the Mediterranean just as we were. I mean to make repairs and resupply in Cartagena, then take *The Thistle* south again to search for her. Anyone who wishes to leave the ship can go ashore in Spain."

"But how will you know where to look? There must be scores of ports along the Berber Coast and they could be bound for any of them."

"The crew recovered some documents in the captain's quarters on that fusta, and Mister De Rivero feels certain they are authorizations to enter and conduct business in one or more Barbary ports. Unfortunately, neither he nor any other member of our crew can read Arabic and thus tell us to which port we should set our heading. I am certain the Arab officers we captured know the answer to that question. Unfortunately, none of them will cooperate with me. I suspect they follow the example of their captain, who steadfastly refuses to say anything at all. I am sure he is the key. If he lives through the night, which, I regret, is doubtful, I will try again with him tomorrow."

"And what if he still refuses?" Molly asked. "What if they all continue to refuse?"

"Duncan's life hangs in the balance, Mol, as well as the lives of every other prisoner now aboard the *Rover*. I cannot not fail them."

12

Sir William returned to *Ban Tigh*, happy to finally be home but finding no happiness within the old manor. The house was devoid of the life and joy and laughter that had always filled it while Douglas and Arabella were there. These days, *Ban Tigh* played host only to Sir William and four others: his cook, who did double-duty as master of the cellar, his scullery boy who also doubled as yeoman waiter, and two field hands whom William rarely saw.

Now that his long journey home had reached its end, he had more time to think and reflect. The terrible ordeal on *The Thistle* haunted him. Every night in his dreams, he saw the murder of his son all over again, watched anew the slaughter of the Campbell men, saw his daughter dragged from the deck of the ship to disappear into its dark holds. When awake, he felt the sting of knowing he might not be able to afford the ransom the brigands would ask for, despite the money received from the rebels and his fellow countrymen.

The running of an estate such as *Ban Tigh* required dozens of actions and decisions daily, from managing the crops and animals to stocking the pantry and cellars to making or directing the numerous repairs and maintenance duties required. All of this went ignored now. Normally a man of action with a great lust for life, the old knight found he had little enthusiasm for anything these days. He spent most of his hours moping about the estate and refusing all visitors. For days on end, he took no comfort in food and too much in drink, and his few servants often heard him sobbing in his great chair before the hearthfires late into the night.

13

The morning after the battle, Arabella went to the large common area of the below decks that had been set up to tend to the wounded. The Arab captain had received a blow that would have killed a lesser man instantly, yet he stubbornly refused to die. And though he was a devout believer in Allah the Merciful and had a strong faith in the rewards of the afterlife for the faithful, he could not yet bring himself to surrender to that beckoning void. Bess had been tending to him and was even now at his side, with Angus standing guard nearby.

"Does he still live?" Arabella asked.

"Aye, but not for much longer now, dear," Bess answered.

"Usain Reis," Arabella said to him in the *lingua franca* of the seas, a mixture of Italian, French, Spanish and Arabic sailors used in order to communicate with their foreign counterparts. Arabella had picked up just enough to communicate in general terms, she hoped. The man's eyes twitched but he refused to acknowledge her. She continued. "As you see, we have cared for you and tended you as we would any of our own wounded. Can you not tell me to which port you planned to take me and my betrothed?"

He said nothing, turning his head away and pretending to sleep.

"The Arabs do not take kindly to women, milady," Angus told her. "And this one is likely to be especially stubborn, seeing as it were you who ran him through."

"Damn it, I need that information," Arabella said.

"I believe I could make him talk," Angus said coldly.

She knew what he meant and actually found herself thinking about it. Then she shook her head. "No, not that. The choice should be his, though I fear I have nothing to offer him to induce such cooperation. For sure'n he is a dead man already and neither I nor anyone else can save him. Although..." She paused as a thought came to her. "He was a warrior in life, and surely a proud one at that. My guess is he would rather not die on his back, helpless and in the dark hold of some ship, but on its decks fighting, at least in what small way he can."

"I do not understand, cap'n," Angus said.

"You will. Bring him up to the main deck. And get his mates up there as well; I want them all to see this."

A short time later, the crew stood assembled around the port gunwale, where a section of railing had been removed and a short plank run out over the water. The winds had calmed slightly, though the ship still made a steady three knots. Usain Reis knelt on the plank, his hands tied behind his back. Angus held his shoulders to prevent him from plunging into the water, not just from the rocking of the ship, but the man's weakness. The other three corsair officers stood on the deck close enough to witness the scene, also bound hand and foot and heavily-guarded.

As soon as she had everyone's attention, Arabella addressed Usain again. "So far, I have asked you nicely to cooperate with me. I give you now one last chance to do so."

The man grunted something in Arabic that she did not understand, though his defiant meaning was clear. Arabella took her dagger from her sheath and sliced the fresh bandages from his stomach, exposing the red, oozing wound below. His blood began to drip, slowly at first and then steadily, running down his thighs and falling into the sea. He groaned loudly, closing his eyes and muttering a prayer. The other prisoners, standing behind them, could not see the severity of the injury nor recognize it for the mortal wound it was. They angrily protested the treatment of their captain. A gray fin pierced the surface of the water. It began circling slowly and, in a moment, was joined by several others. Usain began to pray more fervently, though the blood loss and the hot Mediterranean sun took a heavy toll on him. His words began to slur, his vision dimmed and he slumped more heavily against Angus.

"You do not have to die, Usain," Arabella said loudly. "If you but help us, we will mend your wounds and give you such care that you will surely live. But if you do not cooperate, I will send you to your god right here and now!"

These words seemed to awaken the Arab captain. He struggled to sit up and turned to look directly at her. And though he knew his death was near and thus realized the hollowness of her words, his reeling mind failed to grasp her ploy. All he knew at this moment was that he would die as he lived, fighting this infidel to his last breath. "Daughter of *Shaitan*," he spat. "Christian whore! I do not fear death, for Allah is all-knowing and all-merciful. I will deny you and show you how a brave man dies, and He will judge me and reward me a hundred-fold for it!"

At that, Usain shook himself from Angus' grasp and dove headfirst into the sea. His comrades gasped in horror. As he hit the water, six silver blurs shot toward him. The water boiled and a moment later turned crimson. Arabella tried to hide her shudder by continuing to stare out to sea for a moment before turning back to the prisoners. Though they barked and roared in indignant fury, fear shone in each of their eyes. One corsair, a man named Jamal al Din, trembled so badly he could barely stand.

"Let us see who else is man enough to die like the brave Captain Reis," Arabella said. "Starting with him," she said, pointing to Jamal al Din. Angus grabbed the fellow and dragged him toward the plank. His legs gave out and he dropped to the deck, pleading for mercy. He begged first for his life and then death by any other means, the waters still churning below the plank in blood-red carnage. Arabella saw that he had soiled himself. "If only you would be a bit more cooperative than your captain," she said quietly, almost gently. "I ask so little." He hesitated for only a moment before nodding his head. "Lock the other prisoners below and take this one to my dayroom. By way of the head if you please, Angus."

A short time later, the prisoner sat bound in Arabella's dayroom. He remained there, with only the stoic Angus, for nearly an hour. When Arabella finally entered, she was pleased to see that sweat drenched the captive's clothes and pooled on the planks below his chair. Arabella carried the documents they had seized from the fusta.

"What are these? And no tricks, sir, for one of your comrades has just now answered my questions and I but seek to confirm his information," she lied. "If your answers vary from his, I will know one of you is lying and I will send both of you to the same fate as Usain Reis."

"Please, gentle lady, I will not be false with you," Jamal said, still quaking. "Those are orders of safe conduct through these waters while in the company of our ships, with portage privileges in Algiers and Benghazi."

"You say we must be accompanied by a corsair escort in order to use these?" she asked.

"Yes. The documents mention Abdullah Ibn Rahman Reis and his ship by name, but Usain Reis and Uluj Ali are well known in Algiers and felt confident they would have no trouble selling the Christian slaves without him."

"What really happened to Abdullah?"

"He is dead. Usain Reis and Uluj Ali killed him."

"Why?"

"Greed," the prisoner answered. "Originally, three ships were to meet *The Thistle* and *Sea Rover*, with all five crews receiving an equal share of the proceeds from the sale of the slaves, minus the appropriate shares to the Sultan, may Allah keep and bless him, and the *Taife Reis*."

"The *Taife* what?" Arabella asked.

"The *Taife Reis*. It is - how would you call it? - a guild for all trade activities conducted in waters under the control of the Sultan, may Allah honor his household for a thousand years."

"And this guild gets a share of your treasure?"

"An eighth share, yes. Another share goes to the Sultan, long may he live."

"I take it Usain Reis was not happy with a seventh share?" Arabella asked.

"He was greedy; he wanted more. He urged Uluj Ali and Ibn Rahman to betray the Christians, saying that our honor would not be called into question by breaking an oath with non-believers. Then, not only would we have the treasure all to ourselves, but we would greatly increase our shares by adding the value of the pirates and the two ships. But Usain went too far, for he also insisted we not pay the sultan's share, saying he ruled from far away and was wealthy already beyond compare. Abdullah Ibn Rahman would not hear of it. He was an honorable man and insisted on keeping his promise made to the pirates, nor would he even consider refusing the Sublime Portal his portion.

"Usain saw he would not sway Abdullah and told him it was just an idea, that he would of course follow the original plan. But he and Ali were of one mind and, as soon as we were out to sea, the two captains ordered us to attack Abdullah's ship. Though they meant to kill him, their plan was to capture his ship and spare most of his crew, believing we would need them for the attack on your ships. Regrettably, a wayward shot struck the powder battery and his ship was destroyed. After this, Uluj Ali wanted to call off the plan entirely, but Usain Reis was confident that with surprise and Allah's blessings, our two ships alone could subdue yours. And with but two crews splitting the treasure, he said each man's share would be that much greater."

"Did he still mean to pay the guild?" Arabella asked.

"Of course," Jamal al Din said as if Arabella had asked if the man meant to continue breathing. "One does not fail to pay the *Taife Reis* if one expects to survive long anywhere touched by the Mediterranean's blue waters."

"Of course," Arabella said. "But you mentioned two ports, Algiers and Benghazi; in which were the prisoners to be sold?"

"Our instructions were to sell most of the Christians in Algiers and the rest in Benghazi."

"Why would Abdullah take them to two different places?"

"It was a condition of the deal made by the pirates, and one upon which they insisted. This, of course, seemed foolish to us, for we knew that the *suq* in Algiers would bring the highest prices, it being the largest market in the Sultanate."

"You are right, it makes no sense," Arabella said. "Did anyone say why they wanted to make an additional trip to sell slaves in a market where they would likely fetch less money?"

"They did not, though I can think of but one reason why they would," the prisoner said. "Someone wanted those slaves to disappear - forever. Let me see if I can explain. If one sells a Christian slave in Algiers, they often remain within the city, either as the property of a wealthy merchant or the Beylerbey. Christian ships come and go frequently with the Sultan's protection and blessings, long may he live, seeking to buy them back. Sometimes, they are missionaries who redeem them as a form of charity, though just as often they are European merchants who themselves hope to make a profit by ransoming them back to their families. This happens often in the big *suqs* such as Algiers."

"And Benghazi?"

"Very few European ships ever visit that port, and thus the chances of a slave being returned from there are small indeed. Most of the men and women sold there are purchased by Bedouin tribesmen or other nomads who take them deep into the desert, never to be seen again. That is why someone sells a slave in a place like Benghazi."

Arabella said nothing, wondering just which prisoners the pirates meant to treat so horribly - and why. "Tell me: our consort, the *Sea Rover*, did it reach the rendezvous before us?"

"No. Yours was the first. It was assumed the other ship became separated from you at some point, perhaps in a storm. Usain saw this as a sign from Allah that his plan was favorable to Him since the odds of our victory were now great indeed. Once we had seized your ship, we simply needed to wait for the arrival of the *Sea Rover* and then take her as well."

"And what about those other Arab ships we saw on the horizon, following yours? I take it they were not part of your group?"

"They were not. We could not be certain, but suspected that some of Abdullah's crew survived and managed to alert the bey or even the Janissary's Guild, since many Janissary soldiers served on Abdullah's ship and were murdered by Usain and Uluj's betrayal."

"Gramercy, Jamal al Din," Arabella told him. "Your cooperation will not go unrewarded. I will do what I can to see that you are not sold as a galley slave once we reach port, but are allowed the opportunity to ransom yourself."

***

The Thistle continued sailing toward the coast of Spain. The horizon remained free of sails and it looked as if they were all alone on the Mediterranean. Arabella ordered her lookouts to maintain a sharp eye nonetheless, for either Arab or European ships, as she had not yet given up hope of finding the *Rover* still at sea. The winds remained fair and they made good progress, covering a hundred miles that first day. Early the next morn and before the first rays of the sun had peeked from beneath the blanket of night, one of the lookouts spotted a ship very close to them. He said nothing for a moment, thinking he was dreaming or that perhaps the great white sail was some ghostly phantom. His mate noticed his stare and followed it.

"You see that, right?" the mate asked.

"I do if'n you do," the first answered.

"What is she?"

"I am none too sure, though by her rigging and lines she appears to be a tartan, you know, what the Turks call a *taridha*."

"A tartan? I hear they be wicked fast. Much favored by Barbary Corsairs, they be."

"You speak wisely, brother, for look there: she flies the Sultan's green flag atop her mainmast. Though I cannot help but notice she is alone. Inform the commander of the watch!"

Molly had command of this watch. When the man in the top reported his sighting, she immediately ordered the gun crews roused and the guns run out. She then raced to the captain's cabin to wake her. She found her friend already up, shirtless still but pulling on her boots.

"I heard the gunports banging open and the roll of their carriages across the planks. What is it?" Arabella asked.

"An Arab ship, captain, most likely a corsair. She is alone and roughly our equal in size, though we look to have more guns than her. I have told the helm to keep our distance, awaiting your orders."

"Gramercy, Molly," she said, pulling a shirt on and wrapping her unkempt hair in a kerchief.

She grabbed her belt and baldric and exited the cabin, then quickly climbed the ladder to the quarterdeck. The quartermaster and first mate arrived a moment later. As the sun's light increased and set the horizon aglow, the other vessel finally noticed them. They responded in a similar fashion, preparing for a fight but not committing to one until they had first taken the measure of their foe. Though lower in the water, she was almost certainly faster and, with her oars, could probably outmaneuver them as well. But *The Thistle* indeed had twice her guns, and their greater height would give some advantage. Also, the winds were fresh this morning, though not strong, and the Scottish vessel would be able to maneuver well enough if necessary.

"Why do ye fear to attack them?" O'Bannon asked. "There be no question but we should attack at once; we can easily take them."

"'Tis not fear, Mister O'Bannon, but prudence," Arabella responded, not taking her eyes from the enemy. "Our crew took a hell of a drubbing the other day and just barely came away with a victory. I hesitate because we have many hands wounded, many others new to the ship and because I am loathe to throw any of them back into battle so soon. Still, I will not run from these corsairs, and so we will maintain our course and let them choose to fight or flee." A moment later, the corsair ship altered course, turning directly for them. Her oars hit the water, her speed increased and the crews lit their slow matches. "So be it," Arabella said. "We fight. We fight!" she repeated, this time loud enough for the crew to hear.

The hands immediately jumped to their tasks. The gun crews took aim, the top hands adjusted the sheets to bring the ship into range and at the best angle, and the rest of the crew received their weapons from the quartermaster, bows and slings and cutlasses and boarding axes. The crew was still shorthanded though, even with the addition of the galley slaves, many of whom were weak and undernourished from the brutal privations of their servitude. Arabella shook her head and said a silent prayer. She checked her pistols' powder and primers and made certain her cutlass held a keen edge. After this, she left the quarterdeck and went down to the gun deck, where John Browne and his men stood waiting.

"As long as they can maneuver, they will have the advantage," she told them. "So let us try to take our her rudder and bring her masts and rigging down before concentrating on her crew. Mister Browne, hit them with starshot from the larboard guns and then chainshot from the starboard battery. Topside, we will sweep their decks with grape and sangrenel from the swivels. I doubt you shall get a third volley before we close, but if you do, feel free to scrape her decks. Once the hand-to-hand fighting starts, you know what to do. Wait for my command to fire and may the Good Lord guide your aim!"

"Aye aye, cap'n!" came the answer, as the gunners doled out the appropriate ammunition and the crews loaded their guns.

Back on deck, Arabella saw that all was in readiness. The two ships drew within range, both ships having angled their bows to each other to present a smaller target. Arabella watched the Arab ship and

Master de Rivero watched her. The ships moved another fifty feet closer.

"Hard a' starboard!" she cried.

"Hard a' starboard!" de Rivero repeated.

The Thistle began to heel in a slow, almost ponderous turn. The enemy vessel continued straight at them.

"Now the guns!" Arabella cried to Molly, standing at the hatch over the gun deck.

"Blaze away!" Molly screamed.

A second later, the cannons answered. Great orange tongues of flame shot out, followed by clouds of thick, black smoke. The tartan's small foresail exploded in a hail of splinters and flaming canvas, taking three men with her into oblivion. Another round screamed just over her deck, missing the mainmast and its rigging but cutting the Arab boson clean in half. The ship faltered and heeled slightly to port, though she still had her mainsail and a small lateen-rigged mizzen to guide her. De Rivero yelled to the men handling the sails to quickly turn the ship about so they could bring their port guns to bear. The corsair adjusted her sheets and resumed its headlong charge, now firing its two small bow guns. Shrapnel peppered *The Thistle's* decks, wounding two men but doing little damage otherwise. In either ship's tops, crewmen rained arrows and musket fire onto each other. After several minutes and hundreds of sea yards, *The Thistle* completed her turn and came about. The tartan had drawn very close now, her captain intent on ramming them with his ship's iron-shod prow before boarding her. This would likely be the last shot John Browne and his guns would get. Topside, the peterero unloaded their contents again and again, blasting grape and sangrenel into the enemy.

The big guns spoke again, hurling iron balls connected by a length of chain. These flew straight for a short distance before the tension on the chain set the balls spinning around each other with terrible speed and force. The first shot arced wildly and splashed into the water. The second smashed into the oars, rending half-a-dozen before crashing through the side of the ship and savaging several rowers. The last chainshot tore across the deck of the tartan, ripping the life from several men before finally hitting the mizzenmast and completely severing it from the deck. Wild cheers erupted from *The Thistle* gunners, who refused to acknowledge that luck had likely played the greater part in the shot. The wounded vessel veered sharply away from them, her prow striking only a glancing blow instead of smashing through *The Thistle's* timbers. Still, the corsairs lobbed ropes and hooks and quickly locked the two ships together. Men surged up from her decks and more poured from her holds, racing toward the Thistles. The swivel gun crews unloaded one last volley of hot iron into their masses before drawing their swords. From the tops, musket balls and arrows ripped into both crews one last time. Though a dozen corsairs fell from this action, four score more instantly took their place. To meet them stood less than seventy Thistles, many wounded from the previous battle.

Arabella had not expected to face so many men from such a small vessel. She instantly read the fear and uncertainty on her crew's faces. She leapt to the fore with a wild Highlands battle cry and fired two of her three pistols point blank into the first men to rise above the railing, sending their corpses back into their mates. Molly and Fergus rushed to be on her left while Duff and Angus charged to her right. Arabella threw an empty gun into the face of another man and drew her sword, using the empty pistol in her left hand to either parry blows or deliver them to any within reach. Still, the corsairs poured aboard. This foe fought as fanatically as the last, and they soon gained the deck, pushing *The Thistle* crew back toward the stern. John Browne's gun crews charged from below, throwing their weight into the battle and stopping the retreat. Still, they were not enough to turn the tide and the two groups began to fight a vicious battle of attrition, a battle in which the enemy held the advantage.

The fight raged across the main deck with Arabella and her officers at the center. Arabella lunged forward and cut the life from one of her foes but slipped on the bloodstained wood. She went down to a knee and Molly took a step in her direction to cover her. Arabella gained her feet again but Molly paid for it. The butt of an axe struck her just above the left eye and she went down. She tried to stand but could not, falling flat and laying motionless on the deck. A Turk thrust his scimitar to finish her and Duff threw himself between the blade and his fallen comrade. The sword rent a vicious wound on his thigh and opened him to the attack of another foe, who shoved a pike into his midsection. Duff grabbed the haft and folded his body around the spear tip, but not before an inch or more sank into his flesh. Another corsair kicked him hard in the head and he too went down. Arabella took a sideways step to defend her fallen shipmates, fighting three men at once in a contest she knew could not last long.

A piercing shriek rent the air just then as one of the former galley slaves so recently rescued by Arabella hurled himself headlong into the center of the enemy ranks. He attacked with utter abandon, an axe in one hand and a sword in the other, fighting as a man who feared the certain hell of returning to the oar chains more than the cold embrace of uncertain death. Several of his mates followed his example, either from the same conviction or their affection for Arabella or both. They charged straight into the corsair blades, hewing left and right with savage rage, ignoring the bloody wounds they received in the process. The Arab center faltered under this blistering attack. Slowly, inexorably, they were forced back. Arabella immediately seized the opportunity and charged into that vulnerable middle, once more letting fly her battle cry. Her crew rallied to this and followed behind her. The pirates cut a deadly swath through the Muslims now, quickly reaching the Arab captain and his officers.

The Turk towered head and shoulders above his men and wielded two great scimitars. He struck dead two of the former galley slaves at once, sending their heads bouncing back amongst their mates. Arabella stepped into the gap and the giant smiled, licking his lips in bloodlust. He raised both swords high and Arabella shoved her last pistol against his chest and fired. Even as his blades descended, the ball struck his heart. He tumbled backward like a felled oak and his swords clattered harmlessly to the deck. Before the man's body hit the planks, Arabella dropped the gun, took up her sword again and rammed it through the throat of the stunned corsair lieutenant. Another officer clashed blades with her and the two fought for but a moment before she parried his blade and thrust her steel into his heart. Four of the rampaging freedmen leapt onto another corsair officer and hacked him to death with axes and swords.

With their officers dead and their numbers rapidly dwindling, the courage of the remaining corsairs wavered. A few turned and raced back to their ship, setting off a panicked wave of their comrades behind them. They found no sanctuary there though, for not only did Arabella and her crew give chase, but another foe awaited them. One of their own galley slaves leapt from his oar bench, his chains shattered by the same cannon shot that had killed his seatmates. A giant of a man, he wielded a five-foot length of thick chain like a flail, reaping a swath of death through the panicked corsairs. He claimed a half-dozen single-handedly and the Thistles cut down another score before the remaining foe threw down their weapons and surrendered.

A hearty cheer went up for Arabella, who stood amidst her crew on the Barbary ship's blood-spattered deck, gulping great breaths of air into her wearied lungs. She ordered the prisoners bound and taken to *The Thistle*, then ran back aboard to check on Molly and Duff. Molly was already on her feet, though a bit unsteadily, her head bandaged so that she appeared much as one of their turbaned foes. She told Arabella that Duff was alive and the ship's barber-surgeon believed he would recover. Fergus and Angus had also been wounded several times over but nonetheless were still able to stand. The captain returned her attention to the captured ship. The tartan had carried some twenty galley slaves and, oddly, a half-dozen female prisoners. All but six of the rowers had survived the battle, including the warrior who had wreaked such havoc on his former captives.

Arabella approached and personally thanked the fellow for his assistance in the battle, then offered him a position among her crew if he so wished. He smiled and thanked her, his English clipped and with a heavy French accent, but told her he already served in the navies of Malta. Curious, she opened her mouth to ask him about this when one of the newly liberated females dashed up and embraced him.

"Pierre-Louis!" she cried, also clearly French. She was a young woman, no more than twenty, and very attractive, with short black hair and bright green eyes. "I am so happy you are alive!"

The man returned her embrace but dropped his arms quickly. "Sister Marie Elise, I thank the Lord you are safe."

"His hand has protected and delivered us both," she said before turning to Arabella. "But we must not forget to thank you as well, for it was through you that the Lord brought about our liberation."

"It was my pleasure," Arabella answered. "But did I hear correctly: are you of the cloth?"

"I am. I am a sister of the Order of the Ursoline Nuns Hospitallers, based on the island of Malta. That is how I know Pierre-Louis."

"We are a long way from Malta," Arabella observed. "May I inquire how you came to be off the coast of Spain and imprisoned on a corsair galley?"

"I was sailing to France on behalf of my Order," she said. "Pierre-Louis was one of several knights accompanying me as guard and escort. Our ship was attacked and captured three days ago by the very men you defeated today."

"So are there other knights or sisters among the prisoners?" Arabella asked, looking over the men and women she had just liberated, most of whom now milled about the deck of her ship.

"There were no other nuns on the voyage," Pierre-Louis said. "And I was the only knight to disgrace myself by not dying in battle." He looked away as he said this, clearly shamed.

"Pierre-Louis, do not say such things!" Marie Elise chastised. "You fought most bravely. It is not your fault you were struck unconscious. In fact, I am sure it was God's will, for He must have some greater task yet for you."

"Well, you certainly did a hell of a job with those Arabs today," Arabella said with a smile. "But tell me something, sister: I notice you are not garbed as a nun. In fact, you look no different than the other

women we rescued."

"That was planned," she said. "It is no secret the terrible things the

Muslims do to Christian nuns when they catch them. They delight in

such barbaric and savage…well, I will not even say what they delight

in. When it looked certain our ship would be captured, Pierre-Louis

insisted I change. His counsel saved my honor and very likely my life."

"Well, I am glad for it," Arabella told them. "Just as I am glad my

ship happened to be in these waters this morning and that the corsair

captain chose to fight rather than run. We are bound for Cartagena.

When we arrive, I will see what I can do to find you passage on another

ship so you may complete your journey to France."

Arabella left the two and continued the inspection of their prize.

The Arab ship carried some cargo of value along with the crew's

personal items, and indeed the ship itself was still seaworthy and would

fetch a fine price at market. They made hasty repairs to both ships and

had them underway shortly. They put a skeleton crew aboard the tartan

to man her as she sailed in consort with them toward Spain. Mister De

Rivero told Arabella they should reach their destination by midday

tomorrow.

14

Although the ships did reach the Spanish coast the next day, the strong easterly winds of the Levante prevented them from entering Cartagena's harbor for another two days. Finally though, *The Thistle* and her prize sailed slowly into the port under the shadow of the massive forts ringing the bay, their many guns making clear that hostile ships would receive a very spirited welcome indeed. A tender ship met them and escorted them in. They berthed next to a small, sleek vessel of especially graceful lines, though it looked as if it had been neglected for some time. It flew a flag bearing the crest of the Kingdom of Spain. Her crew was working diligently to make repairs to her masts and woodwork, to replace her canvas and rigging and to generally scrub

and polish every inch of her. Porters and other hands carried bales and

barrels and chests and sacks containing all manner of supplies aboard

her, clearly preparing for a long voyage.

Although it was the ship that had first caught her eye, Arabella

could not help but note the tall, lean man she assumed to be its captain

standing sternly atop the ship's single deck overseeing the work. He

was dressed very elegantly in blue and gold Venetian slops and French-

cut doublet and hose, all of the richest velvets, satins and silks and with

a good deal of lace and gold trim. The large hat on his head sported

several grand and colorful feathers, some of exotic varieties Arabella

had never before seen. He seemed to feel her eyes upon him and turned,

catching her staring. He doffed his hat, revealing a handsome face with

delicate features, flashed her a smile and bowed low. Arabella inclined

her head in return and gave him a smile of her own before joining her

officers on the pier.

"That ship," she said to Duff as they walked toward the

harbormaster's office. "What is it, do you know? I have never seen its

like."

He craned his neck and gave it a long look. "Ah, that is a balinger,

most likely Dutch-built judging by her lines, though she has for sure seen better days. A sweet little rig she is though, and I suspect devilishly fast."

"Gramercy," she told him, marking it in memory and returning to their task at hand.

Mister De Rivero had warned Arabella that the Spanish authorities were chauvinistic to a fault and would likely not believe that a woman commanded a vessel of men. *The Thistle* already had a somewhat questionable status as to its ownership since it had been stolen by pirates from its rightful owner, who was now dead, and had then been taken by Arabella. Nonetheless, when Pierre-Louis identified himself as a Knight of Malta and spoke on Arabella's behalf, the attitude of the harbormaster changed immediately. He quickly extended every courtesy befitting a ship's captain to Arabella and waved away her attempt to explain the convoluted ownership of the vessel. Her word that the ship belonged to Lord Campbell and that she captained it on his behalf was good enough, he said. Arabella next asked if he knew whether any of the ships now in port were bound for France. Several, he told her, and in no time had secured Marie Elise and the French knight passage aboard one of these. The sister and Pierre-Louis again thanked Arabella for their deliverance from bondage and told her they would be returning to Malta in but a few weeks time and she must come visit them. She assured them she would try.

Once she had seen to her guests, she next inquired of the harbormaster if any of the ships currently in port might be traveling to Scotland. She had already written most of a letter to her father, first inquiring as to his health and then informing him she was free and imploring him to not pay any ransoms. She assured him she was safe in Cartagena and would return to Scotland as soon as possible, but could not say when that might be. As such, would he please send word here if he received news of Duncan. The master assured her any inn in Cartagena's harbor area would gladly receive and hold letters for her for a small fee, then gave her the names of a few nearby. She picked one at random, used quill and ink to note it on her letter then sealed it with wax. As to ships bound for Scotland, the official knew of only one, though just where in Scotland she was headed he could not at the moment recall. Arabella told him anywhere was good enough and retrieved the name of the ship and her captain - for a small fee, of course. She quickly found that ship, the *Sara Amanda*, but could not meet with her captain as he was away and not expected to return until tomorrow. She found his first mate though, supervising the provisioning of the vessel, ultimately bound for the Orkney Isles and the fertile fishing waters there. He told her he would gladly deliver her letter to whichever port they stopped in laying nearest to Invernesshire. He asked nothing in return, but Arabella pressed a half-crown into his hand anyway, thanking him profusely before returning to her ship.

Her crew was eager to get into the city and spend the treasure they had taken from the Turks, at least those coins and small items they could immediately trade for necessities such as women and liquor. Each man also knew he had an additional share coming once the captured ship, the prisoners and the goods had been sold at auction. They would return for that money later; for now, the men fled the ship as if it were on fire. Once their hard coin disappeared – and it would not take long, to be sure – they would unerringly begin spending their anticipated future proceeds, using chits or promissory notes for cash and often settling for pennies on the pound. As she watched them go, Arabella knew none of them had any obligation to return and continue serving aboard *The Thistle*. They could remain in Cartagena or seek service on any of the dozens of ships currently in port. She told them all they were welcome to come back, making clear she meant to return to the Barbary Coast as soon as she completed repairs and had acquired sufficient provisions. She assured them formal Ship's Articles would be drawn up by then, ones much fairer than the old ones under Boggs, of course. Arabella was committed to the idea of searching the North

African coast until she either found Duncan and the others or received word they had been ransomed and were safely back home.

Molly and Fergus stood firmly with Arabella on her desire to return to the Barbary Coast, though they were by far the minority. Most of the other officers and masters wanted to leave the Mediterranean and return to the much friendlier Atlantic, though they were divided on what to do then. Some wanted to return straight home, others wanted to continue their piratical ways along the western European coast, while still others advised heading west to the Caribbean to ply their illicit trade in the New World. With Arabella's mind set, the men would have to decide whether to remain with her or offer their services to another captain.

Before any of this could happen, though, they had to first sell their goods from the last voyage. Naturally, Mister De Rivero knew just where to find the best prices for their swag. There was only one public slave auction in Cartagena, held twice a week, so the Muslim prisoners were marched there and placed in the holding pens, where prospective buyers could get a good look at them before the next sale. As for the remaining goods, Arabella hired two wagons and loaded everything aboard, this consisting largely of bales of silk and cotton, some tools and weapons seized but not needed aboard their own vessel, several large ingots of copper and iron, and lastly and most valuable of all, several casks of peppercorn, nutmeg and cinnamon from the Orient. All of the ship's officers accompanied the wagons, along with Seamus who, as quartermaster, would ensure the transaction was conducted fairly and the crew received the appropriate shares.

A few hours later, the haggling and hand-wringing had been completed and the deal was done. Arabella had a large chest of gold and silver and the fence had two wagonloads of booty. A day later, this scene repeated itself with their human 'treasure,' where each prisoner was inspected, prodded, pinched and bartered over ad nauseum until each had found his way into the galley or household of a new owner. The shares were determined and word was put out to the taphouses, gambling dens and stews for the crewmembers to return and recoup their shares, welcome news to the many who had been completely broke within an hour of leaving the ship.

A short time later, the men queued up on deck, where Seamus, Molly and old Thomas sat at a table with a strongbox full of gold and silver coins and a ledger bearing each sailor's name and share. Molly apportioned each take accordingly, the sailor marked the ledger, Thomas noted it and the quartermaster signed off on it as fair. In fact, it was more than fair, with all hands receiving a greater share than any had ever seen under Captain Boggs. Once again, they rushed from the ship as soon as their fingers closed about the coins, with nary a thought to saving any for the morrow. Arabella received her shares last and immediately realized they would last no longer than anyone else's. A frightful number of expenses needed to be paid in order to resupply the ship, everything from purchasing new timbers, canvas, pitch and oakum, to food and beer for several score men for a month or more at sea. As she had promised everyone equal lots with no 'owner's share' but for powder and shot, she had to pay for all the other costs herself. Her share alone was not enough to cover this, but Molly and most of the other former *Thistle* prisoners graciously chipped in.

As repairs started and provisions began to come in, Arabella had word spread about the city that a 'ship for adventure' would soon put to sea and sought able sailors to man her. Arabella could not help but worry that this entire affair was nothing but an enormous gamble, for she had no idea how many, if any, of her former hands would return once she was ready to sail. Her task would have proven more difficult, if not impossible, if she had let on that she was the ship's captain. As it was, the hand bills and town criers simply announced the ship would sail under 'Captain Fraser, a Highlander,' whom of course no one save her own sailors had ever heard of. As soon as she had concluded these duties, she set about one last obligation. She took up a collection from the officers and crew to pay for a return trip to Scotland aboard another vessel for any crewmember or passenger who had sailed with them from Nairn and wished to return home immediately.

Arabella felt certain that both Thomas and Bess would take advantage of this and, though she would hate to see them go, she would certainly understand. Both surprised her by being among the first to sign back on as purser and sailmaker's mate, respectively. And though Thomas greatly desired to return to *Ban Tigh* to attend Sir William in what he knew must be a trying time, he felt the greater obligation was to aid Arabella and ensure her safety. For her part, Bess expressed considerable offense at Arabella's "impudence" for even thinking she would abandon her young charge to a shipload of "filthy, savage pirates." What neither Thomas nor Bess would admit though, was that despite the dangers and hardships, both were having the adventure of their lives sailing these waters as hands aboard a 'pirate' ship. Nonetheless, several of *The Thistle's* former compliment did take Arabella up on her offer, including Isla, Lord Campbell's' seamstress, who had been helping Bess with the sails, George, Lord Campbell's page who had of late been toiling as Mister Browne's gunner's mate, and the surviving minstrels. Arabella would miss them all, though she would especially miss the minstrels and their beautiful music.

Later that evening, Arabella and Molly supped before the great window in the captain's cabin, enjoying the view of the reflected lights of Cartagena twinkling on the water. Duff Selkirk announced himself. Mostly recovered and able to report for duty again, he requested a word with both of them. He limped before the women looking rather sheepish, as if he did not want to say what was on his mind. Arabella had seen that look often this day and said it for him.

"You want to leave *The Thistle* and return home, Mister Selkirk."

"God love you, Arabella," he said. "But I am an honest sailor, not a pirate, and it is for my home and familiar seas I am longing."

"As are we all," she told him warmly. "I will not pretend we do not sorely need your knowledge and experience as first mate aboard this ship. Nonetheless, if it is your desire to go home, then you will do so with my blessings."

"You are still committed to remaining in these parts?" he asked.

"My betrothed and several other innocent men were taken off this ship and brought to these waters. Until I find them or know they are safe elsewhere, the Med is where I intend to stay."

"Honestly, I do not know how you can hope to find them," he said. "Though Algiers be not far from here, Benghazi is all the way across the bloody sea. These waters are bristling with legions of hostile Muslims looking for vessels such as ours. By Mary, the odds are better you will join your fiancé in bondage rather than rescue him."

"To hell with the odds; I must try," Arabella declared.

"So your mind is made up then? No chance of changing it?"

"None."

"And you will for certain stay with her, Molly?" he asked.

"Aye."

Dammit; I feared you might say that. If that is the case, than I will stay on as well, for someone must keep the both of you out of trouble. Though I am likely a damned fool and will regret it later."

"I appreciate your sacrifice, Mister Selkirk," Arabella told him "Rest assured, I too long for the green hills of Scotland and for my hearth and home. I do not intend to keep us in these waters one day longer than necessary."

"I shall hold you to it. Now if you will excuse me, I had best have a word with the pilot about our course," the first mate said, standing and excusing himself. "And you will forgive me if I treble-check our supplies of shot and powder."

A short time later, the bosun and the quartermaster barged into

Arabella's quarters without so much as a knock.

"Word is we are for Algiers and then Benghazi," Fionn MacCumhail said.

Arabella was not surprised these men had heard the news already, as the only thing that traveled faster aboard a ship than the rats was information of a new heading.

"The captain's cabin is not the main deck, gentlemen, to be trod about in without her leave," Molly said before Arabella could answer. "Please remember it."

"We did not come here to talk to you," Mister O'Bannon said shortly. "We be here to talk ship's business with the captain."

"Aye, so run along, girl," Fionn said.

Molly bristled and Arabella placed a restraining hand on her forearm. "Gentlemen, Miss MacBain is a ship's officer and you will show her respect. Now, how may I help you?"

"Is it true ye mean to remain in these heathen waters instead of heading straight away to the Atlantic?" Fionn asked.

"That is my intent."

"To blazes with yer intent," he said. "'Tis the crew who should be deciding our course."

"The crew? You are mistaken, sir," Molly said. "It is the owner of the vessel that sets the course, or in his absence, the captain."

"Ye both be starting to sound like Boggs," the quartermaster said. "Like ye own this ship and everyone who sails aboard her. 'Tis not right."

"There are no slaves chained to *The Thistle*, sir," Arabella answered. "The hands serve at their pleasure and are free to seek employment elsewhere any time they choose. Further, I make no claim of ownership of this vessel; it is the rightful property of Lord Campbell and I merely captain it for him in his stead."

"Lord Campbell? How do yer figure that?" Seamus asked.

"'Tis the law. When John Campbell and his eldest were murdered, by rights this ship passed to Duncan Campbell. As his betrothed and as the duly-appointed captain, I am entitled to choose how best to use it to serve his interests, foremost being his liberation from captivity."

"I am a'feared ye are mistaken about this rig's proper owner, wench," O'Bannon said. "She *used* to belong to Lord Campbell, but was taken a prize by Captain Boggs *and his crew*. Regardless of who captains her, 'tis the crew that owns this ship now. The fact that the men of this vessel are allowing ye to serve at their pleasure as her captain does not confer ownership upon ye."

"I am quite certain the law would say differently," Molly said.

"Bah! There be no law here except that which ye can enforce by the sword," Fionn said.

"Molly is right," Arabella said. "When we docked in Cartagena, we docked under papers declaring the legal owner of this ship as Lord Campbell. The port authority acknowledged that good gentle as the rightful owner and, as far as I am concerned, any who says otherwise is a thief and a pirate and deserves to be treated as such."

"That sounds like a threat," Seamus growled. "I took such threats from Boggs because he could back them, but I will be damned if I take them from a goddamned *baltai*!"

Molly gasped and Arabella's countenance grew ice cold. "I know what that term means and I do not appreciate it. In faith, such insults do not befit us as ship's officers. Let us be civil and discuss this as comrades and mates. Now, if we may set aside the issue of ownership for a moment, may I inquire as to what might be your objection to remaining in the Mediterranean? Is it not as good a place to adventure as any?"

"It is not," Fionn answered. "Nor is traveling across a thousand miles of hostile waters to Benghazi what we had in mind when the crew seized *The Thistle*."

"Funny, that is exactly what you would have done if things had gone as planned and Boggs had remained in command. And you, as one of his sailors, would have gladly gone there with him," Arabella retorted.

"Things have changed since then," Mister O'Bannon said.

"Yes, without our corsair escort there is greater risk in the journey now," Molly said.

"What the hell is that supposed to mean?" O'Bannon barked.

"It means that if any crewman feels he lacks the courage to face such risks, it would be best if he collected his belongings and sought employ on another ship," she replied.

"Ye dare question me courage?"

"I am but trying to find a better fit for you than a fighting ship, sir," Molly told him. "Something more in line with your mettle. I believe I saw along this dock earlier today a sponge barge in need of hands; perhaps you should try them."

"*Pog mo thon*!" Seamus cursed, his face going red and his hands balling into fists.

"We have no aversion to risks, girl, if they be reasonable and bear the promise of being profitable," Mister MacCumhail answered, glaring at her. "Tangling with the Turks unnecessarily be neither. As such, the risk is unacceptable."

"To you, perhaps," Molly retorted. "But not to those of us with hardier constitutions."

"Molly, please; you are not helping," Arabella admonished. "Mister MacCumhail, please know I do not consider this voyage to be unnecessary; in fact, as far as I am concerned, it is crucial. And I do not intend to *tangle* with any corsairs if I can avoid it. However, I accept that we will very likely have to do just that at some point and thus there is some risk. But therein also lies our chance for profit."

"Aye, risk and profit go hand in hand," O'Bannon said. "But Fionn and I says there be less o' the one and more of t'other on the western side of Gibraltar."

"We shall not find the *Sea Rover* in the Atlantic," Arabella said.

"Nor shall we find them here! Christ, ye do not even know if the *Rover* made it to these waters!" Fionn said. "And even if it did, it be a thousand-to-one ye could find her a'fore she reaches port and sells yer loved ones to the Turks. If ye truly want to help them, ye would wisely listen to those experienced enough to know what we speak of and set course for the Atlantic. There at least, ye could be doing some good if'n yer wanted to raise a ransom to purchase yer kin back from the Mussulmans."

"And just how would we raise that ransom?" Arabella asked,

ignoring again his insult and trying hard to retain her composure. "By turning pirate against our fellow countrymen? By preying upon innocent merchants and travelers and bringing terror and ruin into their lives just as was done to mine and the people aboard this very ship? How convenient you are able to cloak such despicable activities in the name of Christian charity as a means of rescuing loved ones."

"The one questions our courage and now t'other questions our integrity," Fionn grumbled to Seamus. "And all because this moist sirrah wants to find her wayward hump-mate!"

"'Tis bad enough you cannot or will not keep a civil tongue with me!" Molly barked, her blood still hot. "But by God you will do so when addressing the captain!"

"Or else what, poppet?" Fionn asked with a smirk.

"Or I will cut it from your mouth and hang it from my belt." Molly looked him in the eye as she said this and her hand moved to her sword.

"Touch that blade and I'll cut you down," Fionn snarled.

"Avast!" Arabella said, standing and placing her own hand on the hilt of her cutlass. "This is getting us nowhere and so I will put an end to it. Gentlemen, if you think me capable of brutalizing innocents even as a means of securing the freedom of those I love, you have sorely misjudged me."

"Bah! It be no different than what ye intend here!" Fionn said.

"It is very different. These corsairs are pirates already, each one a holy soldier for their sultan and his beys in their war against Christianity. They are legitimate prey."

"It is folly!" Seamus said. "The Turks have these seas locked tight as a drum. Even a ship commanded by men would stand little chance of surviving for more than a few weeks along the Barbary Coast. With sirrahs in charge, I doubt *The Thistle* would last two days."

"You impertinent pig!" Molly spat. "Have you witnessed nothing of our battles of late, each led by Arabella and each ending in victory?"

"Aye, with four score old salts backing her," O'Bannon answered.

"I saw ye lying on the deck during our last skirmish," Fionn remarked to her.

"Mister MacCumhail!" Arabella said. "You are no longer welcome on this ship. Pack your sea chest and be gone within the half-hour. Mister O'Bannon, since you were elected by the crew, I cannot relieve you of your position. However, know this: folly or not, I have made up my mind and our course is set. *The Thistle* will stay in the Mediterranean until I say otherwise. Should any *pirate* attempt to wrest her from me, he will taste my steel."

Fionn drew his sword. "'Tis easy to make a threat; let's see yer try to back it!"

Molly and Arabella drew steel as well. Seamus turned quickly and slapped the bar down on the cabin door, locking them in, before drawing his own blade. "Now it's just us; there'll be no help from yer lapdogs Fergus and Duff."

"We will not need them," Arabella growled.

The two men attacked. Arabella and Molly met their charge, parrying the men's swords with their own and slashing back. Metal rang and wood splintered as the men deflected the swords into the cabin walls. The men drew back for another attack and their own blades stabbed the wooden planks of the ceiling. The four combatants quickly realized that the low ceiling and narrow width of the cabin gave little room for the four of them to maneuver, and thus their swords were more hindrance than benefit. Each tossed the weapon aside and drew their dagger. The two pairs faced off again, slowly circling about the small room. The men, being physically stronger than the women, knew they now held the advantage with the close-quarter weapons. O'Bannon feinted left, Molly moved to parry and he lunged right, closing hard and fast. Molly corrected her thrust and stabbed at him. He twisted his body to avoid the blow but was not quick enough; the dagger sliced deeply across the top of his left forearm. Before she could pull back though, his hand trapped hers and he thrust straight at her heart. She caught his wrist with her left hand but was overmatched and had to step back quickly to avoid the razor-sharp tip. After two steps she hit the wall and could go no further.

Fionn tried a similar tactic with Arabella, feinting then lunging, spinning about and thrusting again. Arabella parried each attack but was nonetheless also forced back while doing so. The big man feinted again, allowing an opening in an effort to bait her. She took it and stabbed at him. His hand shot out to catch hers but he misjudged her speed. Her blade bit deeply into his palm. He jerked his hand back even as he struck with the other, thrusting the tip of his knife directly at her chest while still moving forward. Arabella parried the blow but was forced back another step.

O'Bannon pressed his attack against Molly, forcing her against the stern wall as he pushed his knife closer to her bosom. She brought her knee up hard toward his groin but he was ready for this and blocked it with his thigh. He smiled and pressed the knife harder, its tip making contact and slicing into her flesh. Molly brought her booted foot down now with all her might on top of the Irishman's instep. Bones snapped and Seamus screamed in pain, shifting his weight to his other leg. She shoved him hard in that direction and, off-balance, he staggered. She twisted her body from under his as he flicked his blade after her. His knife sliced into the back of her left arm just above the elbow.

Fionn continued his rapid-fire thrusts at Arabella, forcing her ever back across the small cabin. Her foot struck her clothes chest and she stumbled, going down to a knee. She stabbed her dagger up between her and Fionn to keep him at arm's length but he knocked it aside and dove on top of her. He pushed the knife from her grip as they went down, though her blade sliced off one of his fingers in the process. She wrapped her left hand around his right wrist as he tried to drive his knife into her, though she knew she could not match his strength. Her right hand shot forward, her fingers going for his eyes. He tried to catch it but his wounded, bloody left hand could not hold on. Instead, he turned his face away at the last second and she missed. Still, she clutched a handful of his greasy hair and, as he pulled back his dagger with his right hand to gather strength and momentum for another plunge toward her heart, she jerked her head up and forward with all her might. Her skull hit his nose with a sickening crunch. Blood spurted from the shattered organ. Blinded by pain, blood and rage, he stabbed his dagger down. It missed Arabella's heart but sliced through the top of her left shoulder and sank into the wooden deck.

Across the small cabin, Molly grunted in pain and tore her arm from Seamus' dagger. She again stomped down on his injured foot, immediately following this with a knife slash toward his eyes, her momentum spinning her around. Focused down at his feet, he failed to see the dagger until the tip sliced across his left eye. He howled in pain and blindly stabbed his blade toward her, catching her in the buttocks. It did not pierce deeply though before she spun and slammed her dagger into the side of his neck. It sank in all the way to the hilt and erupted from the other side, killing him.

Arabella wrapped her left hand around Fionn's wrist and used her weight to keep his dagger lodged in the wooden planks of the floor. She again lurched upward, this time finding Fionn's neck with her teeth. She clamped down hard and ripped. Fionn shrieked, releasing his dagger and rolling away from her. She had caught an artery and blood spurted from the ragged gash, painting the front of his shirt crimson. He yanked the sash from around his waist to wrap the wound, but Arabella jumped, catlike, on top of him. Before he could reach his throat with the bandage, her knees crashed down on him and pinned him to the floor.

"Nay, you can bleed to death," she told him. He tried to shove her away but no longer had the strength, his life already spent. A moment later, he died.

Arabella looked over her shoulder and saw Molly holding one scarf to her bleeding arm and another to her backside. She looked pale and on the verge of collapsing but gave her friend a brave smile. Arabella returned it and went to join her just as the wooden bar across the cabin door shattered. Fergus Campbell charged into the room with his sword drawn, followed closely by Angus, Duff and several other crewmen. They stopped fast at what they saw. The room was a shambles, its furniture and dinnerware smashed, the table upended and most of the chairs broken. Two men lay dead on the floor in pools of blood while Molly sat in the only usable chair, blood oozing from several wounds. Arabella stood over her, a dead man's blood covering her from nose to knee. Her red hair encircled her like a lion's mane, and Fergus was struck by just how closely she resembled at this moment a lioness fresh from the hunt. None of the men could find their tongues but simply stood in the doorway, staring dumbfounded at the two women.

"Mister Selkirk," Arabella said calmly. "I will be escorting Miss MacBain to the barber-surgeon, and I should think we will both be there for some time. Mister Campbell, please ensure that these men receive a proper burial, and if you could convince some of the hands to tidy up my cabin before I return, I would be ever grateful."

At that, she helped Molly to her feet and the two of them limped from the room without another word.

15

In another week's time, Arabella and Molly were mostly mended and the ship was mostly ready to sail. Arabella knew conducting commerce in the Mediterranean could be a tricky thing; half the nations of Europe were currently at war with the Ottoman Empire and the other half had peace treaties that were tenuous at best, secured primarily by large payments to the regime. The ships of these 'tribute' nations could ply the Mediterranean and conduct trade along the Barbary Coast, but needed to secure the appropriate flag or flags to fly from their mastheads to identify themselves. Even this still allowed any Ottoman ship to stop and board them to ensure they also carried the appropriate writs and authorizations. These came from the Sultan's ambassadors and had to bear the proper, current seals and marks. Naturally, there existed a thriving business in the forging of such documents, with the Turkish ambassadors frequently changing the official seals and emblems to stay one step ahead of the forgers, and the counterfeiters working just as hard to remain current.

Although Arabella possessed legitimate documents, they required *The Thistle* to have an Ottoman escort at all times. As such, she was forced to have the writs redone by a forger to exclude this condition, paying for it with another collection from her officers as well as the promise of a share from any treasure taken on the voyage. She also had the fellow exclude the two destination ports from the documents so she could visit other ports of call as necessary. Now, they would appear to be nothing more than legitimate merchants licensed to conduct trade in all the cities under the Sultan's dominion.

With the ship repaired, restocked and now possessing the proper authorizations, all they needed was a crew. Sign-ups would be held on the morrow.

Arabella sat in her day room studying maps of the North African coast when a messenger requested permission to come aboard. Duff met the lad at the gangplank and, after a moment's conversation, granted him leave. Arabella greeted the boy near the pilot's station, noting the large package he clutched in his hands. He shifted the box precariously to one hand, removed his hat and bowed low before her. The lad's garments looked to be quite expensive and finely tailored, giving him the appearance of one who worked for a nobleman or wealthy merchant. Upon closer observation though, Arabella could not help but notice they were rather threadbare and worn.

"My master begs the pleasure of your company in joining him for supper this evening. He also bade me deliver this gift to you, a small token of his esteem for your unique position as master and commander of this vessel."

"Really?" she said, intrigued. "And who is this master you serve?"

"The captain of yon ship," the lad said, pointing to the balinger Arabella had so admired when she first arrived in Cartagena. "Master Bartholomew Roderick of *The Greyhound*."

Arabella opened the package and found within an absolutely beautiful hat, certainly from one of the finest haberdashers in Cartagena and in the latest style currently popular in Venice and Florence. It bore one of the most handsome feathers she had ever seen.

"You may tell your master I accept his invitation."

Arabella arrived at the Caliz de Oro Inn shortly before the appointed time, resplendent in the finest outfit she could piece together on such short notice. She refused to wear a fancy dress with bodice, as the style of the day dictated, but chose instead to go in garb befitting a sea captain. She wore slops tied with silk ribbons at the knee with stockings below these, tall boots, a man's silk shirt, a surcoat, a waist coat and the hat Captain Roderick had gifted her. Completing the outfit and befitting the danger always present in a city such as Cartagena, she wore her baldric slung athwart her chest, with cutlass and dagger. For added insurance, she also brought Duff and Molly. As they had not been invited to dine with Captain Roderick, she bade them stay in the inn's common room but near the door to the private dining chamber her host had reserved.

Arabella knocked and the door swung open. The young man who had brought her the hat bowed low as she entered. Apparently, he would be performing the duties of a gentleman waiter this evening. Beyond him, Captain Roderick sat regally at the end of a long table. He wore garments similar to the lad's in that they had obviously once been very expensive though now appeared rather sad and timeworn. He rose when Arabella entered, took her offered hand, bowed low and kissed it.

"My dear lady, prithee forgive me for not extending the courtesy of formally introducing myself before now. Alas, ship's business has kept me dreadfully busy these last many days, as I am certain you can understand. Captain Bartholomew Roderick of *The Greyhound*, at your service," he said, his accent Welsh.

"Captain Arabella Fraser of *The Thistle*," she replied, accepting the seat he offered.

"So it is true, then? You are indeed the captain of that fine ship in yonder dock?"

"I am, though for the moment that is not common knowledge."

"Verily, then it shall not pass my lips to any other," he said, filling their glasses with wine. Arabella did not reach for hers immediately and, after a moment's confusion, Roderick smiled and switched glasses, taking a drink from hers to vouchsafe its integrity. "'Tis a remarkable occurrence, your captaincy. Such a thing is extraordinarily rare, as I am sure you must know."

"It is uncommon," she agreed, taking up her new glass. "But not unheard of. History is replete with great female warriors and captains. Was it not Queen Tomyris of the Massagetai who defeated the Persians under Cyrus? Alwilda and Sela were renowned pirate captains on the Baltic but a few centuries ago, and of course my own nation has a long tradition of strong women, including the Countess of Ross who led troops for William Wallace. Why, not forty years past, Lilliard led the Scots at the Battle of Ancrum and personally slew the English commander. And think on Grace O'Malley, who even today commands legions of men and fleets of ships along Ireland's north coast."

"You are well-studied I see, and more so than I. I yield the point," Captain Roderick said, chuckling and raising his glass. "A toast to all such bold and audacious women - yourself included." The two drank deeply and the boy refilled their glasses. Arabella was surprised to note that it was an excellent claret. Her host continued. "If memory serves me though, Grace O'Malley comes from a clan with a long history of piracy on the high seas. Something tells me this is not the case with you."

"Nay, at least no history I am aware of. I find myself in this situation not because of birth, sir, but because of fate."

"Ah yes, fate. I too have danced with her in the past," he said, getting a faraway look in his eyes. He lost his smile for the first time since Arabella had entered the room. He caught himself after but a moment and returned his full, smiling attention back to her. "Please do not feel compelled to explain yourself to me if you do not wish, though I cannot deny I am curious to hear the tale."

"'Tis no great secret and, truly, no epic yarn either. I was en route from Scotland to France for my wedding when pirates set upon our ship. My husband-to-be and I were taken hostage, though put aboard separate vessels. Eventuallly, I learned the pirates had no intention of returning us to our families even if the ransoms were paid. The blackhearts meant instead to carry us to the Barbary Coast and sell us all into slavery."

"Dear God! How dreadful." At that moment, the young waiter brought in a large silver platter containing a variety of appetizers, setting this before the pair and then bringing another bottle of wine. "Please, try some of the *pan de horno* and this wickedly delicious gazpacho," Roderick told her, pushing the platter and its collection of little bowls before her. "And do go on with your fascinating tale, prithee."

"The details are far too sanguine for such a setting as this and, truly, are of little consequence," Arabella said. "If I may suffice to say, when the opportunity arose to change the circumstances of my captivity, I took it. Truly, my plans went no further than saving my life and the lives of my friends, and perhaps place ourselves in a position of strength from which to barter our freedom. However, fortune smiled upon us and we ended up in command of the ship, with me as her captain."

"Led your fellow prisoners in revolt and seized the ship in bloody hand-to-hand fighting! Extraordinary!" Captain Roderick said, gazing at her as if she had just now sprouted wings or had walked on water before his eyes.

"Something like that," she answered. Despite herself, she found that she rather enjoyed the attention and admiration of this handsome fellow. Nonetheless, she did not want to talk about herself all evening but wished to know more about her host. "But pray tell, Captain Roderick, what brings you to these waters?"

"The aforementioned fate, as it were, though aided in no small way by poor judgment on my part and foul betrayal on another's. Let us just say I trusted someone I should not have and ended up running afoul of the Spanish authorities. Luckily, the Crown has of late come to its senses and realized my worth to them is greater on the seas then on a gallows. All they require of me is to satisfy my debt to them, an obligation that fortuitously promises me the opportunity for both adventure and wealth."

"Why, that is an answer worthy of a pirate, sir," Arabella said.

"Heavens no," he answered. "I prefer the term 'gentleman adventurer,' for I carry certain licenses allowing me to engage in acts of hostility against the enemies of the Crown."

"A Letter of Marque!" Arabella said. "You are no pirate; you are a privateer."

"But of course, dear captain. Piracy is illegal," he said with a wink before taking another bite from one of the many delicacies on his platter.

"So how do you find the Mediterranean? Have you had much opportunity to exercise your Letter's authority?" she asked.

"None at all, to be frank, for my writs were only recently issued. You might say the ink upon them is not yet dry. Though rest assured I am no new hand at such ventures, for I have sailed in a similar capacity on both sides of the Pillars and I look forward to feeling the sea brisk upon my face once again. I might ask how you are finding the Mediterranean, but I fear the question is already settled, as I could not help but notice the two large wagonloads of goods you offloaded for market upon your arrival."

"Those goods were legally acquired, I assure you," she told him, smiling coyly.

"I would never suggest otherwise," he said. "Um, and forgive me for repeating base gossip, which I detest and never partake in—"

"Of course," Arabella interjected with a smile.

"Of course. But they say you are more wildcat than woman in

battle; *'Laboua'a-t'Asharq'*," he muttered.

"I beg you pardon?" she said.

"It is something I heard some of your Muslim prisoners in the marketplace say. Roughly translated, I believe it means the 'Lioness of the Levant.'"

Arabella laughed so hard she nearly dropped her wine glass. "So I am a lioness now?" she said, then growled in a fairly good imitation of one. Enchanted, Captain Roderick laughed with her and they both drank another toast.

"Ah, yes, these heathens do have such imaginations," he said. "And yet, I must assume they would not say it if there were not some truth to it. And I must ask your forgiveness once more for repeating rumors, but I am certain I heard some scuttlebutt about a nasty incident involving yourself and some members of your crew the other night in this very port. I believe two men died."

"For one who does not take part in base gossip, you certainly seem to be on very familiar terms with it," Arabella told him. "And now I must ask your forgiveness, but that matter was between myself and my crew and no others."

"Pray forgive my presumption, Captain Fraser," he said earnestly. "Your answer is as appropriate as it was inappropriate for me to ask. I will speak on such topics no more. Ah! I believe dinner is served."

And so it was, as the youth came repeatedly from the kitchen carrying course after course of a sumptuously prepared meal, along with yet another bottle of wine. By the time the lad served dessert, both captains had thoroughly stuffed themselves and were fairly well crocked. Between courses, their discussions continued on a very friendly basis. Finally though, Captain Roderick asked what he had intended to this entire meal.

"If I may be so bold, and please do not think you have to answer this if you wish not to, but what is next in store for *The Thistle* and her *lioness* captain?"

"I mean to keep searching for the prisoners taken from *The Thistle* and placed aboard the second pirate ship, my fiancé among them. And by God, I mean to search every ship and every port in the Mediterranean if I have to until I find them."

"Bravo!" he said, clapping almost giddily. "What a woman! Your betrothed is fortunate indeed. But tell me, dear, do you mean to take this task on by yourself, I mean with your one ship? A fine ship it is, no doubt, and well-manned - or womaned, as the case may be - but a dangerous prospect in any waters and especially the Med."

"I am not opposed to making alliances with other captains when it serves my purpose, if that is what you mean."

"Ah, you have smoked me! Was I so obvious? Pray pardon, perhaps it was the wine. My ship in yonder port, as you have no doubt noticed, is terribly fast, or at least will be once we finish scraping two year's worth of barnacles and neglect from her hull. But it is also small and rather lightly gunned, limiting what I can do with her. If we, you and I, were to join forces, we could be much more effective. All the Crown asks is a very reasonable ten percent. Under a Letter of Marque, you would be completely legal, so long as we focused our efforts solely on the ships of the Sultan or other pirates. Not to imply that you would ever consider doing otherwise, of course."

"The Turks and renegades were my sole intended targets. Your proposal indeed has merit. I am favorable to it, sir, though I wish to consult with my officers prior to giving you my final answer. Let us sup again tomorrow evening, this time aboard my ship, and I will give you my answer then."

The meal concluded, both captains stood — unsteadily — and bowed to each other. Arabella tipped so much she had to grasp the edge of the table to keep from falling. This caused Captain Roderick to giggle and Arabella joined him. She bowed again and finally exited the room. Molly and Duff awaited her, empty platters and dry mugs lining their own board. Arabella's attempt to compose herself failed miserably, but luckily Duff and Molly were nearly as drunk as she and hardly noticed. The three of them left the inn arm in arm, singing sea shanties as they staggered down the cobbled streets back to *The Thistle*.

The morning after her dinner with Captain Roderick found Mister Selkirk and Thomas sitting behind a table atop *The Thistle's* main deck. Another ledger lay open before them, this one yet blank as they awaited the first potential crewmen. Arabella stood at the quarterdeck railing, anxiously watching the docks below and the gangplank leading to her ship. Eventually, one young fellow came hesitatingly down the long wooden pier and boarded. After a brief discussion with Duff and more than a few glances toward Arabella, he made his mark in the logbook and joined the crew. A few moments later, two more fellows came aboard, followed shortly by several others. After this, they saw a steady stream of interested sailors. Of these, some few shook their heads and departed, but the majority signed on.

Arabella noted happily that almost all of the former crew returned, though whether from loyalty or poverty she did not know and decided she did not care. Obviously, the old hands knew their captain was a female, as did many of the new recruits. In fact, some admitted they had signed aboard only because of this novelty, though many had heard of the 'Lioness of the Levant's' ferocity in battle and hoped this would turn their fortunes around. A few hands signed aboard not knowing they would be commanded by a woman only to storm off once they learned the truth, though these were replaced almost immediately. Soon, they had filled their compliment entirely and the officers found they even had to turn away some late comers.

Most of the former Thistles had heard of the incident involving Seamus O'Bannon and Fionn MacCumhail. Few seemed to hold this against Arabella and Molly, and in fact looked upon them now with even greater respect. Arabella promoted Fergus to fill Fionn's position, while the crew again elected a quartermaster from among their ranks. They chose an intelligent and somewhat reserved Oxfordshire man named William Fenimore. Those hands who knew him well just called him Madagascar Jack, as he was one of the few Englishmen to have visited the island of St. Lawrence on the east coast of Africa, known to its native inhabitants as Madagascar. Mister Fenimore had sailed under Captain Boggs, though it was notable that he was one of the few men who had always treated Arabella with great courtesy while she had been a prisoner.

With the crew now settled, Arabella called a meeting with her officers and presented to them Captain Roderick's proposal. The group debated the benefits of having two ships versus the negative of dividing the wealth between two crews. They ultimately decided two vessels would face less risk and likely secure more treasure. Just as important, many liked the legal protections of operating under a Letter of Marque.

"Very well," Arabella announced. "Captain Roderick will be joining us for supper this evening and I would like all of you to join us as well. In the meantime, let us call in dear auld Thomas with quill and parchment and start drawing up our new 'Ship's Articles.'"

The Thistle and *Greyhound* left Cartagena first thing the next morning, plotting a course for Algiers. They hoped to avoid if at all possible any engagements with corsair vessels on this first leg of their trip. It would not do, the captains reasoned, to have Arab goods or Muslim prisoners on board if they were boarded and inspected by Ottoman officials. After Algiers, they planned to sail to Malta before continuing on to Benghazi. Since Malta was not under the control of the Sultan, they would be free to take any Ottoman vessels they could along the way, offloading the booty there before again traveling back into Barbary waters. When dealing with corsairs, either in port or in the open seas, the captains devised a pretense of being merchants seeking to purchase captured Christian slaves to return to their families - at a profit to the ship and crew, of course. This ruse was not without risks of its own, however, for the repatriation trade was currently dominated by the Greeks who often resorted to violence to control their hegemony. Their ships also plied the waters of the Mediterranean and were heavily-gunned, and they would not hesitate to try to stop and board any vessel they thought suspicious.

The Thistle and *Greyhound* sailed south-by-southeast for several days. The winds blustered briskly, causing choppy seas and blowing in the occasional light squall. On the third day out from Cartagena, the lookouts spotted a large Turkish galley skimming the waters to their west. The galley spotted them as well and altered course several points to come in for a closer look. The privateers made certain they flew the proper pennons and these apparently did their job, for the galley turned and headed elsewhere without even boarding them. The next day, three Ottoman warships sailing in consort also crossed their path and these did stop them. Their paperwork proved to be in order though, and the Arab officers and their intimidating Janissary guards returned to their vessels, sailing off in search of other prey.

Late in the evening on the fourth day out from Cartagena, the two privateer ships sailed into the broad Bay of Algiers. They spotted first the *kasbah* high on a hill overlooking the water, its huge cannons pointing menacingly down into the harbor. Rounding the headlands, they next saw the enormous *mole'* jutting into the sea and, beyond this, the city itself, sheltered on the western side of the bay and nestled against the *sahel*, the low, rugged hills running along the coast separating the sea from the endless deserts beyond. Arabella realized now why some sailors called the city *'Alger la Blanche,'* or Algiers the White, for the vast majority of its buildings had been finished in a brilliant white that glowed even in the setting sun.

The two ships made their portage without incident. Benito de Rivero handled the paperwork and formalities, as he had visited this port before. Several Janissaries came aboard to inspect the ship and, after a thorough search, reported finding everything in order. The harbormaster seemed very surprised when he learned that a female captained *The Thistle* and insisted on seeing her for himself. Assured he was not being played the fool, the official's bemusement turned to a sort of sad indignation, with a lot of head shaking and finger wagging, and he muttered something to Benito about the continuing decline in European morality as well as common sense. However, as the vessels were properly licensed by the Sultan to conduct business in his port, he would not refuse her. He did insist, however, that she wear the *hajib*, the traditional dress of the local Muslim women, if she meant to leave the ship and go about the city.

Before the fellow left, Benito inquired if the *Sea Rover* had ported recently. The man said he did recall a foreign ship but not the name, though he would gladly check his logbooks for a small fee. A short time and several coins later, he informed Mister de Rivero that the *Sea Rover* had indeed docked in Algiers some nine days ago. He remembered her now as there had been some problem with her paperwork, though a respected corsair captain by the name of Uluj Ali was with him and vouched for the vessel. They had sold several slaves at the *suq* two days after their arrival, though they remained in port for more than a week, apparently awaiting another ship. According to the logs, the *Rover* had left port only yesterday.

When the harbormaster departed, Arabella turned to Molly, her eyes wide. "I do not believe it! They were here!"

"Aye, and with Uluj Ali," Molly said. "But how can that be? We sank his ship, with him on it!"

"He must have survived and made it to shore," Arabella said. "And then eluded Captain McNamara's men. I can only surmise he was still there when the *Rover* arrived. I would wager the rat made up some cock and bull story to explain what happened to *The Thistle* and then convinced Spotiswoode to come here and sell his captives as originally planned. The question now is where did they go from here? Benghazi or home?"

"I reckon they would only head back to England if they had no more captives to sell," Molly said. "We need to see if we can account for all the *Thistle* prisoners here in Algiers."

"Then let us do so without further delay," Arabella said.

In no time, the proper garments had been found and purchased for Arabella so she could accompany her male officers ashore. Molly remained behind in command of the ship. Arabella wore a long black *abayah* over a *kamiz*, with a scarf covering her head and hair. A veil covered her face so only her eyes were exposed. And though she resented being made to wear such clothing, she actually enjoyed the loose-fitting garments, which protected her from the blazing sun yet allowed air to move about her. In addition, the flowing *abayah* allowed her to keep a sword and pistol concealed upon her as she walked the city. A local merchant gave them directions to the *suq*, telling them the next slave auction would be tomorrow at noon. The ship's officers spent the next several hours searching through the bazaars and alleyways of Algiers for any sign of the *Rover* captives, all the while pretending to be merchants interested in finding and purchasing

Europeans to repatriate. Finding slaves proved surprisingly easy, as the entire economy of the city seemed dependant upon them. Slaves ran shops for their masters or labored as craftsmen for them, doing the work of blacksmiths and coopers and cordwainers. Others toiled as household servants and were often seen running through the town on miscellaneous errands. They cleaned the streets and built the buildings, while others simply accompanied their masters about town as porters and package-bearers.

Several questions and several more pence led the ship's officers to the city's *bagnios*, or slave prison, which lay on the edge of town near the ocean. Arabella found the *bagnios* not at all what she expected, for unlike most dungeons or gaols of Europe, the *bagnios* was a sprawling and open compound. Scores of slaves who were not currently tasked idled about, cooking or sleeping, gaming, dancing, some even whiling away the hours in a small tavern run by yet another slave. The gates to the complex stood open and she watched as several prisoners exited and others returned, seemingly at will.

Master de Rivero explained that things were this way for several reasons, the foremost being that there was no reason for the slaves to try to escape because there was simply nowhere for them to go. A great sea stood before them to the north and the endless, burning sands of the desert surrounded them on the south, east and west. Scowling Janissaries guarded the docks and carefully watched all who came and went into any visiting ships. In addition, slaves were easily distinguished from their Muslim captors because they were not allowed to wear beards, an honor reserved only for 'true believers.' Those who had them when captured were forced to shave. Also, the slaves typically retained the clothing they wore when captured except for any hats, which, like beards, were forbidden. The European style of trousers and shirts stood out markedly against the robes and *imamas* or *kaffiyehs* worn by most Algerians. Finally, each slave in the *bagnios* wore a large iron ring about their neck. This last item was not intended to keep them from trying to escape, but to mark them as belonging to the Beylerbey of Algiers, in effect to the city, as opposed to the many slaves owned by private citizens.

Arabella and her officers entered the *bagnios* under the watchful eyes of the Janissary guards and only then did she remove her veil. Small apartments for rent circled the compound's inner wall. This rent was then added to a person's ransom and, as such, typically only captured nobles or wealthy merchants used them. The remaining prisoners lived in the open, central courtyard, in the middle of which stood a large communal kitchen. As the Thistles entered, various prisoners approached and gave their names and hometowns, hoping they had come specifically to repatriate them. Arabella found it hard to look these men in the eye when she told them no, sorry, not this time. They headed directly for the tavern since this appeared to be the prisoner's main gathering point. Once inside, Arabella bought a round of drinks from the slave working behind the bar and made certain to tip him generously. She noticed that her coins for the ale went into the till but her tip went into a small earthen jug he kept separate. Curious, she asked him how a Christian slave ended up running a tavern in a prison, in a country where alcohol was prohibited by law, no less.

"Oy, thems rules is only for the Mussulmen," he answered, his accent clearly placing him from the southwestern part of England. "We Christians are just heathen sinners to them so long as we do not convert, so the alcohol be just fine and dandy for us. As fer me, I be from a little village in Cornwall name o' Treen. This one day, 'bout, oh, two years ago now, I was a'fishin' off Gurnard's Head when I were taken in a corsair raid. Sure'n I was damned surprised to see them Turks off'a Cornwall, but there they was and here I be. But yer see, miss, funny thing about the Turks is, they be not just holding yer and letting yer sit while a'waitin' yer ransom. No siree, they be smart and if'n yer has a skill they can use, well, then they puts yer to work. If'n ye be a carpenter, than by Pete they put yer to work as a carpenter. But they be fair too, for they often might let a bloke keep a piece of his labor's coin. Sure'n they may take eighteen pence to a shilling, but them other two pence be yers. And that ye can save and put toward yer ransom or ye can buy stuff with it and, ye know, make yer life here a bit more comfortable, least as comfortable as it can be, by the by.

"Well, 'twas no time a'fore they found out I had me a little tavern in Treen, just scraped by, ye know, no mutton for me every night and twice on Sunday, if yer know what I mean. And once I gets here the bloke that buys me has this deal with the Beylerbey where he gets to run this here tavern for the prisoners. Sweet deal for the Turks, it is. Damned if they don't take most o' yer labor for free, let ye earn pennies to the pound for the rest and then take that back from ye in drink! Course, I cannot say I mind too much, for the Good Lord knows we can all use a drink or two now and then. Hell, without, surely more than a few o' us would go mad! Asides, it be helping to pay me way out of here. Yer see, me master takes everything for the ale and food and I gets to keep all the tips, which, mind yer, sure'n be not much. Still, me ransom is not too high and at the rate things be going, in another year or so I should have collected enough to pay me way free. Course, damned if I know what I will find when I get home. Likely me missus has either run me tavern into the ground with her spending or married that damned Albus Filch and now he be half-owner!"

Another customer called for the barkeep just then and he turned away to fill that man's mug. He came right back though, for he knew that the free had more money than slaves and he sensed Arabella had not finished with him. In both he was correct. Arabella pulled another tuppence from her pouch and set it on the board, though she kept her finger on it as she again queried him.

"I would guess a man in your position keeps up on the comings and goings of the prisoners in here," she stated. "Especially the arrival of newcomers. In this you may again be of service to me. Might you know of any men arrived recently off an English merchantman named the *Sea Rover*, which would have come to this port about a fortnight ago?"

"Aye, I know o' one man. We talked shortly after his arrival and I ha' seen him in here a few times. Cannot say for certain that I know of any others from that particular ship, for I ha' not met any, but sure'n we did get a good number o' new arrivals around that time."

"And what happened to those slaves?" she asked, rolling the coin to the tapman. He snatched it up quickly and it disappeared into the jar.

"Most of them was purchased by the Beylerbey and put to work either as galley slaves or laborers here in the city, working on the various construction projects that always seem to be on and on."

"These new arrivals," Arabella continued. "Were any clearly of nobility or at least well enough off to rent one of those private rooms yonder?"

"Nay, cannot say I seen any new tenants there, milady. And I's keeps me eye on them, ye can be sure, for if theys got money to spend on fancy digs, then sure'n they gots it for a pint or two in here."

"What of this one fellow you mentioned, the one you said came off the *Rover*? Did he get sent to the galleys or is he yet here in the *bagnios*?"

"Aye, he be living here, though he be not here right now. He were sent out to work on the breakwater this morning with a whole gang o' men, and they do not usually return until after dark."

"Gramercy, good sir," Arabella told him.

Though the hour was late, she and the other officers ate a meal and had another round as they awaited the return of the work crew. A short time after dusk, a small group of Janissaries marched a large group of slaves back into the compound. The men were filthy, soaking wet from head to toe and covered with mud and muck and stinking of the sea. They were exhausted as well, with some dropping straight to the ground as soon as they reached the compound and falling dead asleep. Most, however, made their way to the cook area to fetch their supper, the only food they had tasted since they left the camp before sunup. Arabella spotted her man at once, for he had until recently served as *The Thistle's* bosun under Captain McMullins. He was a Highlander himself, a man from the desolate part of the West Country simply called the Rough Bounds. Arabella tried for some moments to remember his name, finally recalling it as Indulf Ranald.

"Mister Ranald," she said, stepping before him.

He jumped a little, for none had called him by his formal name for many weeks. He looked up at her and his eyes went wide, his mouth agape, not sure he was really seeing her or was having a waking dream.

"Miss Fraser?" he asked.

"Aye, and I am glad you remember me."

"Ye are hard to forget. Ye're not a prisoner, though," he added, taking in her garb. Finally, he noticed the rest of the officers behind her and he cracked the first smile he had in weeks. "Ye be 'ere to ransom me!"

"Oh, um, about that," Arabella stammered, for she had hoped it would not come to this so soon. Truthfully, they had not the funds to ransom the prisoners taken from *The Thistle* and had only come for information at this point. "Actually, that is not possible just yet, Mister Ranald, though we are working on it. If you will carry your trencher with us back to the tavern, I shall buy you an ale with which to wash down your meal and we can talk."

Arabella led him to the pub, where the barkeep quickly brought everyone a round of thick, dark stout.

"I see's yer found him," he announced. "Told yer right, I did. Told yer."

"And gramercy again, sir," Arabella said, paying him for the ale and including another tip. "That will be all, thank you." The man took the tip and the hint and returned to the bar.

"So ye are not prisoners?" Ranald repeated around a large mouthful of food. "And yet ye are here in Algiers. I do not understand."

"It is a long story," Arabella told him. "Suffice to say we are not prisoners but we are seeking information about the whereabouts of all those taken from *The Thistle* and put aboard Captain Spotiswoode's vessel. Do you know what happened to the others?"

"Aye, most were sold right beside me at auction and are either here or on a galley out there," he said, waving in the general direction of the sea. He finished his too-small supper and downed half his pint in a single draught. Arabella waved her hand to have another tankard brought.

"You say most were sold here," she said. "What of the rest? And do you know what happened to Duncan Campbell?"

"Young Master Campbell? I cannot say I saw much of him once we was aboard the *Rover*. The pirates separated him from us pretty quick, put him in nicer quarters and all owing to his money. Most o' the rest of us ended up in the hold. We arrived here, oh, I really don't know how many days ago, might ha' been a week, might ha' been a month and, like I said, most of us were brought ashore in chains and sold."

"And the rest?" Arabella repeated.

"Stayed on board, I guess. I just assumed they had either already made arrangements for their ransoms or else ol' Spotiswoode had other plans for 'em. Though now I think on it, seems to me the crew did mention something about another port elsewhere up the coast. Perhaps the others was going to be sold there."

"And you are certain Master Campbell is not here in Algiers?"

"Most humbly sorry, miss, but all I am certain of was that he was not taken off the ship with me, nor sold at the same auction. Whether he stayed on board the *Rover* or came ashore to be sold the next day I cannot say. Though for sure I have not seen him here in the compound."

"Did everyone who was sold with you end up in the *bagnios*?"

"Oh, no, not all o' em. Most did, though, bought by the gov'ner - I think they call him a bey - to be property o' the Sultan o' Ottoman. A few got bought by other folks though, and I have not seen 'em since. So, when are ye going to be able to get me out of here?"

"Soon, I hope," Arabella told him. "But I fear we will need to raise your ransom first. But I promise you, you will not be forgotten; none of you will." Arabella pushed a shilling across the table to him. "Thank you for your information and enjoy your drink, Mister Ranald. We will meet again."

On the following day, they found two additional captives from *The Thistle*, Angus MacBrodie, the ship's original cook and cousin to their own Mister Angus Brodie, and Jean Mauleon, one of the deckhands. Their information proved to be similar to Mister Ranald's: neither could recall seeing Duncan since early in their captivity, though Mister Mauleon was certain that several prisoners had been kept aboard the *Rover* when it left Algiers. Arabella again promised the men she would do all she could to secure their ransom, but they would need to be patient a little longer. They found no sign of any of the other men known to have been taken by Captain Spotiswoode. Arabella was torn between remaining in Algiers and continuing the search or heading straight for Benghazi to try to catch up with the *Sea Rover*. Ultimately, she again considered the information Jamal al Din had given her, and decided that if there were more prisoners in Algiers they likely would not be going anywhere, while the men bound for Benghazi faced the greater risk of disappearing as soon as they were sold. And so, though she hated to leave the Algerian captives in the hellish bonds of slavery for even another minute, she gave the order for *The Thistle* and *Greyhound* to depart at once. The trip to Benghazi would take much longer than the trip from Cartagena to Algiers, for they would need to travel to the far side of the Mediterranean Sea, and they would lose at least a day while they visited Malta to resupply.

The ships left the White City with the evening tide, the lamplights from a thousand windows cutting through the dark and reflecting back on the harbor like the starry heavens above. They followed a course of east by northeast, almost the identical path many Barbary pirates themselves took on their raids from Algiers. The corsairs often sailed to Sicily and Corsica, then up to Florence and back down again along the western Italian peninsula, around the boot and finally hard east toward Greece. They avoided Malta, home of their powerful and hated foe the Knights Hospitallers, for the days of the great corsair fleets under commanders such as Barbarosa had long passed. These days, most Muslim raiders sailed alone or in small groups of no more than two or three ships and could rarely take on the mighty Maltese war galleys.

The weather took a turn for the worse shortly after *The Thistle* and *Greyhound* left Algiers. By the time the crew could no longer see the city lights behind them, the rains had come, bringing with them the vestral winds. These gales whipped the seas into a frenzy, battering the ships incessantly, keeping the carpenters ever busy plugging leaks and caulking seams while the crews pumped water from the holds.

16

The week following Sir William's return to *Ban Tigh,* a courier showed up on his front stoop bearing a sealed envelope. It carried no markings other than his name and the word Errogie. He bade the lad stay while he read it. The lad noted his expression change from one of relief to one of concern. As he finished reading, his countenance grew very dark.

"Are you well, sir?" the boy asked.

"What? Oh, fine, fine, lad. Gramercy to ye," he said, handing him a tuppence. He then held out another and said, "Tell me, young man: how did you receive this letter? Who gave it to you?"

"'Twas another courier, sir, down in Moss Side. Truth be told, I thought it a bit strange, a courier delivering a letter to a courier. But he said that was just what had happened with him and that I was to deliver it to you." The lad plucked the coin from Sir William's hand and trotted off down the lane.

William watched him go and then returned to his study. There, he reread the note several times. It first told him Arabella remained alive and was being well cared for and, as of yet, remained unmolested. Next came a very complicated series of instructions for how he was to contact their representative in Edinburgh when he had collected the ransom and was ready to pay. Finally came the amount itself. It was exorbitant, so much so that his thoughts immediately returned to the ships his friends had promised to send in search of the pirates. He knew their odds of actually locating the scoundrels were slim at best, but he also knew that paying the asked-for ransom would ruin him utterly.

And so, for now at least, he would continue to hold out hope for Arabella's rescue.

17

Three days out from Algiers, the morning watch in the crow's nest of *The Thistle* spotted three lateen-rigged ships sailing in convoy due east. Two looked to be medium-sized merchantmen and the third was a large galley. The privateers altered their course slightly to move closer for a better look. The cargo ships were lightly-armed merchant *pincos*, or pinks as the sailors called them, while the third was a large xebec of one hundred fifty tons at least and carrying more than a dozen big guns and numerous peterero. Each of the pinks appeared to have but one small cannon, a falcon or falconet at the most, and a swivel gun. The lookout saw another tall sail several leagues behind the convoy and to the north, though this did not appear to be part of their group or close enough to cause concern. *The Greyhound* adjusted her course and sailed close enough to *The Thistle* for the captains to communicate.

"What say you, Captain Fraser?" Bartholomew called across the frothy chasm.

"'Tis a risk, to be sure," she answered. "That war galley carries a good deal of firepower and likely a large number of corsairs. Yet I think also those merchant ships must be holding a right valuable cargo to require such protection."

"My thoughts exactly. Shall we take them?"

After but a moment's contemplation the Highlander answered. "Aye!"

"Merchants first or the gunship?"

"The gunship, I would say. That will be the more formidable foe."

"We may have a devil of a time catching the pinks if they split up and flee while we are tangling with the galley," Captain Roderick commented. "What say we first rake them with chain and bar to their rigging before we take on the warship?"

"Agreed!"

Both ships turned toward their prey, yet still maintained their current speed in an effort to not appear a threat. After an hour and still many miles from their targets, the Ottoman ships decided they did not like the looks of these two European vessels and increased their speed, spreading all available canvas to the wind. The privateers abandoned their charade and did the same, *The Greyhound* keeping true to her name and leaping quickly to the fore. Miles away and unnoticed by any of them, the ship with the tall sails did the same.

Another hour passed and the great square sails and clinker-built hulls of the European ships proved their worth, as they devoured the distance between themselves and the convoy. The galley had remained between the two pinks, refusing to abandon one to defend the other, but now their prey chose a different course. All three vessels turned hard to starboard and began sailing south by south-east. The pinks continued to sail at maximum speed while the galley reefed her sails, decreasing her speed slightly. Clearly, her captain meant to put himself between their pursuers and the merchant ships with their cargo, possibly sacrificing his own ship to give them the chance to escape. After another hour, the ships had closed to nearly within range of their long guns. The xebec shifted her sails suddenly and racked her oars, beginning a sharp turn to come about and face her pursuers. *The Greyhound* had slowed her speed just enough to allow *The Thistle* to catch up, and now both privateer vessels sailed in line abreast a little over two hundred yards apart. A steady wind from the northwest filled their sails and pushed them at a fair five knots as they closed on the war galley, their guns primed and their slow matches burning.

At the last moment, the ships veered away from the xebec, sailing just beyond the effective range of her guns. They raced past her toward the merchant ships. The xebec let loose with both broadsides anyway, sending stone and metal and chain screaming toward them. Most of her fury hit the water to no effect. One roundshot, however, skipped across the water's surface and smashed a hole in *The Thistle's* side, while a shot of chain went spinning through her upper rigging. This last severed her topsail braces and tore a six-foot gash in her main topsail. To the south and west of *The Thistle,* the nimble *Greyhound* emerged unscathed, cutting the water at more than six knots and racing after the merchants. *The Thistle* lost perhaps half a knot from her damage, but sailors leapt into the tops to make repairs. Down below, the carpenter and his mate worked frantically to patch the hole in her side. The xebec, now behind the two privateers, doused her sails and dipped her oars into the sea in an oft-practiced maneuver to bring her about, the rowers on one side hanging on their sticks and fighting the galley's forward momentum with every ounce of their strength while their mates across the gangway pulled their oars through the water, all while their masters rained lashes across their sun-baked backs to encourage them. The xebec turned quickly. The sailors unfurled her enormous sails again and both sets of oars beat the water together now. The war galley shot forward in pursuit.

The Greyhound closed on the fastest pink while *The Thistle* raced after the other, both merchant ships having veered away from each other in the hope at least one would escape. The xebec's captain ignored *The Thistle* for the time being and went after the smaller *Greyhound*, hoping to disable her quickly and then turn his full firepower on *The Thistle*. The craft moved remarkably fast under both sail and oar, gaining even on *The Greyhound*. Still, Arabella felt reasonably sure Captain Roderick would reach the pink before the xebec reached him. If the Welshman could disable the little merchant ship quickly, he could race back to *The Thistle* and they could take on the big gunship together.

Captain Roderick closed on the pink's starboard side and both ships let fly with their long guns. The merchant sent a stone ball screaming across *The Greyhound's* main deck, where it nicked the main mast but did no real harm. The privateer gunners aimed high, intent on disabling their prey's rigging and bringing her to a halt. Their salvo hit the mark, showering the pink's deck with jagged splinters torn from the masts and spars and dropping sheets and halyards onto her crew.

Nonetheless, the masts remained standing and the sails, though holed, still billowed. Captain Roderick had his swivel guns ready and as soon as they were in range, his gunners let fly. They again fired into the pink's tops while his long guns blasted point blank into the ship's stern. More rigging disintegrated and cascaded down onto the decks, killing several more sailors. One of the big guns also struck home, smashing the merchant's rudder into splinters. In answer, an Arab crewman fired the pink's swivel gun and sent a cloud of hot, jagged iron across *The Greyhound's* deck, tearing the life from four men. Still, the merchant crew could no longer sail their ship, which bobbed atop the water's surface at the mercy of the wind and Captain Roderick. He would come back for her later.

He ordered the helm hard a'larboard the moment their bow passed their disabled foe, steering a course toward *The Thistle* and the second merchant ship. Arabella's ship had lost some speed but was still closing on her. Captain Roderick spotted the war galley fast approaching. Her captain must have realized *The Greyhound's* plan and that the first merchant ship, though helpless, was safe for the time being. The Turk altered his course and moved to cut off the *Greyhound*. *The Thistle* drew within range of the pink and both crews opened fire. Each ship tore into the other's rigging, *The Thistle's* guns shredding everything above the pink's deck. The merchant ship's one cannon managed a lucky shot, piercing *The Thistle's* mizzenmast some eight feet above her deck, snapping it in two. The enormous spar toppled over the starboard bow, immediately becoming a sea anchor and dragging the ship to a crawl.

"Axes to the quarterdeck!" Arabella yelled. "Cut her loose! We can sail with our fore and main!"

The crew jumped to her command as both ships' gunners fired another salvo, this time adding their swivel guns to the longs. The merchant vessel had little effect, but once more suffered terribly under Arabella's guns. Its cannon fell silent and it now lay dead in the water. A moment later, Arabella's crew cut their ship free from the broken, forty-foot timber and they began moving forward again. Arabella immediately looked for the xebec and saw her even now closing on Captain Roderick's ship.

The Greyhound turned its bow to the war galley, coming up fast into the gap between that ship and *The Thistle* at nearly seven knots. Bartholomew knew his ship would not be able to outrun her; his only chance lay in closing fast and fighting, despite the fact the xebec carried at least twice and possibly three times his numbers. Still, he did not have to win this battle; he only needed to hang on long enough for

Arabella to join him. He ordered his top hands to spread every inch of canvas The Greyhound carried to give her the appearance of racing at top speed to beat the xebec. However, he also ordered four immense leather waterskins lowered into the sea on the ship's starboard side, out of sight of the enemy, where they acted as sea anchors and greatly slowed his ship. As such, though she appeared to fly at full sail, she actually made just under five knots. The crew of the xebec took the bait, furiously dipping their oars into the water and increasing their speed even more to ensure The Greyhound did not slip around them and join The Thistle.

Captain Roderick let his deception continue until the two ships drew to nearly within the range of their long guns. He gave a signal to his men to cut free the water bladders while the pilot shoved the helm directly toward the Arab ship. The Greyhound leapt forward now, presenting only her narrow bow as a target, and this at an ever-changing angle. The Arab captain thought briefly of trying to rake her from stem to stern with his forward guns but did not trust his gunners to make such a difficult shot at their present speed. He screamed orders to turn the ship hard to larboard and try to bring her alongside the privateer for a broadside. With both ships sailing at maximum speed, the distance between them shrank much more rapidly than he had wanted, for he had hoped to be able to fire several salvos into the smaller ship before closing for hand-to-hand combat. Now, he would be lucky to get off even one salvo. *The Greyhound* raced toward the huge galley, looking to all the world as if she meant to ram her. As she closed to within mere yards, both captains ordered their gunners to open fire. Captain Roderick's four guns were answered by eight, enveloping the tiny *Greyhound* in a maelstrom of fire and steel. Captain Roderick's pilot shoved the tiller hard to starboard as the upper deck exploded into splinters and rent flesh. The ship turned just enough to strike a glancing blow against the war galley, scraping gunwale to gunwale along her side and snapping her oars like matchsticks. Nearly a half mile away, Arabella heard the thunder and saw the two ships disappear in a cloud of black smoke. She feared the worst and cursed her own ship's slow movement, knowing Captain Roderick could not long withstand the onslaught of the war galley's many guns and legions of corsairs.

"Ship off the starboard stern!" came the loud, surprised cry from the crow's nest. "By Mary, she's right on top of us!"

Arabella spun and saw nothing but yards of sails towering high above her. She quickly recognized the ship as of European origin, thankful it was not an enemy galley until she remembered some corsairs used just such ships, as did any number of pirates in these waters.

"I do not believe it!" Molly cried.

Arabella looked to where she was pointing and stared directly into the smiling face of Liam McNamara. *The Raven* surged past them at full speed, sailing directly toward *The Greyhound*, her gun ports open and her crew ready for battle. As they passed, the Irishman removed his hat and bowed to her.

"How does he keep doing that?" Molly asked.

"I shall ask him later," Arabella said. "Right now my only concern is to put this rig at *The Greyhound's* side while it is still afloat!"

Aboard Captain Roderick's ship, the surviving privateers leapt to their feet and charged to meet their foe. The *Greyhound* gunners fired another broadside and the men in the tops fired a musket volley down into the massed Arabs on her deck. Another group lobbed *grenados*, their fuses sputtering for an agonizing second before the iron cans exploded. The gunners knew they would have no time to reload their slow muskets, and thus cast them aside, drawing swords and axes. Captain Roderick refused to wait for the enemy but bravely led his men onto their ship, knowing the desperate act might be their only hope of surviving. Still, he had one more weapon at his disposal that he now deployed. As his men engaged the corsairs, six lads swung from his tops and landed on the galley's deck behind the combatants. They rushed to the imprisoned rowers with hammer and chisel in hand and began banging away at their chains. As they freed each slave, they handed him an axe or belaying pin and told him now was his chance to exact revenge upon his captors. The freedmen leapt to the task with the same zeal their captors had shown when wielding their whips.

Even with the addition of the slaves, the pirates had little real hope of overcoming the numbers they faced. Bartholomew's men fell rapidly and, in a matter of minutes, half the Greyhounds lay dead or wounded. Captain Roderick saw the futility of his attack and called a retreat. He could only hope the Arabs would pursue him and not simply use the galley's long guns to destroy his ship, the greater value being in taking them alive. His men scrambled back onto *The Greyhound,* and sure enough the corsairs gave chase. The retreating sailors paused just long enough to lob the last of their crude grenades, blasting a devastating hole in the center of the Barbary's charge. Nonetheless, the corsairs still numbered over one hundred against but forty pirates. Cruel smiles spread across their faces and their hearts burned with bloodlust as they leapt aboard.

As their feet touched the deck, a shadow loomed over them and cannon fire erupted. *The Raven* unloaded a broadside of grape and canister-shot directly into the massed flanks of the enemy. The bow crashed against the side of the xebec, and Liam's men blazed away with muskets and bows. Before the smoke had cleared, Liam led more than a hundred men onto the galley, putting their foe between them and the Greyhounds. Captain Roderick stared, open-mouthed at the sudden appearance of *The Raven* and her crew. After but a moment's hesitation, he reversed his retreat and ordered another charge at the Arabs. The raging foes smashed together. Minutes later, *The Thistle* arrived, lending another ninety sailors to the fray. The corsairs now were overmatched and knew it. Still, they continued to fight. Only after another score of them fell and the survivors faced three times their number, did they finally surrender.

Thunderous cheers erupted from the victors, tempered only by their surprise at the unexpected arrival of the Ravens. Captain Roderick marched across the deck to where Captains Fraser and McNamara stood in heated discussion. Without so much as a word, he drew back his fist and slammed it hard into the Irishman's nose. Arabella heard the sound of small bones crunching and saw both men winch, Liam grasping his nose and Bartholomew clutching his fist.

"'Tis some thanks for saving your boney arse, Barty!" Liam said to the Welshman.

"Go to hell, McNamara!" Captain Roderick spat back.

"No wonder you could not handle the Arabs yourself; you hit like a wee lass," Liam mocked, though blood drained from his nose when he took his hand away.

Captain Roderick bristled and reached for his cutlass. He winced again as soon as his smarting hand tried to grasp the hilt. As such, he simply glared at the man. "We were handling them just fine before you showed up, just holding them until *The Thistle* arrived," he spat.

"Bollocks!" Liam said. "No offense to Lady Arabella, but by the time they had reached you, there would have been naught for them to do but collect your boots, after pouring what was left of you out of them!"

"Just what the hell are you doing here anyway, Liam?" Arabella demanded, stung by his comment, perhaps because of the truth in it. She also resented the fact that he had 'come to her rescue' once again, at least, no doubt, in his eyes.

"Trying to steal our prizes, you can bet," Bartholomew growled.

"Were you tailing me again?" Arabella asked.

"Tailing you? Hardly," the Irishman said. "My ship has been following this convoy for days, just waiting for the right moment to slip in and snatch one of those fat little pinks out from under that galley's guns. And sure'n they had finally become spread out enough for me to do just that when you buggers showed up and ruined everything!"

"Save your tears; you will get no sympathy from us," Bartholomew said. "The fact that you either did not possess the strength or the courage to take on the entire convoy is not our concern."

Liam flushed scarlet and jerked his cutlass from its sheath. "Question my courage again and so help me I will cut you down, Barty!"

Captain Roderick now drew his sword, ignoring the pain shooting through his hand.

Arabella pulled hers as well and jumped between them "Avast! If you mean to kill him, then you will have to come through me, Liam!"

Liam's anger fled him as rapidly as it had come. A look of confusion and hurt crossed his face and he lowered his blade. "But I saved him, and helped you win the day. Why do you treat me as an enemy?"

"You butted in where you were not invited and not welcome," she told him.

"Not welcome? How many of your crew would have been killed, Barty, before *The Thistle* arrived to help you? And how many more of yours, Arabella, would have died facing near on a hundred Turks after they had cut down Barty's men? Besides, what was I to do? Reef my sails, pour an ale and just watch the action?"

"If you think this squares us, you are sadly mistaken," Bartholomew said through clenched teeth. "Two years, Liam; two years in a Spanish dungeon is what you owe me, and a good deal more."

"Dammit, Barty! If you would let me explain-" Liam started.

The Welshman cut him off. "I do not think you can and the Lord knows I do not want to hear it. Just go, Liam."

"So do you mean to rob me and my men of our share in this, denying that we contributed in any way to the victory?" McNamara asked, turning from Bartholomew to Arabella. His crew muttered dangerously, their numbers almost equal to Arabella and Bartholomew's combined. Arabella had no desire to see more blood spilled this day, especially between brethren.

"Of course not. You and your men obviously earned a share," she announced firmly. Both pirate captains turned to face her, Liam smiling and Bartholomew frowning. "He is correct that my ship was still a bloody long distance away, while a great host of corsairs yet faced your men, Bartholomew. God knows how many more Greyhounds would have died before we arrived, and sure'n we would have had a hell of a time mopping the rest of them up without you." Captain McNamara's grin grew larger and he made a point of flashing it in Captain Roderick's face.

"But we would have mopped them up to be sure," Arabella continued. "And we all would be the richer for it with fewer shares to spread amongst ourselves. You were not asked to join this fight, Captain McNamara, and your 'claim' to this convoy carries no weight. It is as Captain Roderick said: either you make your move against the entire convoy and accept the risks, or you forfeit any claim to her, as well as the right to complain if someone else does the task. Have your men stand down, Liam; we will make no decision on the division of booty under the threat of your swords. We will adjourn to my dayroom aboard *The Thistle* to discuss the fair division of the prizes in a civilized manner. Meanwhile, our ships will sail out to collect the two pinks. And I mean our talk to be a mannerly discussion; there will be no fisticuffs or swordplay! Mark me: if either of you get out of line, you will answer to me. Understand?" Both captains quickly nodded.

"Good. And that goes for everyone else as well!" Arabella called loudly to the assembled crews. "I will brook no fighting amongst you over the division of booty or any other matter. We will not kill each other over a few Goddamned shillings! First and second mates from all three ships, you are charged with enforcing the peace and you are to shoot the first man that gets out of line! Quartermasters: secure the prisoners and the xebec while we all collect the pinks. And free the rest of the galley slaves, but get the names of those who aided in the battle; those men will receive a share for their assistance. We have not the hands to row the xebec, however, and we will not tow her, so make clear to them they must continue to work the oars if they want to earn their freedom. Finally, dismount all the guns from the galley, for we shall divide them amongst ourselves and bring her into port stripped. Jump to!" She turned and marched back to her ship as the officers and crews did as directed.

Arabella led Liam and Bartholomew into her dayroom and closed the door, stating that none of them would leave until they had settled this matter. Cunningly, she had several bottles of the finest wine her ship carried brought in and placed on the sideboard in buckets of cold seawater, with the promise they would all enjoy a toast or three upon the successful completion of the negotiations - and not a moment before. Things began inauspiciously, for Captain McNamara immediately stated that his crew deserved an equal third share of the prize. Captain Roderick countered that they deserved nothing. Arguments, accusations and insults flew after this and continued for some time, despite Arabella's attempts to rein in their emotions as well as their tongues.

The dry heat of the Mediterranean afternoon grew ever more oppressive within *The Thistle's* cramped dayroom, and Arabella made certain they all had nothing but warm, brackish water from the ship's hold to drink. All the while, the dark green wine bottles perspired seductively but an arm's length away. After two hours they had gotten nowhere. Arabella finally put her foot down, telling them to stop acting like children and focus on the issue at hand. Their past, whatever it may be, was to stay in the past and they would behave like gentlemen or she would have both of them thrown into the ocean to cool off. Negotiations resumed and, after another hour, she finally convinced them to allow her to settle the matter since they obviously could not, and they would abide by whatever she decided. After this, things progressed rather quickly and it was not long before all three captains put their marks on a document Arabella drew up outlining how the seized prizes were to be divided. The chilled wine was served to the delight of everyone, their enjoyment of this being the only other point agreed upon by all.

Once the bottles were drained, Captains Roderick and McNamara returned to their ships and announced the terms of the agreement.

Though there was some grumbling from the crews, both captains had vowed to put the most favorable spin upon it they could and make clear their unequivocal support for the terms. In such a way, the crews were placated and generally happy, since even the most pessimistic among them knew the value of the three ships, their cargo and their prisoners would be great indeed.

The hands spent the remainder of the day making repairs to their respective ships, with Liam repaying Arabella's previous assistance in repairing his damaged mast by helping her replace her own. After the repairs, small crews were put aboard the prize ships to pilot them into port. They left the cargo aboard the merchants, as there was far too much of it to stow aboard their own vessels even if they had wanted to. The guns, however, were removed per Arabella's orders and divided between the three captains. Arabella had John Browne mount many of them right away, increasing her broadside firepower considerably. She also added another long falcon to her cabin in the stern, giving her two chasers, then had Mister Browne ship a gun to the foredeck, just abaft the bowsprit to serve as a bow chaser. He grumbled that the space at the head was terribly limited already and wondered aloud if the decking and knees might need extra bracing to withstand the punishment of a firing gun. Arabella told him she had every confidence the he and the ship's carpenter could accomplish the task.

"*The Thistle* now bristles," Molly quipped, joining Arabella on the quarterdeck.

"Indeed she does," Arabella replied. "I did not like the feeling of near helplessness I experienced facing that great galley and her many guns. She possessed more than twice the firepower of *The Thistle* and *Greyhound* combined. We still are not so powerful as a king's ship, but our *Thistle* has some thorns now to be sure."

"Aye," Molly responded, before going quiet for a time. Finally she looked to Arabella and spoke her mind. "'Tis clear today was not the first meeting between Captains Roderick and McNamara."

"Aye, there be some bad blood between them to be sure, though they did not discuss its roots and I did not pry. But they did not kill each other, and that is something to be thankful for."

Near dusk, the ships unfurled their sails and set out once more, resuming their journey toward Malta. Long cables stretched between them and the prize ships to keep them joined. The captains ordered this not simply to keep a ship from becoming separated or lost in the dark, but because two of them contained the bulk of their treasure while the third was treasure itself. Nobody wanted any of the vessels to give them a 'soft goodbye' in the middle of the night. Each captain made certain the three captured vessels burned bright lanterns stem and stern and they also ordered their gun crews to remain at the ready throughout the night, just in case the temptation grew too strong for any of the crews manning them. The seamen, knowing they protected their own shares of the treasure, were only too willing to remain alert and on guard. Their trust of their 'brothers' clearly went only so far.

Three days later and still many leagues from Malta, the skies darkened ominously and the winds began to gust. Soon a gale arose, howling like the damned and dumping rain down on the privateers in buckets. The captains ordered all sails dropped and turned their bows into the wind, knowing their fate was now at the mercy of the weather and the Good Lord. The storm raged for hours. Sleep was impossible, which was just as well because everyone was kept busy working the pumps or passing buckets hand over hand from the bilge to the main deck scuppers.

The gale ended with the dawn, blowing off to the north as quickly as it had come. The seas turned to glass around them while the sky blazed pink and azure. All of the ships had survived the squall, though each had sustained damage, mostly to their masts and rigging. In addition, six seamen had been lost, four washed overboard and two killed in falls from the tops. The crews again spent the better part of a day making repairs before resuming their journey.

Two days after this, they reached Malta.

18

Though officially a territory of the Kingdom of Sicily, the island nation of Malta effectively belonged to the Order of the Knights of the Hospital of St. John of Jerusalem, the Knights Hospitallers, who dominated it utterly. Now called the Knights of Malta in honor of their recently acquired home, the holy order was one of the few remaining from the days of the Crusades, warrior priests who swore obedience only to their grand master, the pope and God. They had settled in Malta five decades earlier after having been driven from their previous home of Rhodes by the Ottoman warlord Suleiman the Magnificent. Their fee to the King of Sicily for the use of his island was a token one Maltese falcon per year.

The Thistle and her cohorts navigated around the western and southern coasts of the island and back up the eastern seaboard to her capital, Valletta. If the crews had found Cartagena daunting, they found this port city utterly formidable. Valletta sat atop a rocky peninsular plateau carved by hand from Mount Sceberras, which rose between the Grand Harbor and Marsamxett Harbor. The city was one of the newest and most heavily-defended in Europe, if not the world. Its construction had only begun eighteen years prior, after the Turks had laid waste to most of the island's defenses during the Great Siege of 1565. Unlike at Rhodes though, they had failed this time to dislodge the Knights from their rock. Still, the Order had had to rebuild everything, and had embraced the opportunity completely, bringing in the finest architects and military engineers in Europe. Their task was to design not just a new city, but a new kind of city, complete with running water and an effective sanitation system, and fortified beyond any capital in Europe. As *The Thistle* sailed slowly toward her portage in the Grand Harbor, Arabella saw that a massive curtain wall ringed the city and immense fortresses guarded every corner. Atop the walls, the formidable Knights Hospitallers stood watch. There was but one main gate into Valletta, on the far side of the city and past the scores of cannons in the forts and towers, and the gate itself was surrounded by deep defensive ditches and supported by two massive bastions on either side.

Maltese tender ships sailed out to meet them as they approached, wanting to ensure that this large group with its corsair galley was no threat. After meeting with the captains, they raced back to port with news of the privateers' success over the Ottoman ships. *The Thistle, Raven* and *Greyhound* passed at least a dozen Hospitaller galleys of immense size bobbing at rest in the harbor, warships in the Order's quest to defend Christendom and recapture the Holy Lands from their Mohammedan foes. At least, that was the grand purpose they wanted the public and the kingdoms of Europe to believe. In reality, the Knights of Malta used their navy exactly as the sultan used his: to commit piracy on the high seas against their enemies. Arabella counted the massive oars along the sides of the galleys and realized some of the great ships would require many hundreds if not a thousand or more slaves to propel them. It was small wonder the Knights of Malta had such a thirst for purchasing captured Muslims to serve their fleet.

As Arabella and her fellow captains docked their ships, she was surprised at how many people turned out to greet them. A moment later, Arabella realized most were prostitutes and representatives from various alehouses, inns and merchant shops, all hungry for the sailor's newfound wealth and wanting to be the first to help them spend it. The ships' captains and officers waited only briefly before the harbormaster's man, a prim little official named Jardum Bahria, greeted them, accompanied by two very large and intimidating knights. Mister Bahria informed the officers he would be boarding each vessel in turn, meeting her captain and examining their papers and holds. If the ships held Christian captives or had seized the goods of any nation having a treaty with Malta or the Crown of Aragon, the Order would take an extra one-fifth share of the ship's take as a fine. In any event, all cargo and prisoners were to be transferred into the custody of the Order for accounting and auction. Once the auctions had concluded, the Order would take thirteen percent off the top, with ten percent going to the Grand Master and the other three divided amongst the port officials, the auction houses and certain charities such as the Nuns of St. Ursula. In addition, another five percent would be taken this one time since none of the privateer captains had applied for and received license by the Order authorizing them to conduct their 'trade activities' in the Eastern Mediterranean. Though none too pleased with this, the three captains had few alternatives and thus reluctantly agreed to the terms. After the goods, slaves and cargo had been auctioned, the Order would return the rest of the proceeds to the ship's captains for division in accordance with their Ship's Articles.

The official had noted that each ship entered the harbor flying the flags of Spain, an ally of the Knights of Malta in their war against the Mohammedan, and he next confirmed they had the required papers and Letters of Marque to back those flags up. Arabella had her doubts as to whether Captain McNamara had acquired his flags and documents legally, but said nothing of this. When the official came aboard *The Thistle*, First Mate Selkirk escorted him to Arabella. She had prepared herself for the typical male chauvinism and had even prepared a speech threatening that if the officials of Valletta did not want to do business with a female privateer then she would take her goods elsewhere. Mister Bahria indeed expressed great surprise and even some bemusement upon meeting her. However, he carried on about his duties as the professional he was. He did, however, seem uncommonly intrigued by the notion of a female sea captain and privateer no less, and his demeanor changed markedly from the stoic bureaucrat to one of effluent friendliness. Upon completing his inspection, he lingered. He insisted upon providing Arabella with detailed information on where she could purchase the best-priced supplies and materials for her ship, then assured her he would give their captured Arab ships a place of prominence in his harbor for the upcoming auction in order to help them fetch the highest price possible. Arabella warmly thanked him.

The crews spent the next hour or so offloading their cargoes onto the wagons of the Order, grumbling quite a lot and not at all happy to see their booty leaving their possession. The captains assured them they would receive the rest of their shares just as soon as the morrow's auctions had concluded. In the meantime, they were free to leave ship if they wished and could afford to do so and enjoy the island with whatever coin they already possessed. Rumors had already spread amongst the crew and then the townsfolk of the riches contained within the merchant ships. Most of the former galley slaves, having no hard currency in their possession at all, quickly bartered away the expected shares Arabella had promised, and took whatever they could get for them. The captains and quartermasters had, of course, inspected the cargoes days ago and came up with a 'best guess' estimate for the value of their contents. They added to this the expected resale value of the captured ships and then divided the whole by each share owed, minus the percentages to the Crown and the Order. As usual, the ships had not contained sacks of gold and silver coins and chests full of fabulous gems and ambergris, but the typical goods sought and sold in the markets of the Mediterranean. This included butts of wine and barrels of olive oil, craftsmen's tools and weapons, fruits such as dates and raisins, small items of furniture and some lumber and textiles. In addition, several cannon remained that could not be placed on any of their ships and so would be sold. The merchant vessels' greatest treasure, however, were the casks of spices and the bolts of wool and raw silk they carried, each tremendously valuable. Each sailor's share was expected to fetch him in the neighborhood of four pounds English. This would make no one rich, to be sure, but it equaled what many men earned in an entire year of laboring back home. Sadly, the way most sailors spent their money, it might not last many of them the night.

As the crews departed, the captains cautioned them to not run afoul of the island's laws and customs, strictly enforced by the Knights. Arabella made certain her crew knew she intended to continue on to Benghazi the day after tomorrow, and any man not present would be left behind. She spent the remainder of the day seeing to the provisioning of *The Thistle* with victuals and fresh water and other sundry supplies. She oversaw the purchase and delivery of several much-needed spars along with new canvas and rope, authorized Mister Browne to purchase two barrels of gunpowder to replace two others too wet from the storm to be of any use, and generally presided over a host of other small but vital duties necessary to the running of a ship of the sea. One difficulty she encountered was in finding enough beer to replenish the ship's stock, for such was in dreadfully short supply in

Malta. When she did find it, the price was exorbitant. Wine, however, proved to be both cheap and plentiful and of very good quality. The crew, however, might not see things the same way, for the majority of them were English, Irish or Scottish and expected their 'daily allotment' to include beer or ale, not wine. As such, she purchased a small quantity of ale and a good deal of strong wine and decided the crew could discover this once they were well out to sea.

Arabella's tasks carried her all about Valletta. She was impressed with how clean the city was. Beautiful as well, she thought, with its many grand buildings, both secular and religious. She found herself wishing she had more time to spend here, as it clearly offered a great deal to see and explore. Her eyes were drawn to the magnificent St. John's Cathedral, towering over the rest of the buildings, though the nearby Grand Master's Palace also greatly intrigued her. One task she looked forward to was fulfilling her promise to visit Sister Marie Elise and the Knight Pierre-Louis. She quickly found the Saint Mary Magdalene of the Penitents church on lower Merchants Street, the home of the Sisters of the Order of St. Ursula. It was from here they ran their charity, the Magdalene Asylum for the Reception of Reformed Prostitutes. Arabella hesitated and took a self-conscious glance over her shoulder to make certain she was not being watched before she entered.

A small but beautiful chapel opened before her, the bright light of the day shining through the tall, painted-glass windows, bathing the room in a myriad of reds and yellows and blues. Over the altar hung a life-sized carving of Christ crucified. The chapel was empty save for Arabella and an elderly nun kneeling in prayer before the crucifix. At the sound of the door closing, she stood and turned. Her eyes traveled up and down the privateer captain with a knowing and somewhat sad look.

"You have come to the right place, my child," she said. "We can help you."

Arabella did not know whether to be offended or to laugh. After a moment, she realized she was amused and smiled warmly. "Aye, sister, I hope you can help me. I am seeking one of your order by the name of Sister Marie Elise."

"Oh? Yes, she is here, recently returned to us. Who shall I tell her is calling?"

"Captain Arabella Fraser of *The Thistle*."

"You are she?" the sister exclaimed excitedly. "Sister Marie Elise has told all us about you! Oh, forgive my earlier assumption about, er, your purpose for visiting."

"Could I do otherwise under His watchful eyes?" she said, nodding to the crucifix.

The sister smiled and led her from the chapel. They walked down a long hallway lined with doors, going past several before stopping at one as nondescript as the others. The nun knocked.

"Come," Marie Elise called from within. The sister opened the door and announced their visitor. Sister Marie Elise had been writing in a journal at a small desk but jumped to her feet when she heard Arabella's name. "Capitan!" she cried, rushing to embrace her. "I am so glad you have come!"

"And I am glad to see you are well and made it home safely."

"Only thanks to you and of course to Christ our Lord," she said. "How long are you in port? Have you any plans for supper this evening? Oh, you must join us, we would be so honored to have you."

"I would love to sup with you, though I regret in the meantime I cannot linger. I must tend to a host of duties about the city this day, and I only stopped by to say hello and make certain you managed to get back to Malta without me by your side to keep the Turks at bay."

"Of course, of course. We sup when the church bell rings six, and shall not expect you before then. Have you been to see Pierre-Louis yet?"

"Not yet, though I intend to. Do you know the way to the barracks, by chance?"

"Oui. He is in the *Auberge de Provance,* just east of the city gate on Republic Street."

A short time later, Arabella left the little church and walked the short distance to the seven *Auberge* of the Knights Hospitallers. The soldiers stationed on Malta came from all over Europe and were housed in barracks based on their nationality. Arabella stopped by the French barracks and inquired if Pierre-Louis was present. The soldier standing guard at the entrance told her, regrettably, he was not on the island at the moment but was aboard a galley at sea patrolling for Turkish pirates. The sergeant-at-arms assured her he would tell the knight she had called upon him.

Arabella continued seeing to the other tasks requiring her attention. As she did, she noted word of her had quickly spread throughout the city. The novelty of a female privateer captain generated a good deal of attention wherever she went. Arabella graciously refused numerous offers to share a glass of wine or even a meal with scores of gentlemen and even some ladies, each professing fascination with her and longing to hear her story. Shopping became difficult and she quickly concluded her business, retreating to the sanctuary of her ship to await her appointed supper with the sisters. Still, the offers continued to come. She refused each in turn until she received one she could not: an offer to dine at the Palace with the Grand Master himself, tomorrow evening. In truth, the invitation was for all three ship's captains, though Arabella noticed she was the only one addressed by name. She mentioned this to Molly, who immediately became very excited.

"Oh, Ara, can I–"

"Alas, dear Mol, you are not invited."

"But-"

"Nay, 'twould not be proper. A man like the Grand Master stands on ceremony, you can be sure, and as ship's captain I must be careful to not do anything unseemly or seen as insulting of his honor. Not if we mean to ever do business on this island again, or even sail these waters safely."

"Oh, I know," Molly said, giving her friend a smile. "But a girl looks forward to such things, you know, especially when she has been cooped up with a bunch of smelly sailors for weeks on end."

"I am sorry. Though I am guessing if the old goat knew my second mate was a woman, and a handsome one at that, this invitation would have had your name on it as well. I must make a point to mention it to him. Still, I would love to have you accompany me on a bit of shopping tomorrow if I am to look presentable to His Grace."

Arabella's meal with the nuns that evening was simple but very pleasant. She found the wine particularly enjoyable, even if they did limit her to only one small glass. And though the sisters never asked her, she would not leave them without first making a sizable donation to their charity, thus incurring their gratitude even more.

The next morning, she, Liam and Bartholomew attended the auctions that disposed of the captured ships, their cargoes and the prisoners. These affairs proved a great success. The Knights Hospitallers purchased all of the prisoners for their galleys and paid a handsome price for them. Local merchants bought the captured ships, again paying amounts rather higher than their estimated value. Clearly, interest in these ships and these goods, if not the female captain who had captured them, had been above-average. Immediately after this, Arabella and Molly dashed off to the appropriately-named Merchants Street. First stop was a bathhouse, for Arabella's last soaking had been in the cold, salty Mediterranean some days ago. Molly indulged herself as well, joining in a lengthy soak in a hot, heavily-perfumed bath, during which women washed their hair, braiding Arabella's and tying it with gaily-colored silk gallants.

After this, the two women went dress shopping, for the pirates had stolen all of Arabella's dresses along with the wedding presents when they had first seized *The Thistle*. Regrettably, these treasures had not been kept aboard the ship but had been sent across to the *Gunsway* for sale in some other port. There were numerous garment shops in Valletta, all with the latest fashions popular in Europe and at a wide range of prices. Arabella settled on a beautiful red dress in the Venetian style, with slashed and puffed *bollonais* sleeves, a silk neckerchief to cover her shoulders and designed to leave just a hint of cleavage visible. As was the current fashion, she also purchased a laced stomacher and a cartridge-pleated farthingale. She bought a new chemise of cotton lawn with frilled lace cuffs to wear below her finery, and a pair of Florentine *pianelles* for her feet. She was just contemplating whether to spend any more coin on a little bottle of terribly expensive French perfume when Molly bought it for her.

"Bloody pirates stole my other wedding present for you," she said with a smile.

The girls finished their shopping and Arabella stowed her purchases safely aboard ship before rushing to join her fellow captains at the *Banca di Ordine Religioso*. There, the monies collected from the day's auctions would be distributed.

By the time she arrived, the Order had already taken their cut and Captain Roderick was collecting the Spanish Crown's ten percent, as their Letters of Marque called for. Captain McNamara protested that this was totally unnecessary as 'the Crown' would never know they had captured any prizes unless 'someone' told them, and that someone would certainly not be him.

"They will know," Bartholomew said with resigned certainty, ending the discussion.

After this, the captains divided the remaining shares between themselves for issue to their crews. They used one of the many rooms in the heavily fortified bank set up for just this purpose. A long table lay athwart the room and the captains sat behind this, accompanied by their pursers and quartermasters, with a heavy strongbox before them. When ready, the captains ordered the thick iron doors to the room opened. The sailors, some having lined up hours earlier, filed in. Many literally salivated when handed their gold and silver and then nearly trampled their mates rushing from the building to spend it. Others, of course, had creditors waiting for them just outside and were lucky if they had a shilling to their name five minutes later. Arabella felt it did not help matters any that Captain McNamara advised each of his crewmen to "spend it quickly or not at all!" The distribution of shares took the remainder of the afternoon, and Arabella issued the last of hers by lantern light just after dusk. She and her fellow captains began collecting their effects to leave when a courier arrived carrying a very large box. He looked around, saw Captain Roderick and approached.

"Your purchase, sir," he said, setting the box on the table and pulling out a little leather-bound book with quill. Captain Roderick looked into the box, smiled and paid the boy a handful of coins to settle. The youth made a mark in his book, thanked the captain, bowed and departed.

Captain McNamara glanced into the box as well. "Oh, here we go again."

"And what is that you have there in that package, Mister Roderick?" Arabella asked, craning her neck to see. By way of answering, he removed what was without doubt the largest and finest *capitain* hat Arabella had ever seen. Its construction was of the finest velvets, and what must have been yards of piping and lace and frill draped it. Little gems covered it from brim to brim, catching and refracting the lantern light, and a ridiculously large ostrich feather dyed the most shocking shade of turquoise sat atop. Captain Bartholomew proudly placed it on his head and posed for his fellow captains. Liam rudely burst into laughter and Arabella had to fight to not do the same.

"Quite handsome," she finally managed. "I assure you I have never seen its equal."

Still laughing, Liam packed his ship's logbooks and strongbox and stood to leave. "Fair lady, I regret I must bid you a warm adieu," he said with a bow to her. "Barty," he added with a curt nod, skipping the bow.

"Wait! Where are you off to?" Arabella asked. "Will you not be supping with us at the Palace tonight?"

"I must beg your forgiveness but I cannot. Pressing business and all. Please do give my regrets to the head popinjay."

"But why?" Arabella asked, clearly disappointed. "'Tis a great honor to dine with the Grand Master, and sure'n a bit of an insult to refuse such."

"As I said, I have pressing business in other parts to which I absolutely must attend. I need to return to my ship and ensure she is ready to sail as soon as possible."

"But surely you will not depart before the morning tide? Why, your crew is still enjoying their leave," Arabella asked.

"If the man has business more important than the Grand Master of the Knights of St. John, not to mention spending time in your fair company, then my dear, let us not delay him," Bartholomew said.

"But we have not even had a chance to discuss whether you wish to sail in consort with *The Thistle* and *Greyhound*, adding your ship's strength to ours and ours to yours," Arabella said.

"And the better off we are for it," Bartholomew sniped.

"I am truly sorry, Arabella. I mean to sail with the mid-watch tide and my crew knows it. They are to have returned by then or be left behind. I have urgent business-"

"He means 'debts,'" Bartholomew interjected.

"—which I must settle that simply cannot wait," the Irishman finished.

"Counted on a greater share of that convoy's wealth, did you?" Bartholomew asked with a grin. "Left yourself no margin for delays and the added interest they bring, I take it?"

"Besides," Liam continued, ignoring the man. "Although I am certain the Grand Master puts out a handsome board, and the Saints know I love a good meal as much as the next man, I look upon an invite to sup with the head of that order of holier-than-thou knights in his fortress about the same as I would receive an offer to dine with the queen in the Tower of London. No thank you."

"Well then, another time perhaps," Arabella said.

"I shall look forward to it," he told her with a wink. Bartholomew groaned and rolled his eyes. Liam turned to go and then stopped. "Please have a care with the Grand Master, Ara. I have a suspicion a man such as he does not take kindly to other pirates growing too successful in his seas. Competition and all."

"Yes, yes," Bartholomew said. "Good thing Arabella and I are not *pirates*, but licensed privateers, carrying *authentic* Letters of Marque under the authority of the King of Spain. I would advise you to heed your own advice however, as the only pirate in this room. Though I doubt you should ever have to worry about becoming successful enough to raise anyone's envy."

Liam opened his mouth to say something profane but then remembered Arabella. Instead, he bowed again to her and left.

"I wish you would be a bit more civil to him," she said as they finished gathering the last of their things.

"I was civil," Bartholomew replied, flexing the fingers of his bruised right hand. "I didn't kill him."

"Should I even ask why the two of you despise one another so much, or shall I simply assume it had something to do with a woman?"

"Sadly, it was not so romantic as all that. If you must know - and I see that you do or I will never hear the end of it - Captain McNamara and I were once partners, sailing together in consort on various adventures of a quasi-legal nature. I even considered him my friend once, naïve and foolish as I was. He corrected me in that misassumption off the coast of Spain two years ago when the *brave* captain abandoned me to face alone three heavily-armed Spanish galleons while he slipped away with the prize we had just captured. Truly, I expected him to do the same with us the other day."

"He may be a bit of a scoundrel, but he hardly seems a coward," Arabella said.

"Call him an opportunist then. He had the opportunity to escape with the gold, and I had the opportunity to enjoy the hospitality of the Spanish inquisitors for two years."

"I am so sorry. And yet now you serve the Spanish as a privateer," Arabella said.

"I make no apologies for that. Truth is, they offered me the choice to repay my debt to them by sailing under their Letter of Marque or face the gallows. I chose the former. Would you have done any differently?"

Arabella had no answer for him as the two left the small, fortress-like building. They walked in silence back to the docks where, before boarding her ship, she gazed long at *The Raven*, its less-then-full crew scrambling to ready her for sail. Once on her own ship, she changed into her new dress, topping it with the regal hat Captain Roderick had bought her in Cartagena. She did not forget though Liam's warning, and tied a long dirk to her thigh and a *sgian dubh* to her left arm under her sleeve. By the time she exited her cabin, Captain Roderick and a carriage sent by the Grand Master awaited her on the docks.

The Magisterial Palace in Valletta's central square was easily the equal to any castle in Europe in both size and imposing magnificence. Two Knights Hospitallers in their finest ceremonial garb greeted the captains and escorted them into the building. Arabella had not expected such ceremony and felt rather uneasy for it. Bartholomew, on the other hand, looked as if he felt nothing less was his due. The interior of the Palace was even grander than its exterior. Works of art by the finest artists, sculptors and craftsmen in Europe and the Orient lined the walls and filled every niche. Furniture of extraordinary craftsmanship filled the halls and rooms, and beautiful tapestries hung throughout. And everywhere, enormous paintings of the former Grand Masters looked down upon the visitors with their imposing gazes. The main hall had been decorated with frescoes depicting the Great Siege, while other rooms contained friezes of other episodes from the Order's history, including several of its beginning when Pope Paschall II officially recognized the Blessed Gerard as guardian of the Hospice of St. John in

Jerusalem in A.D. 1113. Arabella also noticed the pagan sea god Neptune in numerous paintings and sculptures, which struck her as oddly out of place in a palace so closely tied to a holy order of Christian knights. Apparently, even they were not immune from the superstitions of all who sailed upon and were at the mercy of the sea.

The Grand Master, Hugues Loubenx de Verdalle, met Arabella and Bartholomew in an opulent dining room of immense size, the hall dominated by a table that could easily seat fifty. Tonight, it had been set for only four. The man rose and crossed the room to greet them and Arabella found that again she was surprised, this time by the man's appearance. She had been expecting a tall, powerfully-built knight with broad shoulders and handsome features, something like an older Pierre-Louis. The Grand Master was tall, to be certain, but quite thin and severe, with a pinched face that no one could call handsome. He was clearly bald or balding under his cap, and his neatly-trimmed, pointed goatee showed more gray than black, certainly not unusual for a man in his fifties but again, not what she had imagined. In contrast to his almost completely ordinary physical appearance, however, his eyes blazed black from under his brow with an intensity that immediately made her feel uncomfortable, as if he could peer deeply into her soul and knew at once her every sin and moral failing. Monsieur de Verdalle carried himself with the air of a man who was unmistakably the ruler of his personal corner of the world. His cold expression warmed immediately though as his guests entered the room, and he smiled as he extended his hand to greet them.

"Welcome, honored guests," he announced in a deep and pleasant voice. He spoke his native French and clearly expected his guests to do the same.

Arabella and Bartholomew swept their hats from their heads. Unsure of the proper etiquette for greeting someone of his status, Arabella hesitated then awkwardly tried to shake his hand and curtsy at the same time.

"Arabella Fraser of the Clan Fraser," she said. "Captain of the Scottish privateer ship *The Thistle.*"

Bartholomew bowed deeply and splendidly. "Captain Bartholomew Roderick, Master of the *Greyhound* and kin to the Knights Vaughan of Tretower Court, County Powys, Wales."

The Grand Master smiled and inclined his head just so while raising his eyebrows as if impressed. Arabella had the unmistakable impression though that he placed the 'Knights Vaughan' and other such Welsh gentry on an equal footing, aristocratically speaking, with the men who cleaned his stables.

"Just the two of you?" he asked, looking about. "Will not Captain Smithe be joining us?"

"Captain Smithe?" Arabella asked.

"The third captain in your party. I do hope I am pronouncing his name correctly. Sometimes it can be so difficult to tell by what is listed in the logbooks."

"Oh, Captain *Smithe*!" Arabella said, pronouncing the 'i' long. "Yes, he sends his deepest regrets and most humble apologies. Urgent business has called him away this very eve." Bartholomew said nothing, though Arabella knew without seeing that he rolled his eyes.

"How unfortunate. Though not without a silver lining, for I may now devote more of myself to each of you," the Grand Master said, though he gazed only at Arabella as he said it. "Milady, may I compliment you on your beauty and your stunning dress."

"Gramercy, milord," she answered with another small curtsy.

It was not lost on her that the man said nothing about Captain Roderick's outfit, despite the fact that he had likely spent twice on his garb as she on hers. Still, she felt like a common peasant wearing naught but rags next to the Grand Master. The yards of gold lace in his doublet alone likely cost more than the entire value of *The Thistle*. A stunning garment and perfectly tailored, it was of the finest black velvet, lined with gold silk showing and pulled through *pinkes* and *cuttes* throughout. His trussed doublet sleeves were of the same gold-colored silk, while a crimson shirt of *brocatelle* provided a splash of color beneath. He wore Venetian slops, also of velvet, tied at the knee with garter ribbons, silk stockings under these and boothose over the stockings. He wore tall-heeled shoes in the latest Spanish fashion, though he stayed true to his French roots with a Flemish pill hat atop his head. A white, starched ruff circled his neck and a long, sable-lined cape finished his outfit.

"Please be seated," he said, directing Arabella to the seat on his right before turning and taking his own chair at the head of the table.

Squires dressed in the finest livery stood at the ready to attend them. They immediately filled the chalices with a strong red wine from the Master's own vineyards. Arabella was not surprised to find it an excellent vintage. Other servants brought the first courses without delay, fresh greens and a variety of local vegetables.

"So how do you find Malta, mademoiselle?" Grand Master de Verdalle asked. "I fear those not accustomed to our climate sometimes find it uncomfortably warm this time of year."

"It is a most fair climate you have, sir," Bartholomew piped in.

"Sure'n at times it is warmer than my native Scotland," Arabella answered. "But this makes the seas all the warmer and more pleasant. And in faith, Valletta is a beautiful city, one of the finest I have ever visited, and her people are most friendly."

"Excellent. I would feel personally wounded if you left here with any ill feelings for my island or her people. On that, are you planning to stay long? We have many things to offer the discriminating visitor, including some of the finest shopping anywhere in Europe, as I see you have already discovered."

"I am sorry, sir, but our stay this time must be a short one. We too have rather urgent business to attend to and I mean to sail with the morning tide."

"Yes, our apologies, your lordship," Captain Roderick said. "Though we do hope to return at some point in the near future."

"Leaving so soon? You sea rovers, always dashing off to distant shores. It cannot be postponed, even for a little while?"

"I am afraid not, sir," Arabella answered. "Though, as Captain Roderick says, we certainly hope to return to Malta in the near future if possible."

"You must consider yourself always welcome, my dear," he told her.

Before long, the servants brought the next course, this consisting of large silver trays bearing different pastas. The Master explained the regional varieties to Arabella, pointing out dishes such as *ravjul* and something called *mqarran il-Forn*, which reminded her of a shepherd's pie but filled with pasta and topped with melted cheese. The wine with this course changed to a fortified red Malmsey from Sardinia, heavy and sweet but no less excellent than the first.

"*Captain* Arabella," the Grand Master intoned, savoring the words. "Pardon, mademoiselle, but I am having such a time with the concept of a girl captaining a ship of bloodthirsty privateers on the high seas. And against an enemy who will not even allow their own women to walk side-by-side with their husbands or leave the house without a veil. Why, the very thought of you, so free, so independent, so *dominant*, must arouse in our heathen foe the greatest distress."

"Surely, Your Lordship, I cannot say what they think of me. And to be honest, I care not about their feelings on the matter."

"Splendid," the man said, both amused and impressed. "But tell me: what circumstances did compel you into such a bold and daring role?"

"Desperation, Your Grace. I saw no other way to save the lives of those I cared for from the corsairs' slave markets."

"I take it your loved ones were brought to these waters against their will?"

"As was I."

"And what a price I am certain you would have fetched," he murmured, eyeing her in a way that was not at all becoming of a man who had given himself to God.

"Your lordship is too kind," she told him.

"But I am unclear of something; if, as I am to understand, you were able to free yourself from bondage and take control of your prison ship, how is it that you yet sail the Mediterranean under a Letter of Marque? Perhaps you acquired a taste for adventure and do not yet wish to stop?"

"I remain in these waters only because there was another ship in consort with the one upon which I was held hostage. It is that ship and her hostages I seek still."

"But of course. But come, captain, let us be frank. As a man who has taken part in many campaigns against the infidel, I know the rush, the thrill one feels when they face another warrior in a life and death clash of arms. I know the joy - yes, I can call it joy - one feels when they emerge victorious and can look down upon the destroyed body of their foe. As a humble man of faith, I do so cherish my service to God each time I send one of Satan's Mohammedan minions back to him.

Tell me, dear child, do you feel nothing when you do the same? Is there not some part of you that enjoys the battles, the victories, the blood?"

"Milord," Arabella said, blushing slightly. "Should we really be talking about such things at table?"

"My apologies," he told her, though not before seeing with satisfaction a look in her eyes that told him she did enjoy her victories, at least a little. "Of course, it cannot be denied that, just as I have been very successful in serving God in my way, you also have had your share of victories over the Turks, or so the Banca tells me."

"The Good Lord has looked upon both of us with mercy and generosity," Arabella answered.

"She is modest," Bartholomew said. "In battle, she is a lion."

"As in other activities, I am sure," the Grand Master said in a tone that made Arabella's cheeks flush again. "Perhaps the lady would consider serving under me?"

"I beg your pardon?" she asked.

"I mean, of course, to sail under a Maltese Letter of Marque instead of a Spanish one. I am certain you would find it more rewarding than your current charter."

"Oh, I see. I am flattered you think so highly of my abilities, sir. Truly, I would be a poor captain for you, as the only treasure I seek is the repatriation of my loved ones. I have no desire to amass the gold that a great order such as yours requires to fund its noble mission."

"I am sorry to hear it. Nonetheless, my offer stands. Please do consider it," de Verdalle urged.

"I will, milord."

They continued to converse as the courses arrived one after the other. A fruit tray came and went, followed by a fabulous fish soup the locals called *aljotta*, rich with garlic and onions. After this came the main course: rabbit, beef, fish, even *laham taz-ziemel*, made with stallion meat. Wonderful and rich cheeses and desserts followed, with names Arabella would never remember. And with each course came another wine: Rhenish, claret, Canary and finally, sack

By the end of the meal, Arabella and Bartholomew and even the Grand Master were quite full and more than a little tipsy. The sea captains had some difficulty standing to take their leave. Arabella hoped the carriage would again be made available to them for the trip back to the docks. De Verdalle took her hand, bent low and lingered over a long kiss as he bade her farewell. He insisted she visit him again when next she found herself in Valletta. She said she would, failing to notice as the Master gave no more than a curt nod to Captain Roderick, ignoring the man's outstretched hand before turning on his heel and retreating back into the Palace.

Arabella spent the morning readying her ship to sail. Each time her duties carried her up on deck, she found herself casting long glances to where *The Raven* had berthed the night before. She then invariably turned to the horizon to search for any sign of her sails. There was none, for Captain McNamara had slipped the harbor more than twelve hours earlier. Only half of Arabella's crew had returned to the ship by the first tide. Captain Roderick faced the same problem, and both decided to wait for the rest of the men before sailing, despite having threatened otherwise. Arabella finally had to send Molly and Fergus into town to round them up. All but two of the absent crewmen arrived by noon, four of these so drunk their mates had to carry them aboard. The final two were brought straight from the local gaol by the Knights themselves and released into Arabella's custody, on the condition they not set foot on Maltese soil for the remainder of *The Thistle's* stay in port. This promise was easily kept, as the two ships sailed immediately. Mister de Rivero estimated the journey to Benghazi should take some four days, assuming the tides, the winds and the weather cooperated. Since they were traveling to a Muslim city, Arabella and Bartholomew agreed once again to avoid any naval actions with the Sultan's corsairs if at all possible, lest they show up in port with a hold full of Arab prisoners and goods bearing the Sultan's mark.

Two days into their journey, the winds changed course, now blowing away from Africa. This slowed them somewhat and required a good deal of tacking and wearing to make progress. Their journey of four days stretched into seven before they finally spotted the wide Benghazi harbor and the city beyond, shimmering in the sun-drenched Saharan desert. Two long piers stretched far out into the water on either side of a wide dock harboring a handful of small and large ships and scores of fishing boats. A large fort sat on a gentle bluff overlooking the bay, and several war galleys guarded the harbor. As the two privateer ships approached, one of these unmoored and moved to intercept them. Arabella and Captain Roderick ordered their ships to douse sails and come to a complete stop, wanting to give no appearance of hostility. Their merchant flags streamed in plain sight atop their flagstaffs.

The Arab warship came alongside them, her deck filled with armed men, her great guns ready for action. The Arab captain was friendly though, coming aboard with a half-dozen Janissaries to inspect their papers and holds. Arabella reluctantly assumed the role of ship's cook, letting Duff stand in as captain. Not only was this done to avoid running afoul of the more conservatively-patriarchal customs and laws this deep in the Empire, but Arabella was beginning to grow concerned that word of her, or at least the 'Lioness of the Levant,' might be spreading. The galley captain granted the ships portage rights, again under their guise of ransoming Christian slaves and purchasing other goods as necessary or profitable for resale in Europe. Once they had docked, *The Thistle* officers walked amongst the local fisherman and *suqs*, spreading coins and asking their usual questions. They learned the *Sea Rover* had not yet reached this port, which Arabella found most disturbing.

"But we know they left Algiers some days before us bound for these parts," she told Molly and Captain Roderick later in her day room. "And we were delayed. Where could they be?"

"There are a host of towns along these shores," Bartholomew said. "They could have stopped at any one."

"Aye, but they were to stop nowhere else so far as we know. Heaven forbid something happened to them," Arabella said.

"Perhaps they suffered some damage in the storm," Molly said. "Remember, a few days before we reached Valletta? They may have been damaged and forced to head for the nearest seaport to make repairs."

"Or that same storm could have sunk them," Roderick said.

Arabella gave him a dirty look. "Or maybe not. It could be anything that has delayed them. Maybe they were captured by pirates. These seas are full of them, I hear."

"You are not helping, Mister Roderick," Arabella told him.

"Just trying to state all the possibilities," he answered with a grin.

"Since we cannot know their fate, let us pray they were but delayed briefly and are otherwise well. As for now, there is little we can do but wait here for them," Arabella announced.

The ship captains gave their crews limited leave, allowing them to depart the ship only in small groups and restricting them to the Christian *bagnios* and pubs found there. For her part, Arabella kept mostly to the ship, keeping watch on the horizon and closely studying each arriving vessel as well as their crew and any prisoners aboard. The rest of her time was spent trying to keep her crew busy with the numerous things that always needed tending, such as small repairs or those large ones not capable of being performed while at sea. In addition, stores long in the holds were brought out and inspected in the light of day, often for the first time since being stowed, including some spare timbers and spars and their enormous rolls of sailcloth. Mister Browne brought a good deal of his damp powder up and took almost the entire foredeck on which to dry it, with an admonition from the captain he not blow the front half of the ship off. His retort of "I shall try not to," was not very reassuring.

On the third day after their arrival, Arabella heard a commotion on the docks some distance away. A small group of Arab sailors chattered noisily with a harbor official while pointing at her ship. These men had arrived in the port not an hour ago; she had watched them come in. The harbor man calmed the fellows down and walked them toward his small office at the far end of the docks, taking them slowly past the privateer ships. One of the sailors turned and stared hard at *The Thistle* as he passed. His eyes met Arabella's and a shock of recognition went through her, a look mirrored on his face. It was Jamal al Din!

19

Jamal quickly turned away, whispering excitedly to the harbormaster and the other men with him. All of them turned and looked toward Arabella, but she had already leapt from the quarterdeck to the main deck and out of view. The sailors continued on their way.

"Mister Selkirk! Have we any men ashore?" Arabella called.

"Aye, cap'n; ten hands."

"Send a runner at once to find them and tell them to return to the ship immediately unless they wish to remain in Benghazi."

Duff looked at her for a moment and then grabbed the nearest deckhand, sending him on the mission. "Captain?"

"Ready the ship; we are leaving immediately. And have Mister

Browne charge the guns." With the deck of the pier above *The Thistle's*

gun deck, most of the big guns would be worthless against anyone

approaching on foot, though they would still serve if a vessel

approached them.

"Aye, aye, cap'n," he cried, rushing off to rouse the crew to her

orders.

"Captain Roderick!" she called to *The Greyhound*. A moment later

the captain stepped from his cabin, barefoot and with a mug of short

beer in his hand. "We have been smoked! Have you all your crew

aboard?"

"I do. You say we have been discovered?"

"Aye. We need to flee at once."

"What of your men? Are they all accounted for?"

"Nay, I have ten ashore and have dispatched another to fetch them.

It shall take us some minutes before we can be underway; I pray they

return before then."

"I shall wait for you," he called.

"Please do not; I would not have it on my conscience if things go

badly. Get your erse to sea as quickly as you can. We will be right

behind, I promise."

"Then God speed to you, Ara, and I will see you soon!" He dashed off to ready his ship.

"What is it, Ara?" Molly asked, rushing up on deck.

"We have been smoked. Damned if one of the bloody Turk officers we off-loaded in Cartagena did not just arrive in Benghazi and recognize me and the ship."

"No! Are you certain?"

"Aye. We must to sea, and quickly. Even still, we may yet have to fight our way out of this harbor. Run down below and open the weapons locker, if you would, and arm the hands."

"Aye, cap'n."

Minutes later, the crew had been assembled on deck and put to their tasks. Because of the wind and the tides upon their arrival, *The Thistle* had moored with her bow toward the shore and with the pier on her starboard. They needed to turn about before they could even begin their escape. Unfortunately, the breeze blew onshore today as well, though at an angle. As such, it would take some time to not only come about, but to take *The Thistle* from a dead rest to full sail, with scores of small and large tasks needed to make this happen. Below decks, Arabella heard John Browne barking orders to his gun crews amidst cursing and the occasional thump of a dropped cannonball. He left the gunports closed though on Arabella's orders; no sense tipping their hand just yet. Arabella jumped in and helped ready the ship while keeping a weather eye on the docks. As of yet, she saw no sign of any Janissaries charging to meet them, but also saw no sign of her missing crewmen.

"The wind is against us but the tide is fair," First Mate Selkirk called to the crew alow and aloft. "We must come about and put our head as close-hauled as we can without putting the ship in irons!" The crew jumped to. After a lot of heavy work and a good deal more cursing, all was in readiness to make the dangerous maneuver. "Now back and fill, mates!" Duff cried. "Bear away to larboard! Play the spritsail and mizzen course sheets and reach for the wind!" After a long, agonizing minute, the ship's bow began to slowly swing away from the pier while her stern pivoted in place. Several more minutes later, the ship had nearly completed her arc but now faced the most difficult part of the maneuver. "Now ease and reef!" he yelled. "Ease and reef!"

The crew cut loose the jib and bent a score of oars and gaffs against the docks, arresting the swing of the ship before it smashed against the piers. After a tense moment, the ship now sat facing the open seas with her port side abreast the pier. The *Greyhound* had already warped and was even now moving toward deep water. Seeing that Mister Selkirk had things well in hand on deck, Arabella went to her cabin to check the readiness of her stern chasers, fearing she may yet need them this day.

Just then, a large group of Janissaries, perhaps fifty in all, rushed from behind the harbormaster's building. Each soldier carried a *jezail* musket and several other weapons on his belt, including a pistol and scimitar. Arabella heard another clatter of footfalls on the far side of the dock and saw scores more sailors and their officers charging toward one of the large war galleys tied there. *The Thistle* still sat at the pier, the top hands desperately trying to adjust the sails to catch enough wind to get them moving. Duff realized they would not make it in time, and readied the crew for battle.

Arabella took a step toward the cabin door to join them but stopped. With the ship's stern now facing the shore, her chasers pointed directly at the docks - and the approaching men. Everything she needed lay in a footlocker next to the guns. The question was, could she ready one in time? She leapt to the nearest gun, Lord Campbell's bronze 'Quacker.' She released the breeching lanyards securing it to the wale and threw her shoulder against the carriage. She placed a foot against the cabin wall and heaved the heavy gun back. She grabbed a charge and used the ramrod to force it down the barrel, then packed it tight with a wad. Three iron balls sat in the locker, two solid and one filled with powder and shot. She grabbed the latter and rammed this down the barrel. A glance through the stern windows showed the corsair guards no more than fifty yards away and rapidly closing. Above her, shots rang out from the tops, answered in kind by a withering volley from the Janissaries. Arabella shoved a spike down the gun's touch-hole and pierced the charge. She poured some priming powder into the hole, jumped to open the porthole window and then hauled on the carriage lanyards, slamming the gun forward and into firing position.

On the pier, the Janissaries fired another volley then dove behind wooden crates and sacks of wheat stacked there. The *Thistle* crewmen took the opportunity to reload as well, ducking below the gunwales and grabbing their own powder horns. The Turks were the faster though and fired another round, then resumed their charge, their shots keeping the privateers' heads down.

Arabella grabbed the unlit slow match and realized only then her cabin had neither a portfire nor a lit lantern right now. She let fly a curse that would have made her father blush, and grabbed flint and tinder from the shelf. A second later, a spark leapt to life. The Arabs had nearly reached the ship, carefully peppering the crew with coordinated fire to keep them pinned down. The Janissaries paid particular attention to the hands trying to man the ship's swivel guns, which Arabella had heard fire but once. Above her, the stern gun sat loaded but unmanned, its crew hunkered down under cover and unable to reach it. Arabella shoved her shoulder hard against the gun's carriage and rammed a wedge under the barrel to adjust its elevation. She brought the slow match to the touch hole. The gun roared and the section of pier directly under the Janissaries' feet exploded into jagged, flaming wood. The blast hurled a dozen men high into the air before dropping them into the sea. Wounded men writhed on the shattered pier while those in the water sank below the waves, never to surface again. The remaining soldiers staggered back to their feet and regrouped, bravely charging the ship once more. Arabella knew they would reach it before she could hope to get another round off. She raced from her cabin and joined her crew on deck.

As soon as the Arabs had gone down, Duff and Molly had rallied the Thistles, who leapt back up and fired volley after volley into their foe. The peterero roared again, belching clouds of sangrenel that ripped through the barrels and boxes the Muslims ducked behind, leaving many of them crouched in bloody death. Still, more than two-dozen Janissary continued their charge, hollering and hallooing like savages as they came. They fired their last volley and discarded the weapons, drawing now their long, curved swords and daggers. Across the bay, the large war galley began to move slowly from its moorings, the oars beating the water. On deck, her crew readied a dozen large and small cannon. Several loud splashes from the far side of the pier drew Arabella's attention. She turned and saw her missing crewmen rowing a stolen fishing boat toward *The Thistle*. She leapt down to the midship deck and tossed a rope ladder over the side.

"Any time now, Mister de Rivero!" she yelled to her pilot, who had taken over commanding the tops while Mister Selkirk led the ship's defenders. "I want this ship moving if you have to man a rowboat and tow us!"

"It was next on my list if this last course adjustment does not work, captain!" he answered. "Tops! Close reach, port tack!"

A moment later, the ship began to move slowly away from the pier. Still, their flight was not fast enough to prevent the swiftest of the Janissaries from leaping onto their deck. The Thistles met them just as Arabella dragged the last of her shipmates over the larboard wales. The Janissaries fought with seasoned skill and near-fanatical fury, almost overwhelming the pirates despite being outnumbered four to one. The crewmen just brought aboard grabbed weapons and followed their captain into the fray. Arabella rallied her crew and coordinated their attack, quickly turning the tide against their foe. Moments later, the Arabs lay dead on the deck or had been forced into the sea. The victory had not been without cost, however, as their attack had taken the lives of six Thistles and wounded another eight. This fight had no sooner ended when the next began, as the corsair galley opened fire. Grape, bar and chain tore across *The Thistle's* deck and through her rigging. The broadside had been aimed high, the intent being to disable the ship, not destroy her crew. Still, two more men joined their mates in cold death, while shattered spars and torn sheets crashed to the planks.

"Mister Browne!" Arabella called through the main hatch. "We are not concerned with capturing that ship; I want her sunk!"

"Aye, aye, captain!" he answered.

The larboard guns erupted, hurling their stones with thunderous force. Two of the rounds struck home, though neither below the waterline. Just then, another set of sails appeared beyond the galley as the *Greyhound* joined the fight. A moment later, more explosions erupted aboard the warship as Captain Roderick's first volley struck home. John Browne and his gunners quickly reloaded and fired another broadside, pounding three more holes into the galley's sheer strakes above and below her waterline. The Arabs returned fire, again savaging *The Thistle's* rigging and the men within it. The *Greyhound* quickly came about to run parallel with the galley on her larboard side, with *The Thistle* on her starboard. The three ships ran north-by-northeast and continued to bang away at each other as the gap between them narrowed. Mister De Rivero tried to tack *The Thistle* away from the warship but could not outrun their rowers. The two privateer ships fired round after round into the massive galley's hull, with several more striking below her waterline. Seawater flooded into her, but still she came on, driven forward by scores of slaves who worked her oars to the tune of the bosuns' whips.

On the deck of *The Thistle*, the crews loaded and fired their peterero as rapidly as they could, sweeping the galley's deck with grape and sangrenel to horrible effect. Below them, John Browne screamed and cursed and egged on his men to work faster. The galley lurched to within ten yards of them and a dozen Muslims hurled grappling hooks. Ten of these struck home and scores of hands hauled on them, dragging the two ships together. Hundreds of corsairs swarmed about the galley's deck, preparing to board her. As the ships' hulls smashed together, both gun crews fired a volley point-blank into the other. *The Thistle's* guns sent their rounds blasting through the galley's lower hull, while several yards of *The Thistle's* planking disintegrated, opening a gaping wound in her gun deck, destroying two cannon and killing five men. The

Ottoman warship, already flooding, instantly shuddered and listed hard to starboard, her deck canting toward the sea. The corsairs fought for footing, with some sliding into the ocean and others leaping aboard Arabella's ship. The galley slaves, chained to their oars, screamed in terror and prayed for salvation. The Thistles hacked away at the grappling lines to separate their ship from the sinking hulk. Arabella glanced at the galley, her eyes meeting those of one of the oarsmen. Horror and revulsion filled her, knowing she had just condemned him and his mates to death. She saw then *The Greyhound* coming up hard and fast on the galley's far side, her captain standing on deck and directing their attack.

"Bartholomew!" she yelled at the top of her lungs, catching his eye. "The slaves! Help them!" He nodded his head and Arabella turned back to the action aboard her own ship. Scores of agile Arab warriors had leapt aboard or swung over from their ship's rigging to drop onto the deck. *The Thistle's* peterero burped a final volley of death into them before the gunners drew their swords. Arabella severed the last of the lines connecting the two ships and *The Thistle* began to drift away. The remaining corsairs on the galley jumped into the sea, some swimming toward them and others swimming for the shore.

Captain Roderick ordered his pilot to bring them directly alongside the galley and was the first to leap aboard her. His boarding party raced up and down the rowers' benches, hacking and smashing at the slaves' chains as the brackish water sloshed about their legs. Some of those still confined panicked and attacked their would-be rescuers, and Captain Roderick's men were forced to club them into unconsciousness before they could save them. Each man freed though, if he had control of his wits, joined in the effort to save his brothers.

At least three score Turks had made it aboard *The Thistle*. Arabella led her crew and met their charge head on. The battle raged across the main deck amid the smoke of muskets and pistols fired once and then tossed aside in favor of swords, axes, belaying pins, gaffs and daggers. The battle surged and ebbed and many on both sides dropped screaming to the wooden planks. The privateers' numbers quickly shrank, though for every corsair who fell another took his place as more crawled out of the sea and up the ship's ratlines to join their comrades.

Aboard the galley, the Greyhounds scurried on all fours to free the last of the prisoners, the deck pitching so steeply they could no longer stand. At the last, Captain Roderick ordered all hands into the water. Most of those who could swim made for the ratlines and rope ladders dangling from *The Greyhound*, while oar boats darted in to pluck out those who could not. A moment later, the galley rolled over and slipped beneath the waves.

"Stand firm, Thistles!" Arabella yelled. "The Greyhounds will join us in but a moment!"

Indeed, some were already doing so. A few of Captain Roderick's men and dozens of the newly-freed oarsmen had ignored the *Greyhound* and swam straight for *The Thistle*. The rowers had seen their oppressors board that ship and intended to exact upon them what revenge they could. A few corsairs remained in the water, swimming for the ratlines. Dozens of rowers leapt on top of them and shoved them below the waves, holding them there until they drowned. The Muslims on deck realized what was afoot and redoubled their efforts, knowing they had to seize the ship quickly or else all was lost. Arabella knew this as well and now switched tactics, directing her crew into a slow, defensive retreat. As the galley slaves clambered onto the ship, they took up weapons from the dead or grabbed fishing nets, block and tackle or any heavy object they could lay their hands on and charged toward their hated foe. The course of battle swung once more in the favor of the privateers. Arabella halted her retreat and ordered another advance. Her men and the freed slaves swept the Turks from the deck in minutes, with the remaining few throwing down their weapons and beseeching Arabella to protect them. She could not refuse.

"Avast, free men! Victory is ours!" she yelled, stepping between the oarsmen and her Muslim prisoners. The former galley slaves stopped their attack but looked none too pleased about it. Arabella ordered the prisoners locked below - for their own safety.

Thunder rent the air and geysers of water shot skyward near the privateer ships as the Turkish fort on the hill, which had hitherto held its fire, let loose. The fort's massive guns went quiet for but a moment as the gunners reloaded and adjusted their aim. *The Thistle* and *Greyhound* turned to the open sea once more and sheeted their sails for maximum speed. Another volley narrowly missed the ships, racing desperately to move beyond range. On shore, two more war galleys filled with rowers and corsairs and prepared to slip their moorings and give chase. By the time the fort managed another salvo, the privateer vessels had moved just beyond her reach. The fort stopped firing but the war galleys now moved into the bay, speeding toward the privateers with a vengeance. The warships gained quickly, their rowers driving them faster than *The Thistle* and *Greyhound* could sail in the light winds of the bay. The privateers had a sizable lead, however, and as they moved around the headlands of the bay, their sails filled once more, pushing them faster yet. Even still, the galleys slowly closed the distance.

The chase continued for hours, with the galleys gaining foot by foot as they chewed up the miles. Meanwhile, the privateer crews used the time to make much-needed repairs to their rigging and sails, slowly increased their own speed even as the galley slaves tired. As the sun sank low in the western sky, the rowers approached the limits of human endurance. The Arab captains realized they would not catch the European ships this time and gave up the chase, turning for home. As they did so, they fired a final broadside toward the ships in desperation and defiance, the shots plunging harmlessly into the sea.

In the light of the following morn, the captains brought their ships alongside each other and reduced sail. Certain repairs still needed to be made and could only be done while the ships idled. Also, Captain Roderick desperately needed to send some of the rescued galley slaves over to *The Thistle*, as the more than one hundred men coupled with his own threatened to swamp his small craft. Arabella took sixty of them, many of whom agreed to join her crew. This made quarters aboard her ship tight, but she shuffled her officers' and masters' quarters, doubling up where she could and readily giving up her dayroom to her pilot and sailing master. Even so, both captains agreed they needed to quickly find a port where they could deposit the remaining men.

By the next morning, their repairs had been completed and the ships continued their journey. The skies shone clear, with no rain clouds in the offing, just a few high wispy cotton balls here and there. They traveled throughout the day without encountering any other vessels and, that evening, the captains supped together aboard *The Greyhound.*

"So much for awaiting the *Sea Rover* in Benghazi," Captain Roderick remarked. "What now?"

"I have given it some thought," Arabella said. "If the *Rover* is yet bound for these waters, she would have to travel east and thus most likely cross through the Gulf of Sirte to reach Benghazi. I suggest we sail west through the Gulf as far as, say, Misratah before turning north and sailing to Malta to drop off our extra hands. We should still have plenty of provisions and water and so should be able to turn right about and sail again on the next tide."

"To where?"

"Straight back to Benghazi. Upon our return to that port, assuming we have not yet encountered the *Rover*, we should be able to sail close enough to see if any European-built ships lie at anchor."

"It is a fair plan and sure'n I do not have better. Are we to take any prizes on our journeys?"

"I think we should. We still have plenty of powder and shot and God knows we could use the coin. Besides, any ship we take may have information on the *Rover* or her prisoners."

"And if, upon our return to Benghazi, we have still failed to find her?"

"I intend to keep searching. At some point, we must either find the ship and her prisoners or discover some information as to their fate."

"Indeed. But the question is, how long do you intend to keep looking, Ara?"

"As long as it takes," she told him. "As long as it takes."

The two ships soon reached the emerald waters of the Gulf of Sirte. Lookouts kept a weather eye on the horizon at all times. The Gulf stretched some three hundred miles from end to end and over one hundred thirty miles to the south and the golden deserts of North Africa. Arabella knew the odds of encountering the *Sea Rover* in such a tremendous span of ocean were long indeed, but felt she had to try. The ships managed to avoid unwanted conflicts by continuing their ruse as licensed merchants free to trade within the Empire. Two days out, an Ottoman galley accompanied by three other ships stopped and boarded them. The Turks found their holds empty of swag and their papers in

order and let them continue on their way. An inquiry as to whether the
Janissaries had seen their 'sister ship' the *Sea Rover*, separated from
them recently in a storm, netted no new information. After another two
days, the privateers reached Misratah. There had been no trace of the
Rover and so they turned north, beginning their journey back to Malta.
This leg of their trip also proved uneventful and the ships arrived
several days later. Here, they deposited their excess mariners and, with
no goods or prisoners to sell at auction, were back at sea within hours -
much to the chagrin of the Grand Master, whose dinner invitation to
Arabella was, regrettably, declined.

They again sailed south, directly back to the African coast. They
sighted those shores several days later and turned east-south-east near
the tiny village of Bu'ayrat al Hasun, notable only for the ancient
Roman ruins visible high on a hill overlooking the town, under which
some shepherds were seen taking shelter from the noonday sun. The
next day, near the port town of Sirte, the privateers overtook and
captured a fat, Arab merchant ship before it could outrun them into the
safety of the harbor. The vessel was unarmed and surrendered without a
fight, yielding up a valuable cargo of raw cotton and finished textiles,
barley and wheat, olives, dates, grapes, iron ingots, barrels of fish and
even livestock, for the deck of the merchantman had carried not only

the crew, but six bleating goats and two cows with great, sleepy eyes.

The next day proved fortunate for the hunters as well, as they captured a lone Turkish corsair vessel as it left Marsa al Uwayjah. Her crew, however, put up a very fierce fight despite being outnumbered and outgunned. The fight did not last long though, and the privateers captured another thirty prisoners, took two cannon, two swivel guns and a goodly amount of shot and powder. They also freed two-and-twenty Christians from the oars. They found the greatest bounty, however, in the ship's hold, for she had sailed from Algiers and had of late been raiding Christian ships along the Spanish and Italian coasts. Among other goods, she carried ivory, gold, silk and barrels of spices such as cinnamon, nutmeg, cloves and saffron, some of which were worth more than their weight in gold in the right markets. Regrettably, the xebec itself had been badly damaged in the encounter and, after looting her, they were forced to leave her to sink.

Some two weeks after first fleeing Benghazi, *The Thistle* and *Greyhound* returned to that port city. They did not enter the great harbor, however, but sailed just outside, scanning it for any sign of the *Sea Rover*. They saw her not, and on their second pass aroused the suspicion of the locals. Two large war galleys raised their great central sail and ran out their oars. The privateers quickly put their helms to the wind and departed. The ships sailed west once more, heading back toward Misratah. This time, however, they did not turn about there but continued west. Arabella intended to fulfill her vow to search every mile of the Barbary Coast if necessary to find Duncan and the others. The ships sailed first to Tripoli, where they took at sea a local fishing vessel. Their questions gained them no useful information on the fate of the *Sea Rover* or her prisoners, though they did learn something of value: the port of Tripoli offered no safe harbor for the 'Lioness of the Levant', as her infamy had by now reached these parts. As if to confirm this, several Turkish warships raised sail and moved from the city toward them. The privateers set the fishermen free and quickly left. From Tripoli, *The Thistle* and *Greyhound* continued west along the coast, scanning the various ports along the way for any sign of the *Rover*. When they could, they questioned local fishermen and other European merchant vessels, though otherwise left them unmolested. Between ports, they continued to hunt for corsair prey, engaging a few galleys and merchant ships. They captured some, sank others and occasionally had to flee when they found they had bitten off more than they could chew.

After many weeks, they reached Tangier, Morocco, on the Atlantic coast. The *Rover* had not visited here, they learned, though they did have the incredible fortune of finding and purchasing one of the *Thistle* prisoners who had been brought here by a Turkish merchant. From Tangier, the two ships turned about and headed back into the Mediterranean. The privateers spent many more months prowling the waters of the Barbary Coast, continuing to seize smaller or lightly-gunned Ottoman merchant ships. Eventually, Arabella found and rescued almost all of the *Sea Rover's* former captives, including – finally - Misters Ranald, MacBrodie and Mauleon. She ransomed some and took others by force, questioning each at length to learn anything she could about where Duncan and the few remaining others might be. Details proved scarce, but she grasped onto any crumb of information and pursued it doggedly, chasing it until it either produced results or led to yet another dead end. She spent chests of gold searching for and liberating hostages, though she found only disappointment and false leads when it came to Duncan.

The Thistle and *Greyhound* did not spend all their time hunting on the Barbary Coast, though. As often as they could, they ported in Cartagena or one of the other friendly harbors of Europe. There, they put ashore the men they had rescued, took on fresh supplies and made any necessary repairs. The captains allowed their crews the chance to take much-needed and well-earned breaks to relax and spend some of their hard-earned coin. Whenever she was in Cartagena, Arabella made regular deposits in various banks of both her shares of treasure and 'Duncan's share,' since he was legally the owner of The Thistle and the Ship's Articles allotted him a share of any captured valuables. She also made it a point to check for messages from her father or anyone else, each time coming away empty-handed. She knew mail delivered by ships at sea was both slow and unreliable, with messages frequently going astray for months or years even depending on the fate of the ship carrying them. Still, she could not shake the feeling that something was amiss. She longed to set a course for home to check on her father, and the thought of again seeing *Ban Tigh* always brought a tear to her eye. Nonetheless, she steeled her resolve and refused to let anything distract her from continuing her search for Duncan.

20

The last of the ships sent in search of Sir William's daughter and her captors returned to Invernesshire some two months after he had received the pirates' ransom demand. Their captains wasted no time in sending word to *Ban Tigh* that, regrettably, they had found no sign of the *Gunsway, The Thistle* or the *Sea Rover* around the coasts of the whole of Scotland, England and Ireland, nor had they discovered any word of Arabella or Duncan. They had, however, seized a suspicious ship in waters near the Cheswick Black Rocks and hanged twelve of her crewmen as suspected pirates. The ships' sponsors promised William they would prepare another expedition, in a few months or perhaps early next year, and he was welcome to come along if he wished. He sent word of his profound gratitude for their efforts and expressed his enthusiasm and support for a future venture. The truth, though, was that the auld knight had not the heart for another failed expedition and resolved to raise the rest of the funds needed to pay the ransom. He continued to receive letters from his friends and associates beseeching him to let them know if he needed any assistance raising those funds. He thanked them all for their support and their offers, promising he would and having no intention whatsoever to do so. Sir William was a proud man and, despite his financial difficulties, he would go hat in hand to neither friend nor foe.

Some time after this, William heard the extraordinary news that Duncan Campbell was in Edinburgh, a free man! The young lord had finally been able to raise his ransom and, upon paying this, was released by the pirates as promised. He had traveled straight away to Edinburgh to petition the Royal Court for his lands and title as Thane of Cawdor. A mere formality, for the matter had already been introduced in Parliament and approved in his absence. Sir William anxiously awaited any word from him regarding Arabella. None came and William decided Duncan must have intended to deliver such in person. The knight fretted over whether this meant good or ill and continued to await Duncan's return to Cawdor. Regrettably, some sort of legal or financial trouble delayed him in the city and his stay soon stretched from days to weeks and finally to the better part of a month. Finally, Duncan departed Edinburgh for Cawdor and home. Troubles aside, he brought with him his father's title and was now legally master of the estate. Within hours of hearing of his return, William set out to meet him.

Two days later, the old gentleman entered the beautiful grounds and was quickly granted entrance to Thane Campbell. He found the lad quite busy, still trying to get a handle on his late father's legal and financial affairs. Deeds and titles of holding and scores of tattered old scrolls and chits and promissory notes surrounded him, strewn about the great table in the main hall. Duncan pushed all of this aside when his page announced Sir William.

"William!" he called out, rising to embrace the man. "I had not expected you so soon."

"I am sorry; you expected me?"

"Yes, I sent my man to fetch you just yesterday."

"I see. No, I came as soon as I heard you had returned home; no doubt I missed him on the road. I give thanks to Heaven for your safe return and am most glad to see you in very good health. This gives me comfort in the kidnappers' care for their captives. Now if you will forgive my directness, have you any news of Arabella?"

"I regret I have none, William. I was kept entirely isolated during my confinement,, and neither saw nor heard mention of her, though I asked often. I am sorry."

"You heard nothing in all your months of captivity?"

"Nothing useful, and nothing on Arabella specifically. The pirates talked occasionally of 'the prisoners' or 'the ransoms' but made certain to never let slip details while in my presence. I could not even tell where they kept me or how far from where they attacked us I might have been, for I was blindfolded most of the time or kept in rooms with no windows."

"Were you a'ship?"

"For the first few weeks, yes. After that, they took me ashore somewhere, though I neither saw nor heard anything useful as the bloody dogs put me in the bottom of a hay cart while transporting me. I am certain they took me in circles and down many lanes to keep me ignorant, though by then we could have been but a league from Cawdor and I would not have known it. But what of you Sir William: have you heard anything of my Ara?"

"Only their ransom demand. They contacted me via messenger

some months ago with the amount, assuring me she was being well-cared for."

"Well that is certainly good news! I assure you, they did not abuse me whilst I was in their care, and I must assume they are treating Arabella in kind."

"Gramercy, Duncan," William told him. "I most appreciate your comforting words. I can only hope her captors have great patience."

"Patience?" Duncan asked.

"Aye; their ransom demand is exorbitant and I am having a devil of a time raising it."

"I am most sorry to hear it. But, and pray pardon my familiarity, are not your house and lands worth a good deal?"

"In these times, I regret that may not be the case; so many of our brothers are being forced to sell that values have dropped drastically. Nay, my plan right now is to keep working my fields and bring in a fat harvest in the fall. Then I can add its value to the coin I have already gathered and the money I yet hope to raise by selling some acres and most of my livestock. I tell you though, I mean to hold on to *Ban Tigh* if at all possible."

"Even if doing so increases the time Arabella remains apart from us?" the Thane asked.

"Even so, for I refuse to let a filthy gaggle of thieves and cowards rob me of my home and legacy. I mean to bring my daughter *home*, Duncan, not to bring her to *homelessness*."

"William, rest assured, Arabella will ever have a home so long as I possess Cawdor Castle," Duncan told him, laying a strong hand on his shoulder. "As will you."

"Gramercy again, good sir. That is most kind of you."

"It is too little by far and you are a gentleman for not saying it. You must know I would have gladly paid Arabella's ransom myself if I could have. My captors made it clear they would not allow this though, for they seemed to know I could not afford both her fee and mine. And since no one else would pay my ransom, the greater of the two I am sure, they would have lost my value. So I was forced to pay mine first, in its entirety, and this has wreaked havoc on my finances. Truth be told, I have had to let go numerous servants, empty my accounts and auction nearly every piece of art and jewelry I just inherited." Sir William looked about and noticed that indeed, the walls seemed rather barren, with many portraits and tapestries usually present gone. Large pieces of furniture he remembered from his last visit to the castle were also missing. "Even that was not nearly enough," Duncan continued. "I was forced to sell off a goodly portion of my lands as well. Luckily, I discovered a group of investors based in Edinburgh currently hungry for arable land in these parts and only too willing to acquire all I was willing to sell. I tell you, I was fortunate to find them, for they pay a fair price, perhaps because they are not locals and do not yet know the current depressed value of things here. You may wish to consider them yourself, William. I will put their man in touch with you if you but ask."

"You have my leave."

"Consider it done, friend. Now, let us break bread together and have a *quaiche* or three of scotch in anticipation of Arabella's speedy return."

More months passed and Sir William continued to work tirelessly to raise Arabella's ransom. He called in old debts and even had to sue a cousin for repayment of a small loan granted some years ago. Occasionally, an anonymous friend or relation would send him a few pounds or even a few pennies. He was loathe to accept this but begrudgingly did so, knowing each shilling brought him closer to freeing his daughter. In addition, he sold off every acre of land not presently sowed, and worked the rest from sunrise to sunset. Despite needing additional hands to work his fields, he could not afford them and was in fact forced to lay off the two he had. His efforts paid off though. The fall harvest was a good one. Immediately after selling his crops at market, he sold off most of his remaining livestock and then contacted the Edinburgh investors to make arrangements to sell off the acres he had just reaped.

But he had waited too long, he learned. The businessmen had grown savvy to the region's property values, and the prices they offered him were far less than he had hoped for. As such, he chose instead to sell them fewer acres, just enough to buy more seed and the other supplies he would need to replant in the spring. He would reap another harvest and pray that by then, things would have turned around enough that his lands would fetch a greater value. Sir William's estate, humble to begin with, was now reduced to *Ban Tigh*, in great disrepair, a handful of mangy animals no one wanted and a few paltry acres.

The land speculators approached him once more with an offer for the house and the rest of the Fraser lands. Their offer was not a great one, but Sir William calculated it would be just enough to secure Arabella's freedom. Still, it would leave him with nothing. He and Arabella would be broke, homeless paupers entirely dependent on others for their food, their shelter and their very survival. William struggled with the decision for near a fortnight before finally sending word of his decision. He would not sell *Ban Tigh*. He would sow his

remaining acres as planned, praying for warm rains, the pirates'

patience and Arabella's forgiveness.

21

The hot, sticky days of summer gave way to the cool breezes and longer nights of autumn, and still Arabella continued her search. The rains came, bathing the world as if to wash away its sins, and *The Thistle* and *Greyhound* continued their peripatetic ways. Soon, even fall became a memory, replaced by the Mediterranean winter. Now came howling winds and dangerous seas, and always the rain. The ships spent weeks at a time locked in ports while the wind and waves raged, slipping free between storms to brave the desperate seas once more. Through it all, Arabella's crew remained faithful and Captain Roderick stoically stayed at her side. They did not find Duncan Campbell, though they occasionally found and rescued one of the few remaining prisoners. In addition, they continued to have success against their Ottoman foes, and everyone continued to profit from Arabella's leadership. The privateers sailed from one end of the Mediterranean to the other, from north to south and back again. When they needed safe ports in which to sell their prizes, make repairs or acquire supplies, they were welcomed in not only Cartagena and Valletta, but Cagliari and Sassari on Sardinia, the Italian ports of Livorno, Naples and Palermo, Sicily and even tiny La Sabina in the Balearic Islands. In this latter port, Arabella always expected to find *The Raven* and Captain McNamara, and was always disappointed when she did not.

As the privateers ported in the tiny village of Hawmat as Suq, a filthy hovel on the Barbary Coast populated mainly by flies and maggots and the sad people they fed on, they finally learned what had kept the *Sea Rover* from Benghazi so many months ago. She had limped into this tiny port after losing her main and mizzen masts in the same storm that had so battered *The Thistle* and *Greyhound*. The ship had no spares and none were to be found in this small village. Even finding a tree from which to carve one was impossible in this desert wasteland. And so they waited, essentially trapped here until another ship happened by with a cargo of raw timber. The *Rover* finally reached

Benghazi after *The Thistle* and *Greyhound* had left, missing them by mere days.

Captain Liam McNamara jumped to his feet when the three-masted merchant vessel sailed into the narrow harbor of La Sabina.

"'Tis *The Thistle!*" he exclaimed, drawing curious looks from the other patrons in the tiny dockside bar. He watched as it drew closer and it was only when the ship docked and he took a really good look at her that he saw otherwise. Same build, same size and similar markings, yes, but a different figurehead and a bit more rake to her mizzen. Still, he watched with interest as her captain and several officers came ashore and made their way toward this, the only tavern within sight. Englishmen they looked to be, though if God smiled upon him, Liam thought, they would be Irish and would have a bottle or two of whiskey they did not mind sharing with a brother.

Liam had been in La Sabina for more than a month now, ever since the winter rains had come and brought the unpredictable *Levante* winds with them. He learned he had once again just missed Arabella and *The Thistle* by a few days, and decided to remain in port, hoping for her return. The excuse he gave his men, however, was the precarious nature of the seas right now, and in this at least his words had some truth. On some days, the temperature dropped below freezing and the waves topped sixteen feet, keeping even the mightiest ships bottled up in the bay. Not only this, but with the winter, merchant shipping all but stopped, taking with it a pirate's source of income. Liam had thought about returning to Ireland or even sailing west to the Caribbean and Hispaniola, where folks said the Spanish treasure ships were easy prey. "Sure they were," he said. "The ships were always easy prey – somewhere else." He had given in to the lure of 'easy' gold once before and it had cost him a good friend, his ship and nearly his life. So he stayed in the Mediterranean, in La Sabina, drinking wine and thinking often of a certain red-haired female. He nearly jumped once more hearing Arabella's name spoken aloud in the tiny tavern, thinking for a moment his thoughts had just leapt from his mind into reality.

"Arabella Fraser?" the bent and wrinkled old man behind the bar repeated. "Sure, I know her; most folk in these parts do."

Liam turned and saw it was the newly-arrived sea captain who had made the inquiry. At a glance, Liam disliked him; something in his eyes said he had given a lot of people pain and had more to give before he was through.

"Looks like the harbormaster in Cartagena told us right," he said. Scottish, Liam recognized, becoming more interested. Could this be

Duncan, captain of his own ship now and in search of his affianced?
"Be she here now?"

"Nay, not for a month or more," the tapman answered. "Course, she could show up tomorrow or two months from now, or never again. Sure'n I cannot say. But if I do see her and do so before you, who shall I say was looking?"

"We are kin of hers from Edinburgh and bring important news from home," the sea captain said, slapping a shilling down on the board. Liam's ears pricked up even more, though he pretended not to listen. "Word is she has been traveling about the Med on the privateer ship *Thistle*, searching for her missing fiancé. That true?"

"Aye, 'tis no secret, that," the barkeep said, palming the coin.

"Near brings a tear to me eye, the thought of her pining away all these months for her long-lost love," the Scotsman said with a sneer. "Word also is she does not simply sail aboard the ship as a passenger, but actually commands the vessel. Sure'n there be no truth to that and some wag was having a bit of fun with me."

"'Twas no lie, good sir," the barkeep said. "Miss Arabella does indeed captain *The Thistle* and command her crew."

"God's teeth!" the Scotsman said. "What boatload of dunderheads would make a wench their captain?"

"From what I hear, it was not really put to a vote," the bar man said, his demeanor going noticeably icier. "Though it was not disputed much neither."

"Oh, I see. She must be financing this little venture. And since she's the one paying, she gets to play at captain. How cute."

"Softly, good sir," the barkeep said. "Many in these parts have a fondness for the lady, meself included."

"Well of course you do," the captain said, softening his tone. "We all do, for did I not say we were kin? I was just having a bit of fun, that is all. So tell me: might ye know where *Captain* Fraser be now?" Another shilling accompanied his question.

The barkeep hesitated a moment before taking it. "East. Think I remember hearing something about Sardinia, though I make no promises."

"Ye heard him, men," the captain said, turning to the sailors accompanying him. "We be sailing east as soon as this wind drops enough to let us leave this bloody harbor."

The men turned to leave and the barkeep called after them. "Your news?"

"Pardon?"

"Your news? This important news that brought you clear from

Scotland. I mean, if I do talk to Captain Fraser before you do, what shall I tell her?"

"Tell her she can stop scouring the seas for Duncan Campbell; he is a free man again, his ransom paid. He is on the Island of Malta, hoping to be reunited with his fiancé. He is like to be there for some months, so that is where she should go if she truly wants to find him."

The captain and his men left, heading directly to their ship. Liam threw back his wine and followed them. If he could round up enough of his crew, he might not be spending Christmas in La Sabina after all.

Two days later and on the morn of Christmas Eve, *The Raven* left port precisely two hours after the Scottish ship *Phoenix*, which so resembled *The Thistle*. Captain McNamara directed his helmsman to follow at a lengthy and discreet distance. In fact, since he knew where the *Phoenix* was heading, they need not even keep her in sight. One week later, *The Raven* sailed into the *Gulfo degli Angeli* on the southern tip of the island of Sardinia. The large and bustling Port of Cagliari spread before them, its namesake city rising above the storm-wracked waters atop her seven hills. Liam spotted the *Phoenix* at once, at anchor near the west end of the harbor. Dozens of large and small ships filled the bay, including an immense Maltese war galley. There was no sign of *The Thistle*. Captain McNamara steered his ship to the opposite end of the docks.

With a few questions and a few coins to the harbormaster's mate, he learned Arabella had not ported here in many weeks, though she was rumored to be in these waters, perhaps as close as Livorno. The captain of the *Phoenix* likely learned this as well, yet his ship remained in port. Liam soon learned why. The locals had planned a grand festival to welcome the new year, just as they had done annually for centuries. Many of the ships in the harbor had come especially for the gala, for it was no sedate affair, but a drunken bacchanal of epic scale. It took place in the town's ancient Roman amphitheatre and was fueled by enough wine to fill the bay and attended by almost every citizen in town. Liam knew his crew would never forgive him if he made them remain on *The Raven* and miss it, and in fact he wanted to go to the damned thing as much as any. He told them to go and have a good time, but to be back on the ship early the next day.

The gala exceeded anything Liam had ever seen or even heard about. It raged all night and on into morning and still gave no sign of letting up. Luckily, Liam and a few other Ravens were lucid enough to spot the crew of the *Phoenix* slip quietly away shortly after sunrise. Liam rounded up his men, and the lot of them staggered back to their ship just in time to see the Maltese man-of-war sail from the bay in escort of a large merchant carrack also flying the flag of the Knights of Malta. Just before the ships rounded the eastern cape, the *Phoenix* shipped her anchor and followed them. Shortly after this, *The Raven* unfurled her own sails.

The Raven shadowed the *Phoenix* for several days, even as the Scottish ship shadowed the Maltese, all of them sailing north-east. Their current course, if maintained, would take them to the port city of Livorno on the Italian peninsula, the last rumored location of *The Thistle*. Yet the way the *Phoenix* sailed, hanging back from the war galley and merchant ship when she could have easily passed them, looked to Liam as if she were stalking a prey she meant to take and was but waiting for the opportune moment. He himself had done the same thing countless times. This made no sense, though, for it would be folly for a ship of the *Phoenix's* size to even attempt to take such an enormous and powerful galley by herself. No, her captain must have some other purpose in mind, he decided.

As the sun dipped to the horizon on the third day of this curious chase, the light silhouetted the *Phoenix* side by side with the galley and the merchant ship. All three vessels had hove to. Liam listened intently for the sound of cannon fire but heard none, nor did he see the flashes and smoke that would accompany a naval action. No hostile confrontation this, the Irishman surmised. Perhaps the captain of the *Phoenix* had simply drawn alongside the vessels to inquire if their crews had any knowledge of where *The Thistle* might be. Perhaps he had not actually been pursuing them at all, but had merely been traveling in their same direction at a leisurely pace. Either way, this was a mystery that would not be solved any time soon, for Liam's ship was several hours behind the *Phoenix*. Liam told his helmsman to hold their course steady and maintain their present speed. He would be in his cabin and was to be alerted should there be any news, or when they were within close range of the other ships.

The pounding of footsteps across the wooden planks awoke him before the man's knock on his door. It was dark out, the deep, sluggish time several hours before dawn. Liam pulled open the door just as his first mate reached for it.

"Oh, ye are awake. Yer better come see this, cap'n."

In a moment, Liam stood with the fellow on the quarterdeck. He followed his mate's outstretched arm through the foggy gloom and saw an orange glow miles ahead of them. Clearly, a ship - or ships - blazed.

"Rouse the hands," Liam directed. "Bring us to full sail and put us alongside that brig fierce quick."

Two hours later, they reached two smoldering hulks, their thick black smoke mixing with the haze of the early morning and giving the entire area an other-worldly look. By their size and shape, Liam knew at once they were the Maltese merchant vessel and her escort. The *Phoenix* was nowhere to be seen. A few other ships had seen the flames as well and had reached them before *The Raven*, mostly fishing vessels from Sardinia and Corsica. *The Raven* sailed close to the largest one, her captain standing on deck and watching them with a wary eye.

"Ahoy there!" Liam called. "Do you know what happened here?"

"They was attacked," the man called back. "By pirates!"

Captain McNamara gave a look to his first mate before continuing. "Any survivors?"

"Three."

"Were they able to name the ship that did this?"

"Aye. 'Twas *The Thistle!*"

"*The Thistle?*" Liam repeated incredulously. "It cannot be! There was another ship in these waters last night, a ship that bears a strong resemblance to Captain Fraser's ship. Were the survivors certain 'twas *The Thistle?*"

"There was no mistaking her, according to the hands we pulled from the wreckage," the sea captain replied. "Each man swears that Captain Fraser herself was present for the attack."

"Bloody hell!" Liam swore. "Was she alone, *The Thistle*? She is known to sail in consort with another vessel, and sure'n I cannot see how only one ship could have defeated that galley and her escort."

"The survivors made no mention of another ship, though none was needed from what they say."

"How so?"

"'Twas not firepower that took the galley, but treachery. The men say Captain Arabella sent over several barrels of wine as a token of her esteem for and fellowship with the knights. But it were poisoned. As the knights lay dying and helpless, the Thistles attacked."

"Bloody hell!" Liam swore again. "Did the survivors say what course she took afterward?"

"North."

"Helm: north it is!" Liam called.

Late the following day, *The Raven* sailed into the narrow port of Livorno. A long quay jutted far into the water, sheltering the bay and channeling approaching ships between a gauntlet of guns from three small forts on the shore. At a glance, Captain McNamara saw that neither *The Thistle* nor the *Phoenix* was anchored here. Still, he made port and quickly sounded out the harbormaster regarding either ship.

"No, no *Phoenix*," the man told him. "But *The Thistle*, you just missed her."

"She was here?"

"Si, she arrived late yesterday and departed first thing this morning."

"Are you certain?"

"I am not blind, fool," the man told him gruffly. "*The Thistle* has ported here in the past and I can damn well recognize Captain Arabella's fiery red mane, even at a distance."

"What did she do while here?"

"Offloaded a good deal of cargo and sold it. Cheap too. They seemed to be in a hurry."

"I do not suppose you heard mention of where next they were headed?"

"Sorry, but I did not."

"Gramercy," Liam told him, leaving the man to his business and turning to his first mate. "Everyone remains aboard; we are not staying. As soon as the tide shifts, we make sail."

"What heading, captain?"

"Malta."

A gale raged across the whole of the eastern Mediterranean, and *The Thistle* and *Greyhound* raced to find a port. Master De Rivero warned that this blow was just the first of many greater tempests that would ravage these seas in the coming weeks and months. Any ship foolish enough to remain out now that winter had truly arrived would surely pay the price. The crews of both ships, brave and experienced hands all, echoed this sentiment and made clear that this was the time to find a safe port for the winter. They had by now recovered every single prisoner taken from *The Thistle* by Captain Spotiswoode save one: Duncan Campbell. Arabella refused to give up the hunt, feeling that with the very next ship or port, her fortunes must turn and she must finally find her fiancé. Images of him filled her dreams almost constantly now. Each night he came to her, beseeching her to keep trying, to find him and set him free from the hellish torment in which he languished. But each waking day Arabella failed him. The search and the frustrations weighed heavily upon her. Late this night as the ship rocked in the grips of the tempest, Molly sought her out. She found her in her chart room, pouring over maps of the Mediterranean

Sea yet again.

"Ah, Mol," Arabella said, barely looking up. "I am glad it is you. I wanted to run our new course by you."

"I would be happy with any course that takes us directly to the nearest safe harbor where we may port for the winter."

"Surely you jest. No, I was just mulling over the possible reasons behind our lack of success at finding my Duncan on the Barbary Coast."

"And?"

"I have come to the conclusion that Captain Spotiswoode and the *Rover* must in fact never have brought Duncan to these shores."

"That is my thinking as well," Molly said.

"I see we are of the same mind." Arabella turned the map over so it faced Molly. Newly-inked plotlines showed a course from their present position due east, deep into the Aegean Sea and into the very heart of the Ottoman Empire. "Clearly, the pirates must have feared depositing Duncan anywhere from which he had any hope of rescue, and likely carried him farther east, to Crete or Rhodes or even the Turkish mainland. Our journey into the Aegean will be more hazardous than any we have yet undertaken and I want to ensure that every officer and every sailor knows-"

"Are you mad?" Molly interrupted. "You are not seriously considering taking us to the very shores of the Sultanate are you? And in winter?"

"That is exactly my intention."

"Then you have answered my question: you are indeed off your head."

"Am I?" Arabella said. "Why? For trying to rescue my fiancé? Because the seas are a bit rough and I continue the search instead of running and hiding in some port? Because I refuse to give up and quit simply because we have encountered a few setbacks in our quest? For this you accuse me of being deranged?"

"Perseverance and fortitude are admirable, Ara, but only within reasonable limits," her friend said. "You have gone far beyond those limits. You are obsessed, and I fear that obsession has made you lose touch with reality. We have scoured every inch of the Barbary Coast many times over and have found or accounted for every person aboard this ship when Spotiswoode seized her except Duncan. Not one person we have met over the last year, Christian or Turk, reports ever seeing Lord Campbell aboard the *Rover* once it reached the Mediterranean. Ara, I believe the reason we have not found him in these seas is because he never reached them!"

"That is preposterous. Why would they bring everyone else here and not him?"

"How should I know? It could be any of a hundred reasons. He could have worked out a deal with Spotiswoode or else quickly paid his ransom. Perhaps he stole an oar boat in the dead of night and pulled for the coast of Spain. Maybe he and the pirates quarreled and they cut his throat!"

"Do not say that!" Arabella yelled, shooting to her feet. "Duncan Campbell is not dead! I would know it if he were; I would feel it."

"I am sorry, Ara. Like I said, I do not know why he did not pass through the Pillars of Hercules with the rest of us, I only know he could not have. You say you feel that he yet lives, well so too do I feel just as certain that he never reached these seas. And I am not alone in this, for every man and woman aboard this ship and *The Greyhound* knows it also and wonders why the devil you do not! And now you talk of taking us directly into the maws of the Sultan's navy, and in the middle of winter no less, through straights and shoals dangerous in even the best weather? And all because you refuse to face the truth!"

"So the fact that a few fainthearts believe Duncan is not in the Med makes it the truth?"

"That is not the truth I am speaking of, Ara. There is another behind why you refuse to admit that we will never find Duncan in these seas."

"You are making no sense, Mol."

"I make no sense? I am not the one who insists we continue searching for a phantom we can neither see nor grasp, ever endangering this ship, her crew and yourself. And all because you cannot admit that searching for Duncan and never finding him is easier than actually facing him."

"What the hell are you talking about?" Arabella asked, turning her back on her friend and staring out at the storm through the porthole. The darkness hid the pallor that suddenly came onto her face.

"I have known you too long for you to hide your true feelings from me," her friend said softly. "You do not want to marry Duncan. I think you regretted your decision almost as soon as you made it, though you are unwilling to admit it, perhaps even to yourself."

"To hell you say!" Arabella said, still looking away from her friend and now fighting back tears. "I love Duncan!"

"Do you?" Molly asked, stepping close and placing a comforting hand on her friend's shoulder. "Not that it matters, for I do not think you could love any man so much, because getting married for you means giving up too much freedom, too much independence. And I think every day you spend sailing the seas, master of this ship and her crew, you realize it more and more. To find Duncan means to confront that truth and the choice it presents: give up the seas and your independence, or break the heart of the man you love most in this world - your father."

Arabella said nothing. She turned and faced her friend, tears filling her eyes. Still, a slight smile pulled at her lips. She accepted the offered hug and held it. After a while she stepped back and picked up the map. Her finger traced a new course — straight to Malta, but a few days journey from their present position. "My dearest Mol, I am sorry. I have been a fool and a coward and I have endangered all of us needlessly. We shall go to Valletta and remain there for the winter; come the spring, we will go home."

The *Greyhound* and *Thistle* reached that fair city three days later, their holds filled with swag and with two captured prize ships in tow. The port tenders met them outside the harbor as usual and raced back to the city with their news. As before, a crowd gathered to greet them. This time, however, a large number of ordinary citizens lined the docks in addition to the usual prostitutes, ale hawkers and merchants, and this despite the foul weather. Everyone wanted to see *Laboua'a-t'Asharq* and hear the tales of her latest conquests over the hated Mohammedans. Arabella even spotted several sisters of the Order of St. Ursula among the throngs, including Marie Elise.

"I say, I believe they intend to make you a saint," Captain Roderick said pointing them out.

"I doubt it; my family is Presbyterian. Perchance they are not here for me at all but for you, sir, for I do not believe you made a donation to them the last time we visited."

"It must have slipped my mind; I shall attend to it post haste," he said with little conviction before hastily changing the subject.

The crews headed into town and the ships were soon deserted of all but a few stubborn hands. As the captains collected a few personal belongings for their stay in town, they received another invitation to dine with the Grand Master. Arabella was pleasantly surprised to see that this time, the invitation extended to all of their fellow officers as well. Unfortunately, these had scattered to the four winds moments after their arrival in port. As such, the captains alone boarded the carriages sent for them by the Grand Master. As the wooden wheels clattered over the cobblestone streets, Arabella and Bartholomew watched the sun slip below the massing clouds of another rising storm, its rays turning the sky from gray to the most vivid orange and pink.

Arabella sighed as the orb sank below the horizon just as the horses clopped to a halt before the Palace. Two Knights of the Order again escorted them into the main dining hall. Unlike last time, however, de Vernalle was not alone to greet them. A dozen knights including Pierre-Louis stood with him, wearing their battle armor and carrying swords. The table had not been set for supper.

"Where are the rest of your officers?" de Verdalle barked. "I expected them as well."

"They were regrettably unavailable, Your Grace," Bartholomew said. "May I ask what is going on here?"

"Arrest them," de Verdalle said to his men. The knights stepped forward and seized the two captains, who offered no resistance. "And search the town for their officers and masters."

"Grand Master!" Arabella cried. "What is the meaning of this?"

"This is what we do in Malta to pirates, Miss Fraser!"

22

"Pirates? But we carry Letters of Marque!" Bartholomew protested.

"Exactly," de Verdalle said. "The provisions of which require you to attack only Turkish shipping or unlicensed pirates. You violated those provisions ten days ago when you attacked two Maltese ships off the coast of Naples!"

"We did no such thing!" Arabella exclaimed.

"That is a lie!" the Grand Master shouted. "We have learned of your treachery, of how you attacked a ship carrying goods belonging to my Order as well as her escort. We know you slaughtered the knights and sailors aboard both vessels, looted their cargoes and then set them ablaze to conceal your crimes."

"This is madness! We were not even in those waters ten days ago," Arabella cried. "If Your Grace says an evil thing befell your ships, then I will not dispute it, but why suspect us in the matter?"

"Because as bloodthirsty as you were, you failed to silence all of the merchant ship's crew. Three men survived, two by leaping overboard and a third by hiding underneath the corpses of his murdered shipmates, then clinging to a piece of wreckage after you sank his ship from under him. These men were rescued and returned here. Each of the survivors has identified the ship that attacked them as *The Thistle*, with you present and commanding her, Miss Fraser!"

"Preposterous!" Bartholomew shouted. "My ship has sailed in consort with Arabella's every day for months, and I and my crew can vouch they did no such thing."

"So you admit you were with her when she committed this crime!" the Grand Master said. "Then you are guilty as well. Take them from my sight!"

"You cannot do this!" Captain Roderick cried.

"Where is justice? I demand a trial!" Arabella called as the guards began to drag them away.

"And you shall have it!" de Verdalle called after them. "Do not expect the matter to be more than a formality, however, for I am certain it will allow you the opportunity to do little more than confirm openly the confession my inquisitors shall have already drawn from you!"

The knights quickly stripped the prisoners of their swords and daggers, then tightly bound their hands. Pierre-Louis made certain he was one of the knights holding Arabella. She looked pleadingly to him and saw nothing but cold hardness etched on his handsome face. The knights dragged them from the castle and threw them into the back of a waiting wagon. They carried them away from Valletta and to the nearby city of Vittoriosa. Their destination was the Fort St. Angelo, an ancient fortress now housing the Order's dungeons. Arabella could not help but notice it stood directly across the lane from the Inquisitors' Palace.

Once inside the prison, the guards separated Arabella and Bartholomew. Pierre-Louis and the other knight led Arabella deep into the dungeons below the keep, down to a place where no sunlight and no fresh air dared intrude. They marched her down a narrow hallway, its stone walls slick with slime and stench. Cell doors, some of iron bars and some of solid, iron-bound oak lined the corridor. Arabella could not tell if any were occupied. The men led her to a small cell with a heavy wooden door, removed her bonds and shoved her inside. The straw on the floor stank of urine, dried blood and fear.

"Remove your clothes," the first knight commanded.

"I beg your pardon," Arabella said.

"Your dress and your boots will be of no use to you here. But take comfort, pirate, for they will not go to waste. They will be sold to feed the orphans of the men you murdered."

"I did not murder your knights!" Arabella cried, looking Pierre-Louis in the eyes as she said this.

She barely had time to see the other soldier's hand before it slammed against her cheek. Though openhanded, the slap caused stars to explode and sent her staggering. "Lying whore!" he cried.

"No, Gaston," Pierre-Louis said, restraining his friend. "It is not right."

"But she is a pirate," he protested. "She murdered our brothers!"

"She is a prisoner in our care and she has not yet been tried. She is not to be abused."

Gaston glared at his friend a moment then shrugged his shoulders. "It matters not. The inquisitors will do far worse than I could," he muttered, before turning back to her. "Your dress and your boots. Now."

Arabella hesitated for a moment and then turned away. She did as they asked, keeping only her thin chemise and thanking Heaven she had grown accustomed to wearing bloomers under her clothes. Gaston took the items and slammed the door shut, sealing her in. He and Pierre-Louis walked away without another word. No more than a sliver of light reached her through the small, barred window in the door, this from a wall sconce some distance away down the corridor. Once the knights' footsteps died away, the silence fell heavy within her prison.

One week after leaving Livorno, *The Raven* limped into Valletta's harbor, most of her sails torn to shreds and the rest close-reefed, her rigging in shambles. Captain McNamara focused on bringing his ship safely alongside the docks, fighting the powerful storm surges that threatened to smash his vessel against the pier. Once docked, he looked for *The Thistle, Greyhound* or *Phoenix*, but saw none of them. Liam once again presented forged papers and gave a false name to the harbormaster, disappointing the man with his news that he had no cargo to sell. The fellow informed him in answer to his questions, though, that yes, *The Thistle* and *Greyhound* had arrived in port just two days before him.

"I did not see them as I entered the harbor," Liam commented. "Do not tell me she has set out once more in these wicked seas."

"Heaven forbid, sir," Mister Bahria said. "No, the captains made arrangements to port in Malta through the winter. Their ships were moved last night across the harbor to Vittoriosa, where they now lay under the protective guns of the Fortress St. Angelo."

"Ah, I see. And might you know where I can find Captain Fraser?"

"I am sorry, sir, but I do not."

A short time later, Liam left his ship and walked into the city, a cloak wrapped around his shoulders as meager armor against the wind and rain. He found the citizens abuzz with news, talking animatedly amongst themselves and rushing about to spread some particularly juicy bit of new gossip. Not fluent in the local tongue, he could not make out just what excited them so. He noticed a large crowd gathered in the central square and made his way over. A thick, wooden pillar stood there, serving as a central message board upon which a handful of official-looking parchments hung, each copied into several languages. He pushed his way through the throng and read the newest one. It announced the arrests of Captains Fraser and Roderick by the Order for the crime of piracy on the high seas, a crime carrying the penalty of death! It further stated that both ships' officers and masters were sought in connection with this crime as well, with rewards to anyone who aided in their capture – and severe punishments for any who aided in their escape from justice.

Liam staggered back to his ship in a daze, the iniquity and utter absurdity of the matter battering his mind. As he stepped from the gangplank onto the slick deck, his first mate approached him.

"Ye 'ave two guests in yer dayroom, captain, a'waitin' yer."

"Who are they?"

"Best not to talk here, sir," the man intimated quietly, as if the ship's hull could not be trusted to keep her secrets. "They be friends, though."

Liam saw he would get no more from the man and knew from long years of working with him that this was certainly for the best. If his guests wanted their presence kept mum, then so be it. He entered his cabin a moment later and saw two figures standing uneasily within. Heavy cloaks covered them from head to toe, damp from the rains, and their drawn hoods concealed their faces. Upon seeing him enter, both drew back their wraps.

"Thank God you are here!" Molly MacBain said. "I could not believe our luck when we spotted your ship in the harbor."

"I trust you have heard the news?" Duff Selkirk asked.

"I have learned it just now," Liam told them, waving them to some nearby chairs. He crossed to his writing table and unlocked a small chest holding a decanter of brandy and several goblets. He handed two of these to his grateful visitors. "It is an abomination."

"We had nothing to do with the attack on those ships!" Molly said. "If it even happened at all and is not simply a fabrication by the Grand Master to get his hands on Arabella or our ship or both."

"It happened all right," Liam told her. "I saw the ships burning with my own eyes. But you do not need to convince me of your innocence, Mol, for I know Arabella would never do such a thing. In faith, I have a fair idea who actually did commit this crime."

"Who?" both Molly and Duff blurted.

"There is a Scottish merchant vessel named *Phoenix* plying these waters of late, and I have noted she bears the damnedest resemblance to your *Thistle*. I saw her make contact with the Maltese ships just before they burned. I would wager my weight in gold they were the ones who did what you now stand accused of. Which raises another question: I know Arabella and Captain Roderick have been arrested, but who else among your crews was also taken?"

"None that I know of, and a fair spot o' luck it was," Duff told him. "Molly and I were in an alley across from the Palace when the guards dragged Arabella and Bartholomew out and tossed them in a prison cart."

"Wait; what the hell were the two of you doing in an alley across from the Palace?" Liam asked.

"Never you mind," Molly said. "What matters is that I followed them to see where they were being taken, while Duff alerted as many of our fellow crewmembers as he could and told them what had happened. Sure'n we did not know what sort of tomfoolery was afoot, but we knew enough to go into hiding right away. And not a moment too soon, for the knights took to the streets that very evening, going from tavern to tavern and inn to inn. So far, we have managed to avoid them."

"You are welcome to remain aboard my ship as long as you like, and the same holds for the rest of the crews," Liam told them. "I only wish we could get away from this island and the danger she presents to you. Unfortunately, this weather may keep us pinned to these shores for some time, perhaps even the entire bloody winter."

"'Tis not myself I worry about," Molly said. "'Tis Arabella. And Captain Roderick, of course. I fear the knights will not accept their word that they had nothing to do with the attack on their ships, but will torture them until they 'confess.' And once that happens, they will surely be hanged. We must save them."

"I agree," Liam said. "Though I hold no false hope such a thing will be easy. It may not even be possible. This entire island is a fortress, locked tight by the Order. And then there is the fact that even if we did, somehow, manage to free them, where could we go? Even the weather works on the side of the knights just now, for we cannot make it off this rock while these storms rage."

"We must still try," Molly declared.

"Aye," Liam said. His tone was that of a man who knew he had to do a task that not only would likely fail but would also probably result in his death. "Sit tight here and let me do a bit of scouting around. I will try to come up with some semblance of a plan."

Liam spent the next day walking about Vittoriosa, her streets, her hills, even her sea cliffs. He did not walk alone though, for his Irish stubbornness proved no match for Molly's Scottish stubbornness. Despite the danger to herself, she insisted on going with him. She dressed as a man and acted as no more than one of the captain's mates, a difficult task for a woman with her curves, but plenty of hay stuffed within a set of oversized men's clothes made the disguise passable. The two hiked the docks below and hills surrounding the little fort, studying and committing to memory every detail about the nearby coastline, the comings and goings of the knights and any visitors to the keep. They studied the types of materials used in its construction, the stone and

iron and wood and its potential strengths and weaknesses, the latter,

sadly, being all too few. Soon, the two sailors began to form a plan,

though even they admitted it was a desperate, implausible scheme with

little hope for success.

For the first few days, the knights left the prisoners alone except to

bring them their meals. On the third day, Arabella asked one of the

guards if what the Grand Master had said was true, that she and Captain

Roderick would be 'questioned' by the inquisitors. The knight smiled

coldly and told her it would happen soon, once they had finished their

interviews with the witnesses and any others who were able to give

testimony against them. Soon, he said, she would be taken across the

lane to that dark, windowless keep, and may God have mercy on her

soul when that happened, for her interrogators certainly would not. The

next day, the guards came for her.

The rain poured from the sky in buckets and the wind screamed as

the knights, including the grim-faced Pierre-Louis, marched Arabella

and Bartholomew in irons out into the courtyard. Despite the hour

being nearly noon, the day was as dark as night, as if the sun refused to

allow any of its light to reach the world below. Arabella held her head high, ignoring the stinging rain as she marched purposefully across the muddy ground. It took every ounce of strength and willpower she possessed, however, to keep from collapsing or turning and trying to flee back into the fortress. She was strong, she knew, and had faced many dangers and challenges, but this would be different. The inquisitors were experts in pain and would not stop until she begged them to accept her confession for attacking the Maltese ships, and any other crime they wanted. She stole a quick glance at Captain Roderick and saw that he was not holding up nearly as well as she. His face had a very gray-green pallor, looking as if he would be sick at any moment. Perhaps he already had. His knees buckled with almost every other step and his guards, one on either side, supported more than restrained him. But then, he had been through something similar before, in Spain, and knew better than she what was coming. The four knights escorted the prisoners across the sodden courtyard to the massive iron gate. Six more knights awaited the little group at the portcullis, two within and four without. The inner guards unlocked the heavy door and swung it open, letting the two prisoners and their escort pass and join the others before slamming the gate shut once more.

As the procession stepped into the muddy lane to cross to the Inquisitors Keep, the green grasses lining the road around them rose skyward, as if fantastically come alive. Thirty tall, misshapen towers of brown mud, green leaves, grasses and creepers emerged from the earth, ringing the knights. One stepped forward, sloughing off its frondescent coat to reveal a human underneath, albeit one only slightly less shaggy and mud-covered than before. He held a sword in his hand.

"Stand and deliver, lads!" Liam McNamara barked, waving his blade before him. "We are relieving you of your prisoners. You will offer no resistance if you know what is good for you!" A look of stunned incredulity came over the face of each knight. Each knight hesitated for but a moment before, almost as one, they drew their swords, the rasping steel ringing through the air as the eight heavy blades appeared. The remaining ambushers immediately cast off their cloaks of shredded hemp and sackcloth, heavily-adorned with mud and vegetation, so they too could draw steel. The two fortress guards, locked behind their gate, turned and raced back toward the fort, clearly to fetch more guards. Pierre-Louis took a step toward Liam. "You look a right dangerous swordsman, and I would hate to face you in fair fight," the Irishman told him, sliding his cutlass back into his sheath. "Which is why I brought these." He drew two pistols from his belt, cocked them and pointed both straight at the Frenchman's chest. The knight stopped. Several more pistols appeared in the hands of the other ambushers, each of them pointing at the guards. "Time is short, gentlemen," Liam continued. "We have no desire to kill you, but rest assured, we will burn every one of you down if we have to. The prisoners, now!"

Pierre-Louis looked the captain in the eye. He saw only cold resolve there and knew the man made no hollow threat. He sheathed his sword and indicated his comrades should do the same. He produced a ring of iron keys and quickly unlocked Arabella and Bartholomew's shackles. "Have them, then," he said, pushing the prisoners toward their mates. The pirates collected them and quickly led them away. "You will never get off this island, monsieur. They will soon be back behind the walls of this fortress, and you will be with them!"

"Then you will not hold it against me if I ask that you do not pursue us right away so I may enjoy my momentary freedom," Liam said. "In fact, I insist upon it unless you wish to sacrifice your life foolishly." At that, he turned and raced after the fleeing group. Two large hay wagons waited a short distance away. The fugitives leapt into the carts and the drivers cracked their whips, urging the horses into a gallop. A short time later, the two carts stopped at a crossroads. "You know the plan, men," he called. "Jump to!"

Everyone disembarked save Liam, Bartholomew, Arabella and the two wagon drivers. The other sea dogs put on fresh clothes and split up into several small groups. They stepped briskly toward different villages spread all across Malta. The drivers cracked their whips and the heavy carts began moving again, the empty one following the road leading toward the southernmost point of the island while the other headed straight toward Valletta.

"Jesus and Mary bless you, Liam McNamara!" Arabella cried, giving the Irishman a fat kiss on the lips. Liam, at first stunned, quickly reciprocated. She pushed him away. "That was a 'thank you,' captain, not a marriage proposal," she told him.

"I shall not kiss you," Captain Roderick told him stiffly. "Though you also have my thanks."

"You are both very welcome," he told them sincerely.

Arabella opened her mouth to ask him what his plan was when thunder rolled over them. She looked to the sky and heard it again. The roar repeated itself and she realized it was not thunder at all but the roar of cannon fire, coming from the direction of Fort St. Angelo.

"Dear God! Are they firing at us?" she asked.

"Nay, Ara," Liam answered with a grim smile. "They are no doubt firing at Molly and some of our lads rescuing *The Thistle* and *Greyhound* from their captivity in the docks below the fort."

"They mean to sail them in this weather? Is it safe?" Bartholomew asked.

"Not at all. But we will need those ships before long, and if we do not take them now we will forever lose the opportunity. Thankfully, they do not have a great distance to travel. They, as well as *The Raven* and the rest of my crew, are bound for a small island just to the northwest of this one. I have learned of a sheltered cove on her lee side just deep enough to safely hold ships such as ours. Apparently, there are no villages nearby, so is quite possible their arrival and presence there will go completely unnoticed — assuming, of course, they get there." Liam cast an apprehensive glance at the iron sky, "The sea is a right nasty bitch today and I fear for them all, to be sure."

"And what of us?" Bartholomew asked. "Should we not be on those ships as well?"

"I wish we could, despite the peril. But no, they cannot sit off shore and wait for us while those forts pound away at them and the Order mans their war galleys to give chase. No, they must race straight for the open seas where the tide and wind will carry them quickly away from Malta. As for us, I regret we must remain on this rock for a little while longer."

"But they will be searching for us!" the Welshman protested. "It is not safe to remain here!"

"Nor can we leave," Liam growled, "Unless you are hiding a galleon up your arse that you have failed to tell us about, Barty. But do not worry; I know of a place we can hide. And speaking of hiding, you best crawl under here with me for the rest of the trip." Liam pushed some of the hay at the bottom of the cart aside to reveal a concealed door. He lifted it and Arabella and Bartholomew saw a narrow, coffin-like space under a false floor.

"Where the hell are you taking us?" Bartholomew asked, eyeing the crawlspace suspiciously.

"Tarry not, fool! We are even now approaching the city gates," Liam told him, disappearing into the hole. After a moment's hesitation, Arabella followed him. With a heavy sigh and a shake of his head, Bartholomew joined them.

The wagon stopped briefly at the entrance to Valletta while her driver chatted with the guards. Though concerned about the distant cannon fire from across the bay, no word had yet reached them regarding the prisoners' escape. As such, they gave the cart only a cursory glance before waving it through. The cart clopped and clattered across the stones for several minutes before stopping again. The hatch over their hiding place opened and they saw sky once more, though only a narrow, gray strip between the buildings of the alley in which they found themselves.

"Quickly, now," Liam urged, crawling out of the cubbyhole and helping the others out as well. Their feet had no sooner hit the ground than the wagon shot forward again, moving quickly back toward the city gates.

Liam led them to a steep stairwell cut directly into the street and leading into the basement of one of the buildings. The dark little passage ended after a few feet at a stout wooden door bound in iron. The portal stood open, though more than this Arabella could not see in the inky darkness beyond. She nearly jumped when she heard a female voice from within.

"Follow me," the woman whispered, lifting the cover on a hooded lantern just enough to allow those behind to see their way.

Liam closed and bolted the door as he passed, and the woman led the small group for some distance through the low, narrow passage. She eventually stopped at another heavy wooden door. She pushed this open to reveal a small root cellar, and beyond this, what appeared to be a room for aging wine. A ladder led from the first room to a hatch in the ceiling. The woman lifted the shield on her lantern higher and allowed the light to shine completely. Arabella gasped.

"Sister Marie Elise!" Arabella rushed forward to embrace her savior, but the sister stopped her with an uplifted hand. The nun reached into her habit and pulled out a large, silver cross.

"I told your friend I would help you," she said sternly. "But my help is conditional. Tell me you did not do this foul deed you have been accused of. Swear it upon this cross."

Arabella took the holy object in her hands without hesitation and knelt before the sister, looking up into her eyes. "I swear in the name of Christ I had no hand in the attack upon the Knights' vessels. Please believe me, sister."

"I do. I do!" Sister Marie Elise said, smiling now as she pulled Arabella to her feet and embraced her. "I am sorry I ever doubted you. You will be safe here for as long as you need. Nobody but our order knows these rooms exist."

"Not even the knights?" Bartholomew asked.

"No. Although we love our brothers, we trust them only slightly more than the Turks," she said with a smile.

"You will not get in trouble for this?" Arabella asked.

"No, it is fine. The mother superior is aware of the situation and I have her full support. She asks - or rather, insists - only that the men stay in one room and you remain in the other. There is food and water here already and I will bring more when I can. Oh, and messieurs, we have counted the wine bottles and measured the casks." She said nothing more, but turned and climbed the ladder.

"Thank you, sister," Arabella called to her. "And God bless."

She disappeared from sight and the hatch concealing their hiding place closed with a heavy thud. Liam stared at it for a moment before moving to inspect the food their host had left them.

"That is the second time of late you have risked your safety, even your life, to save mine," Captain Roderick said in a hesitant voice, as if the words pained him. "The first time, with the corsair galley, I was suspicious of your motives, convinced you had only done so for profit."

"You believe otherwise now?" Liam asked, looking at the man.

"Over the last several days, I have had many hours to reflect upon a lot of things. It occurred to me that, regardless of your motives, you faced a tremendous risk taking on that galley, which was near twice your size and carried more men. And I think you knew you would receive but a small share of the proceeds, while the *Greyhound* and *Thistle* claimed the lion's share. It further occurred to me you could just as easily stayed out of the fight entirely and waited until all three ships had battered ourselves into bloody splinters, then swooped in and had your way with whoever remained."

"And how do you know I was not only interested in saving fair Arabella here, as opposed to your ugly hide?" the Irishman asked with a grin.

"She was not the one in mortal danger when you attacked; I was. And now we come to today, where even a fool can see there was no profit in your actions, lest not the kind you can spend in a tavern. And sure, I do not know if you would have risked all if only I and not Arabella had been in those dungeons, but I would like to think so. And yet…"

"Still chewing on Spain, are you?" Liam asked.

"Do you deny that you abandoned me to face three Spanish galleons alone, and after the gold we had taken had been put aboard *your* vessel?"

"I will concede that you were abandoned to a terrible fate, Bartholomew, but you must know it was not my decision."

"Were you not the master of your own ship?" the Welshman asked.

"For all of about five minutes after that gold came aboard. I saw those galleons surrounding you and knew *The Greyhound* could not hope to escape. I gave the order to come to your aid, all guns blazing and damn the consequences. Three ships or three hundred, I had no intention of abandoning you. My crew, on the other hand, felt differently. We had the gold, they said, and those ships were focused on you while we were clear of the action and had the wind at our backs. They had already decided the matter, you see, and I could either go along with them or fight them. Well, one should never give that choice to an Irishman, for we are stubborn and will always choose the fightin'. I think I cut down three of them before the rest got me in a rush. Somebody broke a belaying pin over my noggin, and the next thing I remember was waking up in the water. I swam for the shore and reached it just in time to see my *Raven* sailing away."

"Christ, man!" Bartholomew exclaimed. "In faith?"

"As God is my witness, friend."

"Curse me! I have been a fool to judge you so foully and ever deny you the chance to explain all to me!" the Welshman cried. "Can you ever forgive me?"

"Sure'n you are already forgiven, mate. You could not have known."

"And yet you once more captain *The Raven*," Arabella said. "Might I inquire as to how you won her back?"

"Violently," Liam said. He wore a smile, but his eyes were cold. He said nothing more.

The three captains remained in hiding for more than a month. At one point, Liam told Arabella and Bartholomew what the captain of the *Phoenix* had said about Duncan being on Malta, and all agreed it was simply a ruse to lure them into the hands of the Grand Master. Sister Marie Elise brought them what news she could, including word that several bodies had washed ashore some days after *The Thistle, Raven* and *Greyhound* had fled Malta, accompanied by a good deal of wreckage. She also informed them the knights had found the wagons used in the escape abandoned on the beach the very next day, along with the shattered remains of several oarboats. Although no bodies were found with them, most were of the opinion that the fleeing prisoners had not survived the journey beyond the breakers, and their bones would likely wash up only with the spring tides. The Order announced the end of their search for the outlaws on Malta, but made clear that once the weather permitted, their ships would go far and wide in an effort to try to confirm their fate.

Arabella, Liam and Bartholomew remained sequestered in their dark cellar for several more weeks due to the weather. Finally, the winds and waves calmed enough for them to make the trip. They left the town the same way they had entered, hiding beneath the floor of a hay wagon. The sisters loaded this one with Sacramental wine and other items used by the little churches and chapels spread throughout the island. It was a common journey for them, and the knights waved them through the city gates with hardly a glance. The fugitives traveled north and reached the shire of Mellieha near dusk. On the far side of the town, they found a longboat and a smiling Molly MacBain awaiting them. She told them all three of the ships had reached the nearby island of Gozo and its safe harbor, though they had suffered a great deal of damage and had lost several hands. The privateers remained on Gozo throughout the harsh winter, living off their ships' stores and adding to this fresh-caught fish and what fruits, vegetables and game they could find in the uninhabited parts of the island. They kept look-outs on watch at all times and their cannons at the ready, expecting any moment to see a flotilla of Maltese war galleys sailing into the cove.

The crews remained undiscovered the entire time they stayed on the tiny island, though it was May before the seas settled enough for them to safely leave. They wasted no time putting Malta and the Knights of Jerusalem in their wake. They sailed directly to the port city of Gela on the island of Sicily, a journey of but two days. They remained only a short time, just long enough to replenish their stores and bring aboard certain other supplies and material they needed for a longer voyage. The ships set sail once more, this time for Cartagena. Arabella announced that she intended to return to Scotland as soon as possible, to see her father and, hopefully, find Duncan there. Both captains told her they would accompany her — purely to ensure her safety, of course.

The three ships sailed in consort from Gela and soon reached Spain. Still under a death sentence there, Captain McNamara kept *The Raven* outside the harbor while Arabella and Bartholomew entered and took on fresh water. Arabella also collected her gold from the various banks and moneylenders where she had deposited it. Luckily, they had reached Cartagena before any Maltese ships carrying news of them, though surely this would happen soon and any of her accounts would be ordered seized. The amount she now retrieved was sizable indeed, despite the amount of gold she had spent keeping *The Thistle* in food and drink and powder and timber during her voyages. Duncan's share alone filled three heavy chests. Regardless of what the future held in store for them, whether it be marriage or not, she meant to make sure he received his due. And he would need it she knew, for if he was indeed ransomed, it had not come cheaply.

Many days later, *The Thistle*, *The Raven* and the *Greyhound* passed through the Pillars of Hercules and entered the Atlantic. A vast stretch of ocean separated Arabella from her home. Still, she meant to be there in time to help her father bring in the fall crops.

23

The late summer sun beat down cruelly on Sir William's bare back. He stood in his fields and beat at the hard soil with a pick to dig a new irrigation ditch. The knight stood alone, having no one else in his employ these days to do such work. Grunting with the effort, he did not hear the approaching horses until they were nearly upon him. He spun about, pickaxe in hand, and saw five men approaching. They were elegantly dressed, though the lead rider was much more so. As the men drew near, William recognized with a shock that James Stewart, the Earl of Arran, was at their fore, accompanied by his men-at-arms.

"Thou idle lay-abouts could learn a few lessons from Sir William," James said to the riders with him. "A man of his advanced age, working his own fields. Truly, it is inspiring!"

The earl's fellows laughed heartily. William stewed, the heat of the day seeming to grow by the second.

"I see you still have not learned that gentlemen do not laugh at the misfortune of others," William said. "Though of course, you never were a gentleman. What do you want?"

"Have some respect, old gaffer!" one of the knights growled, moving his horse closer. William raised his pick a little higher.

"Stay, Jonathan," the earl said. "He cannot help it. All Highlanders are little more than uncivilized savages to begin with, and Sir William here has the added angst of his daughter's loss to addle his wits."

William gripped his pick so tightly his knuckles turned white. "Again, what do you want?"

"Why, to help you, of course."

"Oh, come to drown yourself in me well then?"

Two more knights moved forward but James stopped them with an upraised hand.

"Clever. No, actually, I have heard of your struggles to raise your dear daughter's ransom and, as a father myself, my heart weeps for you and your situation." One of the knights failed to suppress a snicker and the earl shot him a withering glare before continuing. "As one of my subjects, I want only to help you. And in return, you can help me."

"Oh? How so?"

"I know you were close to the Ruthven Rebels, though I could never prove it. I can only assume the situation has not changed. As such, you may have heard something that would assist me in locating and bringing to justice the traitors who fled from me at Stirling Castle, Earls Mar and Angus."

"Hah! What makes you think I would tell you a damned thing? Not that I know anything, of course."

"Because I am not a fool, William. I know how desperately you need money to ransom your daughter. If you help me, I will see that you get it."

"As I said, I have no information on the men you speak of. Besides, I am raising her ransom just fine. Good day." William turned his back on them and returned to his digging.

"As I can see," the earl said. William said nothing, though he stopped working to listen. "It is a shame how dry these fields get in the summer. The least spark can set them ablaze and cause all to be lost." William heard the unmistakable sound of flint and tinder being struck and he spun about. One of the knights held a glass and tin oil lamp in his hand, its wick flaming brightly even in the sunlight. "Oh, have you remembered something, then?" James asked.

Sir William stared at the burning lantern for a long moment. "No," he croaked finally. "Sure'n I have not heard anything worth repeating."

"Pity," the earl spoke. His man hurled the lamp.

"No!" William shouted, dropping his pick and rushing into the field. The fragile lantern smashed to the ground before he reached it, splattering its flaming contents over the dry stalks. Flames erupted at once.

The earl and his men had already turned their horses about and were racing away. "You know how to contact me if you happen to remember something, William!" Arran called to him. "Today was but a gentle warning. I have other sources and will discover what I need without you if I must. And if I learn you have been false with me this day, or have aided the rebels in any way, I promise you that you will hang alongside them!"

Sir William cursed the man at the top of his lungs. The fire spread rapidly. His crops were lost and he knew it. He turned and ran down the trail back toward *Ban Tigh*. The old knight spent a long, exhausting night fighting the flames and embers that constantly menaced his home. A narrow swath of green grass lay between the fields and the manor, and this proved its salvation. Still, his crops were laid waste and most of his remaining animals had either run off or been destroyed by the inferno. As the morning sun rose over the charred ruin that was once his livelihood, Sir William collapsed on the grass, sobbing until merciful sleep finally took him.

***

Some days later, a messenger arrived at *Ban Tigh*. He looked about the destruction of the farm and the charred outbuildings and smoke-blackened manor and almost forgot why he had come. Sir William, standing at the open door, had to twice clear his throat loudly before the lad finally handed him the folded, wax-sealed letter. William gave him a few coins and the youth handed them back.

"Keep them for your master," he said. "Looks like he needs them more than I." The kid turned and trotted off down the lane, singing Four-and-Twenty Blackbirds with lyrics to make a sailor blush.

William opened the envelope and read its contents. He had recognized the handwriting already as belonging to the kidnappers. The letter started by berating him for the amount of time he was taking to raise Arabella's ransom, mentioning the great expense it took to provide for her and how this sum was being added daily to her ransom. The letter next spoke of the pirates' failing patience and how something 'unfortunate' might happen to her if payment was not received soon.

Lastly, it carried a new ransom amount, this one a full fifty percent greater than their original demand. Sir William wept once more.

The first thing next morn, he sat at his desk before a blank piece of parchment, inked quill in hand. He sat unmoving for over an hour, unsure of whether to address his missive to the Earl of Arran or the Edinburgh investors. Finally, he wrote to Edinburgh, asking the businessmen to come to *Ban Tigh* at their convenience to assess its value, along with all its contents.

Many days later, the agents arrived. They inspected his house, the furnishings and the few minor works of art William possessed, mostly portraits of long-dead relatives. A lot of 'tsk-tsking' and head shaking accompanied their otherwise silent task. At the conclusion of the tour, they provided him with their estimate. The old knight felt it shamefully low but noted it would cover the ransom, even if just barely. He told the men he needed to think about it for a few days and they told him their offer was good for one week only, at which time it would either be withdrawn or substantially reduced. They would return for his answer then.

Five days after this meeting, another messenger arrived. Sir William bristled. Why had the land agents not given him the full seven days, he wondered, and why had they not come in person? Was *Ban Tigh* worth so little to them? He accepted the scroll and unfurled it, hating himself for knowing he was about to sign away the last of his family lands and possessions. The scroll, however, was not a legal contract for the purchase of *Ban Tigh*, but was in fact its salvation. The first sheet contained a note from Earl Mar telling William he had heard of the knight's great loyalty to him and his cause when confronted by the Earl of Arran. How he had heard of this encounter was not mentioned. The letter continued that, as a token of his gratitude, he had authorized a loan to be made to Sir William at once in an amount nearly double what the Edinburgh agents had just offered him for *Ban Tigh*. The second sheet of parchment was a legal writ containing the details of the loan, drawn on the earl's accounts in London and redeemable at any goldsmith-banker in Scotland.

That very day, Sir William wrote a letter to Lord Campbell informing the young man of his extraordinary news. He had but to collect the money, contact the kidnapper's agent in Edinburgh and then await his daughter's safe return. Sir William splurged and paid to have his message delivered by a fast horse as opposed to a swift boy. Three days after this, he received Duncan's reply. The letter expressed his ineffable delight at William's good fortune, giving thanks to God and

Mary and all the saints in Heaven. He begged to be allowed to accompany William on his trip to Edinburgh, where he would gladly stay with the old knight to attend him until Arabella returned. In addition, Duncan would bring several men-at-arms as protection during the journey and when they made the ransom transaction. Sir William was to reply as soon as possible so the thane could begin making the necessary arrangements. William had secretly hoped as much, for he had no desire to travel back to Edinburgh alone, especially on such a dangerous road. And the company of the thane, a young man well known to be very adept with a blade, would be as welcome as any two men-at-arms. William delivered his reply in person to Cawdor Castle. Duncan, surprised but overjoyed, immediately began making preparations.

One week later, Sir William and Thane Campbell stood waiting to board a ship at the very port in Nairn where they had walked onto *The Thistle* more than a year ago.

"Really, my good man, another ship?" William asked, trying to look as if he did not think it a terribly good idea. He may not have pulled it off convincingly though, as his old bones were already quite stiff and he in fact welcomed a leisurely boat ride instead of many more days in the saddle.

"'Twas an opportunity I could not pass up, one of most fortuitous luck," Duncan told him as they clambered aboard. "A business acquaintance of mine had need to take this vessel to Edinburgh and was set to depart Nairn when he heard of my need for swift transportation. As a favor to me, he has delayed here just for us."

"I trust she is more heavily-armed than that rig of your father's, may God rest his soul."

"She is exceptionally well-armed, William, so do please put your mind to rest on that account."

Sir William looked about the decks and saw the ship fairly bristled with cannons both large and small. And her crew looked to be hard men all. Satisfied, William let his friend lead him below decks for a game of cards.

The two men disembarked six days later in Edinburgh, delayed slightly by stubborn winds. Sir William followed the instructions provided him by Arabella's captors and left word of his arrival in the half-dozen named taverns. He then contacted a local goldsmith-banker and withdrew the necessary funds. He and Duncan finally proceeded to a seventh pub as directed and waited, Duncan's four men-at-arms ever close. A few hours later, a messenger approached and handed William a note bearing his final instructions. He was to proceed at once to an old church not far from the docks, the building in disrepair and no longer used for services. The note stated he was free to bring his 'armed escort,' but must not attempt to double-cross the kidnappers if he ever hoped to see his daughter alive again.

Sir William, Duncan and the swordsmen immediately traveled to the ancient parish church, its roof gone and its walls crumbling. It appeared deserted. Finally, Duncan spotted the soft glow of a lantern within. The men entered the building, holding before them their own lamps. William's heart pounded in his chest, not from fear but from the joy he felt at the prospect of being reunited with his daughter once more. A man stood in the nave, close to the light but not so close he could be recognized. He appeared to be alone, but William doubted this was the case. The old knight felt a tinge of recognition and squinted into the darkness, trying to discern the man's features. *Was it that devil Spotiswoode?* he wondered. As Duncan and Sir William entered the gentle orb of light, the man stepped forward. Sir William recognized him now, though it was not who he expected.

"Welcome to Edinburgh, Sir William," the Earl of Arran said, though his smile was anything but welcoming. William was too stunned to respond, so he continued. "You seem surprised, old soul. Were you expecting someone else: your daughter perhaps?" The earl laughed, as did Duncan, oddly. William turned to his friend and saw the same smile as the earl's, the grin of a wolf that has just brought down its prey and is preparing to feast. "Did he bring the ransom, Duncan?"

"Aye, milord. Every shilling of it," Thane Campbell answered.

"Excellent. You should have accepted my offer when you had the chance, William," the earl told the stunned knight. "You would have saved your money and your lands. As it is, you will not now even save your life. Take him."

The four swordsmen Duncan had brought stepped forward, two of them seizing William and the other two disarming him and placing shackles about his wrists and ankles.

"You scheming, black-hearted son of a whore!" William exclaimed, finding his voice at last. "You were behind the kidnapping! Spotiswoode was working for you!"

"That is a shilling to you, Duncan," the earl said. "I did not think you clever enough to figure that out, William. Now, lest you mistakenly think this but another act of piracy against your person, know this: by my Royal authority, I am placing you under arrest for the act of treason against Scotland and her king. Witnesses have come forward who will confirm that you recently met with the rebels Mar and Angus in the Border Marches."

"Witnesses? You mean spies and traitors!" William spat.

"Patriots!" James shot back. "Men who know where their true loyalties should lie and who are not so stubborn or ignorant as you. Men such as Lord Campbell here. As soon as your trial is concluded - a mere formality, I assure you - he shall be the new master of *Ban Tigh* and the Fraser lands."

"Gramercy, my lord," Duncan said with a bow. "Attaining them through royal seizure is so much more profitable than purchasing them through an anonymous 'investor's group.'"

Both men laughed as William fumed, still restrained by the guards. "You were behind the land agents as well?"

"Aye, though actually it was Duncan's idea. He is quite a crafty lad. You see, he had first come to me shortly after the Ruthven Raid to sell me information about the conspirators, many of whom were good friends of his father. His information was most useful and helped send many of them to their death. When I told him it was his father's head that I really wanted, he surprised me by offering not only him but his brother Colin as well, so long as he was allowed to keep the Campbell title and lands. So much for filial piety," the earl said with a laugh.

"Regrettably, Lord Campbell proved a most cautious and clever foe, never giving me enough evidence to move against him directly. And then came Duncan's master stroke of brilliance: he would woo your daughter and win her hand in marriage, with a convenient trip to France for the ceremony. The idea to use pirates to murder both elder Campbells en route most impressed me. I have not seen one so ruthless since, well, myself!"

"So depraved, you mean!" Sir William said.

"Which brings me to the Frasers," the earl continued. "Originally, the plan was to simply kidnap Arabella to squeeze enough ransom from you to ruin you, using the phony investor's group to purchase your lands at a fraction of their worth. But then dear Duncan met my daughter Alexandria."

"What does she have to do with this?" William asked.

"Now William, you cannot admit that she is most fair, so much more so than that daughter of yours," the earl said.

"And it does not hurt that her father is the most powerful man in Scotland, while you are little more than a penniless peasant, William," Duncan interjected.

"Ever the cunning player," the earl said. "Well, at this point, the plan was altered slightly to ensure that Arabella would never be returned from her captors, but would instead be sold into slavery along the Barbary Coast. It was quite ingenious, really. With one stroke, I would eliminate three traitors and gain a loyal subject with estates cutting through the heart of the Highlands. In addition, we would both share in the fees paid by the Muslim slavers for the prisoners *and* collect any ransoms paid by you and the other families. It was absolutely brilliant."

"'Twas despicable! Cowards and curs you both are!" William cursed.

"And the plan has, for the most part, gone off exceptionally well," James continued. "To be sure, there was a bit of a mix up concerning upon which ship my daughter should have been placed, though this was quickly dealt with. The one thing we sadly failed to account for was the God-awful pigheadedness that seems to infect every one of you damned Frasers. I do not know who is worse: you for holding on to your pathetic estates for so long, or your daughter for somehow freeing herself from Captain Boggs before the drunken idiot could sell her to the Turks."

"You have no idea how hard it was to keep that information from you," Duncan added. "Thank God her first letter came through Cawdor on its way to you and my man had the foresight to seize it."

"You mean to tell me my daughter is free?"

"Sadly, no," Duncan told him. "She *was* free. You see, she had the graciousness to remain in the Mediterranean and, God love her, acquire a ship to search for me, believing that I, like her, had also been transported to the Barbary Coast. Once I returned home and learned she was free, I sent Captain Spotiswoode right back to find her. And while this proved challenging to say the least, we eventually managed to make certain she would never set foot on Scottish soil again. I dare say she is even now either still rotting in a Maltese dungeon for the charge of piracy, or else they have hanged her already. So sorry, William."

"God no!" the old knight said.

"I promised you, William," James said. "That you would hang alongside Mar and Angus, and that is one promise I intend to keep."

"Well then, if that is my fate than I shall prepare for a very long life in your dungeons," Sir William told him defiantly. "For certes you will never capture those good earls and their followers, even with all your accursed spies."

The Earl of Arran and Duncan laughed again, cooling Sir William's confidence.

"That may have been true if the traitors had been wise enough to remain hidden in the Marches or in England, beyond my reach. But I have learned they intend to unite their pitiful band of drunken rebels with another traitor hiding in the Borders, one with his own band of curs and cowards. Once their two groups become one, I have it on good authority they mean to march north to challenge me directly!" James said with a laugh. "And though I have no fear of facing the rebels united, it will be so much easier to destroy their forces separately, before they rendezvous. And thanks to my informants, I know exactly the route they are taking, and young Lord Campbell and my forces will be waiting for them."

"Burn in hell!" Sir William said. "Both of you!"

"You first, William," the earl said quietly. "You first."

24

The Thistle, Raven and *Greyhound* entered the broad Atlantic and

turned north into the *Gulfo de Cadiz* along the southwestern coast of

Spain. As they sailed up the coast, they found their Spanish Letters of

Marque served them well, for it seemed they could not go a day

without being stopped and boarded by that nation's gunships. Arabella

and Bartholomew managed to divert careful inspection of Captain

McNamara and *The Raven* on several occasions, owing to their own

legitimacy and the fact he sailed in consort with them. In a few

instances, however, the only thing that saved the Irishman from a dance

with the rope were his forged identification papers and the fact that

they had been expertly crafted. The ships turned west at Huelva and north again at Cabo de Sao Vicente on the extreme southwestern tip of Portugal. Here, southerly winds reduced their speed to a crawl. In addition, violent storms frequently chased them into ports along the coast and kept them bottled up for days on end.

The warm days of summer passed and it was mid-autumn before they finally reached England's shores. Another fortnight found them in the waters near Berwick-upon-Tweed, where Arabella had last seen her father and Duncan so very long ago. As *The Thistle* sailed slowly past Sharper's Head, she stood on the deck and had Mister Browne fire the guns in salute of her brother and the slain Campbell men. Late the next day, they turned west into the Firth of Forth and toward Edinburgh, where they would port and spend the night before resuming the last leg of their journey. Because *The Raven* had on occasion operated in these waters in a less-than-legal status, her captain suggested the ships not berth at the Port of Leith in Edinburgh proper, but rather a bit south and east of there. The docks at Fisherrow Sands in Musselburgh, on the mouth of the River Esk, should serve them just as well, he said. Arabella agreed and the three ships steered toward this port just as the last rays of the sun sank below the Lammermuir Hills.

After porting, the three captains decided to stretch their legs and take a meal in town. They walked to a nearby inn and had no sooner stepped inside when Captain McNamara gasped and ducked into the shadows, dragging Arabella and Bartholomew with him.

"What the-"

"Shh! That man," Liam said, pointing to a fellow at the bar having a pint. "I recognize him. He was a sailor on the *Phoenix*!"

"You mean the ship that sacked the Maltese vessels and blamed it on *The Thistle*?" Arabella asked.

"The very one."

"Are you certain you recognize him as belonging to that ship?" Bartholomew asked.

"I am; I marked well many of their officers and hands in the various ports we shared as they chased you across the Mediterranean."

"Do you think the *Phoenix* is here as well?" Arabella asked.

"I think it is worth taking a look in the harbor at Leith, for sure," Liam answered.

"I agree," Arabella said through clenched teeth. "And if we find her there, I shall fetch my *Thistle* and send her to the briny deep!"

"That's my girl," Liam said. "Now let us step over to Leith and have a look about."

The three departed the building and turned north; Leith was but a few miles away. Their hunger left them, replaced by a cold desire to settle a score with those who had wronged them. Sometime later, they reached the harbor's southwest end, each surveying the masts of the tall ships peeking over the waterfront. As they rounded the corner of a large warehouse, both Liam and Arabella stopped short.

"The *Phoenix*!" Liam cried.

"The *Sea Rover*!" Arabella said.

"What?" Liam asked. "Where?"

"That ship," she said, pointing to it.

"No, that is the *Phoenix*. I know her."

"And I know Goddamned well the ship that took my Duncan from me, and that is her! And if she is here, likely so too will be her captain, the man who murdered in cold blood Lord Campbell and his eldest son."

"Wait. Describe her captain," Bartholomew said to Arabella. She did and Liam announced that was the very man who captained the *Phoenix*.

"By God, the two ships are one and the same!" Liam said.

"Then our mission has changed," Arabella said. "We may yet send this brig to the bottom of the harbor, but I will settle with her captain first."

"We need to know if he is aboard, then," Liam said.

"Give me but a moment," Bartholomew replied, setting off toward the ship. He strolled up its gangplank and was met by one of the hands standing guard. A few minutes and a few coins later, he returned. "The captain is staying at Lauriston Castle, just this side of the borough of Cramond."

"That is west of here," Arabella said. She turned and began walking in that direction at once.

"Have we any semblance of a plan?" Liam asked as he and Bartholomew joined her.

"My plan is to give the man the killing he deserves, then return to my ship and send his to the bottom of the firth."

"Did you not hear ol' Barty? The captain is in a castle. How will we get to him?"

"Castles are meant to defend against armies, and only then when they are expecting a siege and have their defenses up. We should have little trouble slipping in if we do so quietly."

"And what if they have guards or dogs or both?" Bartholomew asked.

"Then you may have to create a little diversion," Arabella stated.

The trio soon left the docks behind. They walked through the gloom the short distance to the grand tower house known as Lauriston

Castle, surrounded by acres of fenced parkland. The captains made a fast trip around the perimeter, confirming the presence of a guardhouse at the front gate and at least two large mastiffs prowling the yard. After but a moment's conference over their plan, the two men left Arabella alone at the rear of the property as they walked around to the front.

Once there, Liam and Bartholomew began singing loudly and holding each other as if for support as they staggered down the lane near the stone fence. Liam rapped his belaying pin loudly on the rock wall surrounding the property as he walked. Soon, he heard dogs barking from the other side. Arabella watched from atop the wall as the dogs raced from the rear of the property. She dropped down from the wall into the yard and sprinted across the vast lawn, darting from tree to tree as she moved closer to the manor house. In the distance, she heard the dogs barking and Liam and Bartholomew loudly singing. In moments she stood before the first of many windows dotting the manor's rear façade. The third one she tried opened to her touch. A quick glance inside showed it to be a study or library, currently unoccupied. Light glowed softly from a nearby room, peeking in through the far doorway. Arabella climbed inside silently, sword in hand. She heard voices coming from the next room, though she could not make out the words over the crackle of a fire in the hearth. She padded to the far door, slightly ajar, and pressed her ear to the crack.

"This would be easier if we still had Boggs and *The Thistle*," a man spoke.

Arabella recognized the voice at once as belonging to Captain Spotiswoode. Her blood went cold and she tightened the grip on her cutlass.

"The earl assures me the ships we have shall be enough to handle the rebels," another voice responded. "We have twice their guns, greater maneuverability and of course, the element of surprise."

Arabella recognized this voice as well, her heart nearly stopping: it was Duncan Campbell!

"Easy for him to say. The earl will not be with us and thus his arse will not be on the line at Redshin; ours will. We should have more ships," Spotiswoode said. "Or at least more gold."

"Damn your greed, man," Duncan chuckled. "You are beginning to sound like my Alex."

"Do not talk about me as if I am not even in the room," a female voice said. Arabella's surprise turned into stunned incredulity now, for that voice belonged to a dead woman. "I still have not forgiven either of you for leaving me stuck in that damned, stinking hold aboard *The Thistle* for all those days. I nearly died!"

"I had nothing to do with that, dearest," Duncan protested. "'Twas Spottiswoode's fault."

"To hell it was," he said. "It was that fat, drunken bastard Boggs' doing!"

"How convenient; the only one to blame is a dead man. Well, there may yet be another dead man – or two," Alexandria said, glaring first at Spottiswoode and then Duncan, "if you two idiots continue to make similar mistakes."

"I assure you, there will be no more mistakes," Duncan said.

"See to it there are not if you ever want daddy to make you a viscount," Alexandria said. "I cannot keep saving the both of you from your own ineptitude."

"My ineptitude?" Spotiswoode said, bristling. "I am the one that-"

"That let that bitch Arabella elude you for so long, until I agreed to dye my beautiful blond hair that disgusting shade of red. I saved your mission from utter failure with those red tresses, they and my most-convincing acting at playing *Captain* Arabella Fraser."

Spottiswoode opened his mouth to say more but Duncan cut him off. "Of course you are correct, my sweetest - as usual. And James, how can you ask for more gold for our upcoming task? Surely you could not have spent your portion of the gold we procured from Sir

William before the earl carted him off to Stirling! By Mary, 'twas but a day ago we acquired it."

"Course not," the man answered. "Though I noticed your share was bigger than mine despite it being me who has been taking the risks and doing most of the nasty work all these months."

"Pish posh," Duncan said. "By my benevolence, you have been made a wealthy man, and you stand to prosper still more in the near future. Quit your grousing and enjoy this moment of peace and tranquility before the coming storm."

Arabella could not believe her ears. Was this madness, or some crazy, terrible dream? Her head swam as she tried to comprehend what she was hearing.

"I for one shall be glad when all of this is over and daddy hangs the old knight along with Mar and Angus," Alexandria said. "I do so love a hanging; I hope we can be there to watch it. I only wish you could have been more competent and had captured Arabella so she could swing next to her father."

"Oh, get off it, already," Spotiswoode protested. "You was out there, you know how slippery she was. Still, we took care of her, we did, took care of her real good. Nay, we will not see the likes of her again."

Arabella had heard enough - more than enough, in fact. She swung the door open and stepped into the room. "I beg to disagree."

The look of shock on their faces would have been laughable had the situation not been more serious. The glass Duncan held slipped from his fingers and shattered on the stone floor. Alexandria gasped and took a faltering step back, looking for all the world as if she was seeing a ghost. Only Spotiswoode seemed to retain some semblance of wits. He set his snifter down and drew his blade, stepping away from the fireplace.

"I thought you said she was dead?" Alexandria spat, her beautiful face ugly with mingled fear and hatred.

"Me dead? Speak for yourself; I attended your funeral," Arabella said.

"I was right about you: ignorant, ugly peasant girls are so easily fooled," the girl said. "As it is, I will be witnessing yours!"

"Not if I kill you first!" Arabella snarled, stepping foward.

Spottiswoode stepped between them as Alexandria screamed and raced from the room. Duncan finally awoke from his stupor and leapt to his feet, pulling his own sword.

"I am, to say the least, surprised to see you, Ara," Duncan said, eyeing her ship captain's garb and weaponry with amused wonder.

"Apparently, you failed me yet again, James."

"'Twas not me; goddamned Knights of Malta must have let her go," he sputtered. "That were not my fault, Master Duncan, surely it were not! But now be our chance to finish her."

"Come and try, Spotiswoode," Arabella growled. "And die like the pig you are!"

"Looks like her time at sea has made her believe she really is a pirate," Duncan said with a smirk. "Drop your weapons, please, Ara; girls who play with swords can get hurt. And despite what my dear fiancée thinks, seeing you again reminds me that I really do not wish you dead."

"To hell with your sentiments," Spotiswoode growled. "Let's kill her now and be done with it!"

"Oh, 'tis not sentiment, James. You know what Alexandria is like; there are ice sculptures with more warmth than that bitch. No, I fear I will need other women to keep me satisfied, not to mention sane. Arabella will make a marvelous plaything. I may even keep her in the castle, right under Alexandria's feet, locked tight in my dungeons. Lucky for me, my betrothed detests dark and dreary places and so should never discover my - pet."

"You make me sick!" Arabella said, raising her weapon and

preparing to attack. "I can no longer say which one of you I shall enjoy killing more."

She did not get the chance to find out. Something hard smashed against the back of her skull. White lights exploded and she could not stop herself from sliding to the ground. Just before she lost consciousness, she saw a pair of boots belonging to one of the castle guards, and remembered the window to the study she had left open behind her.

Liam and Bartholomew entertained the guards with an impromptu 'drunken' jig, arm in arm and feet flying. The dogs did not seem quite so amused and kept up a constant barking. Suddenly, a high-pitched shriek from the manor house pierced the din, ending all. The guards made certain the gate was locked then turned and raced toward the house, the mastiffs following.

"That was a woman's scream," Liam said. "Either someone has discovered Spotiswoode's corpse, or things have gone to hell in a handbasket for Ara."

"Quickly, to the back wall!" Bartholomew cried, dashing off in that direction. Liam followed.

Moments later, they arrived at the point where they had left

Arabella. She was not there. They looked across the lawn toward the house and saw four men moving through the shadows, accompanied by the two huge mastiffs. Two of the men appeared to be carrying a body toward one of the stone outbuildings behind the manor. The gloom and thick foliage prevented them from seeing clearly just who was being carried and whether they were alive or dead.

"Fie!" Liam cursed quietly.

"Now what?"

"Now what? How can we know the answer to that until we know where Arabella is and in what condition?" Liam replied. He marched back and forth twice before stepping to the wall and starting to climb. "To hell; I am going in there."

"No, wait!" Bartholomew said, grabbing his arm. "'Tis a fool's errand. Let us quickly make a circuit about the property to see if she escaped from another exit and yet awaits us elsewhere."

"'Tis a large parcel; perhaps if we split up and take different sides, meeting near the front gate?"

"Agreed."

"But if she is not to be found without, I am going in there."

"And I will be at your side."

The two rogues separated and raced quickly but quietly around the large estate. They stopped at frequent intervals to call softly to Arabella, listening intently for any reply. They heard none. After a short time, they met back at the front. As they discussed whether to scale this wall or head around back once more, the heavy iron gates swung open with a crash. A carriage pulled by a team of horses raced out, turning sharply on the cobblestone street and heading off in the direction of the harbor.

"Did you see who was within?" Liam asked, pressed flat in the shadows.

"Nay, the curtains were drawn."

"Arabella could be in that coach."

"Aye, or she could still be in that castle. So which is it, mate: do we follow the wagon or check the manor?"

"You trust me to make that decision?" Liam asked, looking his old comrade in the eye.

"I do, brother," Bartholomew answered. "Though often a fool, I find you have good instincts."

"I might hit you for that later; I shall have to think on it. As for now, my gut tells me the castle. We saw what looked to be a body being carried from the house, and for sure Arabella is not outside these walls. I want to check that first, and I am praying that if we find a corpse, it belongs to Spotiswoode."

The two men raced around to the back of the house once again, pausing only long enough to catch their breath before scaling the wall. As they alighted on the wet grass, a low growl told them they were not alone. One of the huge mastiffs charged from the shadows straight at them. Liam jerked his belaying pin from his belt and stepped forward to meet the charge. The beast leapt and the captain spun sideways, the slavering jaws rending empty air an inch from his throat. He brought the heavy wooden club down hard on the dog's skull. The mastiff hit the ground and rolled several times, unconscious. They heard another dog barking from somewhere within the castle.

"Quickly!" Liam whispered. He did not need to tell his friend twice.

Another moment brought them to the squat building of fitted stone to which the men had carried the body. It had windows on three sides, each laced with wrought iron bars, and a stout oak door on the fourth. A large padlock secured it.

"Can you pick it?" Captain Roderick asked.

"As simple as dancing a jig," the Irishman told him, dropping to a knee and pulling a finely-wrought iron tool from a pouch at his belt. The jig lasted a rather long time, the lock clearly more difficult than he had anticipated. Finally though, the clasp popped free and Liam pulled the heavy door open.

The room inside was almost completely dark, but by the little light the windows provided, they could see it was a storage shed used for dry-aging meat. Dozens of slabs of beef, pork and fowl hung from hooks in the near-freezing room. Something - or someone - hung from one of these. Liam stepped inside and instantly recognized the shapely figure of Arabella, her hands tied tightly and looped over the metal crook, her toes barely touching the floor. A cloth gag had been tied around her mouth. Liam felt her neck and breathed a sigh of relief to find it still warm, a strong pulse beating within.

"She is alive! Her hair is sticky with blood, though; someone must have hit her. Help me get her down."

The men freed Arabella and, a moment later, had gently roused her. They helped her from the shed and across the yard, then lifted her over the wall as she filled them in on what she had seen and heard in the castle.

"The bastard!" Liam spat when she finished her story. "Your own fiancé."

"Clearly, his lust for power exceeded his tenuous grasp of morality," Bartholomew said. "I am sorry, Arabella."

"Gramercy," she said. "But this is no time for pity. You say you saw a carriage leave the house heading toward the docks?"

"They were headed in that direction, to be sure," Liam answered.

"Duncan and Spotiswoode were plotting something when I came upon them. I have to stop them."

"But you are wounded," Bartholomew protested. "You need care and rest."

"I have time for neither. They mentioned the Earls Mar and Angus and spoke of a trap the Earl of Arran had set for them and their followers at a place called Redshin. They also said the earl was holding my father at Stirling and means to hang him. I know I cannot expect either of you to help me and risk your ships in what is likely a profitless venture, but I must do everything in my power to stop the earl and save my father, and I would be ever so grateful for your assistance."

"A profitless venture? On the contrary," Liam said. "I can think of few things potentially more profitable than coming to the aid of a couple of fat, wealthy earls. I am all for it."

"As am I," Bartholomew said. "Though the only 'profit' I desire is to help you and your father in your time of need, even if I earn nothing more than your gratitude."

"'Tis my only true concern as well," Liam sputtered. "When I spoke of profits, sure'n I meant only your happiness, Ara, which is worth more to me than all the gold in Spain."

"Nice try, Liam," Bartholomew said with a smirk.

"Stuff it, Barty. Do not think you fooled anyone with your fancy speech and your feigned altruism. Arabella is-"

"Enough!" she cried. "You can fight over me later. Right now, there is fighting of another sort to be done. Now quickly, let us back to our ships. If we are swift, we may yet catch Spotiswoode before the *Rover* or the *Phoenix* or whatever its true name is slips the harbor."

The trio raced back to Fisherrow Sands at a sprint. Once there, however, they realized they had another problem. A good portion of their crews had been granted shore leave until the following morning, and most were still in town. Those few who were now aboard ship were there mainly because they had spent all their coin on drink and could not afford to rent a room anywhere; most were far too drunk to be of any use. The captains had no choice but to go into town and search the taverns and stews for their sailors, advising them they were to return to ship at once or be left behind. An hour later and from their vantage point east of Leith, the captains watched the *Sea Rover* and two other ships leave the harbor and head out to sea.

"Dammit!" Bartholomew swore, watching them sail away. "Now

we shall have to give chase and pray we reach their destination while there is still time to make a difference. Where did they say they were headed again?"

"They mentioned a place called 'Redshin,' though the name means nothing to me," Arabella said.

"Nor to me," Liam said, seeing the same befuddled expression on Bartholomew's face. "Let us ask the harbormaster; perhaps the old salt has heard of it."

They sent Arabella to do the job, beauty and charm often working quicker and cheaper than coin alone.

"Redshin?" the auld gaffer repeated. He scratched his salt-and-pepper whiskers and looked to the sky as if the answer might be written in the stars. "Redshin…Redshin. You know, I seem to recall there being a Redshin Cove 'tween the Cheswick Black Rocks and Sharper's Head, near Berwick. 'Tis about two days south of here by sail."

"You can think of no other Redshin?" Arabella asked.

"Nay."

"Then I shall pray 'tis the correct one. Gramercy, good sir," she said, giving the man a coin and a peck.

Just before dawn, *The Thistle, Raven* and *Greyhound* finally set sail. They carried their full crews, though most of them were as bleary-eyed and disagreeable as wet cats. They cleared the harbor and spread every inch of canvas they carried. A stiff breeze blew and the swift *Greyhound* leapt to the fore. When the masts of the older, heavier *Raven* creaked in protest, the bosun pleaded with Captain McNamara to reduce sail, just a bit. Liam refused, ordering triple backstays rigged about the timbers for extra strength. By the time all three ships were in the deep water of the firth, they were running at a very respectable six knots. A mist played on the waters this day, reducing visibility to less than a league. The lookouts in the mastheads caught no sight of the *Sea Rover* or her consorts. Despite her injury, Arabella remained on deck the entire day, more than once saying a silent prayer that she led them in the right direction.

The three ships sailed south along the Scottish coast for the remainder of the day and well into the evening. Darkness forced them to slow considerably to avoid any shoals or other hazards in the shallow, coastal waters. At first light, the captains again increased their speed to maximum. Just past noon, they rounded Meadow Haven at the tip of Sharper's Head. Redshin Cove lay just to their west. They saw not her rocky shores though, for their focus was drawn instead to the flashes of orange flame before them and the roar of cannons echoing across the water. Two groups of warships blazed away at each other in pitched battle.

25

Captains Fraser, McNamara and Roderick each gave the same order: continue at full speed, guns and boarders at the ready! In another ten minutes, they had cut the distance in half and could clearly see the action. The *Sea Rover* was accompanied by the *Gunsway* and another ship, a large English war galleon. They battered away at three immense carracks even as two smaller vessels burned brightly nearby, destroyed beyond any hope of rescue. The fat, slow-moving carracks carried little in the way of heavy armament, as they were primarily troop carriers, their decks teeming with sailors and soldiers. Now that Duncan and Spottiswoode's faster, more maneuverable ships had obliterated the carracks' armed escorts, they could easily stay out of boarding range and pound mercilessly at their foe with their long guns.

"The *Rover* is mine!" Arabella yelled across the water to Captains McNamara and Roderick. Both men tipped their hats to her in acknowledgement.

"I shall take the *Gunsway*," Bartholomew called.

"Oh great; I guess that leaves the war galleon for me. Thank you," Liam said.

Despite the mists and the battle, the approach of the three new ships did not go unnoticed. *Rover* let fly a final broadside at the largest of the carracks, the convoy's flagship, then turned into the wind to come about and face *The Thistle*. The carrack listed badly, clearly taking on water as hundreds of soldiers dashed frantically about her decks readying boats that could not hope to carry but a fraction of their number. *The Thistle* and *Rover* closed fast on each other, and Arabella let fly her broadside first. Captain Spotiswoode immediately answered back. *The Thistle's* guns proved the more accurate, but both salvos took a heavy toll, littering the ships' decks with shattered timbers and rent flesh. The *Rover* maneuvered her helm to begin a long, arching turn to bring her other broadside to bear as Arabella's helmsman did the same.

"Avast that!" she yelled. She knew the two ships could pound away at each other for hours if they wanted, as the big carrack slipped slowly below the waves. "Helm, bring me fast alongside the *Rover*; we will board her!" The man did as she asked, turning *The Thistle* back and directly into the path of the other ship. "Ropes and hooks!" Arabella cried over the roar of the battle. "Thistles, hear me! There are the men who brought shame upon our good name in the Mediterranean! There is the crew that accused us of being murderers, of being without honor or courage! Now is our chance to see that they are repaid in full! Swivel guns and muskets alow and aloft at the ready! One shot and then we board, then let all be blood and iron!"

The *Rover* helmsman saw what *The Thistle* intended. He bent the whipstaff while his crew adjusted the sails, seeking to pull away and keep using their longs. *The Thistle*, still moving at nearly full speed, proved the swifter and drove her bow hard at them. Dozens of grappling hooks flew and both ships fired their swivel guns. Amid the smoke and carnage, the two crews launched themselves at each other, Arabella in the center of it all. Metal rang, men screamed and powder smoke stung the eyes and burned the lungs of the living and dying alike. Limbs were hewed and lives extinguished and the decks soon grew slick. The combatants, equal in numbers, surged first forward and then back, only to advance again a moment later. Arabella fought always in the fore, her pistols spent but her sword arm strong, a cutlass in one hand and a boarding axe in the other. The men before her fell like lambs before a lion. She cut a swath of death all around her, intent only on reaching her real objective: the quarterdeck and the men standing upon it. She opened a gap in the *Rover* lines and raced for the stern ladder. A second later, the shifting tide of battle closed behind her, stopping her crew's advance and cutting off any hope of retreat for Arabella.

She cared not, flying up the ladder and leaping onto the command deck. Captain Spotiswoode shoved a pistol into her face and pulled the trigger. She jerked her head to the side just as the powder exploded. The deadly ball screamed past her ear, tearing a ragged gash in her scalp as the burning powder singed her raven tresses. She buried her cutlass to the hilt in the man's bowels then shoved him aside. Duncan stood behind him, sword in hand, his eyes wide at the sight of his one-time fiancée bloody and burnt, her hair smoldering while fire burned in her eyes.

"Sure'n you are a demon from hell!" he cried. "And hell is where I am sending you back to!"

He lunged at her. She parried with her axe and jerked her cutlass from Spotiswoode's guts. She knew Duncan was an experienced and deadly fighter and he proved it immediately, following his thrust with another even more rapid than the first. She just managed to deflect it but had no chance to launch her own attack. He came at her hard and fast, driving her back across the quarterdeck. His sword shot forward again and again, the quick, powerful blows relentlessly seeking to end her life. She continued to dodge and parry these, her hatred of him giving her strength. With a growl, she smashed his sword away with a blow that rang his bones from finger to shoulder, then followed up with her axe. It missed his brow by a fraction of an inch as he grotesquely contorted to avoid it. An unsettled look came into his eyes, behind which she caught a hint of fear.

"God be damned!" he spat. "What devilry is this?"

"Surprised to find a woman your equal?" she asked, a cold smile on her lips.

"You are no equal of mine, bitch!" he snarled, coming at her once more.

Her parry with the axe came almost too fast to see, followed up with a slashing thrust from her cutlass that flayed open a six-inch gash on his left cheek and very nearly ended his life.

"I stand corrected," she said. "I am not nearly so low as you!"

The battle continued, the two combatants thrusting, lunging, feinting and parrying again and again. They maneuvered about the small quarterdeck, the ship below them rocking and bobbing on the waves. They circled the tiny platform three times, unable to find any weakness in the other's defenses, hoping only that their foe would tire or drop their guard for but a second. As Arabella moved near the fallen Spotiswoode a fourth time, the sea captain roused himself from drifting into that eternal sleep and grabbed her ankle. She stumbled and Duncan pounced. She saved her life only by letting gravity take her, the tip of his blade flaying her shirt but nothing more. She hit the deck hard and her boarding axe bounced from her hand. Duncan again drove his blade toward the downed woman, aiming for her heart. She just managed to parry the blow, then viciously kicked out at him. He danced away, feinted toward her exposed foot then lunged for her neck. She twisted her body aside but not fast enough, the blade slicing into the flesh of her shoulder. She twisted and rolled sideways even as Spotiswoode reached for her again. He wrapped his arm around her throat, intent on dragging her with him into the Abyss. Her parry came slower this time and the tip of Duncan's sword sliced into her upper thigh. In fury and desperation, she whipped her sword toward Duncan's face and jerked her dagger from her belt. The young nobleman was forced to parry her powerful sword thrust and failed to see the dagger. She slammed it with all her strength through the toe of his tall riding boots - the very ones she had so admired in Paris.

He screamed in pain and his blade sheered off course, stabbing the deck and sinking deeply into the wood. Arabella wrenched the dagger from his foot and stabbed it up and over her head, piercing Spotiswoode through the eye and finally sending him to hell. She then threw herself sideways, rolling from the dead man's grasp and coming up in a crouch. Duncan yanked his trapped sword free from the planks, but his injured foot refused to support his weight. He staggered and Arabella's blade shot forward, sinking into his stomach. He pulled away even as his sword flew forward, slashing deeply into the flesh of her sword arm. Arabella threw herself back and stood, blood oozing from her wounds and her head growing light.

The two glared hatefully at each other from opposite ends of the quarterdeck. Arabella's strength threatened to fail her but she refused to fall, not while Duncan still breathed. She had spent more than a year searching for him, during which countless lives had been risked and scores lost. His greed and vile treachery had murdered her brother and the senior Campbell men, and might yet cost her father his life. His betrayal of her was beyond unspeakable. These thoughts steeled her and wiped away all her fatigue, her pain, everything except one all-powerful and all-consuming desire: to make Duncan Campbell pay. He sagged weakly against the railing, his face contorted in rage as a crimson stain quickly spread across his doublet and slops. Though he yet stood, the color drained from his face. He clasped his free hand to his wound, stealing a glance down just long enough to see black bile oozing between his fingers. He knew he had been dealt a mortal blow.

"Damn you!" he snarled. "I was going to be a count!" With the last of his strength, he lunged for her, his blade aimed directly for her throat.

Arabella brought her cutlass up and smashed his sword aside, then reversed the motion and shoved her blade into his jugular. "And I was going to be your wife. Funny old world, isn't it?"

He sprawled over the railing and died, his beautiful blue eyes fixed on her own. She gazed at him for a moment and then turned to face the main deck. Her crew and the Rovers still battled, their numbers fewer but their ferocity undiminished. The combatants remained roughly equal, with neither side holding a clear advantage. Arabella meant to change this. She grabbed Spotiswoode's corpse and shoved it from the quarterdeck onto the main, then did the same with Duncan's. The first body struck two Rovers and knocked them from their feet. As the second corpse came tumbling over the railing, the combatants parted en masse to avoid it. The two sides faced each other now in eerie silence across a chasm of death, ready to resume their battle at any moment. Their eyes went to the corpses and then traveled up to the warrior who had cast them down. The Thistles smiled and took heart; the Rovers looked as if their courage stood on the brink.

"Who. Is. Next?" Arabella growled, her lioness' gaze sweeping across the main deck and piercing each potential foe.

A Rover's sword clattered to the planks, dropped as if its touch burned the holder. A few more did the same and a moment later, not a man among the Rovers held a weapon.

A short distance away, the crews of *The Raven* and *Greyhound* continued to battle their foes. Captain Bartholomew had chosen to stand off from the *Gunsway* and fight with his long guns. The more nimble of the two ships, he was firing three broadsides for every two of theirs. Still, both vessels were savaging each other, and Arabella could not tell which now held the advantage, if either. Captain McNamara had followed Arabella's tactic and fired an initial broadside at the more heavily-armed galleon then moved in close to board. His men now fought a fierce, pitched battle against a foe of at least equal his numbers and likely more. Closer to shore, the wounded carracks could not assist their would-be rescuers, as their crews devoted all of their efforts to keeping themselves afloat long enough to ferry everyone to safety.

Arabella looked about and saw that Duff had been wounded a dozen times over though yet remained on his feet. Molly, also bloodied and battered, looked to have fared little better.

"Secure the prisoners in the lower hold," Arabella commanded. "After that, I want you Duff to take some hands and every oarboat, dinghy and gig from the *Rover* and *Thistle* and help get those troops to shore. Molly, take the *Rover* with the first and second watch and go assist *The Raven*. Everyone else, follow me back to *The Thistle* and to our brothers on *The Greyhound*. By God there is more work yet to be done this day!"

The men, women and guns of *The Thistle* and *Rover* proved the deciding factor in the battle, forcing the surrender of what was left of Duncan and Spotiswoode's fleet within the hour. Each of the privateer captains emerged from the savage, hand-to-hand fighting wounded and bleeding from scores of cuts and gashes, and counted themselves lucky for it, as many had not survived at all. In the meantime, the carracks had managed to offload all of their troops with the privateers' help. Arabella was stunned to see just how many men crowded the beaches, several thousand at least.

Arabella, Bartholomew and Liam came ashore in their oar boats and were met at once by a small group of swordsmen, also bloodied and battle-weary. The gentleman at the fore stood out as the most elegantly garbed, though blood smeared his handsome face, his doublet hung in burnt and bloody tatters and his silk stockings were shredded. His hat was gone and thus he had nothing to remove as he bowed to Arabella and the other captains.

"Milady, gentlemen. I know not who thou be nor why you saw fit to come to my aid. Still, you have done a noble and heroic deed this day, not just for myself but for all of Scotland. For that, I am in your debt."

"'Twas our pleasure, good sir," Arabella told him. "Though I gather you are neither the good Earl Mar nor Angus, for there is not a hint of the Highlands in your voice. To whose aid, I am wondering, did we just come?"

"Prithee forgive my manners. But let me assure you you did just aid Earls Mar and Angus, though neither is on this beach today. I am Lord Maxwell, their friend and ally, and am even now on my way to join forces with them in their battle against the Earl of Arran."

"Your Lordship," Arabella said, curtsying. Liam and Bartholomew bowed as well. "I am Arabella Fraser of the Clan Fraser, captain of the privateer ship *Thistle*. My comrades: Captain Roderick of the

Greyhound and Captain McNamara of *The Raven*."

"Good gentles," Lord Maxwell said, returning the bows. "Fraser is it?" he asked, his eyes widening. "Your father is Sir William Fraser?"

"You know of him?"

"I do indeed, and am proud to count him among my allies."

"I am glad to hear it, though I regret to inform Your Lordship I have learned the earl is holding him captive within Stirling Castle, awaiting only the Earls Mar and Angus to join him at the gallows."

"Then it is fate indeed that brought you to Redshin Cove this day," Lord Maxwell said. "Once my army joins with that of Earls Mar and Angus, we mean to seize Stirling and shake that rat Arran from within its sheltering walls."

"If my sword and my courage can be of further assistance to you in that effort, milord, you have it," Arabella pledged.

"We could always use additional experienced blades," he told her with a smile.

The battle for Stirling Castle was over before it began. After several days march, the combined armies of the rebel lords advanced upon the fortress. At once, the Earl of Arran knew his scheme had failed. He abandoned his king and fled. King James, alone of counsel now, outnumbered and surrounded by a larger army, immediately sued for peace. After hearing the rebel lords' grievances, he shrewdly agreed they had been most foully abused by Arran. He promptly issued royal pardons to the rebel earls, Lord Maxwell and all who had supported them, restoring their lands and titles in the process.

Sir William was freed from the dungeons below the castle and, upon being reunited with his daughter, wept without shame. Earl Mar declared his loan to William forgiven, then he, Earl Angus and Lord Maxwell delivered in gratitude an entire chest of gold coins to the three privateer captains to divide amongst themselves and their crews. Feasting and revelry followed at Stirling Castle for several days, during which Liam quipped that it was for certain not the first time a band of rogues, outlaws and pirates had occupied the fortress, and would likely not be the last.

26

The festivities eventually concluded, and the time came for everyone to return home, or at least to wherever they chose to call home. Sir William, Arabella, Liam and Bartholomew walked together back to the beach, their oar boats ready to carry them to their respective ships. William shook the hands of Liam and Bartholomew, telling them they would always be welcome at *Ban Tigh* should they ever find themselves in the Highlands. They assured him they would find excuse in the near future to take him up on the invitation.

"Well, daughter," the old knight said, turning to Arabella. "I for one shall be glad to have you and Thomas and Bess back home with me again. That drafty auld *bothy* seems empty without you. And who knows: it may not be too late to find you a good husband."

At this, both Liam and Bartholomew puffed out their chests and jostled for prominence before William and his daughter. Arabella laughed at them.

"I believe Thomas and some of the others may join you, father," she said. "And I think they shall bring home a few coins I collected for someone else that should now go to you. As for me though, I do not think I shall return to *Ban Tigh* just yet."

"But I do not understand," he replied. "I am safe, the Earl of Arran is exiled to France, and Duncan and Spotiswoode are dead. What possible reason could now remain for you to continue living as a privateer?"

"Freedom, father," Arabella answered. "And adventure. Sure'n a Highland lass could settle for nothing less."

END

About the Author:

KJ Fay lives in the beautiful Sierra Nevada foothills of northern California. KJ grew up reading old action-adventure 'classics' by the likes of Dumas, Sabatini and Burroughs, and still enjoys more contemporary authors like Philippa Gregory and Arturo Perez-Reverte. And while this novel may evoke the classic action-adventure yarns of yesteryear, it is at its core a character-driven story about a young woman's search not just for the man she loves, but for herself.

If you enjoyed this novel, please tell a friend and consider leaving a review on Amazon. Thank you!

Made in the USA
Coppell, TX
14 July 2021